"A novel for people w

expectations for lite

written with brilliance, incomparable talent
and obvious artistic power, [and] a wide knowledge
of the human nature, mind, and soul."
—*Berlingske Tidende* (Denmark)

"A sensation. *The best book of the last ten years*
. . . A novel of incredible clarity and beauty."
—*Bücher* (Germany)

"A rare reading pleasure."
—*San Francisco Chronicle*

"Rich, dense, star-spangled. . ."
—*Harper's Magazine*

treat for the mind. One of the best books I have read in a long time."—Isabel Allende

Praise for NIGHT TRAIN TO LISBON:

"A meditative novel that builds an uncanny power through a labyrinth of memories and philosophical concepts that illuminate the narrative from within . . . a rare reading pleasure."

—*San Francisco Chronicle*

"Contains style, narrative richness, and philosophy . . . I read it in three nights. Then I was convinced to change my life."

—*Süddeutsche Zeitung* (Germany)

"Celebrates the beauty and allure of language . . . adroitly addresses concepts of sacrifice, secrets, memory, loneliness, infatuation, tyranny, and translation."

—*Chicago Sun-Times*

"I was hooked—I read the book in no more than two sittings. Two long sittings, I might add, for I was forever putting the book down to ruminate on something a character said. . . . More than any mystery I can remember since, say, Umberto Eco's *The Name of the Rose, Night Train to Lisbon* challenges the reader, both intellectually and philosophically."

—*BookPage*

"This book, powerful, serious, and brilliant, constitutes one of the true revelations of this season."

—*L'Humanité* (France)

"The reader quickly becomes as obsessed as Gregorious, following breathlessly as the narrator plunges down one well of the past after another. . . . A book so intent on answering the larger questions of existence that if readers give it a chance, it could be life-altering. A brilliant book that manages to excite the mind and the heart in equal measure."

—Betsy Burton, The King's English Bookshop, Salt Lake City, UT

"A book in which poetry and philosophy are intimately intertwined."

—*Tages-Anzeiger* (Switzerland)

"As mesmerizing and dreamlike as a Wong Kar-Wai film, with characters as strange and alienated as any of the filmmaker's . . . [Mercier] is a master at mixing ideas and plot. . . . Unforgettable moments of crystalline, even poetic, insight." —*Bookforum*

"After reading this whirlwind of philosophical reflections, you are not the same person as when you started. It's likely the biggest compliment you may give a novel—and this book deserves it."
—*Kristeligt Dagblad* (Denmark)

"Impressive . . . a life lesson and a model of lucidity."
—*La Quinzaine* (France)

"A thriller of a philosophical novel. You cheat yourself not bringing this book with you on vacation." —*Weekendavisen* (Denmark)

"Taps into some of the oldest veins of story, the primal ones of night journeys, of a distant land, of being stuck in-place, and yet adrift and confused in life purpose, and then the startling summons to seek it in all its deeper histories and mysteries. . . . Mercier does all of this and more, masterfully, alertly, intelligently. . . . [*Night Train to Lisbon*] has helped remind this reader of what it is to really read."
—Rick Simonson, Elliott Bay Book Company

"Absolutely recommended." —*De Telegraaf* (Netherlands)

"Has the coloration and feel of Alan Lightman's *Einstein's Dreams* or Peter Handke's *Crossing the Sierra de Gredos* . . . the stuff of fine fiction."
—TheMorningNews.com

"The artful unspooling of Prado's fraught life is richly detailed: full of surprises and paradoxes, it incorporates a vivid rendering of the Portuguese resistance to Salazar. . . . comes through on the enigmas of trying to live and write under fascism." —*Publishers Weekly*

"A serious and beautiful book about the examined life."

—*Le Monde* (France)

"An elegant narrative of the exploration of one human being by another. Its composition unites inner and outer journeys in the most beautiful manner, and on its way gets to throw as much light as possible on the inexhaustible question: what does it mean to be a human being, and to what extent we manage to get to know each other—and ourselves."

—*Børsen* (Denmark)

"A clever novel about the search for freedom."

—*Vrij Nederland* (Netherlands)

"Patient readers will be rewarded . . . by the involving, unpredictable, and well-constructed plot and Mercier's virtuosic orchestration of a large and memorable cast of characters. As the stories of Gregorius and de Prado draw together, this becomes a moving meditation on the defining moments in our lives, the silent explosions that change everything."

—*Library Journal*

"A fantastic internal train ride . . . An impressive book, a conscious detective novel." —*Die Zeit* (Germany)

"An elegant, meditative book . . . the age-old intellectual's dilemma, considered in a compelling blend of suspenseful narrative and discursive commentary. . . . An intriguing fiction." —*Kirkus Reviews*

"An intense novel . . . for refined palates." —*La Repubblica* (Italy)

"Philosophical and spell-binding . . . *Night Train to Lisbon* is a novel for absorption . . . One and a half million German readers can't be wrong: philosophy can go to the heart!" —*Politiken* (Denmark)

NIGHT TRAIN TO LISBON

NIGHT TRAIN TO LISBON

PASCAL MERCIER

Translated from the German
by
Barbara Harshav

Grove Press
New York

The publisher gratefully acknowledges the Swiss Council for the Arts PRO HELVETIA for their generous support of this translation.

The epigraphs are taken from:
Coplas de don Jorge Manrique by Jorge Manrique, translated by Henry Longfellow (Boston: Allen & Ticknor, 1833)
The Complete Essays of Montaigne by Michel de Montaigne, translated by Donald M. Frame (Stanford: Stanford University Press, 1948)
The Selected Prose of Fernando Pessoa by Fernando Pessoa, translated by Richard Zenith (New York: Grove Press, 2002)

First published in the German language in 2004 by Carl Hanser Verlag

Published simultaneously in Canada
Printed in the United States of America

FIRST PAPERBACK EDITION

ISBN-10: 0-8021-4397-0
ISBN-13: 978-0-8021-4397-6

Grove Press
an imprint of Grove/Atlantic, Inc.
841 Broadway
New York, NY 10003

Distributed by Publishers Group West

www.goveratlantic.com

08 09 10 11 12 13 10 9 8 7 6 5 4 3 2

Nuestras vidas son los ríos
que van a dar en la mar,
qu'es el morir

Our lives are rivers, gliding free
to that unfathomed, boundless sea,
the silent grave!

Jorge Manrique

Nous sommes tous de lopins et d'une contexture si informe et diverse, que chaque piece, chaque momant, faict son jeu. Et se trouve autant de difference de nous à nous mesmes, que de nous à autruy.

We are all patchwork, and so shapeless and diverse in composition that each bit, each moment, plays its own game. And there is as much difference between us and ourselves as between us and others.

Michel de Montaigne, Essais, *Second Book, 1*

Cada um de nós é vários, é muitos, é uma prolixidade de si mesmos. Por isso aquele que despreza o ambiente não é o mesmo que dele se alegra ou padece. Na vasta colónia do nosso ser há gente de muitas espécies, pensando e sentindo diferentemente.

Each of us is several, is many, is a profusion of selves. So that the self who disdains his surroundings is not the same as the self who suffers or takes joy in them. In the vast colony of our being there are many species of people who think and feel in different ways.

Fernando Pessoa, Livro Do Desassossego

NIGHT TRAIN TO LISBON

PART I
THE DEPARTURE

1

The day that ended with everything different in the life of Raimund Gregorius began like countless other days. At quarter to eight, he came from Bundesterrasse and stepped onto the Kirchenfeldbrücke leading from the heart of the city to the Gymnasium. He did that every workday of the school term always at quarter to eight. Once when the bridge was blocked, he made a mistake in beginning Greek class afterward. That had never happened before nor did it ever happen again. For days, the whole school talked of nothing but this mistake. The longer the discussion lasted, the more it was thought to be a mistake in hearing. At last, this conviction won out even among the students who had been there. It was simply inconceivable that Mundus, as everyone called him, could make a mistake in Greek, Latin or Hebrew.

Gregorius looked ahead at the pointed towers of the Historical Museum of the City of Bern, up to the Gurten and down to the Aare with its glacier green water. A gusty wind drove low-lying clouds over him, turned his umbrella inside out and whipped the rain in his face. Now he noticed the woman in the middle of the bridge. She had leaned her elbows on the railing and was reading in the pouring rain what looked like a letter. She must have been holding the sheet with both hands. As Gregorius came closer, she suddenly crumpled the paper, kneaded it into a ball and threw the ball into space with a violent movement. Instinctively, Gregorius had walked faster and was now only a few steps away from her. He saw the rage in her pale, rain-wet face. It wasn't a rage that could be dumped into words and then blow over. It was a grim rage turned inward that must have been smoldering in her for a long time. Now the woman leaned on the railing with outstretched arms, and her heels slipped out of her shoes. *Now she jumps.* Gregorius left the umbrella to a gust of wind that drove it over the railing, threw his briefcase full of school notebooks to the ground and uttered a string of curses that weren't part of his usual vocabulary. The briefcase opened up and the notebooks slid onto the wet pavement. The woman turned around. For a few moments, she watched unmoving as the notebooks darkened with the water. Then she pulled a felt-tipped pen from her coat pocket, took two steps, leaned down to Gregorius and wrote a line of numbers on his forehead.

"Forgive me," she said in French, breathless and with a foreign accent. "But I mustn't forget this phone number and I don't have any paper with me."

Now she looked at her hands as if she were seeing them for the first time.

"Naturally, I could have . . ." And now, looking back and forth between Gregorius's forehead and her hand, she wrote the numbers on the back of the hand. "I . . . I didn't want to keep it, I wanted to forget everything, but when I saw the letter fall . . . I had to hold onto it."

The rain on the thick eyeglasses muddied Gregorius's sight, and he groped awkwardly for the wet notebooks. The tip of the felt pen seemed to slide over his forehead again. But then he realized it was now the fingers of the woman, who was trying to wipe away the numbers with a handkerchief.

"It is out of line, I know . . ." And now she started helping Gregorius gather up the notebooks. He touched her hand and grazed her knee, and when the two of them reached for the last notebook, they bumped heads.

"Thank you very much," he said when they stood facing each other. He pointed to her head. "Did it hurt?"

Absently, looking down, she shook her head. The rain beat down on her hair and ran over her face.

"Can I walk a few steps with you?"

"Ah . . . yes, of course," Gregorius stammered.

Silently they walked together to the end of the bridge and on toward the school. The sense of time told Gregorius that it was after eight and the first hour had already begun. How far was "a few steps"? The woman had adjusted to his pace and plodded along beside him as if she would go on like that all day. She had pulled the wide collar of her coat so high that, from the side, Gregorius saw only her forehead.

"I have to go in here, into the Gymnasium," he said and stood still. "I'm a teacher."

"Can I come along?" she asked softly.

Gregorius hesitated and ran his sleeve over his wet glasses. "In any case, it's dry there," he said at last.

She went up the stairs, Gregorius held the door open for her, and then they stood in the hall, which seemed especially empty and quiet now that classes had started. Her coat was dripping.

"Wait here," said Gregorius and went to the bathroom to get a towel.

At the mirror, he dried the glasses and wiped off his face. The numbers could still be seen on his forehead. He held a corner of the towel under the warm water and wanted to start rubbing when he stopped in the middle of the movement. *That was the moment that decided everything,* he thought when he recalled the event hours later. That is, all of a sudden, he realized that he really didn't *want* to wipe away the trace of his encounter with the enigmatic woman.

He imagined appearing before the class afterward with a phone number on his face, he, Mundus, the most reliable and predictable person in this building and probably in the whole history of the school, working here for more than thirty years, impeccable in his profession, a pillar of the institution, a little boring perhaps, but respected and even feared in the university for his astounding knowledge of ancient languages, mocked lovingly by his students who put him to the test every year by calling him in the middle of the night and asking about the conjecture for a remote passage in an ancient text, only to get every time off the top of his head information that was both dry and exhaustive, including a critical commentary with other possible meanings, all of it presented perfectly and calmly without a soupçon of anger at the disturbance—Mundus, a man with an impossibly old-fashioned, even archaic first name you simply *had to* abbreviate, and *couldn't* abbreviate any other way, an abbreviation that revealed the character of this man as no other word could have, for what he carried around in him as a philologist was in fact no less than a whole world, or rather several whole worlds, since along with those Latin and Greek passages, his head also held the Hebrew that had amazed several Old Testament scholars. *If you want to see a true scholar,* the Rector would say when he introduced him to a new class, *here he is.*

And this scholar, Gregorius thought now, this dry man who seemed to some to consist only of dead words, and who was spitefully called *the Papyrus* by colleagues who envied him his popularity—this scholar would enter the room with a telephone number painted on his forehead by a desperate woman apparently torn between rage and love, a woman in a red leather coat with a fabulously soft, southern voice, that sounded like an endless hesitant drawl that drew you in merely by hearing it.

When Gregorius had brought her the towel, the woman clamped a comb between her teeth and used the towel to rub the long black hair lying in the coat collar as in a bowl. The janitor entered the hall and, when he saw Gregorius, cast an amazed look at the clock over the exit and then at his watch. Gregorius nodded to him, as he always did. A student hurried past, turned around twice and went on.

"I teach up there," Gregorius said to the woman and pointed up through a window to another part of the building. Seconds passed. He felt his heart beat. "Do you want to come along?"

Later, Gregorius couldn't believe he had really said that; but he must have, for all at once they walked to the classroom next to each other; he heard the screech of his rubber soles on the linoleum and the clack of the boots when the woman put her foot down.

"What's your mother tongue?" he had asked her just now.

"Português," she had answered.

The *o* she pronounced surprisingly as a *u*, the rising, strangely constrained lightness of the *é* and the soft *sh* at the end came together in a melody that sounded much longer than it really was, and that he could have listened to all day long.

"Wait," he said now, took his notebook out of his jacket and ripped out a page: "For the number."

His hand was on the doorknob when he asked her to say the word once more. She repeated it, and for the first time he saw her smile.

The chatter broke off abruptly when they entered the classroom. A silence of one single amazement filled the room. Later, Gregorius remembered precisely: He had enjoyed this surprised silence, this speechless incredulity, that spoke from every single face, and he had also enjoyed his delight at being able to feel in a way he would never have believed possible.

What's up now? The question spoke from every single one of the twenty looks that fell on the peculiar couple at the door, on Mundus, standing with a wet bald head and a rain-darkened coat next to a hastily combed woman with a pale face.

"Perhaps there?" said Gregorius to the woman and pointed to the empty chair in the back corner. Then he advanced, greeted them as usual, and sat down behind the desk. He had no idea how he could have explained, and so he simply had them translate the text they were working on. The translations were halting, and he caught some curious looks. There were also bewildered looks for he—he, Mundus, who recognized every error even in his sleep—was overlooking dozens of errors, half measures, and awkwardness.

He managed not to look over at the woman. Yet, every second he saw her, saw the damp strands stroking her face, the white hands clenched, the absent, lost look going out the window. Once she took out the pen and wrote the phone number on the notebook page. Then she leaned back again and hardly seemed to know where she was.

It was an impossible situation and Gregorius glanced at the clock: ten more minutes until the break. Then the woman got up and walked softly to the door. When she got there, she turned around to him and put her finger on her lips. He nodded and she repeated the gesture with a smile. Then the door fell shut with a soft click.

From this moment on, Gregorius no longer heard anything the students said. It was as if he were all alone and enclosed in a numbing silence. At some time he stood at the window and watched the red female figure until she had disappeared around the corner. He felt the effort not to run after her reverberate in him. He kept seeing the finger on her lips that could mean so many things: *I don't want to disturb,* and *It's our secret,* but also, *Let me go now, this can't go on.*

When the bell rang for the break, he stood still at the window. Behind him, the students left more quietly than usual. Later he went out too, left the building through the back door and sat down across the street in the public library, where nobody would look for him.

For the second part of the double class, he was on time as always. He had rubbed the numbers off his forehead, written them down in the notebook after a minute of hesitation and then dried the narrow fringe of gray hair. Only the damp spots on his jacket and pants still revealed that there had been something unusual. Now he took the stack of soaked notebooks out of his briefcase.

"A mishap," he said tersely. "I stumbled and they slipped out, in the rain. Nevertheless, the corrections should still be legible; otherwise, you have to work on your conjectures."

That was how they knew him and an audible sigh of relief went through the room. Now and then, he still caught a curious look, and a remnant of shyness was in a few voices. Otherwise, everything was as before. He wrote the most frequent errors on the board. Then he let the students work silently on their own.

Could what happened to him in the next quarter hour be called a decision? Later, Gregorius was to keep asking the question and never was he sure. But if it wasn't a decision—what was it?

It began when he suddenly looked at the students bending over their notebooks as if he were seeing them for the first time.

Lucien von Graffenried, who had secretly moved a piece in the annual chess tournament in the auditorium, where Gregorius had played simultaneous matches against a dozen students. After the moves on the other boards, Gregorius had stood before him again. He noticed it immediately. He looked at him calmly. Lucien's face flamed red. "That's beneath you," said Gregorius and then made sure this game ended in a draw.

Sarah Winter, who had stood outside the door of his flat at two in the morning because she didn't know what to do with her pregnancy. He had made her tea and listened, nothing else. "I'm so glad I followed your advice," she said a week later. "It would have been much too early to have a baby."

Beatrice Lüscher with the regular, precise handwriting who had grown old frighteningly fast under the burden of her always perfect achievements. René Zingg, always at the lowest end of the scale.

And naturally, Natalie Rubin. A girl who was stingy with her favor, a bit like a courtly maiden of the past, reserved, idolized and feared for her sharp tongue. Last week, after the bell rang for the break, she had stood up, stretched like someone at ease in her own body, and taken a piece of candy out of her shirt pocket. On the way to the door, she unwrapped it and when she passed him, she put it to her mouth. It had just touched her lips when she broke off the movement, turned to him, held the bright red candy to him and asked: "Want it?" Amused at his astonishment, she had laughed her strange light laugh and made sure her hand touched his.

Gregorius went through them all. At first he seemed to be only drawing up an interim balance sheet of his feelings for them. Then, in the middle of the rows of benches, he noticed that he was thinking more frequently: *How much life they still have before them; how open their future still is; how much can still happen to them; how much they can still experience!*

Português. He heard the melody and saw the woman's face as it had emerged with closed eyes behind the rubbing towel, white as alabaster. One last time, he slid his eyes over the heads of the students. Then he stood up slowly, went to the door where he took the damp coat off the hook, and disappeared, without turning around, from the room.

His briefcase with the books that had accompanied him a lifetime remained behind on the desk. At the top of the steps, he paused and thought how he had taken the books to be rebound every couple of years, always to the same shop, where they laughed at the dog-eared, worn-out pages that felt almost like blotting paper. As long as the case lay on the desk, the students would assume he was coming back. But that wasn't why he had left the books or why he now resisted the temptation to get them. If he left now, he also had to go away from those books. He felt that very clearly, even if at this moment, on the way out, he had no idea what it really meant: to go away.

In the entrance hall, his look fell on the little puddle that had formed when the woman in the dripping coat had waited for him to come back from the bathroom. It was the trace of a visitor from another, faraway world, and Gregorius regarded it with a devotion usually reserved for archaeological finds. Only when he heard the janitor's shuffling step did he tear himself away and hurry out of the building.

Without turning around, he walked to the corner, where he could look back unseen. With a sudden force he wouldn't have expected of himself, he felt how much he loved this building and everything it stood for and how much he would miss it. He checked the numbers again: Forty-two years ago, as a fifteen-year-old Gymnasium student, he had entered it for the first time, wavering between anticipation and apprehension. Four years later, he had left it with his diploma in hand, only to come back again four years later as a substitute for the Greek teacher who had been in an accident, the teacher who had once opened the ancient world to him. The student substitute turned into a permanent student substitute, who was thirty-three by the time he finally took his university exams.

He had done that only because Florence, his wife, had urged him. He had never thought of a doctorate; if anyone asked him about it, he only laughed. Such things didn't matter. What did matter was something quite simple: to know the ancient texts down to the last detail, to recognize every grammatical and stylistic detail and to know the history of every one of those expressions. In other words: to be *good.* That wasn't modesty—his demands on himself were utterly immodest. Nor was it eccentricity or a warped kind of vanity. It had been, he sometimes thought later, a silent rage aimed at a pompous world, an unbending defiance against the world of show-offs who made his father suffer all his life because he had been only a museum guard. Others, who knew much less than he—ridiculously less, to tell the truth—had gotten degrees and solid positions: they seemed to belong to another, unbearably superficial world with standards he despised. In the school, no one would ever have come up with the idea of dismissing him and replacing him with somebody with a degree. The Rector, himself a philologist of ancient languages, knew how good Gregorius was—much better than he himself—and he knew that the students would have risen in revolt. When he finally did take the examination, it seemed absurdly simple to Gregorius, and he handed it in in half the time. He had always held it against Florence a bit that she had made him give up his defiance.

Gregorius turned around and walked slowly toward Kirchenfeldbrücke. When the bridge came into view, he had the amazing feeling, both upsetting and liberating, that, at the age of fifty-seven, he was about to take his life into his own hands for the first time.

2

At the spot where the woman had read the letter in the pouring rain, he stood still and looked down. For the first time, he realized how deep the drop was. Had she really wanted to jump? Or had that only been an impetuous apprehension on his part going back to Florence's brother who had also jumped off a bridge? Except that Portuguese was her mother tongue, he didn't know the slightest thing about the woman. Not even her name. Naturally, it was absurd to want to recognize the scrunched-up letter from up here. Nevertheless he stared down, his eyes tearing with the effort. Was that dark dot his umbrella? He felt in his jacket to make sure the notebook with the number written by the nameless Portuguese woman on his forehead was still there. Then he walked to the end of the bridge, uncertain where to turn next. He was in the course of running away from his previous life. Could somebody who intended to do that simply go home?

His eye fell on Hotel Bellevue, the oldest, most distinguished hotel in the city. Thousands of times he had passed by without ever going in. Every time he had felt it was there and now he thought that, in some vague way, it had been important to him that it was there; he would have been upset to learn that the building had been torn down or had stopped being a hotel—or even:

this hotel. But it had never entered his mind that he, Mundus, had any reason to be in there. Timorously, he now approached the entrance. A Bentley stopped, the chauffeur got out and went inside. When Gregorius followed him, he had the feeling of doing something absolutely revolutionary, indeed forbidden.

The lobby with the colored glass dome was empty and the carpet swallowed all sound. Gregorius was glad the rain had stopped and his coat wasn't dripping. With his heavy, clumsy shoes he went on into the dining room. Only two of the tables set for breakfast were occupied. Light notes of a Mozart divertimento created the impression that one was far away from everything loud, ugly and oppressive. Gregorius took off his coat and sat down at a table near the window. No, he said to the waiter in the light beige jacket, he wasn't a guest at the hotel. He felt scrutinized: the rough turtleneck under the worn-out jacket with the leather patches on the elbows; the baggy corduroy trousers; the sparse fringe of hair around the powerful bald head; the gray beard with the white specks that always made him look a bit unkempt. When the waiter had gone off with the order, Gregorius nervously checked whether he had enough money on him. Then he leaned his elbows on the starched tablecloth and looked over at the bridge.

It was absurd to hope she'd surface there once again. She had gone back over the bridge and then vanished in an Old City alley. He pictured her sitting at the back of the classroom absently gazing out the window. He saw her wringing her white hands. And again he saw her alabaster face surface from behind the towel, exhausted and vulnerable. *Português.* Hesitantly, he took out the notebook and looked at the phone number. The waiter brought breakfast with silver pitchers. Gregorius let the coffee grow cold. Once he stood up and went to the telephone. Halfway there, he turned around and went back to the table. He paid for the untouched breakfast and left the hotel.

It was years since he had been in the Spanish bookstore on Hirschengraben. Once, every now and then, he had gotten a book for Florence that she had needed for her dissertation on San Juan de la Cruz. On the bus, he had sometimes leafed through it, but at home he had never touched the books. Spanish—that was her territory. It was like Latin and completely different from Latin, and that bothered him. It went against his grain that words in which Latin was so present came out of contemporary mouths—on the street, in the supermarket, in the café. That they were used to order Coke, to haggle and to curse. He found the idea hard to bear and brushed it aside quickly and violently whenever it came. Naturally, the Romans had also haggled and cursed. But that was different. He loved the Latin sentences because they bore the calm of everything past. Because they didn't make you say something. Because they were speech beyond talk. And because they were beautiful in their immutability. Dead languages—people who talked about them like that had no idea, really no idea, and Gregorius could be harsh and unbending in his contempt for them. When Florence spoke Spanish on the phone, he shut the door. That offended her and he couldn't explain it to her.

The bookstore smelled wonderfully of old leather and dust. The owner, an aging man with a legendary knowledge of Romance languages, was busy in the back room. The front room was empty except for a young woman, a student apparently. She sat in a corner at a table and read a thin book with a yellowed binding. Gregorius would have preferred to be alone. The sense that he was standing here only because the melody of a Portuguese word wouldn't leave his mind, and maybe also because he hadn't known where else to go, that feeling would have been easier to bear without witnesses. He walked along the shelves without seeing anything. Now and then, he tilted his glasses to read a title on a high shelf; but as soon as he had read it, he had already forgotten it. As so often, he was alone with his thoughts, and his mind was sealed toward the outside.

When the door opened, he turned around quickly and at his disappointment that it was the mailman, he realized that, contrary to his intention and against all reason, he was still waiting for the Portuguese woman. Now the student shut the book and got up. But instead of putting it on the table with the others, she stood still, let her eyes slide again over the yellowed binding, stroked it with her hand, and only a few seconds later did she put the book down on the table, as softly and carefully as if it might crumble to dust with a nudge. Then, for a moment, she stood at the table and it looked as if she might reconsider and buy the book. But she went out, her hands buried in her coat pockets and her head down. Gregorius picked up the book and read: AMADEU INÁCIO DE ALMEIDA PRADO, UM OURIVES DAS PALAVRAS, LISBOA 1975.

The bookdealer came in, glanced at the book and pronounced the title aloud. Gregorius heard only a flow of sibilants; the half-swallowed, hardly audible vowels seemed to be only a pretext to keep repeating the hissing *sh* at the end.

"Do you speak Portuguese?"

Gregorius shook his head.

"*A Goldsmith of Words.* Isn't that a lovely title?"

"Quiet and elegant. Like dull silver. Would you say it again in Portuguese?"

The bookdealer repeated the words. Aside from the words themselves, you could hear how he enjoyed the velvety sound. Gregorius opened the book and leafed through it until the text began. He handed it to the man who looked at him with surprise and pleasure and started reading aloud. As he listened, Gregorius shut his eyes. After a few sentences, the man paused.

"Shall I translate?"

Gregorius nodded. And then he heard sentences that stunned him, for they sounded as if they had been written for him alone, and not only for him, but for him on this morning that had changed everything.

Of the thousand experiences we have, we find language for one at most and even this one merely by chance and without the care it deserves. Buried under all the mute experiences are those unseen ones that give our life its form, its color, and its melody. Then, when we turn to these treasures, as archaeologists of the soul, we discover how confusing they are. The object of contemplation refuses to stand still, the words bounce off the experience and in the end, pure contradictions stand on the paper. For a long time, I thought it was a defect, something to be overcome. Today I think it is different: that recognition of the confusion is the ideal path to understanding these intimate yet enigmatic experiences. That sounds strange, even bizarre, I know. But ever since I have seen the issue in this light, I have the feeling of being really awake and alive for the first time.

"That's the introduction," said the bookdealer and started leafing through it. "And now he seems to begin, passage after passage, to dig for all the buried experiences. To be the archaeologist of himself. Some passages are several pages long and others are quite short. Here, for example, is a fragment that consists of only one sentence." He translated:

Given that we can live only a small part of what there is in us—what happens with the rest?

"I'd like to have the book," said Gregorius.

The bookdealer closed it and ran his hand over the binding as affectionately as the student.

"I found it last year in the junk box of a secondhand bookshop in Lisbon. And now I remember: I took it because I liked the introduction. Somehow I lost sight of it." He looked at Gregorius, who awkwardly felt for his briefcase. "I give it to you as a gift."

"That's . . ." Gregorius began hoarsely and cleared his throat.

"It cost pretty much nothing," said the bookdealer and handed him the book. "Now I remember you: San Juan de la Cruz. Right?"

"That was my wife," said Gregorius.

"Then you're the classical philologist of Kirchenfeld, she talked about you. And later I heard somebody else talk about you. It sounded as if you were a walking encyclopedia." He laughed. "Definitely a popular encyclopedia."

Gregorius put the book in his coat pocket and held out his hand. "Thank you very much."

The bookdealer accompanied him to the door. "I hope I haven't . . ."

"Not at all," said Gregorius and touched his arm.

On Bubenbergplatz, he stood still and looked all around. Here he had spent his whole life, here he knew his way around, here he was at home. For someone as nearsighted as he, that was important. For someone like him, the city he lived in was like a shell, a cozy cave, a safe structure. Everything else meant danger. Only someone who had such thick eyeglasses could understand that. Florence hadn't understood it. And, maybe for the same reason she hadn't understood that he didn't like to fly. Getting on an airplane and arriving a few hours later in a completely different world with no time to take in individual images of the road—he didn't like that and it bothered him. *It's not right,* he had said to Florence. *What do you mean—not right?* she had asked, irritated. He couldn't explain it and so she had often flown by herself or with others, usually to South America.

Gregorius stood at the display window of Bubenberg Cinema. The late show was a black-and-white film from a novel by Georges Simenon: *L'homme qui regardait passer les trains*. He liked the title and looked for a long time at the stills. In the late '70s, when everybody bought a color television, he had tried in vain for days to get another black-and-white set. Finally he had brought one home from the dump. Even after he got married, he had held on to it stubbornly, keeping it in his study, and when he was by himself, he ignored the color set in the living room and turned on the old rattletrap that flickered, the images rolling occasionally. *Mundus, you're impossible,* Florence had said one day when she found him before the ugly, misshapen crate. When she started addressing him like the others, and even at home he was treated like a factotum of the city of Bern—that had been the beginning of the end. When the color television had vanished from the flat with the divorce, he had breathed a sigh of relief. Only years later, when the black-and-white picture tube broke altogether, did he buy a new color set.

The movie stills in the display window were big and crystal clear. One showed the pale alabaster face of Jeanne Moreau, stroking damp strands of hair off her forehead. Gregorius tore himself away and went into a nearby café to examine more closely the book of the Portuguese aristocrat who had tried to articulate himself and his mute experiences in words.

Only now, as he leafed slowly one by one through the pages, with a bibliophile's careful attention, did he discover the portrait of the author, an old photo, yellowed at the time the book was printed, where the once black surfaces had faded to dark brown, the bright face on a background of coarse-grained shadowy darkness. Gregorius polished his glasses, put them back on and, within a few minutes, was completely engrossed in the face.

The man may have been in his early thirties and radiated an intelligence, a self-confidence, and a boldness that literally dazzled Gregorius. The bright face with the high forehead was thatched with luxuriant dark hair that seemed to shine dully and was combed back like a helmet, with some strands falling next to the ears in soft waves. A narrow Roman nose gave the face great clarity, supported by strong eyebrows, set like solid beams painted with a broad brush, soon breaking off at the edges so that a concentration on the middle emerged, where the thoughts were. The full curved lips that wouldn't have been surprising in the face of a woman, were framed by a thin mustache and a trimmed beard, and the black shadows it cast on the slim neck gave Gregorius the impression of a certain coarseness and toughness. Yet, what determined everything were the dark eyes. They were underscored by shadows, not shadows of weariness, exhaustion or illness, but shadows of seriousness and melancholy. In his dark look, gentleness was mixed with intrepidity and inflexibility. The man was a dreamer and a poet, thought Gregorius, but at the same time, someone who could resolutely direct a weapon or a scalpel, and you'd better have gotten out of his way when his eyes flamed, eyes that could keep an army of powerful giants at bay, eyes that were no stranger to vile looks. As for his clothing, only the white shirt collar with the knot of a tie could be seen, and a jacket Gregorius imagined as a frock coat.

It was almost one o'clock when Gregorius surfaced from the absorption the portrait evoked in him. Once again, the coffee had grown cold in front of him. He wished he could hear the voice of the Portuguese man and see how he moved. Nineteen seventy-five: If he was then in his early thirties, as it seemed, he was now slightly over sixty. *Português*. Gregorius recalled the voice of the nameless Portuguese woman and transposed it to a lower pitch in his mind, but without turning it into the voice of the bookdealer. It was to be a voice of melancholy clarity, corresponding precisely with the visage of Amadeu de Prado. He tried to make the sentences in the book resonate with this voice. But it didn't work; he didn't know how the individual words were pronounced.

Outside, Lucien von Graffenried passed by the café. Gregorius was surprised and relieved to feel that he didn't flinch. He watched the boy go by and thought of the books on the desk. He had to wait until classes resumed at two o'clock. Only then could he go to the bookstore to buy a Portuguese language textbook.

3

As soon as Gregorius put on the first record at home and heard the first Portuguese sentences, the phone rang. The school. The ringing wouldn't stop. He stood next to the phone and tried out sentences he could say. *Ever since this morning I've been feeling that I'd like to make something different out of my life. That I don't want to be your Mundus anymore. I have no idea what the new one will be. But I can't put it off anymore. That is, my time is running out and there may not be much more of it left.* Gregorius spoke the sentences aloud. They were right, he knew that, he had said few sentences in his life that were so precisely right as these. But they sounded empty and bombastic when they were spoken, and it was impossible to say them into the phone.

The ringing had stopped. But it would start again. They were worried and wouldn't rest until they had found him; something could have happened to him. Sooner or later, the doorbell would ring. Now, in February, it always got dark early. He wouldn't be able to turn on a light. In the center of the city, the center of his life, he was attempting to flee and had to hide in the flat where he had lived for fifteen years. It was bizarre, absurd, and sounded like some potboiler. Yet it was *serious,* more serious than most things he had ever experienced and done. But it was impossible to explain it to those who were searching for him. Gregorius imagined opening the door and inviting them in. Impossible. Utterly impossible.

Three times in a row, he listened to the first record of the course, and slowly got an idea of the difference between the written and the spoken, and of all that was swallowed in spoken Portuguese. His unerring, facile memory for word formation kicked in.

The phone kept ringing at ever shorter intervals. He had taken over an antiquated phone from the previous tenant with a permanent connection he couldn't pull out. He had insisted that everything remain as it was. Now he took out a wool blanket to muffle the ringing.

The voices guiding the language course wanted him to repeat words and short sentences. Lips and tongue felt heavy and clumsy when he tried it. The ancient languages seemed made for his Bern mouth, and the thought that you had to hurry didn't appear in this timeless universe. The Portuguese, on the other hand, seemed always to be in a hurry, like the French, which made him feel inferior. Florence had loved it, this breakneck elegance, and when he had heard how easily she succeeded, he had become mute.

But now everything was different all of a sudden: Gregorius *wanted* to imitate the impetuous pace of the man and the woman's dancing lightness like a piccolo, and repeated the same sentences over to narrow the distance between his stolid enunciation and the twinkling voice on the record. After a while, he understood that he was experiencing a great liberation; the liberation from his self-imposed limitation, from a slowness and heaviness expressed in his name and had been expressed in the slow measured steps of his father walking ponderously from one room of the museum to another; liberation from an image of himself in which, even when he wasn't reading, he was someone bending myopically over dusty books; an image he hadn't drawn systematically, but that had grown slowly and imperceptibly; the image of Mundus, which bore not only his own handwriting, but also the handwriting of many others who had found it pleasant and convenient to be able to hold on to this silent museum-like figure and rest in it. It seemed to Gregorius that he was stepping out of this image like a dusty oil painting on the wall of a forgotten wing in the museum. He walked back and forth in the dim illumination of the lightless flat, ordered coffee in Portuguese, asked for a street in Lisbon, inquired about someone's profession and name, answered questions about his own profession, and conducted a brief conversation about the weather.

And all at once, he started talking with the Portuguese woman of the morning. He asked her why she was furious with the letter writer. *Você quis saltar? Did you want to jump?* Excitedly, he held the new dictionary and grammar book before his eyes and looked up expressions and verb forms he lacked. *Português.* How different the word sounded now! Before, it possessed the magic of a jewel from a distant, inaccessible land and now it was like one of a thousand gems in a palace whose door he had just pushed open.

The doorbell rang. Gregorius tiptoed to the phonograph and turned it off. They were young voices, student voices, conferring outside. Twice more, the shrill ring cut through the dim silence where Gregorius waited stock-still. Then the footsteps receding on the stairs.

The kitchen was the only room that faced the back and had a Venetian blind. Gregorius pulled it down and turned on the light. He took out the book of the Portuguese aristocrat and the language books, sat down at the table and started translating the first text after the introduction. It was like Latin and quite different from Latin, and now it didn't bother him in the slightest. It was a difficult text, and it took a long time. Methodically and with the stamina of a marathon runner, Gregorius selected the words and combed through the tables of verbs until he had deciphered the opaque verb forms. After a few sentences, he was gripped by a feverish excitement and he got some paper to write down the translation. It was almost nine o'clock when he was finally satisfied:

PROFUNDEZAS INCERTOS. UNCERTAIN DEPTHS. *Is there a mystery under the surfaces of human action? Or are human beings utterly what their obvious acts indicate?*

It is extraordinary, but the answer changes in me with the light that falls on the city and the Tagus. If it is the enchanting light of a shimmering August day that produces clear, sharp-edged shadows, the thought of a hidden human depth seems bizarre and like a curious, even slightly touching fantasy, like a mirage, that arises when I look too long at the waves flashing in that light. On the other hand, if city and river are clouded over on a dreary January day by a dome of shadowless light and boring gray, I know no greater certainty than this: that all human action is only an extremely imperfect, ridiculously helpless expression of a hidden internal life of unimagined depths that presses to the surface without ever being able to reach it even remotely.

And to this amazing, upsetting unreliability of my judgment is added another experience that, since I have come to know it, steeps my life continually in a distressing uncertainty: that, in this matter, the really most important one for us human beings, I waver even when it concerns myself. For when I sit in front of my favorite café, basking in the sun, and overhear the tinkling laughter of the passing Senhoras, my whole inner world seems filled down to the deepest corner, and is known to me through and through because it exhausts itself in these pleasant feelings. Yet, if a disenchanting, sobering layer of clouds pushes in before the sun, with one fell swoop, I am sure there are hidden depths and abysses in me, where unimagined things could break out and sweep me away. Then I quickly pay and hastily seek diversion in the hope that the sun might soon break out again and restore the reassuring superficiality.

Gregorius opened the picture of Amadeu de Prado and leaned the book against the table lamp. Sentence after sentence, he read the translated text into the bold, melancholy eyes. Only once had he done something like that: when he had read Marcus Aurelius's Meditations as a student. A plaster bust of the emperor had stood on the table, and when he worked on the text, he seemed to be doing it under the aegis of his mute presence. But between then and now there was a difference, which Gregorius felt ever more clearly as the night progressed, without being able to put it into words. He knew only one thing as two o'clock approached: With the sharpness of his perception, the Portuguese aristocrat had granted him an alertness and precision of feeling that didn't come even from the wise emperor, whose meditations he had devoured as if they were aimed directly at him. In the meantime, Gregorius had translated another note:

PALAVRAS NUM SILÊNCIO DE OURO. WORDS IN GOLDEN SILENCE. *When I read a newspaper, listen to the radio or overhear what people are saying in the café, I often feel aversion, even disgust at the same words written and spoken over and over—at the same expressions, phrases, and metaphors repeated. And the worst is, when I hear myself and have to admit that I too repeat the eternally same things. They're so horribly frayed and threadbare, these words, worn out by being used millions of times. Do they still have any meaning? Naturally, the exchange of words functions, people act on them, they laugh and cry, they go left or right, the waiter brings the coffee or tea. But that's not what I want to ask. The question is: Are they still an expression of* thoughts*? Or only effective sounds that drive people here and there because the worn grooves of babble incessantly flash?*

Then I go to the beach and hold my head far into the wind, which I wish were icy, colder than we know it in these parts: May it blow all the hackneyed words, all the insipid language habits out of me so I could come back with a cleansed mind, cleansed of the slag of the same talk. But the first time I have to say something, it's all as before. The cleansing I long for doesn't come by itself. I have to do *something, and I have to do it* with words. *But what? It's not that I'd like to get out of my own language and into another. No, it has nothing to do with linguistic desertion. And I also tell myself something else: You can't invent a new language. But is that what would I like?*

Maybe it's like this: I'd like to reset *Portuguese words. The sentences that would emerge from this new setting might not be odd or eccentric, not exalted, affected or artificial. They must be archetypal sentences of the Portuguese that constitute its center so that you would have the feeling that they originated directly and undefiled from the transparent, sparkling nature of this language. The words must be as unblemished as polished marble, and they must be pure as the notes in a Bach partita, which turn everything that is not themselves into perfect silence. Sometimes, when a remnant of conciliation with the linguistic sludge is in me, I think, it could be the pleasant silence of a cozy living room or the relaxed silence between lovers. But when I am utterly overcome by rage at the sticky habits of words, then it must be no less than the clear, cool silence of the unlighted outer space, where I pull my noiseless orbits as the only one who speaks Portuguese. The waiter, the barber, the conductor—they would be puzzled if they heard the newly set words and their amazement would refer to the beauty of the sentences, a beauty that would be nothing but the gleam of their clarity. They would be—I imagine—cogent sentences, and could even be called inexorable. Incorruptible and firm they would stand there and thus be like the words of a god. At the same time, they would be without exaggeration and without pomposity, precise and so laconic that you couldn't take away one single word, one single comma. Thus they would be like a poem, plaited by a goldsmith of words.*

Hunger made Gregorius's stomach ache and he forced himself to eat something. Later he sat with a cup of tea in the dark living room. What now? Twice more the doorbell had rung, and the last time he had heard the stifled buzz of the phone was shortly before midnight. Tomorrow they would file a missing person's report and then the police would appear at the door sometime. He could still go back. At quarter to eight he would walk across the Kirchenfeldbrücke, enter the Gymnasium and wipe out his enigmatic absence with some story that would make him look ludicrous, but that was all, and it suited him. They would never learn anything of the enormous distance he had covered internally in less than twenty-four hours.

But that was it: he *had* covered it. And he didn't want to let himself be forced by others to undo this silent journey. He took out a map of Europe and considered how you got to Lisbon by train. Train information, he learned on the phone, didn't open until six o'clock. He started packing.

It was almost four when he sat in the chair, ready to leave. Outside, it started snowing. Suddenly all courage deserted him. It was a crackpot idea. A nameless, confused Portuguese woman. Yellowed notes of a Portuguese aristocrat. A language course for beginners. The idea of time running out. You don't run away to Lisbon in the middle of winter because of that.

At five, Gregorius called Constantine Doxiades, his eye doctor. They had often called each other in the middle of the night to share their common suffering from insomnia. Sleepless people were bound by a wordless solidarity. Sometimes he played a blind game of speed chess with the Greek, and afterward Gregorius could sleep a little before it was time to go to school.

"Doesn't make much sense, does it?" said Gregorius at the end of his faltering story. The Greek was silent. Gregorius was familiar with that. Now he would shut his eyes and pinch the bridge of his nose with thumb and index finger.

"Yes, ideed, it does make sense," said the Greek now. "Indeed."

"Will you help me if, on the way, I don't know how to go on?"

"Just call. Day or night. Don't forget the spare glasses."

There it was again, the laconic certainty in his voice. A medical certainty, but also a certainty that went far beyond anything professional; the certainty of a man who took time for his thoughts so they were later expressed in valid judgments. For twenty years, Gregorius had been going to this doctor, the only one who could remove his fear of going blind. Sometimes, he compared him with his father, who, after his wife's premature death, seemed—no matter where he was or what he did—to dwell everywhere in the dusty safety of a museum. Gregorius had learned young that it was very fragile, this safety. He had liked his father and there had been moments when the feeling was even stronger and deeper than simple liking. But he had suffered from the fact that the father was not someone you could rely on, could not hold on to, unlike the Greek, whose solid judgment you could trust. Later, he had sometimes felt guilty about this accusation. The safety and self-confidence he didn't have weren't something a person could control or be accused for lacking. You had to be lucky with yourself to be a self-confident person. And his father hadn't had much luck, either with himself or with others.

Gregorius sat down at the kitchen table and drafted letters to the Rector. They were either too abrupt or too apologetic. At six, he called railroad information. From Geneva, the trip took twenty-six hours. It went through Paris and Irún in the Basque region, and from there with the night train to Lisbon, arriving at eleven in the morning. Gregorius ordered the ticket. The train to Geneva left at eight-thirty.

Now he got the letter right.

Honored Rector, Dear Colleague Kägi,

You will have learned by now that I left class yesterday without an explanation and didn't come back, and you will also know that I have remained incommunicado. I am well, nothing has happened to me. But, in the course of the day yesterday, I had an experience that has changed a great deal. It is too personal and still much too obscure for me to put it on paper now. I must simply ask you to accept my abrupt and unexplained act. You know me well enough, I think, to know that it does not happen out of imprudence, irresponsibility or indifference. I am setting off on a distant journey and when I will return and in what sense is wide open. I don't expect you to keep the position open for me. Most of my life has been closely intertwined with this Gymna-

sium, and I am sure I will miss it. But now, something is driving me away from it and it could well be that this movement is final. You and I are both admirers of Marcus Aurelius, and you will remember this passage in his Meditations: "Do wrong to thyself, do wrong to thyself, my soul; but later thou wilt no longer have the opportunity of respecting and honoring thyself. For every man has but one life. But yours is nearly finished, though in it you had no regard for yourself but placed thy felicity in the souls of others. . . . But those who do not observe the impulses of their own minds must of necessity be unhappy."

Thank you for the trust you have always shown me and for the good cooperation. You will find—I'm sure—the right words for the students, words that will let them know how much I liked working with them. Before I left yesterday, I looked at them and thought: How much time they still have before them!

In the hope of your understanding and with best wishes for you and your work, I remain yours,

Raimund Gregorius

P.S. I left my books on the desk. Would you pick them up and make sure nothing happens to them?

Gregorius mailed the letter at the railroad station. Then at the ATM, his hands shook. He polished his glasses and made sure he had his passport, ticket and address book. He found a seat at the window. When the train left for Geneva, it was snowing big, slow flakes.

4

As long as possible, Gregorius's eyes clung to the last houses of the city. When they had finally and irrevocably disappeared from view, he took out the notebook and started writing down the names of the students he had taught over time. He started with the previous year and worked backward into the past. For every name he sought a face, a characteristic gesture and a telling episode. He had no trouble with the last three years, then he kept having the feeling that somebody was missing. In the mid-nineties, the classes consisted of only a few faces and names, and then the chronological sequence blurred. What remained were only a few boys and girls who stood out.

He shut the notebook. From time to time, in the city, he had run into a student he had taught many years earlier. They weren't boys and girls now, but men and women with spouses, professions and children. He was taken aback when he saw the changes in their faces. Sometimes just because of change: a premature bitterness, a harried look, a symptom of serious illness. But what usually startled him was the simple fact that the altered faces indicated the incessant passing of time and the merciless decline of all living things. Then he looked at his hands with their first age spots, and sometimes he took out photos of himself as a student and tried to visualize how it had been to cover this long stretch to the present, day after day, year after year. On such days, he was jumpier than usual and then would appear unannounced at Doxiades's office so he could once again dispel his fear of going blind. Encounters with students who had lived many years abroad, on other continents, in other climates, with other languages, threw him off balance the most. *And you? Still in Kirchenfeld?* they asked, and their movements showed their impatience to go on. At night after such an encounter, first he would defend himself against these questions and later against the feeling of having to defend himself.

And now, with all this going through his head, he sat in the train, after more than twenty-four hours without sleep, and traveled toward a future as uncertain as he had ever had before him.

The stop in Lausanne was a temptation. Across the same platform was the train to Bern. Gregorius imagined getting off in the Bern railroad station. He looked at the clock. If he took a taxi to Kirchenfeld, he could still make the fourth period. The letter—he had to catch the mailman tomorrow or ask Kägi to give him back the envelope unopened. Unpleasant but not impossible. Now his look fell on the notebook on the compartment table. Without opening it, he saw the list of student names. And all of a sudden, he understood: what had started as the temptation to hold on to something familiar after the last Bern houses slipped away, had become more a farewell as the hours passed. To be able to part from something, he thought as the train started moving, you had to confront it in a way that created internal distance. You had to turn the unspoken, diffuse self-understanding it had wrapped around you into a clarity that showed what it meant to you. And that meant it had to congeal into something with distinct contours. Something as distinct as the list of the many students who had meant more to his life than anything else. Gregorius felt as if the train now rolling out of the railroad station also left a piece of him behind. He seemed driven onto an ice floe that had come loose in a mild earthquake, onto an open cold sea.

As the train picked up speed, he fell asleep and woke up only when he felt the car come to a stop in the Geneva railroad station. On the way to the French high-speed train, he was as excited as if he had set out for a trip on the Trans-Siberian Railroad. As soon as he had taken his seat, the car filled up with a French tour group. A chatter of hysterical elegance filled the car, and when someone in an open coat bent over him to put a suitcase on the storage shelf, Gregorius's eyeglasses were torn off. Then he did something he had never done on his own: he took his things and moved into first class.

The few opportunities he had had to travel first class were twenty years ago. It had been Florence who had urged it, he had gone along and sat down on the expensive cushion with a feeling of fraud. *Do you find me boring?* he had asked her after one of those trips. *What? But Mundus, you can't ask me such a thing!* she had said and ran her hand through her hair as she always did when she was at a loss. Now, when the train started moving, as Gregorius stroked the elegant cushion with both hands, his act seemed like a belated, childish revenge he didn't really understand. He was glad nobody was sitting nearby who could have witnessed the foolish feeling.

He was afraid of the extra fee he had to pay the conductor, and when the man had gone, he counted his money twice. He whispered the pin number of his credit card to himself and wrote it in the notebook. Shortly after, he tore out the page and threw it away. In Geneva, it had stopped snowing and now he saw the sun again for the first time in weeks. It warmed his face behind the windowpane and he calmed down. He had always had much too much money in his checking account, he did know that. *What's going on with your money?* said the bank teller when she saw again what had accumulated because he withdrew so little. *You must be* doing *something with your money!* She invested it for him and so, over the years, he had become a prosperous man who seemed oblivious to his prosperity.

Gregorius thought of his two Latin books he had left on the desk this time yesterday. *Anneli Weiss* was on the flyleaf, written in ink in a childish hand. At home there wasn't money for new books, so he had scoured the city until he found used copies in a second-hand bookstore. When he produced his find, his father's Adam's apple had moved fiercely, it always moved fiercely when something weighed on his mind. At first, he was bothered by the strange name in the book. But then he had imagined the previous owner as a girl with white kneesocks and windblown hair, and soon he wouldn't have traded the used book for a new one at any price. Nevertheless, he had later enjoyed being able to buy old texts in beautiful, expensive editions with the money he started earning as a substitute teacher. That was now more than thirty years ago, and still seemed a little unreal to him today. Just recently, he had stood at the bookshelves and thought: I can afford such a library!

Slowly, the memory images in Gregorius were distorted into dream images in which the thin book where his mother wrote down what she earned by cleaning kept popping up like a tormenting will-o'-the-wisp. He was glad when he was awakened by the noise of a smashing glass.

An hour to Paris. Gregorius sat down in the dining car and looked out into a bright, early spring day. And there, all of a sudden, he realized that he was in fact making this trip—that it wasn't only a possibility, something he had thought up on a sleepless night and that could have been, but something that really and truly was taking place. And the more space he gave this feeling, the more it seemed to him that the relation of possibility and reality were beginning to change. Kägi, his school and all the students in his notebook really had existed, but only as possibilities that had been accidentally realized. But what he was experiencing in this moment —the sliding and muted thunder of the train, the slight clink of the glasses moving on the next table, the odor of rancid oil coming from the kitchen, the smoke of the cigarette the cook now and then puffed—possessed a reality that had nothing to do with mere possibility or with realized possibility, which was instead pure and simple reality, filled with the density and overwhelming inevitability marking something utterly real.

Gregorius sat before the empty plate and the steaming cup of coffee and had the feeling of never having been so awake in his whole life. And it seemed to him that it wasn't a matter of degree, as when you slowly shook off sleep and became more awake until you were fully there. It was different. It was a different, new *kind* of wakefulness, a new kind of being in the world he had never known before. When the Gare de Lyon came in sight, he went back to his seat and afterward, when he set foot on the platform, it seemed to him as if, for the first time, he was fully aware of getting off a train.

5

The force of memory hit him unprepared. He hadn't forgotten that this had been their first railroad station, their first arrival together in a foreign city. Naturally he hadn't forgotten that. But he hadn't figured that, when he stood here, it would be as if no time at all had elapsed. The green iron girders and the red pipes. The arches. The translucent roof.

"Let's go to Paris!" Florence had suddenly said at the first breakfast in his kitchen, arms wound around a drawn-up leg.

"You mean . . ."

"Yes, now. Right now!"

She had been his student, a pretty, usually disheveled girl who turned all heads with her provocative moodiness. From one semester to the next, she had become first-rate in Latin and Greek, and the first time he entered the optional Hebrew class that year, she was sitting in the first row. But Gregorius would never have even dreamed it could have anything to do with him.

The matriculation exam came and another year went by before they met in the university cafeteria and sat there until they were thrown out.

"What a blind worm you are!" she said when she took off his glasses. "You didn't notice anything! *Everybody* knew! *Everybody!*"

It was correct, thought Gregorius, sitting now in the taxi to Gare Montparnasse, that he was one who didn't notice such a thing—one who was so inconspicous even to himself that he couldn't have believed that someone could have a strong feeling for him—*him*! But with Florence he was right in the end.

"You never really meant *me,*" he had said to her at the end of their five-year marriage.

Those were the only accusing words he had said to her the whole time. They had burned like fire and everything seemed to turn to ashes.

She had looked at the floor. In spite of everything, he had hoped for denial. It hadn't come.

LA COUPOLE. Gregorius hadn't expected to go down Boulevard Montparnasse and see the restaurant, where their separation had been sealed without a word. He asked the driver to stop and looked silently for a while at the red awning with the yellow letters and the three stars left and right. It had been an honor for Florence, a doctoral student, to be invited to this conference on Romance literature. On the phone, she had sounded ecstatic, almost hysterical, he thought, so he hesitated to meet her for the weekend as arranged. But then he had gone and had met with her new friends in this famous resturant, whose reputation for the most exquisite food and the most expensive wines had proved to him as soon as he entered that he didn't belong here.

"One more moment," he said to the driver and crossed the street.

Nothing had changed, and he immediately saw the table where he, very unsuitably dressed, had faced these literary hotshots boldly. They had been talking about Horace and Sappho, he remembered as he now stood in the way of the hurrying and irritated waiter. Nobody could keep up with him as he quoted verse after verse, crushing to dust the witty aperçus of the well-dressed gentlemen of the Sorbonne with his Bern accent, one after the other, until the table grew silent.

On the way back, Florence had sat alone in the dining car while the aftershock of his rage slowly ebbed and gave way to a sadness that he had needed to stand up to Florence like that; for that's what it was naturally about.

Lost in those distant events, Gregorius had forgotten the time and now the taxi driver had to drive at breakneck speed to get to Gare Montparnasse on time. When he finally sat breathless in his seat and the train for Irún started moving, a sense that had assaulted him in Geneva returned: that it was the train and not he who decided that this very awake and very real trip carrying him further out of his former life, hour after hour, station after station, would go on. For three hours, to Bordeaux, there would be no more stops, no possibility of turning around.

He looked at the clock. At school, the first day without him was coming to an end. In these minutes, the six students of Hebrew were waiting for him. At six, after the double class, he had sometimes gone with them to a café, and then he had talked to them of the historical growth and contingency of the biblical texts. Ruth Gautschi and David Lehmann, who wanted to study theology and worked the hardest, kept finding a reason not to go along. A month ago he had talked to them about it. They had the feeling that he was taking something away from them, they had answered evasively. Naturally, these texts could also be examined philologically. After all, they were the Holy Scriptures.

Behind closed eyes, Gregorius recommended to the Rector to hire a theology student for Hebrew, one of his former students. With her copper-colored hair, she had sat in the same place as Florence once had. But his hope that that might not be accidental had been in vain.

For a few moments his head was perfectly empty, then Gregorius pictured the face of the Portuguese woman emerging white, almost transparent, behind the rubbing towel. Once again, he stood in the school bathroom at the mirror and felt that he didn't want to wipe away the phone number the enigmatic woman had drawn on his forehead. Once again, he stood up at his desk, took the damp coat off the hook and went out of the classroom.

Português. Gregorius started, opened his eyes, and looked out at the flat French landscape, where the sun was bending down to the horizon. The word that had been like a melody lost in a dreamy expanse, all of a sudden had lost its force. He tried to retrieve the magical sound of the voice, but what he managed to grasp was only a rapidly fading echo, and the vain attempt only strengthened the feeling that the precious word, the basis of this whole crazy trip, had slipped away. And it didn't help that he still knew precisely how the speaker on the language record had pronounced the word.

He went to the bathroom and held his face under the chlorinated water for a long time. Back in his seat, he took the book of the Portuguese aristocrat out of his bag and started translating the next passage. At first, it was mainly an escape, the desperate attempt, despite the fear, to keep on believing in this trip. But after the first sentence, the text fascinated him again as much as it had in the kitchen at night.

NOBREZA SILENCIOSA. SILENT NOBILITY. *It is a mistake to believe that the crucial moments of a life when its habitual direction changes forever must be loud and shrill dramatics, washed away by fierce internal surges. This is a kitschy fairy tale started by boozing journalists, flashbulb-seeking filmmakers and authors whose minds look like tabloids. In truth, the dramatics of a life-determining experience are often unbelievably soft. It has so little akin to the bang, the flash, or the volcanic eruption that, at the moment it is made, the experience is often not even noticed. When it deploys its revolutionary effect and plunges a life into a brand-new light giving it a brand-new melody, it does that silently and in this wonderful silence resides its special nobility.*

From time to time, Gregorius glanced up from the text and looked out to the west. In the remaining brightness of the twilight sky, it seemed the sea could now be imagined. He put the dictionary away and shut his eyes.

If I could see the sea just once, his mother had said half a year before her death, as if she felt that the end was near; *but we simply can't afford that.*

What bank will give me a loan, Gregorius heard the father say, *and for such a thing.*

Gregorius had been angry at him for this placid resignation. And then, he, who was still a student in Kirchenfeld, had done something that surprised him so much he never got rid of the feeling that maybe it really didn't happen.

It was late March, early spring. People hung their coats over their arms, and mild air streamed into the annex through the open window. The annex had been put up a few years earlier because there was no room in the main building of the Gymnasium, and it had become a tradition to put the seniors there. Changing to the annex seemed the first step toward graduation. Feelings of liberation and fear balanced each other. *One more year and then it was finally over . . . One more year and then you had to . . .* These alternating feelings were expressed in the way the students strolled to the annex, nonchalant and scared at the same time. Even now, forty years later in the train to Irún, Gregorius could feel how it had been to be in his body back then.

The afternoon began with Greek. It was the Rector who taught, Kägi's predecessor. He had the most beautiful Greek handwriting you could imagine, he drew the letters ceremonially, especially the loops—as in Omega or Theta, or when he pulled the Eta down—were the purest calligraphy. He loved Greek. *But he loved it in the wrong way*, thought Gregorius at the back of the classroom. His way of loving it was a conceited way. It wasn't by celebrating the words. If it had been that—Gregorius would have liked it. But when this man wrote out the most remote and difficult verb forms as a virtuoso, he celebrated not the *words*, but rather *he himself* as one who knew them. The words thus became ornaments for him, he adorned himself with them, they turned into something like the polka-dotted bow tie he wore year in, year out. They flowed from his writing hand with the signet ring as if they too were a kind of signet ring, a conceited jewel and just as superfluous. And so, the Greek words really stopped being *Greek* words. It was as if the gold dust from the signet ring corroded their Greek essence that was revealed only to those who loved it for its own sake. Poetry for the Rector was something like an exquisite piece of furniture, a fine wine or an elegant evening gown. Gregorius had the feeling that he robbed him of the verses of Aeschylus and Sophocles with this smugness. He seemed to know nothing of Greek theater. Or no, he knew everything about it, was often there, guided educational tours and came back with a suntan. But he didn't *understand* anything about it—even if Gregorius couldn't have said what he meant by that.

He had looked out the open window of the annex and thought of his mother's sentence, a sentence seething with his rage at the Rector's conceit, even though he couldn't have explained the connection. He felt his heart beat in his throat. A look at the board assured him that it would take the Rector a while to finish the sentence he had started and turn around to the students to explain. Without a sound, he pushed the chair back, as the others went on writing with bent backs. He left the open notebook on the desk. With the tense slowness of someone preparing a surprise attack, he took two steps to the open window, sat down on the sill, swung his legs over and was outside.

The last thing he saw inside was the amazed and amused face of Eva, the girl with red hair, freckles, and the squint that had always rested on him mockingly, to his despair, on the boy wearing the thick eyeglasses with the cheap and ugly frames. She turned to her bench mate and whispered something in her hair. "Unbelievable!"

she would say. She said it all the time. And so she was called *Unbelievable.* "Unbelievable!" she had said when she found out her nickname.

Gregorius had walked quickly to Bärenplatz. It was a market, one stand after another, and you made your way slowly. When the crowd forced him to stop at a stand, his eye fell on the open cashbox, a simple metal case with one compartment for coins and another for bills, which formed a thick pile. The market woman was now bending over, fiddling with something under the display, her broad behind jutting out in the coarse cloth of a checked dress. Gregorius had slowly pushed toward the cashbox, his look circling over the people. With two steps, he was behind the counter, grabbed the bundle of bills and plunged into the crowd. When he went up the street to the railroad station, panting, and forcing himself to walk calmly, he expected somebody to call him from behind or take hold of him. But nothing had happened.

They lived on Länggasse, in a gray apartment house with dirty plasterwork, and when Gregorius entered the staircase, which smelled of cabbage from morning to night, he saw himself entering the room of the sick mother he wanted to surprise with the announcement that she would soon see the sea. Only on the last landing before the apartment door did he realize that the whole thing was impossible, absolutely ludicrous. How was he to explain to her and later to the father where he had suddenly gotten so much money? He, who had no practice in lying?

On the way back to Bärenplatz, he bought an envelope and stuck the bundle of bills inside. The woman in the checked dress had a tear-stained face when he came back to her stand. He bought some fruit, and when she was busy with the scale in the other corner, he pushed the envelope under the vegetables. Shortly before the end of recess, he was back at school, climbed into the annex through the open window and sat down in his seat.

"Unbelievable!" said Eva when she saw him and she began to regard him with more respect than before. But that was less important than he had thought. More important was that the discovery about himself given by the last hour didn't inspire any horror in him, but only a great amazement that reverberated for weeks.

The train left the railroad station of Bordeaux for Biarritz. Outside it was almost night, and Gregorius saw himself in the window. What would have become of him if the one who had taken the money out of the cashbox back then had determined his life instead of the one who began to love the ancient silent words so much that he granted them sovereignty over everything else? What did that breakout have in common with this one now? Anything?

Gregorius reached for Prado's book and searched for the laconic note the bookdealer in the Spanish bookstore on Hirschengraben had translated for him:

Given that we can live only a small part of what there is in us—what happens with the rest?

In Biarritz, a man and woman got on, stood at the seat in front of Gregorius and discussed their seat reservation. *Vinte e oito*. It took him a while to identify the repeated sounds as Portuguese words and to confirm his assumption: twenty-eight. He concentrated on what they were saying and now and then he managed to make out a word in the next half hour, but only a few. Tomorrow morning, he would get out in a city where most of what the people said would swoosh by him incomprehensibly. He thought of Bubenplatz, Bärenplatz, Bundesterrasse, the Kirchenfeldbrücke. Meanwhile, it had become pitch-dark outside. Gregorius felt for the money, the credit cards, and the spare glasses. He was anxious.

They came to the railroad station of Hendaye, the French border town. The car emptied out. When the Portuguese couple noticed that, they were jolted and grabbed the suitcases from the shelf. *"Isto ainda não é Irún,"* said Gregorius: This isn't yet Irún. It was a sentence from the language course record, only the name of the town was different. The Portuguese people hesitated about his awkward pronunciation and the slowness with which he strung the words together. But they looked out and now they saw the railroad station sign. *"Muito obrigada,"* said the woman. *"De nada,"* replied Gregorius. The Portuguese couple sat down, the train went on.

Gregorius was never to forget this scene. They were his first Portuguese words in the real world and they worked. That words could cause something in the world, make someone move or stop, laugh or cry: even as a child he had found it enigmatic and it had never stopped impressing him. How did words do that? Wasn't it like magic? But at this moment, the mystery seemed greater than usual, for these were words he hadn't even known yesterday morning. A few minutes later, when he set foot on the platform of Irún, all fear had vanished, and he walked confidently to the sleeping car.

6

It was ten o'clock when the train that would cross the Iberian Peninsula the next morning started moving, the dreary railroad station lamps slid past one after another into the dark. The two compartments next to Gregorius had remained empty. Two compartments down, toward the dining car, a tall slim man with graying hair was leaning on his door. *"Boa noite,"* he said when their eyes met. *"Boa noite,"* said Gregorius.

When he heard the awkward pronunciation, a smile flitted over the stranger's face. It was a chiseled face with clear, definite features, and there was something distinguished and reserved about it. The man's dark clothing was conspicuously elegant and made Gregorius think of the lobby of an opera house. Only the loosened tie didn't fit. Now the man folded his arms over his vest, leaned his head against the door and shut his eyes. With his eyes shut, the face looked very white and radiated fatigue, a fatigue that must have come from other things than the late hour. When the train had reached its full speed a few minutes later, the man opened his eyes, nodded to Gregorius, and disappeared into his compartment.

Gregorius would have given anything to be able to fall asleep, but even the monotonous beat of the wheels coming through the bed didn't help. He sat up and pressed his forehead against the window. Desolate little railroad stations slid past, milky, diffuse lightbulbs, darting past, illegible place names, parked baggage carts, a head with a cap in a railroad guard hut, a stray dog, a rucksack on a pillar, with a blond mop of hair on top. The certainty granted by the first Portuguese words began to crumble. *Just call. Day or night.* He heard Doxiades's voice and thought of their first meeting twenty years earlier, when he still had a strong accent.

"Blind? No. You just got a bad break with your eyes. We check the retina regularly. Besides, there are lasers now. No reason to panic." On the way to the door, he had stood still and looked at him intensely. "Any other concerns?"

Gregorius had shook his head mutely. Only a few months later did he tell him he had seen the divorce from Florence coming. The Greek had nodded, it seemed not to surprise him. *Sometimes we're afraid of something because we're afraid of something else,* he had said.

Shortly before midnight, Gregorius went into the dining car. The car was empty except for the man with graying hair playing chess with the waiter. In fact, the car was closed, the waiter indicated, but then he got Gregorius a mineral water and beckoned him to join them. Gregorius quickly saw that the man, who had put on a pair of gold-framed glasses, had fallen into the waiter's cunning trap. With his hand on the piece, the man looked at him before he moved. Gregorius shook his head and the man withdrew his hand. The waiter, a man with calloused hands whose coarse features didn't seem to conceal a brain for chess, looked up surprised. Now the man with the gold eyeglasses turned the board toward Gregorius and gestured to him to play. It was a long, tough struggle and it was two o'clock when the waiter gave up.

Afterward, when they stood at his compartment door, the man asked Gregorius where he was from and then they spoke French. He took this train every two weeks, said the man, and only once had he been able to beat this waiter, while he usually beat others.

He introduced himself: José António da Silveira. He was, as he said, a businessman and sold porcelain in Biarritz and since he was afraid of flying, he took the train.

"Who knows the real reasons for his fear," he said after a pause and now the exhaustion Gregorius had noted earlier appeared again on his face.

Then, when he told how he had taken over his father's little business and had built it into a big firm, he talked about himself as about somebody else, who had made thoroughly understandable but altogether wrong decisions. And it sounded the same when he talked of his divorce and the two children he hardly got to see anymore. Disappointment and sadness were in his voice, and what impressed Gregorius was that they were devoid of self-pity.

"The problem is," said Silveira, as the train stopped in the railroad station of Valladolid, "that we have no grasp of our life as a whole. Neither forward nor backward. If something goes well, we simply had good luck." An invisible hammer tested the brakes. "And how do you come to be in this train?"

They sat on the bed of Silveiras's compartment as Gregorius told his story. He left out the Portuguese woman on the Kirchenfeldbrücke. That was something he could tell Doxiades, not a stranger. He was glad Silveira didn't ask him to take out Prado's book. He didn't want anybody else to read it and say something about it.

There was silence when he had finished. Silveira's mind was busy, Gregorius saw from the way he turned his signet ring and the brief, shy glances he cast at him.

"And you just got up and left the school? Just like that?"

Gregorius nodded. Suddenly he regretted talking about it; something precious had been endangered. Now he wanted to try to sleep, he said. Silveira took out a little notebook. Would he repeat to him the words of Marcus Aurelius about the impulses of one's soul? When Gregorius left his compartment, Silveira sat bent over the notebook going along the words with the pen.

Gregorius dreamed of red cedars. The words *cedros vermelhos* kept flickering through his restless sleep. It was the name of the publisher of Prado's notes. He hadn't paid any special attention to it previously. It was only Silveira's question of how he wanted to find the author that reminded him he would first have to look for this publishing house. Maybe he had published the book privately, he had thought as he fell asleep; then the red cedars would have had a meaning known only to Amadeu de Prado. In the dream, he wandered with the mysterious name on his lips and the phone book under his arm, through twisted, steeply rising streets of Lisbon, lost in a faceless city, knowing only that it was set on hills.

When he woke up at six o'clock and saw the name SALAMANCA before his compartment window, out of the blue, a sluice gate of memory opened that had remained closed for four decades. The first thing it released was the name of another city: *Isfahan*. Suddenly it was there, the name of the Persian city where he had wanted to go after he finished school. The name bearing so much mysterious strangeness touched Gregorius at this moment, like the code of another possible life he hadn't dared live. And as the train now left the Salamanca station, once again after so long, he lived through the feelings back then when that other life had both opened and closed.

It had started when the Hebrew teacher had them read the Book of Job after a year. For Gregorius, it had been intoxicating when he started understanding the sentences and a path opened for him leading into the Orient. In Karl May, the Orient sounded very German, not only because of the language. Now, in the book read from back to front, it sounded like the Orient. Eliphaz of Telman, Bildad of Shuach, Zofar of Na'ama. Job's three friends. Even the names, in their bewitching foreignness, seemed to come from beyond all oceans. What a wonderful, dreamlike world that was!

Afterward, for a while, he had wanted to become an Orientalist. Someone who knew his way around in *Morgenland*, the East, he loved the German word, it led out of Länggasse into a bright light. Shortly before graduation, he had applied for the position of tutor to the children of a Swiss industrialist in Isfahan. Reluctantly—worried about him, but also fearing the void he would leave behind—the father had given him the thirteen francs thirty for the Persian grammar, and he had written the new codes of the Orient on the small blackboard in his room.

But then a dream had begun haunting him, a dream he seemed to dream all night long. It had been a very simple dream and part of the torment was this simplicity, which seemed to increase the more often the image returned. For in fact the dream had consisted of only one single image: hot Oriental sand, desert sand, white and scorching, had blown on his eyeglasses from the smoldering breath of Persia and had settled there as a white-hot crust robbing him of all sight, melting the lenses and gnawing his eyes.

After two or three weeks when the dream kept popping up and haunting him far into the day, he had taken back the Persian grammar and given the money back to the father. The three francs thirty he could keep, he had kept in a small box, and it had been as if he now possessed Persian money.

What would have become of him if he had overcome the fear of the scorching dust of the Orient and had gone? Gregorius thought of how cold-bloodedly he had reached into the cashbox of the market woman. Would that have been enough to cope with everything that would have assailed him in Isfahan? *The Papyrus.* Why did that decades-old joke that couldn't get to him hurt so much all of a sudden?

Silveira's plate was empty when Gregorius entered the dining car, and the Portuguese couple with whom he had exchanged his first Portuguese words in the early evening, were already on their second cup of coffee.

He had spent an hour lying awake in bed, thinking about the mailman who would enter the lobby of the Gymnasium at nine and give the mail to the janitor. Today, his letter would be there. Kägi wouldn't believe his eyes. Mundus was running away from his life. Anybody else, but not him. The news would make the rounds, upstairs and down, and the students on the steps at the entrance would talk of nothing else.

Gregorius had gone through his colleagues in his mind, imagining what they'd think, feel and say. As he did, he had made a discovery that jolted him: he wasn't sure of a single one of them. At first, things had looked different: Burri, for instance, an army major and enthusiastic churchgoer, found it incomprehensible, downright deviant, and reprehensible, for what was to happen now with the teaching; Anita Mühletaler, who had just gone through a divorce, tilted her head pensively, she could imagine such a thing, even if not for herself; Kalbermatten, the skirt-chaser and secret anarchist from Saas-Fee, might say in the teachers' lounge: "Why not?"; while Virginie Ledoyen, the French teacher, whose prissy appearance contrasted glaringly with her sparkling name, would react to the news with an executioner's look. All that seemed quite clear at first. But then it occurred to Gregorius how he had seen the devout paterfamilias Burri a few months ago with a blond in a short dress who seemed to be more than an acquaintance; how petty Anita Mühletaler could be when students raised hell; how cowardly Kalbermatten was about resisting Kägi; and how easily students who knew how to flatter her could wind Virginie Ledoyen around their little finger and make her drop her strict plans.

Could something be inferred from that? Something about the attitude to him and his surprising act? Could concealed understanding or even secret envy be assumed? Gregorius had sat up and was looking out at the landscape steeped in the silvery shimmering green of the olive groves. His familiarity with his colleagues all these years turned out to be curdled ignorance that had become deceptive habit. And was it indeed important—really *important*—to know what they thought? Was it only because of his bleary head that he didn't know that or was he becoming aware of a strangeness that had always existed, but had been hidden behind social rituals?

Compared with the face that had become open in the dim light of the compartment at night—open to the feelings that thrust out from inside, and open to the look from outside that sought to fathom them—this morning, Silveira's features were shut. At first glance, it looked as if he regretted opening himself up to a total stranger in the intimacy of the compartment smelling of wool blankets and disinfectant, and Gregorius sat down hesitantly at his table. But he soon understood: It wasn't retreat and rejection that was expressed in the firm, controlled features, but rather a pensive sobriety revealing that the encounter with Gregorius perplexed Silveira, had evoked surprising feelings he was now trying to figure out.

He pointed to the phone next to his cup. "I've reserved a room for you in the hotel where I put up my business partner. Here's the address."

He handed Gregorius a business card with the information on the back. He had to look through some papers before they arrived, he said, and prepared to stand up. But then he leaned back again and the way he looked at Gregorius proved that something had started in him. Had he never regretted devoting his life to ancient languages, he asked. That surely meant a very quiet, withdrawn life.

Do you find me boring? It occurred to Gregorius how the question he had asked Florence back then had preoccupied him on the trip yesterday and something of that must have been shown on his face, for Silveira said hastily, please don't misunderstand, he was only trying to imagine how it would be to live such a life that would be so completely different from his own.

It had been the life he had wanted, said Gregorius, and even as the words took shape in him, he feared there was defiance in his firm expression. Only two days ago, when he had stepped on the Kirchenfeldbrücke and seen the Portuguese woman reading, he wouldn't have had any reason for this defiance. He would have said exactly the same thing, but the words wouldn't have had the trace of obstinacy, but would have come from him as an inconspicuous, calm breath.

And why are you sitting here, then? Gregorius was afraid of the question and for a moment, the elegant Portuguese man looked like an inquisitor.

How long does it take to learn Greek, Silveira asked now. Gregorius breathed a sigh of relief and plunged into an answer that was much too long. Could he write down a few words for him in Hebrew, here on the napkin, asked Silveira.

And God said, Let there be light; and there was light, wrote Gregorius and translated it for him.

Silveira's phone rang. He had to go, he said, when he finished his conversation. He thrust the napkin into his jacket pocket. "What was the word for light?" he asked, standing up, and he repeated it to himself on his way to the door.

The broad river outside must already have been the Tejo. Gregorius started: that means they would soon arrive. He returned to his compartment, which had been converted back into a regular compartment with a cushioned bench, and sat down at the window. He didn't want the journey to end. What was he to do in Lisbon? He had a hotel. He would give the bellhop a tip, close the door, rest. And then?

Hesitantly, he picked up Prado's book and leafed through it.

SAUDADE PARADOXAL. PARADOXICAL YEARNING. *For 1,922 days I attended the Liceu where my father sent me, the strictest one in the whole country, they said. "You don't need to become a scholar," he said, and tried a smile that, as usual, failed. By the third day, I realized that I had to count the days so as not to be crushed by them.*

As Gregorius was looking up *to crush* in the dictionary, the train pulled into the Santa Apolónia railroad station of Lisbon.

The few sentences had captivated him. They were the first sentences that revealed something about the external life of the Portuguese man. Student of a strict Gymnasium, who counted the days, and son of a father whose smile usually failed. Was that the origin of the restrained rage conveyed in the other sentences? Gregorius couldn't have said why, but he wanted to know more about this rage. He now saw the first brushstrokes in a portrait of somebody who lived here in this city. Somebody he wanted to know. The city seemed to grow toward him in these sentences. As if it just stopped being a thoroughly strange city.

He took his suitcase and stepped out onto the platform. Silveira had waited for him. He took him to the taxi and gave the driver the address of the hotel. "You have my card," he said to Gregorius and waved a brief good-bye.

7

When Gregorius woke up, it was late afternoon and twilight was sinking over the cloud-draped city. Right after he arrived, he had gotten under the bedspread in his clothes and had slipped into a leaden sleep, clasped by the feeling that he really couldn't allow himself any sleep, for there were a thousand things to do, things with no name, but no less urgent for that, on the contrary, their eerie namelessness made them something that had to be tackled at once to keep something bad from happening, something that couldn't be named. Now as he washed his face in the bathroom, he felt with relief that the fear of missing something and feeling guilty about it fell away along with his numbness.

During the next hour, he sat at the window and tried in vain to bring order into his thoughts. Now and then, his look grazed the suitcase still packed in the corner. When night fell, he went down to the reception and had them inquire at the airport if there was still a flight to Zurich or Geneva. There weren't any, and when he went up in the elevator, he was amazed at how relieved he felt. Then he sat on the bed in the dark and tried to interpret the surprising relief. He dialed Doxiades's number and let the phone ring ten times before he hung up. He opened the book by Amadeu de Prado and read on from where he had stopped at the railroad station.

Six times a day I heard the jingle of the tower bells announcing the beginning of class and sounding as if monks were called to prayers. Thus it was 11,532 times that I clenched my teeth and went back into the gloomy building from the courtyard instead of following my imagination, which sent me through the courtyard gate out to the port, to a ship's rail, where I would then lick the salt from my lips.

Now, thirty years later, I keep coming back to this place. There isn't the slightest practical reason for it. So why? I sit on the mossy, crumbling steps at the entrance and have no idea why my heart is in my mouth. Why am I full of envy when I see the students with brown legs and light hair going in and out as if they were at home here? What is it, why do I envy them? Recently, when the window was open on a hot day, I listened to the various teachers and heard the stuttering answers of anxious students to questions that had made me tremble too. Sitting inside there once more—no, that was certainly not what I wanted. In the cool dark of the long corridor, I met the janitor, a man with a protruding, birdlike head, advancing toward me with a suspicious look. "What are you searching for here?" he asked, when I passed him. He had an asthmatic falsetto that sounded as if it came from a court in the hereafter. I stood still, without turning around. "I went to school here," I said and was filled with contempt for myself when I heard how hoarse it sounded. For a few seconds, a perfect, eerie silence reigned in the corridor. Then the man behind me shuffled off. I had felt caught red-handed. But why?

On the last day of finals, we had all stood behind our benches, the school caps on our heads, as if we were lined up for morning roll call. With measured tread, Senhor Cortês went from one to another, announced the overall grades with his usual strict expression and with the same look, he handed us our diploma. Joyless and pale, my assiduous bench mate took it and held it in his folded hands like a Bible. Giggling, the boy at the bottom of the class, the girls' suntanned favorite, let his fall to the floor like a piece of trash. Then we went out into the midday heat of a July day. What could, what should be done with all the time now before us, open and unshaped, feather-light in its freedom and lead-heavy in its uncertainty?

Neither before nor after have I experienced anything that revealed so cogently and impressively as the following scene how different people are. The boy at the bottom of the class was the first to take off his uniform cap, spun around and threw it over the fence of the schoolyard into the pond next door where it was slowly soaked and finally disappeared under the water lilies. Three or four others followed his example and one cap remained hanging on the fence. My bench mate then straightened his cap, anxious and indignant, you couldn't tell which feeling predominated in him. What would he do tomorrow morning when there was no more reason to put on the cap? But what was most impressive was what I observed in the shadowy corner of the courtyard. Half hidden behind a dusty bush, a boy was trying to stow his cap in his schoolbag. He didn't simply want to stuff it in, that was plainly seen in the hesitant movements. He tried this and that to place it carefully; finally he made room by taking out a few books he now wedged helplessly and awkwardly under his arm. When he turned and looked around, you could read in his eyes the hope that nobody had observed him in his shameful act, along with a last trace of the childish thought, wiped out by experience, that you could become invisible by averting your eyes.

I can still feel today how I twisted my own sweaty cap back and forth. I sat on the warm moss of the entrance steps and thought of my father's imperious wish that I might become a doctor—one who might release people like him from pain. I loved him for his trust and cursed him for the crushing burden he imposed on me with his touching wish. Meanwhile, the students from the girls' school had come over. "Are you glad it's over?" asked Maria João and sat down next to me. She examined me. "Or are you sad about it, after all?"

Now I finally seem to know what keeps compelling me to undertake the trip to the school: I'd like to go back to those minutes in the schoolyard when the past had dropped off of us and the future hadn't yet begun. Time came to a halt and held its breath, as it never again did. Was it Maria João's brown knees and the fragrance of soap in her light dress that I'd like to go back to? Or is it the wish—the dream-like, bombastic wish—to stand once again at that point in my life and be able to take a completely different direction than the one that has made me who I am now?

There's something peculiar about this wish, it smacks of paradox and logical peculiarity. Because the one who wishes it—isn't the one who, still untouched by the future, stands at the crossroads. Instead, it is the one marked by the future become past who wants to go back to the past, to revoke the irrevocable. And would he want to revoke it if he hadn't suffered it? To sit once more on the warm moss and hold the cap—it's the absurd wish to go back behind myself in time and take myself—the one marked by events—along on this journey. And is it conceivable that the boy back then would have defied the father's wish and not gone to medical school—as I sometimes wish today? Could he have done it and be me*? There was in me back then no perspective of experience suffered that could have made me want to take another fork at the crossroads. So what good would it do me to turn back time and, extinguishing one experience after another, to turn myself into the boy who was addicted to the fresh fragrance of Maria João's dress and the sight of her brown knees? The boy with the cap—he would have had to be quite different from me to take another direction as I wish for myself today. But then, if he had, he wouldn't have become a man who would later wish to return to the previous crossroads. Can I wish myself to be him? I don't think I could be satisfied to be him. But this satisfaction can be mine only because I am not him, only as the fulfillment of wishes that aren't his. If, in fact, I were him—I couldn't wish for what would satisfy me as him, as my own wishes might, as long as I forget that I wouldn't have them at all if they had been fulfilled.*

Yet I am certain I will soon wake up again with the wish to go to the school and give in to a yearning whose object can't exist because you can't even think it. Can there be anything more absurd than this: to be moved by a wish that has no conceivable object?

It was nearly midnight when Gregorius was finally sure he understood the difficult text. So Prado was a doctor and had become one because the father, whose smile usually failed, had had this imperious wish, a wish that had originated not in dictatorial arbitrariness or paternal vanity, but had developed out of the helplessness of chronic pain. Gregorius opened the phone book. There were fourteen listings under the name of Prado, but there was no *Amadeu* among them, no *Inácio* and no *Almeida*. Why had he assumed that Prado lived in Lisbon? Now he looked in the business directory for the publisher *Cedros Vermelhos:* nothing. Would he have to search through the whole country? Did that make sense? Even the slightest sense?

Gregorius set out in the nighttime city. To walk in the city after midnight—he had done that since his middle twenties when he lost the capacity to fall asleep easily. Countless times, he had walked through the empty streets of Bern, had stood still from time to time and listened like a blind man to the few steps coming or going. He loved to stand at the dark display windows of the bookshops and feel that, because the others were sleeping, all these books belonged only to him. With slow steps, he now turned the corner out of the side street of the hotel into the broad Avenida da Liberdade and went toward the Baixa, the lower part of town where the streets were arranged like a chessboard. It was cold, and a fine fog formed a milky halo around the old-fashioned streetlamps with their gold light. He found a coffee shop where he had a sandwich and coffee.

Prado kept sitting down on the steps of his school and imagining how it would have been to live a completely different life. Gregorius thought of the question Silveira had put to him and to which he had answered defiantly that he had lived the life he wanted. He felt how the image of the doubting doctor on the mossy steps and the question of the doubting businessman in the train shifted something in him, something that would never have shifted in the certain, familiar streets of Bern.

Now the only other man in the café paid and left. With a sudden inexplicable haste, Gregorius also paid and followed the man. He was an old man who dragged one leg and stood still every now and then to rest. Gregorius followed him at a long distance into Bairro Alto, the upper part of the city, until he disappeared behind the door of a narrow, shabby house. Now the light went on in the first floor, the curtain was pushed aside, and the man stood at the open window, a cigarette between his lips. From the protective dark of a doorway, Gregorius looked past him into the lighted flat. A sofa with cushions of worn-out needlepoint. Two unmatched armchairs. A glass cabinet with crockery and small, colorful porcelain figures. A crucifix on the wall. Not a single book. How was it to be this man?

After the man had shut the window and pulled the curtain shut, Gregorius emerged from the doorway. He had lost his orientation and took the next street down. Never had he followed anybody like this with the thought of how it would be to live this strange life instead of his own. It was a brand-new kind of curiosity that had just broken out in him and it suited the new kind of alertness he had experienced on the train ride and had gotten out with in the Gare de Lyon in Paris, yesterday or whenever it was.

Now and then he stood still and looked straight ahead. The ancient texts, his ancient texts, they were also full of characters who lived a life, and to read and understand the texts had always also meant reading and understanding this life. So why was everything so new now when it concerned both the Portuguese aristocrat and the limping man? On the damp cobblestones of the steep streets, he put one uncertain foot before the other and breathed a sigh of relief when he recognized the Avenida da Liberdade.

The blow caught him unprepared for he hadn't heard the roller-blader coming. He was a giant who hit Gregorius on the temple with his elbow as he overtook him and ripped off his glasses. Dazed and suddenly sightless, Gregorius stumbled a few steps and felt to his horror that he stepped on the glasses and ground them to a pulp under his feet. A wave of panic washed over him. *Don't forget the spare glasses,* he heard Doxiades say on the phone. Minutes passed until his breathing grew calm. Then he knelt down on the street and groped for the glass splinters and the fragments of the frame. What he could feel he brushed together and knotted into his handkerchief. Slowly he groped along the walls to the hotel.

The night porter jumped up frightened, and when Gregoius approached the mirror of the lobby, he saw blood dripping from his temple. In the elevator, he pressed the porter's handkerchief to the wound and then ran through the corridor, opened the door with trembling fingers and tumbled onto the suitcase. He felt tears of relief when his hand touched the cool metal case of the spare glasses. He put the glasses on, washed the blood off, and stuck the Band-Aid the porter had given him on the scratch on his temple. It was two-thirty. At the airport nobody answered the phone. At four he fell asleep.

8

If Lisbon hadn't been steeped in that bewitching light the next morning, Gregorius thought later, things might have taken a completely different turn. Maybe he would have gone to the airport and taken the next flight home. But the light allowed no temptation to turn back. Its glow made the whole past into something very distant, almost unreal, the will lost every shadow of the past under its luminosity, and the only possibility was to depart into the future whatever it might consist of. Bern and its snowflakes were far away and it was hard for Gregorius to believe that only three days had passed since he had met the enigmatic Portuguese woman on the Kirchenfeldbrücke.

After breakfast, he dialed José António da Silveira's number and reached his secretary. Could she recommend an ophthalmologist who spoke German, French, or English, he asked. Half an hour later, she called back, gave him greetings from Silveira and the name of a doctor his sister went to, a woman who had worked for a long time at the university clinics in Coimbra and Munich.

Her office was in the Alfama quarter, the oldest part of the city, behind the citadel. Gregorius walked slowly through the luminous day and avoided in time anybody who could have bumped into him. Sometimes he stood still and rubbed his eyes behind the thick lenses: So this was Lisbon, the city he had come to because, while looking at his students, he had suddenly seen his life from the end, and because the book of a Portuguese doctor had fallen into his hands and its words sounded as if they were aimed at him.

The rooms he entered an hour later didn't look like a doctor's office at all. The dark wood paneling, the original paintings, and the thick carpet gave the impression that you were in the home of a noble family, where everything had its solid form and life proceeded without a sound. It didn't surprise Gregorius that nobody was in the waiting room. No one who lived in such rooms needed to accept patients. Senhora Eça would come in a few minutes, said the woman at the reception desk. Nothing about her indicated a medical assistant. The only thing that hinted at commercial matters was a bright monitor full of names and numbers. Gregorius thought of Doxiades's sober, slightly shabby office and the cocky medical assistant. Suddenly he had the feeling of committing treason and now when one of the high doors opened and the doctor appeared, he was glad he didn't have to remain alone any longer with the unreasonable feeling.

Doutora Mariana Conceição Eça was first of all a woman with big dark eyes you could trust. In fluent German, with a mistake only here and there, she greeted Gregorius as a friend of Silveira, and already knew why he was here. How had he come up with the bizarre idea of having to apologize for his panic about the broken glasses, she asked? Naturally, somebody as nearsighted as he had to feel he had a spare pair of glasses.

All at once, Gregorius calmed down, sank deep into the chair at her desk and wished he never had to stand up again. The woman seemed to have unlimited time for him. Gregorius had never had this feeling with any doctor, not even Doxiades, it was unreal, almost as in a dream. He had expected her to measure the spare glasses, make the usual eye tests, and then send him to the optician with a prescription. Instead, she had him tell the history of his nearsightedness, stage after stage, concern after concern. When he finally handed her the glasses, she gave him a searching look.

"You're a man who doesn't sleep well," she said.

Then she asked him to come to the instruments in the other part of the room.

The examination lasted more than an hour. The instruments looked different from those of Doxiades, and Senhora Eça studied the background of his eyes with the detail of somebody becoming familiar with a brand-new landscape. But what impressed Gregorius the most was that she repeated the test for visual acuity three times. In between were pauses when she had him walk back and forth and started a conversation about his profession.

"How well one sees depends on so many things," she said smiling when she noted his amazement.

At last, there was a diopter number that was clearly different from the usual one and the value for the two eyes was farther apart than usual. Senhora Eça saw his confusion.

"Let's just try it out," she said and touched his arm.

Gregorius wavered between resistance and trust. Trust won. The doctor gave him the business card of an optician and then she called there. With her Portuguese voice, the magic he had felt when the enigmatic woman on the Kirchenfeldbrücke had pronounced the word *português* came back. Suddenly being in this city made sense, a sense that couldn't be named, on the contrary, it was part of this sense that it mustn't be violated by trying to capture it in words.

"Two days," said the doctor after she hung up. "With the best will in the world, says César, it can't go any faster."

Now, Gregorius took the little volume with Amadeu de Prado's notes out of his jacket pocket, showed her the peculiar name of the publisher and told of the futile search in the phone book. Yes, she said distracted, it sounds like a private publisher.

"And the red cedars—it wouldn't surprise me if they were a metaphor for something."

Gregorius had also said that to himself: a metaphor or a code for something secret—bloody or beautiful—hidden under the colorful, wilted foliage of a life story.

The doctor went into another room and came back with an address book. She opened it and ran her finger along a page.

"Here. Júlio Simões," she said, "a friend of my late husband, a secondhand book dealer who always seemed to us to know more about books than anyone else alive, it was really weird."

She wrote the address and explained to Gregorius where it was.

"Give him my best. And come by with the new glasses, I'd like to know if I've done it right."

When Gregorius turned around on the staircase, she was still standing in the door, with one hand on the lintel. Silveira had called her. Then she might also know that he had run away. He would gladly have told her about it and as he went down the stairs, his steps were hesitant, like someone who isn't happy to leave a place.

The sky was coated with a fine white veil that softened the gleam of the sunlight. The optician's shop was near the ferry across the Tagus. César Santarém's surly face lit up when Gregorius told him who sent him. He looked at the prescription, weighed the glasses Gregorius gave him in his hand and then said in broken French, these glasses could be made of lighter material and put in a lighter frame.

That was the second time in a short period that someone had cast doubt on the judgment of Constantine Doxiades, and it seemed to Gregorius that his former life was taken out of his hand, a life, as long as he could remember, with heavy glasses on his nose. Uncertainly, he tried on frame after frame and finally let himself be tempted by Santarém's assistant, who knew only Portuguese and talked like a waterfall, to choose a narrow reddish frame that seemed much too stylish and chic for his broad, square face. On the way to the Bairro Alto, where Júlio Simões's secondhand bookshop was, he kept telling himself that the new glasses could be spare glasses and didn't need to be worn, and when he finally stood before the used book shop, he had recovered his internal balance.

Senhor Simões was a wiry man with a sharp nose and dark eyes emanating a mercurial intelligence. Mariana Eça had called and told him the issue. Half the city of Lisbon, thought Gregorius, seemed to be concerned with calling for him and sending him on, you could almost talk of a ring-around-the-roses of calls, he couldn't remember ever experiencing such a thing.

CEDROS VERMELHOS—there was no such publisher, said Simões, in the thirty years that he had been in the book business, of that he was sure. UM OURIVES DAS PALAVRAS—no, he had never heard of that title either. He leafed through it, read a sentence here and there, and it seemed to Gregorius that he was waiting for memory to bring something to light. Finally, he looked once more at the year of publication. Nineteen seventy-five—he had still been in college in Porto and wouldn't have heard anything of a book that appeared in a private publication, especially not if it had been printed in Lisbon.

"If there is anybody who knows," he said and filled his pipe, "it's old Coutinho, who had the shop here before me. He's close to ninety and is nuts, but his memory for books is phenomenal, a genuine miracle. I can't call him because he can barely hear; but I'll write you a few lines to give him."

Simões went to his desk in the corner, wrote something on a notepad, and put it in an envelope.

"You have to be patient with him," he said when he gave Gregorius the envelope. "He's had a lot of bad breaks in his life and is a bitter old man. But he can also be very nice when you take the right tone with him. The problem is that you never know in advance what the right tone is."

Gregorius stayed in the used bookshop a long time. Getting to know a city through the books in it—he had always done that. His first trip abroad as a student had been to London. On the way back to Calais, he had realized that, except for the youth hostel, the British Museum and the many bookshops around it, he had seen practically nothing of the city. *But the same books could also be anywhere else!* said the others and shook their heads at all the things he had missed. *Yes, but in fact they* weren't *anywhere else,* he had replied.

And now he stood before the ceiling-high shelves with all the Portuguese books he really couldn't read and felt how he established contact with the city. When he had left the hotel in the morning, he thought he had to find Amadeu de Prado as fast as possible to give a meaning to his stay here. But then there had been Mariana Eça's dark eyes, reddish hair and black velvet jacket and now there were all these books with names of previous owners that reminded him of Anneli Weiss's handwriting in his Latin book.

O GRANDE TERRAMOTO. Except that it took place in 1755 and had devastated Lisbon, he knew nothing about the great earthquake that had shaken faith in God for so many people. He took the book off the shelf. The next book, standing crooked, was titled A MORTE NEGRA about the plague of the fourteenth and fifteenth centuries. With both books under his arm, Gregorius went to literature on the other side of the room. Luis Vaz de Camões; Francisco de Sá de Miranda; Fernão Mendes Pinto; Camilo Castelo Branco. An entire universe he had never heard of, not even from Florence. José Maria Eça de Queirós, O CRIME DO PADRE AMARO. Hesitantly, as if it was something forbidden, he took the volume off the shelf and added it to the two others. And then, all of a sudden, he stood before it: Fernando Pessoa, O LIVRO DO DESASSOSSEGO. It really was unbelievable, but he had gone to Lisbon without thinking that he was going to the city of the assistant bookkeeper Bernardo Soares, who worked on Rua dos Douradores and where Pessoa wrote down thoughts that were lonelier than all thoughts the world before him and after him had heard of.

Was it so unbelievable? *The fields are greener in description than in their green.* This sentence by Pessoa had led to the shrillest episode between him and Florence in all the years.

She had sat in the living room with colleagues, laughter and glasses clinking were heard. Gregorius had gone there reluctantly because he needed a book. As he entered, somebody was reading the sentence aloud. *Isn't that a brilliant sentence?* one of Florence's colleagues had called out. Shaking his artist's mane and putting his hand on Florence's bare arm. *Only very few will understand this sentence,* Gregorius had said. All at once, the room filled with an embarrassed silence. *And you're one of these chosen ones?* Florence asked in a cutting tone. With exaggerated slowness, Gregorius had taken the book off the shelf and had gone out without a word. It took some minutes until he heard anything from there again.

Afterward, when he had seen THE BOOK OF UNREST somewhere, he had quickly passed by. They had never spoken of the episode. It was part of everything that wasn't yet worked out when they split up.

Now, Gregorius took the book off the shelf.

"Do you know what this unbelievable book seems like to me?" asked Senhor Simões, tapping the price into the cash register. "It's as if Marcel Proust had written the essays of Michel de Montaigne."

Gregorius was dead tired when he came with his heavy bags up to the memorial to Camões on Rua Garrett. But he didn't want to go back to the hotel. He had come to this city and he wanted more of this feeling so he could be sure he wouldn't call the airport again tonight to book a return flight. He drank a coffee and then boarded the streetcar that would take him to the Cemitério dos Prazeres, near the home of Vítor Coutinho, the crazy old man who might know something about Amadeu de Prado.

9

In the hundred-year-old streetcar of Lisbon, Gregorius traveled back to the Bern of his childhood. The trolley that took him, bumping, shaking and ringing through Bairro Alto, looked just like the old trolley he had ridden through the streets and alleys of Bern for hours when he was still too young to have to pay the fare. The same lacquered wooden slat benches, the same bell pulls next to the strap handles hanging down from the ceiling, the same metal lever the driver operated to brake and accelerate and whose workings Gregorius understood as little today as back then. At some time, when he was already wearing the cap of the sixth form, the old trolleys were replaced with new ones. Their ride was quieter and smoother, the other students scrambled to ride in the new cars, and not a few were late to class because they had waited for one of the new cars. Gregorius hadn't trusted himself to say it, but it bothered him that the world changed. He mustered up all his courage, went to the trolley depot and asked a man in a work coat what happened to the old cars. They would be sold to Yugoslavia, said the man. He must have seen the boy's unhappiness, for he went into the office and came back with a model of the old car. Gregorius still owned it and guarded it as a precious, irreplaceable find from a prehistoric time. He pictured it as the Lisbon streetcar rattled and screeched to a stop in the final loop.

That the Portuguese aristocrat with the intrepid look could be dead had never crossed Gregorius's mind. Only now did the thought come to him as he stood before the cemetery. Slowly and apprehensively, he went through the lanes of the necropolis lined with simple little mausoleums.

It may have been half an hour later when he stood still before a tall sepulcher of white weather-spotted marble. Two tablets with ornate corners and edges had been hewn in the stone. AQUI JAZ ALEXANDRE HORÁCIO DE ALMEIDA PRADO QUE NASCEU EM 28 DE MAIO DE 1890 E FALECEU EM 9 DE JUNHO DE 1954, was written on the top tablet, and AQUI JAZ MARIA PIEDADE REIS DE PRADO QUE NASCEU EM 12 DE JANEIRO DE 1899 E FALECEU EM 24 DE OUTUBRO DE 1960. On the bottom tablet, which was clearly lighter and less mossy, Gregorius read: AQUI JAZ FÁTIMA AMÉLIA CLEMÊNCIA GALHARDO DE PRADO QUE NASCEU EM 1 DE JANEIRO DE 1926 E FALECEU EM 3 DE FEVEREIRO DE 1961, and under that, with less patina on the letters, AQUI JAZ AMADEU INÁCIO DE ALMEIDA PRADO QUE NASCEU EM 20 DE DEZEMBRO DE 1920 E FALECEU EM 20 DE JUNHO DE 1973.

Gregorius stared at the last number. The book in his pocket had appeared in 1975. If this Amadeu de Prado was the doctor who attended the strict Liceu of Senhor Cortês and had later kept sitting on the warm moss of its steps because he asked himself how it would have been to become somebody else—then he wouldn't have published his notes himself. Somebody else had done it, probably a private publisher. A friend, a brother, a sister. If this person was still there after twenty-nine years, that was who he had to find.

But the name on the tomb could also be a coincidence. Gregorius wanted it to be a coincidental congruence, he wanted it with all his might. He felt how disappointed he would be and how dejected he would become if he couldn't meet the melancholy man who had wanted to reset the Portuguese language because it was so hackneyed in its old form.

Nevertheless, he took out his notebook and wrote down all the names along with the dates of birth and death. This Amadeu de Prado had been fifty-three. He had lost his father at the age of thirty-four. Had that been the father whose smile had mostly failed? The mother had died when he was forty. Fátima Galhardo—that could have been Amadeu's wife, a woman who had been only thirty-five and had died when he was forty-one.

Once more Gregorius let his eyes slide over the tomb and only now did he notice an inscription on the pedestal, half covered with wild ivy: QUANDO A DITADURA É UM FACTO A REVOLUÇO É UM DEVER. *When dictatorship is a fact, revolution is a duty.* Had the death of this Prado been a political death? The Revolution of the Carnations in Portugal, the end of the dictatorship, had taken place in the spring of 1974. So this Prado hadn't lived through it. The inscription sounded as if he had died as a resistance fighter. Gregorius took out the book and looked at the picture: It could be, he thought, it would suit the face and the restrained rage behind everything he wrote. A poet and a language mystic who had taken up arms and fought against Salazar.

At the exit, he tried to ask the man in uniform how you could find out who a grave belonged to. But his few Portuguese words weren't adequate. He took out the notepaper on which Júlio Simões had written down the address of his predecessor, and set out.

Vítor Coutinho lived in a house that looked as if it could tumble down any minute. Set back from the street, it was hidden behind other houses and its lower part was overgrown with ivy. There was no bell and Gregorius stood helpless in the courtyard a while. Just as he was about to go away, a voice barked from one of the upper windows:

"O que é quer?" What do you want?

The head in the window frame was framed with white locks that merged seamlessly into a white beard, and on the nose was a pair of glasses with broad, dark frames.

"Pergunta sobre livro," Gregorius called out as loud as he could and held up Prado's notes.

"O quê?" the man asked and Gregorius repeated his words.

The head disappeared and the door buzzed. Gregorius entered a corridor with overflowing bookshelves up to the ceiling and a worn-out Oriental rug on the red stone floor. It smelled of old food, dust and pipe tobacco. On the creaky steps, the white-haired man appeared, a pipe between dark teeth. A coarse checked shirt of washed-out indefinable color drooped over his baggy corduroy trousers, his feet were stuck in open sandals.

"Quem é?" he asked in the exaggerated loudness of the hard of hearing. The light brown, amberish eyes under the gigantic eyebrows looked annoyed like someone whose rest was disturbed.

Gregorius handed him the envelope with the message from Simões. He was Swiss, he said in Portuguese and added in French: A philologist of ancient languages and searching for the author of this book. When Coutinho didn't react, he started on a loud repetition.

He wasn't deaf, the old man interrupted him in French, and now a cunning grin appear on the lined, weatherbeaten face. Deafness—that was a good role to play, with all the twaddle you had got to hear.

His French had an eccentric accent, but the words came, albeit slowly, in a confident order. He scanned Simões's lines, then pointed to the kitchen at the end of the corridor and led the way. On the kitchen table, next to an open can of sardines and a half-full glass of red wine, lay an open book. Gregorius went to the chair at the other end of the table and sat down. Then the old man came to him and did something surprising: He took Gregorius's glasses off and put them on. He blinked, looked here and there, while swinging his own glasses in his hand.

"So, we've got that in common," he said at last and returned the glasses to Gregorius.

The solidarity of those who go through the world with thick glasses. All of a sudden, all the annoyance and defensiveness had disappeared from Coutinhos's face, and he reached for Prado's book.

Without a word, he looked at the portrait of the doctor for a few minutes. He stood up now and then, absent as a sleepwalker, and once poured Gregorius a glass of wine. A cat slipped in and sidled around his legs. He didn't notice it, took off his glasses, and grasped the bridge of his nose with thumb and index finger, a gesture that reminded Gregorius of Doxiades. From the next room, the ticking of a grandfather clock was heard. Now, he emptied his pipe, took another from the shelf and filled it. More minutes passed until he began to speak, softly and in the timbre of distant memory.

"It would be wrong if I said I knew him. You can't even speak of an encounter. But I did see him, twice, in the door of his treatment room, in the white coat, his brows raised waiting for the next patient. I was there with my sister, whom he was treating. Jaundice. High blood pressure. She swore by him. Was, I think, a little bit in love with him. No wonder, a fine figure of a man, with a personality that hypnotized people. He was the son of the famous Judge Prado, who took his own life, many said, because he could no longer bear the pains of his hunched back, others conjectured that he couldn't forgive himself for staying in office under the dictatorship.

"Amadeu de Prado was a beloved, even esteemed doctor. Until he saved the life of Rui Luís Mendes, a member of the secret police, the one called the butcher. That was in the mid-sixties, shortly after I turned fifty. After that, people avoided him. That broke his heart. From then on, he worked for the resistance, but nobody knew it; as if he wanted to atone for the rescue. It came out only after his death. He died, as I remember, quite surprisingly of a cerebral hemorrhage, one year before the revolution. Lived at the end with Adriana, his sister, who idolized him.

"She must have been the one who had the book printed, I even have an idea who did it, but the press closed a long time ago. A few years later, the book popped up in my secondhand bookstore. I put it in some corner, didn't read it, had an aversion to it, don't really know why. Maybe because I didn't like Adriana, even though I hardly knew her, but she assisted him and both times I was there her overbearing way with patients got on my nerves. Probably unfair of me, but that's how I've always been."

Coutinho leafed through it. "Good sentences, it seems. And a good title. I didn't know he wrote. Where did you get it? And why did you come looking for him?"

The story Gregorius told now sounded different from the one he had told José Antonio da Silveira on the night train. Mainly because now he also spoke of the enigmatic Portuguese woman on the Kirchenfeldbrücke and of the phone number on his forehead.

"Do you still have the number?" asked the old man, who liked the story so much that he opened another bottle of wine.

For a moment, Gregorius was tempted to take out the notebook. But then he felt this was too much; after the episode with the glasses, he wouldn't put it past the old man to call there. Simões had said he was nuts. That couldn't mean that Coutinho was confused; there was no question of that. What he seemed to have lost in his solitary life with the cat was the sense of distance and proximity.

No, said Gregorius now; he no longer had the number. Too bad, said the old man. He didn't believe a word of it, and suddenly they sat across from each other like two total strangers.

There was no Adriana de Almeida Prado in the phone book, said Gregorius after an embarrassed pause.

That didn't mean anything, growled Coutinho. If she was still alive, Adriana had to be close to eighty, and old people sometimes got unlisted numbers, he had also done that recently. And if she had died, her name would also have been on the tombstone. The address where the doctor had lived and worked, no, he no longer knew that after forty years. Somewhere in Bairro Alto. It couldn't be too hard for him to find the house, for it was a house with a lot of blue tiles on the façade and far and away the only blue house. Back then at any rate. *O consultório azul,* the blue practice, it was called.

When Gregorius left the old man an hour later, they had gotten close again. Gruff distance and surprising complicity alternated irregularly in Coutinho's behavior, without any obvious reason for the abrupt changes. Stunned, Gregorius went through the house that was a single library down to the last corner. The old man was uncommonly well-read and possessed a huge number of first editions.

He was well-versed in Portuguese names. The Prados, Gregorius learned, were a very old tribe that went back to João Nunes do Prado, a grandson of Alfonso III, king of Portugal. Eça? Went back to Pedro I and Inês de Castro and was one of the most distinguished names in all of Portugal.

"My name is indeed even older and also linked with the royal house," said Coutinho, and through the ironic refraction, the pride was evident.

He envied Gregorius for his knowledge of ancient languages and on the way to the door, he suddenly pulled a Greek-Portuguese edition of the New Testament off the shelf.

"No idea why I give this to you," he said, "but that's how it is."

As Gregorius went through the courtyard, he knew he would never forget that sentence. Or the old man's hand on his back softly pushing him out.

The streetcar rattled through the early dusk. At night he would never find the blue house, thought Gregorius. The day had lasted an eternity, and now, exhausted, he leaned his head against the misted panes of the car. Was it possible that he had been in this city only two days? And that only four days, not even a hundred hours, had passed since he had left his Latin books on the desk? At Rossio, the most famous square in Lisbon, he got out and trudged to the hotel with the heavy bags from Simões's second-hand bookstore.

10

Why had Kägi talked with him in a language that sounded like Portuguese, but wasn't? And why had he complained about Marcus Aurelius without saying a single word about him?

Gregorius sat on the edge of the bed and rubbed the sleep out of his eyes. Then the janitor had been there, in the corridor of the Gymnasium, hosing down the place where he had stood with the Portuguese woman when she dried her hair. Before or after, you couldn't tell, Gregorius had gone with her into Kägi's office to introduce her to him. He must not have opened a door to it, suddenly they had simply been standing before his gigantic desk, a little like petitioners who had forgotten their petition; but then the Rector suddenly wasn't there anymore, the desk and even the wall behind it had disappeared, and they had had a clear view of the Alps.

Now Gregorius noted that the door to the minibar was ajar. At some time, he had woken up from hunger and had eaten the peanuts and the chocolate. Before that, the overflowing mailbox of his Bern flat had tormented him, all the bills and junk mail, and all of a sudden, his library was in flames before it became Coutinho's library, where there were nothing but charred Bibles, an endless row of them.

At breakfast, Gregorius took second helpings of everything and then sat there to the annoyance of the waiter, who was preparing the dining room for lunch. He had no idea how it should go on. Just now he had listened to a German couple making their tourist plans for the day. He had also tried and had failed. Lisbon didn't interest him for sightseeing, as a tourist setting. Lisbon was the city where he had run away from his life. The only thing he could imagine was taking the ferry over the Tagus to see the city from this perspective. But he really didn't want that either. What did he want?

In his room, he assembled the books he had collected: the two about the earthquake and the Black Death, the novel by Eça de Queirós, *The Book of Disquiet,* the New Testament, the language books. Then he packed his bag tentatively and put it at the door.

No, that wasn't it either. Not because of the glasses he had to pick up the next day. To land in Zurich now and get off the train in Bern: It wasn't possible; it wasn't possible anymore.

What else? Was this what came from thoughts of time running out and death: that all of a sudden you didn't know anymore what you wanted? That you didn't know your own will anymore? That you lost the obvious familiarity with your own wishes? And in this way became strange and a problem to yourself?

Why didn't he set off in search of the blue house where Adriana de Prado might still be living, thirty-one years after her brother's death? Why was he hesitating? Why was there suddenly a barrier?

Gregorius did what he had always done when he was unsure: He opened up a book. His mother, a country girl from the flatlands around Bern, had seldom picked up a book, at most a sentimental novel by Ludwig Ganghofer and then it took her weeks to read. The father had discovered reading as an antidote to boredom in the empty halls of the museum, and after he had acquired the taste, he read everything that came to hand. *Now you're escaping to books, too,* said the mother when the son also discovered reading. It had hurt Gregorius that she saw it like that and that she didn't understand when he spoke of the magic and luminosity of good sentences.

There were the people who read and there were the others. Whether you were a reader or a nonreader—it was quickly noted. There was no greater distinction between people. People were amazed when he asserted that and many shook their head at such crankiness. But that's how it was. Gregorius knew it. He *knew* it.

He sent the chambermaid away and in the next few hours he sank into the attempt to understand a note by Amadeu de Prado, whose title had leaped to his eye as he leafed through the book.

O INTERIOR DO EXTERIOR DO INTERIOR. THE INSIDE OF THE OUTSIDE OF THE INSIDE. *Some time ago—it was a dazzling morning in June, the morning brightness flooded unmoving through the streets—I was standing in the Rua Garrett at a display window where the blinding light made me look at my reflection instead of the merchandise. It was annoying to stand in my own way—particularly since the whole thing was like an allegory of the way I usually stood by me—and I was about to make my way inside through the shadowy funnels of my hands, when behind my reflection—it reminded me of a threatening storm shadow that changed the world—the figure of a tall man emerged. He stood still, took a pack of cigarettes out of his shirt pocket, and stuck one between his lips. As he inhaled the first drag, his look strayed and finally fixed on me.* We humans: what do we know of one another? *I thought and acted—to keep from meeting his reflected look—as if I could easily see the display in the window. The stranger saw a gaunt man with graying hair, a narrow, stern face and dark eyes behind round lenses in gold frames. I cast a searching glance at my reflection. As always, I stood with my square shoulders straighter than straight, my head higher than my size really allowed, and leaning back a trace and it was undoubtedly correct what they said, even those who liked me: I looked like an arrogant misanthrope who looked down on everything human, a misanthrope with a mocking comment ready for everything and everyone. That was the impression the smoking man must have gotten.*

How wrong he was! For sometimes I think: I exaggerate standing and walking that way to protest my father's irrevocably crooked body, his torment, to be pressed down by Bechterev's disease, to have to aim your eyes at the ground like a tortured slave who didn't trust himself to meet his master with a raised head and a direct look. It is then perhaps, as if, by stretching myself, I could straighten my proud father's back or, with a backward, magical law of effect make sure his life would be less bowed and enslaved to pain than it was in fact—as if through my attempt in the present, I could strip the tormented past of its reality and replace it with a better, freer one.

And that wasn't the only delusion my appearance must have produced in the stranger behind me. After an endless night when I had remained without sleep or consolation, far be it from me to look down on another. The day before, I had informed a patient in the presence of his wife that he didn't have long to live. You have to, I had persuaded myself before I called the two of them into the consulting room, they have to plan for themselves and the five children—and anyway: part of human dignity consists of the strength to look your fate, even a hard one, in the eye. It had been early evening, through the open balcony door a light warm wind brought the sounds and smells of a dying summer day, and if this soft wave of brightness could have been enjoyed in freedom and oblivion, it could have been a moment of happiness. If only a sharp, ruthless wind had whipped the rain against the windowpane! I had thought, as the man and woman across from me sat on the very edge of their chairs, hesitating and full of scared impatience, eager to hear the verdict that would release them from the fear of an impending death, so they could go downstairs and mix with the strolling passersby, a sea of time before them. I took off my glasses and pinched the bridge of my nose between thumb and forefinger before I spoke. The two must have recognized the gesture as a harbinger of an awful truth, for when I looked up, they had grasped each other's hands, which looked as if they hadn't sought each other for decades—and that idea choked me so that the anxious wait became even longer. I spoke down to these hands, hard as it was to hold out against the eyes expressing a nameless horror. The hands clenched each other, the blood leached from them, and it was this image of a bloodless, white knot of fingers that robbed me of sleep and that I tried to drive away when I broke out for my walk that had led me to the reflecting display window. (And I had tried to drive away something else in the lighted streets: the memory of my rage at my clumsy words announcing the bitter message that had later been turned against Adriana only because she, who takes care of me better than a mother, had forgotten to bring my favorite bread. If only the white gold light of the morning would extinguish this injustice that wasn't untypical for me!)

The man with the cigarette, now leaning on a light pole, let his look wander back and forth between me and what was happening in the street. What he saw of me could have revealed nothing about my self-doubting fragility that didn't accord much with my proud, even arrogant posture. I put myself into his look, reproduced it in me, and from that perspective absorbed my reflection. The way I looked and appeared—I thought—I had never been that way for a single minute in my life. Not in school, not at the university, not in my practice. Is it the same with others: that they don't recognize themselves in their outside? That the reflection seems like a stage set full of crass distortion? That, with fear, they note a gap between the perception others have of them and the way they experience themselves? That the familiarity of inside and the familiarity of outside can be so far apart that they can hardly be considered familiarity with the same thing?

The distance from others, where this awareness moves us, becomes even greater when we realize that our outside form doesn't appear to others as to our own eyes. Humans are not seen like houses, trees and stars. They are seen with the expectation of being able to encounter *them in a specific way and thus making them a part of our own inside. Imagination trims them to suit our own wishes and hopes, but also to confirm our own fears and prejudices. We don't even get safely and impartially to the outside contours of another. On the way, the eye is diverted and blurred by all the wishes and fantasies that make us the special, unmistakable human beings we are. Even the outside world of an inside world is still a piece of our inside world, not to mention the thoughts we make about the inside world of strangers and that are so uncertain and unstable that they say more about ourselves than about others. How does the man with the cigarette see an exaggeratedly upright man with a gaunt face, full lips and gold-framed eyeglasses on the sharp, straight nose that seems to me to be too long and too dominant? How does this figure fit into the framework of the pleasure and displeasure and into the remaining architecture of his soul? What does his look exaggerate and stress in my appearance, and what does it leave out as if it didn't even exist? It will inevitably be a caricature the smoking stranger forms of my reflection, and his notion of my notional world will pile up caricature on caricature. And so we are doubly strangers, for between us there is not only the deceptive outside world, but also the delusion that exists of it in every inside world.*

Is it an evil, this strangeness and distance? Would a painter have to portray us with outstretched arms, desperate in the vain attempt to reach the other? Or should a picture show us in a pose expressing relief that there is this double barrier that is also a protective wall? Should we be grateful for the protection that guards us from the strangeness of one another? And for the freedom it makes possible? How would it be if we confronted each other unprotected by the double refraction represented by the interpreted body? If, because nothing separating and adulterating stood between us, we tumbled into each other?

As he read Prado's self-description, Gregorius kept looking at the portrait at the front of the book. In his mind, he turned the doctor's helmet of combed hair gray and put gold-framed glasses with round lenses on him. Haughtiness, even misanthropy, others had seen in him. Yet, as Coutinho said, he had been a beloved, even esteemed doctor. Until he had saved the life of the member of the secret police. After that, he was despised by the same people who had loved him. It had broken his heart and he had tried to make up for it by working for the resistance.

How could a doctor need to atone for something every doctor did—had to do—the opposite of a transgression? Something, thought Gregorius, couldn't be right in Coutinho's account. Things must have been more complicated, more involved. Gregorius leafed through the book. *Nós homens, que sabemos uns dos outros? We humans: what do we know of one another?* For a while, Gregorius kept leafing through it. Maybe there was a note about this dramatic and regrettable turn in his life?

When he found nothing, he left the hotel at twilight and made his way to Rua Garrett, where Prado had seen his reflection in the display window and where Júlio Simões's secondhand bookshop was.

There was no more sunlight to make the display window into a mirror. But after a while, Gregorius found a brightly lit clothing store with an enormous mirror where he could look at himself through the windowpane. He tried to do what Prado had done: to put himself into a stranger's look, to reproduce it in himself and absorb his reflection from this look. To encounter himself as a stranger one just met.

That was how the students and colleagues had seen him. That was what their Mundus looked like. Florence had also seen him like that, first as an infatuated student in the first row, later as a wife, to whom he had become an increasingly ponderous and boring husband, who used his learning more often to destroy the magic, the high spirits and the chic of her world of literary celebrities.

They all had the same image before them and yet, as Prado said, they each had seen something different because every piece of a human's outside world seen was also a piece of an inside world.

The Portuguese man had been sure that in not one single minute of his life had he been as he appeared to others; he hadn't recognized himself in his outside—familiar as it was—and was deeply frightened at this strangeness.

Now a boy hurrying by bumped into Gregorius who recoiled. Fear at being shoved coincided with the upsetting thought that he had no certainty equal to the doctor's. Where had Prado gotten his certainty that he was completely different from the way others saw him? How had he acquired that? He talked about it as of a bright light inside that had always illuminated him, a light that had meant both great familiarity with himself and great strangeness in the view of others. Gregorius shut his eyes and sat again in the dining car on the trip to Paris. The new kind of wakefulness he had experienced there, when he realized that his trip was actually taking place—was it somehow connected with the amazing wakefulness the Portuguese man had possessed about himself, a wakefulness whose price had been loneliness? Or were these two completely different things?

He went through the world in a posture, as if he were always bent over a book and constantly reading it, people said to Gregorius. Now he stood up straight and tried to feel how it was to straighten the pain-crooked back of your own father with an exaggeratedly straight back and an especially high head. In the sixth form, he had had a teacher who suffered from Bechterev's disease. Such people shoved their head into their neck to keep from having to look at the ground all the time. They looked the way Prado had described the janitor he met on his visit to the school: like a bird. Horrible jokes about the crooked figure made the rounds and the teacher took revenge with a malicious, punishing strictness. How was it to have a father who had to spend his life in this humiliating posture, hour after hour, day after day, at the judge's bench and at the dinner table with the children?

Alexandre Horácio de Almeida Prado had been a judge, a famous judge, as Coutinho had said. A judge who had administered the law under Salazar—a man who had broken every law. A judge who perhaps couldn't forgive himself and therefore sought death. *When dictatorship is a fact, revolution is a duty,* was on the pedestal of the Prados' tomb. Was it there because of the son who had gone into the resistance? Or because of the father who had recognized the truth of the sentence too late?

On the way down to the big square, Gregorius felt that he wanted to know these things and that he wanted to know them in other, more urgent ways than the many historical things he had dealt with through the ancient texts all his life. Why? The judge had been dead for half a century, the revolution was thirty years ago, and the son's death was also part of that distant past. So why? What did all that have to do with him? How could it have happened that a single Portuguese word and a phone number on his forehead tore him out of his orderly life and involved him far from Bern in the life of Portuguese people who were no longer alive?

In the bookstore on Rossio, a photo biography of António de Oliveira Salazar, the man who played a crucial, perhaps fatal role in Prado's life, leaped to his eyes. The dust jacket showed a man dressed all in black with an overbearing but not insensitive face, with a hard, even fanatic look that did however reveal intelligence. Gregorius leafed through it. Salazar, he thought, was a man who had sought power but not one who had seized it with blind brutality and dull violence, nor one who had enjoyed it like the voluptuous, excessive fullness of rich food at an orgiastic banquet. To get it and hold it for so long, he had sacrificed everything in his life that hadn't suited the inexhaustible wakefulness, the absolute discipline, and the ascetic ritual. The price had been high, you could tell that from the stern features and the effort of the rare smile. And the repressed needs and impulses of this barren life amid the sumptuousness of government—distorted beyond recognition by the rhetoric of state—had been vented on merciless execution orders.

Gregorius lay awake in the dark and thought of the great distance there had always been between him and world events. Not that he hadn't been interested in political events abroad. In April 1974, when the dictatorship of Portugal came to an end, some of his generation had gone there and were offended by him for saying he didn't care for political tourism. Nor was he uninformed, like a blind shut-in. But it always felt a little bit as if he were reading Thucydides. A Thucydides in the newspaper and later on the news. Was it connected with Switzerland and its pristine position? Or only with him? His fascination with words, covering horrid, bloody and unjust things? And maybe with his nearsightedness?

When the father, who hadn't gone further than noncommissioned officer, spoke of the time when his company had been stationed on the Rhine, as he said, he, the son, always had the feeling of something unreal, something a little funny, whose meaning was mainly that it could be remembered as something exciting, something that stood out from the banality of the rest of life. The father had felt that, and once he blurted out: *We were scared, scared to death,* he had said, *for it could easily have been different and then maybe you wouldn't even exist.* He hadn't shouted, the father never did that; nevertheless, they had been furious words the son heard with shame and had never forgotten.

Was that why he now wanted to know how it had been to be Amadeu de Prado? To move closer to the world through this understanding?

He turned on the light and reread sentences he had just read.

NADA. NOTHING. *Aneurysm. Every moment can be the last. Without the slightest premonition, in total ignorance, I will walk through an invisible wall, behind which is nothing, not even darkness. My next step can be the step through this wall. Isn't it illogical to be afraid of it knowing that I shall no longer experience this sudden extinction?*

Gregorius called Doxiades and asked him what an aneurysm was. "I know the word means a dilation. But of what?" It was a diseased expansion of an arterial blood vessel through innate or acquired changes in the wall, said the Greek. Yes, in the brain, too, quite often. People didn't usually notice anything and it could be fine for a long time—decades. Then the vessel would suddenly burst and that was the end. Why did he want to know that in the middle of the night? Was anything wrong? And where was he anyway?

Gregorius felt he had made a mistake to call the Greek. He didn't find the words that would have suited their long intimacy. Stiff and hesitant, he said something about the old streetcar, about an odd secondhand bookseller, and the cemetery where the dead Portuguese man lay. It made no sense and he heard it. There was a pause.

"Gregorius?" Doxiades asked at last.

"Yes?"

"How do you say chess in Portuguese?"

Gregorius could have hugged him for the question.

"*Xadrez,*" he said and the dryness in his mouth had disappeared.

"Everything all right with the eyes?"

Now the tongue stuck to the palate again. "Yes." And after another pause, Gregorius asked:

"Do you have the impression that people see you as you are?"

The Greek burst out laughing. "Of course *not*!"

Gregorius was flabbergasted that somebody, Doxiades of all people, laughed about that when Amadeu de Prado was deeply horrified. He picked up Prado's book, as if to hold on to himself.

"Is everything really all right?" the Greek asked into the new silence.

Yes, said Gregorius, everything's fine.

They ended the conversation in the usual way.

Gregorius lay in the dark, distraught, and tried to figure out what had come between him and the Greek. He was after all the man whose words had given him the courage to make this trip, despite the snow that started falling in Bern. He had put himself through the university by working as a taxi driver in Thessaloniki. *A pretty rough bunch, the taxi drivers,* he had once said. Now and then, a coarse word would flash out in him. As when he cursed or dragged fiercely on a cigarette. The dark stubble and the thick black hair on his arms looked wild and uncontrollable at such moments.

So he considered it natural that others failed to see him as he was. Was it possible that this didn't matter at all to someone? And was that a lack of sensibility? Or a desirable internal independence? It was growing light when Gregorius finally fell asleep.

11

It can't be, it's impossible. Gregorius took off the new, feather-light glasses, rubbed his eyes and put them back on. It *was* possible: He saw better than ever. That was especially true for the top half of the glasses, through which he looked out at the world. Things literally seemed to jump at him, as if they were crowding up to attract his look. And since he no longer felt the previous weight on his nose, which had made the glasses a protective bulwark, they seemed importunate, even threatening in their new clarity. The new impressions also made him a little dizzy, and he took the glasses off. A smile flitted over César Santarém's gruff face.

"And now you don't know if the old or the new ones are better," he said.

Gregorius nodded and stood before the mirror. The narrow, reddish frames and the new lenses that no longer looked like martial barriers before his eyes made him into somebody else. Somebody whose looks were important. Somebody who wanted to look elegant, chic. OK, that was an exaggeration; but still, Santarém's assistant, who had talked him into buying the frames, gestured her appreciation in the background. Santarém saw it. "*Tem razão,*" he said, she's right. Gregorius felt rage rising in him. He put on the old glasses, had the new ones packed up, and quickly paid.

Mariana Eça's office in the Alfama quarter was half an hour's walk. It took Gregorius four hours. It began with him sitting down whenever he found a bench, sitting and changing his glasses. With the new glasses the world was bigger and for the first time, space really had three dimensions where things could extend unhindered. The Tagus was no longer a vague brownish surface, but a river, and the Castelo de São Jorge projected into the sky in three directions, like a real citadel. But the world was a strain like that. Indeed it was also lighter with the light frame on the nose, the heavy steps he was used to no longer suited the new lightness in his face. But the world was closer and more oppressing, it demanded more of you, but its demands weren't clear. When they became too much for him, these obscure demands, he retreated behind the old lenses that kept everything at a distance and allowed him to doubt whether there really was an outside world beyond words and texts, a doubt that was dear to him and without it he really couldn't imagine life at all. But he could no longer forget the new view either and in a little park, he took out Prado's notes and tried out the new glasses.

O verdadeiro encenador da nossa vida é o acaso—um encenador cheio de crueldade, misericórdia e encanto cativante. Gregorius didn't believe his eyes: he hadn't understood any of Prado's sentences so easily: *The real director of our life is accident—a director full of cruelty, compassion and bewitching charm.* He shut his eyes and gave in to the sweet illusion that the new glasses would make all the Portuguese man's other sentences accessible to him in this way—as if they were a fabulous magical instrument that made the meaning of the words visible through their external contours. He grasped the glasses and adjusted them. He was beginning to like them.

I'd like to know if I've done it right—the words of the woman with the big eyes and the black velvet jacket; words that had surprised him because they had sounded like those of an ambitious schoolgirl with little self-confidence and didn't suit the certainty she radiated. Gregorius watched a girl on Rollerblades. If the rollerblader had held his elbow a teensy little bit different that first evening—right past his temple—he wouldn't now be on the way to this woman—or torn between an imperceptibly veiled and a dazzling clear field of vision that lent the world this unreal reality.

In a bar, he drank a coffee. It was lunchtime; the room was full of well-dressed men from an office building next door. Gregorius looked at his new face in the mirror, then the whole figure, as the doctor would see it afterward. The baggy corduroy pants, the rough turtleneck and the old windbreaker contrasted with the many tailored jackets, the matching shirts and ties. Nor did they suit the new glasses, not at all. It angered Gregorius that the contrast bothered him; from one sip to another, he became more furious about it. He thought of the way the waiter in the Hotel Bellevue had scrutinized him on the morning of his flight, and how it hadn't mattered to him; on the contrary with his shabby look, he had felt he was standing up to the hollow elegance of the surroundings. Where had this certainty gone? He put on the old glasses, paid, and left.

Had the noble houses next to and across from Mariana Eça's office really been there on his first visit? Gregorius put on the new glasses and looked around. Doctors, lawyers, a wine company, an African embassy. He was sweating under the thick sweater, and at the same time he felt in his face the cold wind that had swept the sky clear. Behind which window was the treatment room?

How well one sees depends on so many things, she had said. It was quarter to two. Could he just go up there at this time? He walked on a few streets and stood still before a men's clothing shop. *You really might buy something new for a change.* For the schoolgirl Florence, the girl in the first row, his indifference to his outward appearance had been attractive. For the wife, it had soon gotten on her nerves, this attitude. *After all, you don't live alone. And Greek isn't enough for that.* In the nineteen years he had lived alone again, he had been in a clothing store only two or three times. He was glad that nobody scolded him for that. Were nineteen years enough defiance? Hesitantly, he entered the shop.

The two saleswomen took all conceivable pains with him, the only customer, and finally they brought out the manager. Gregorius kept looking at himself in the mirror: first in suits that made him into a banker, an operagoer, a bon vivant, a professor, an accountant; later in jackets, from the double-breasted blazer to the sport coat suitable for a ride in the castle grounds; finally leather. Of all the enthusiastic Portuguese sentences pelting him, he didn't understand a single one, and he kept shaking his head. Finally, he left the shop in a gray corduroy suit. He looked at himself uncertainly in a display window a few buildings away. Did the fine scarlet turtleneck he had let himself be pressured into match the red of the new eyeglass frames?

Quite suddenly, Gregorius lost his nerve. With fast, furious steps, he walked to the public toilet on the other side of the street and put his old things back on. When he passed an entryway with a mountain of junk towering behind it, he put down the bag with the new clothes. Then he walked slowly in the direction where the doctor lived.

As soon as he entered the building, he heard the door open upstairs and then he saw her coming down in a flowing coat. Now he wished he had kept the new clothes.

"Oh, it's you," she said and asked how the new glasses were.

As he was telling, she came to him, grasped the new glasses and tested whether they were sitting right. He smelled her perfume, a strand of her hair stroked his face, and for a tiny moment, her movement merged with that of Florence the first time she had taken off his glasses. When he spoke of the unreal reality things had assumed all of a sudden, she smiled and then looked at her watch.

"I have to take the ferry to make a visit." Something in his face must have made her wonder, for she paused as she was leaving. "Were you ever on the Tagus? Would you like to come along?"

Later, Gregorius no longer remembered the drive down to the ferry. Only that, with a single liquid motion, she had pulled into a parking place that seemed much too small. Then they were sitting on the upper deck of the ferry and Mariana Eça was telling about the uncle she wanted to visit, her father's brother.

João Eça lived up in Cacilhas in a nursing home, barely spoke a word and replayed famous chess games all day long. He had been an accountant in a big firm, a modest, unprepossessing, nearly invisible man. It never occurred to anybody that he was working for the resistance. The disguise was perfect. He was forty-seven when Salazar's thugs got hold of him. As a communist, he was sentenced to life in prison for high treason. Two years later, Mariana, his favorite niece, came to pick him up him at the prison.

"That was in the summer of 1974, a few weeks after the revolution. I was twenty-one and was studying in Coimbra," she said now, her face averted.

Gregorius heard her swallow, and now her voice became raw, so as not to break.

"I never got over the sight. He was only forty-nine, but torture had made him into a sick old man. He had had a full, deep voice; now he spoke in a hoarse soft voice, and his hands that had played Schubert, mainly Schubert, were disfigured and constantly shaking." She took a breath and sat up very straight. "Only the incredibly direct, fearless look from his gray eyes—it was unbroken. It took years until he could tell me: they had held white-hot irons before his eyes to make him talk. They kept coming closer, and he had expected to sink into a wave of white-hot darkness any minute. But his eyes didn't turn away from the iron, he went through its hardness and burning and came out the other side of his torturers' faces. This unbelievable inflexibility gave them pause. 'Since then, nothing can scare me anymore,' he said, 'literally nothing.' And I am sure: he didn't reveal anything."

They landed.

"Over there," she said, and now her voice recovered its usual firmness; "that's the home."

She pointed to a ferry that described a big arc, so the city could be seen from another perspective. Then she stood still, hesitant a moment, a hesitation revealing the awareness of an intimacy between them, which had happened surprisingly fast, but couldn't go on now, and perhaps also the frightening doubt about whether it had been right to expose so much of João and herself. When she finally went off toward the home, Gregorius looked after her for a long time and imagined how she had stood before the prison at the age of twenty-one.

He went back to Lisbon and then made the whole trip over the Tagus again. João Eça had been in the resistance, Amadeu de Prado had worked for the resistance. *Resistência:* The doctor had naturally used the Portuguese word—as if, for this matter, this holy matter, there could be no other word. In her mouth, the word, softly urgent, had an intoxicating sonority, a word with a mythical gleam and a mystical aura. An accountant and a doctor, five years apart. Both had risked everything, both had worked with a perfect disguise, both had been masters of silence and virtuosos of sealed lips. Had they known each other?

When he was back on land, Gregorius bought a city map with an especially precise inset of Bairro Alto. As he ate, he laid out the route of search for the blue house where Adriana de Prado, old and without a telephone, might still be living. When he left the pub, darkness was falling. He took a streetcar to the Alfama quarter. After a while, he found the entryway with the heaps of junk. The bag with his new clothes was still there. He picked it up, hailed a cab and was driven to the hotel.

12

Early the next morning, Gregorius went out into a day that began gray and foggy. Quite contrary to habit, last night he had fallen asleep quickly and plunged into a flood of dream images of an incomprehensible sequence of ships, clothes, and prisons. Even though it was incomprehensible, the whole thing had not been unpleasant and was far from a nightmare, for the confused, rhapsodic changing scenes were set off by an inaudible voice that possessed an overwhelming present and belonged to a woman whose name he had sought with feverish haste, as if his life depended on it. Just as he woke up, the word he had been hunting came to him: *Conceição*—the beautiful, fairy-tale part in the doctor's full name on the brass plate at the entrance to the office: Mariana Conceição Eça. When he spoke the name softly to himself, another dream scene surfaced from forgetting, in which a woman of quickly changing identity took off his glasses while pressing them solidly on his nose, so solidly that he still felt the pressure.

It had been one in the morning and getting back to sleep was inconceivable. So he had leafed through Prado's book and got stuck on a note titled CARAS FUGAZES NA NOITE. FLEETING FACES IN THE NIGHT.

Encounters between people, it often seems to me, are like crossings of racing trains at breakneck speed in the deepest night. We cast fleeting, rushed looks at the others sitting behind dull glass in dim light, who disappear from our field of vision as soon as we barely have time to perceive them. Was it really a man and a woman who flitted by there like phantoms in an illuminated window frame, who arose out of nothing and seemed to cut into the empty dark, without meaning or purpose? Did they know each other? Did they talk? Laugh? Cry? People will say: that's how it may be when strangers pass one another in rain and wind; there might be something to the comparison. But we sit across from a lot of people longer, we eat and work together, lie next to each other, live under the same roof. Where is the haste? Yet everything that gives the illusion of permanence, familiarity, and intimate knowledge: isn't it a deception invented to reassure, with which we try to cover and ward off the flickering disturbing haste because it would be impossible to bear it every moment? Isn't every glance of another and every exchange of looks like the ghostly brief meeting of eyes between travelers who glide by one another, intoxicated by the inhuman speed and the fist of the air pressure that makes everything shudder and clatter? Don't our looks perpetually bounce off the others, as in the hasty encounter of the night, and leave us behind with nothing but conjectures, slivers of thoughts and fictional qualities? Isn't it true that it's not people who meet, but rather the shadows cast by their imaginations?

How would it have been, Gregorius had thought, to be the sister of somebody whose loneliness spoke from such giddy depths? Of somebody who in his reflections had revealed such a merciless consistency, but whose words did not sound despairing or even agitated? How would it have been to assist him, give injections and help bandage? What he thought in writing about distance and strangeness between people: What had it meant for the atmosphere in the blue house? Had he kept it completely hidden in himself or had the house been the place, the only place, where he had let these thoughts out? In the way he went from room to room, picked up a book and decided what music he wanted to hear? What sounds did he think fit the lonely thoughts that felt clear and hard as glass figures? Had he sought sounds that were like a confirmation or had he needed melodies and rhythms that were like balm, not lulling and veiling, but softening?

With these questions in his mind, Gregorius slipped back into a light sleep toward morning and had stood before an unreal narrow blue door, in himself the wish to ring the bell and at the same time the certainty that he had no idea what he would say to the woman who opened the door. After he woke up, he went to breakfast in the new clothes and with the new glasses. The waitress gave a start when she noticed his changed appearance, and then a smile flashed over her face. And now, on this gray, foggy Sunday morning, he was on his way to seek the blue house old Coutinho had talked about.

He had inspected only a few streets in the upper part of the city when he saw the man he had followed the first evening smoking at a window. Now in daylight the house looked even narrower and shabbier than back then. The interior of the room was in shadow, but Gregorius caught a glimpse of the tapestry of the sofa, the glass cabinet with the colorful porcelain figures and the Crucifix. He stood still and tried to catch the man's eye.

"Uma casa azul?" he asked.

The man held his hand to his ear and Gregorius repeated the question. A surge of words he didn't understand was the answer, accompanied by gestures with the cigarette. As the man spoke, a bent, very old woman came to his side.

"O consultório azul?" Gregorius asked now.

"Sim!" shouted the old woman in a creaky voice and then once again: *"Sim!"*

She gesticulated excitedly with her stick-thin arms and shriveled hands and after a while, Gregorius caught on that she was waving him inside. Hesitantly, he entered the house that smelled of mold and rancid oil. He felt that he had to push through a thick wall of repulsive smells to get to the door where the man was waiting, a new cigarette between his lips. Limping, he led Gregorius into the living room, mumbled some question and gestured a vague invitation to sit on a tapestry-covered sofa.

In the next half hour, Gregorius struggled to find his way around in the mostly incomprehensible words and ambiguous gestures of the two people who tried to explain to him how it had been forty years ago, when Amadeu de Prado had treated the people of the quarter. There was adoration in their voices, an adoration you feel for someone far above you. But another feeling also filled the room, which Gregorius recognized only gradually as shyness originating in a long-ago accusation you'd like to deny, but can't get out of your memory. *After that people avoided him. That broke his heart,* he heard Coutinho say, after he had told how Prado had saved Rui Luís Mendes, the butcher of Lisbon.

Now the man pulled up a pants leg and showed Gregorius a scar. *"Ele fez isto," he* did it, he said and ran his nicotine-stained fingertips over it. The woman rubbed her temples with her shriveled fingers and then made the gesture of flying away: Prado had made her headaches disappear. And then she too showed a small scar on a finger where a wart had probably been.

Later, when Gregorius asked himself what had been the decisive factor that had finally made him ring the bell at the blue door, he always recalled these gestures of the two people with traces on their bodies left by the doctor who was adored, then ostracized and finally adored again. It had been as if his hands had come back to life.

Now the way to Prado's former office was described to Gregorius and he left the two of them. Head to head, they watched him from the window and it seemed to him that there was envy in their look, a paradoxical envy that he could do something they couldn't do anymore: meet Amadeu de Prado brand new, by making his way into his past.

Was it possible that the best way to make sure of yourself was to know and understand someone else? One whose life had been completely different and had had a completely different logic than your own? How did curiosity for another life go together with the awareness that your own time was running out?

Gregorius stood at the counter of a small bar and drank a coffee. It was the second time he stood here. An hour ago, he had pushed up to Rua Luz Soriano and had stood a few steps before Prado's blue office, a three-story house that seemed altogether blue first because of the blue ceramic tiles, but even more because all the windows were covered with high arches painted dark blue. The paint was old, the color was crumbling and there were damp places where black moss grew rampant. The blue color was also crumbling on the cast-iron bars on the bottom of the windows. Only the blue front door had an impeccable coat of paint as if someone wanted to say: This is what matters.

The doorbell had no nameplate. His heart pounding, Gregorius had looked at the door with the brass knocker. *As if my whole future were behind this door,* he had thought. Then he had gone to the bar a few houses down and struggled against the threatening feeling that he was losing his grip. He had looked at his watch: it had been six days ago that he had taken the damp coat off the hook in the classroom and had run away from his very certain, clear life, without turning around even once. He had reached in the pocket of this coat and groped for the key to his Bern flat. And suddenly, violent and physically tangible as an attack of ravenous hunger, he was assailed by the desire to read a Greek or Hebrew text; to see the foreign beautiful letters that hadn't lost any of their Oriental, fabulous elegance for him even after forty years; to make sure that, during the six confusing days, he hadn't lost any of the ability to understand everything they expressed.

In the hotel was the New Testament, in Greek and Portuguese, that Coutinho had given him; but the hotel was too far, it was being able to read here and now, not far from the blue house that threatened to swallow him up, even before the door had opened. He had paid quickly and set off in search of a bookstore where he could find such texts. But it was Sunday and the only one he found was a closed religious bookstore with books in the display window with Greek and Hebrew titles. He had leaned his forehead on the fog-damp windowpane and felt overcome again by the temptation to go to the airport and take the next plane to Zurich. It was a relief to see that he could experience the oppressing wish as a surging and ebbing fever and patiently let it pass, and finally he had slowly gone back to the bar near the blue house.

Now he took Prado's book out of the pocket of his new jacket and looked at the bold, intrepid face of the Portuguese man. A doctor who had practiced his profession with rock-hard consistency. A resistance fighter, who tried under mortal danger to wash away a guilt that didn't exist. A goldsmith of words whose deepest passion had been to rescue the silent experiences of human life from their muteness.

Suddenly Gregorius was assailed by the fear that someone quite different might now live in the blue house. He quickly laid the coins for the coffee on the counter and rushed to the house. Before the blue door, he took two deep breaths and very slowly let the air escape from his lungs. Then he rang the bell.

A rattling chime that sounded as if it came from a medieval distance reverberated excessively loud through the house. Nothing happened. No light, no steps. Once again, Gregorius forced himself to be calm, then he rang again. Nothing. He turned around and leaned against the door, exhausted. He thought of his flat in Bern. He was glad it was over. Slowly, he shoved Prado's book in his coat pocket, touching the cool metal of the house key as he did. Then he broke away from the door and was about to leave.

At this moment, he heard steps inside. Someone was coming down the stairs. Behind a window, a lamp could be seen. The steps approached the door.

"*Quem é?*" called a dark, hoarse female voice.

Gregorius didn't know what he should say. He waited in silence. Seconds passed. Then a key was turned in the lock and the door opened.

PART II
THE ENCOUNTER

13

In her strict nunlike beauty the tall woman all in black who stood before him seemed to come from a Greek tragedy. The pale gaunt face was framed by a crocheted kerchief she held together under her chin with a hand, a slim, bony hand with protruding dark veins that revealed her old age more clearly than the features of her face. From deep-set eyes shining like black diamonds, she examined Gregorius with a bitter look that spoke of deprivation, self-control and self-denial, a look like Moses admonishing all those whose life consisted of letting themselves be driven passively. These eyes could flame, thought Gregorius, if someone opposed the mute unbending will of this woman, who held herself straight as a candle and bore her head a little higher than her size really allowed. An icy glow came from her and Gregorius had no idea how he was to face up to her. He didn't even know how to say "Good morning" in Portuguese anymore.

"Bonjour," he said hoarsely as the woman kept looking at him mutely and then he pulled Prado's book out of his coat pocket, opened it to the portrait and showed it to her.

"I know that this man, a doctor, lived and worked here," he went on in French. "I . . . I wanted to see where he lived and to talk with somebody who knew him. They're such impressive sentences that he wrote. Wise sentences. Wonderful sentences. I'd like to know what the man was like who could write such sentences. What it was like to be with him."

The change in the woman's stern white face, glowing faintly against the black of the kerchief, could hardly be seen. Only someone with the special wakefulness Gregorius possessed at that moment could have seen that the taut features relaxed a little—a tiny bit—and the look lost a trace of its chilly sharpness. But she remained mute and time began to stretch.

"Pardonnez-moi, je ne voulais pas . . . ," Gregorius now began, took two steps away from the door and fumbled in his coat pocket, which suddenly seemed too small to take the book back. He turned to go.

"Attendez!" said the woman. The voice now sounded less irritated and warmer than just now, behind the door. And in the French words, the same accent resonated as in the voice of the nameless Portuguese woman on the Kirchenfeldbrücke. Nevertheless, it sounded like an order you didn't dare refuse, and Gregorius thought of Coutinho's comment about the overbearing way Adriana had treated the patients. He turned back to her, the bulky book still in his hand.

"Entrez," said the woman, moved back from the door and pointed upstairs. She locked the door with a big key that seemed to come from another century, and then followed him. Upstairs, when she released the hand with the white knuckles from the banister and went past him into the parlor, he heard her gasping and he was grazed by an astringent fragrance that could have come from either a medicine or a perfume.

Never had Gregorius seen such a parlor, not even in the movies. It stretched over the whole depth of the house and seemed endless. The immaculately shining parquet floor consisted of rosettes with a lot of various kinds and tints of wood alternating, and when the eye reached the last one, another one was beyond it. In the end, the look then went out to the trees that now, at the end of February, presented a tangle of black boughs rising into the blue-gray sky. In one corner was a round table with French-style furniture—a sofa and three chairs, the seats of olive green, silvery glimmering velvet, the curved backs and legs of reddish wood—in another a shiny black grandfather clock, whose gold pendulum was still, the hands stopped at six twenty-three. And in the corner by the window was a grand piano, covered down to the keyboard with a heavy throw of black brocade, laced with shining gold and silver threads.

Yet, what impressed Gregorius more than anything else were the endless shelves of books built into the ocher-colored walls. They ended on top with small Art Nouveau lamps, and from wall to wall, with a coffered ceiling arching above them that picked up the ocher tone of the walls mixed with dark red geometric patterns. *Like a monastery library,* thought Gregorius, *like the library of a former pupil of classical education from an affluent home.* He didn't dare walk along the walls, but his eye quickly found the Greek classics in the dark blue, gold-inscribed Oxford volumes, further back Cicero, Horace, the writings of the Church Fathers, the OBRAS COMPLETAS of San Ignacio. He hadn't been in this house even ten minutes and was already wishing he never had to leave it again. It simply *must* be Amadeu de Prado's library. *Was* it?

"Amadeu loved the room, the books. 'I have so little time, Adriana,' he often said, 'much too little time to read, maybe I should have become a priest.' But he wanted the office to be open at all times, from morning to night. 'Anyone who has pain or fear can't wait,' he used to say when I saw his exhaustion and tried to restrain him. Reading and writing he did at night when he couldn't sleep. Or maybe he couldn't sleep because he had the feeling that he had to read, write, and meditate, I don't know. It was a curse, his sleeplessness, and I'm sure: without this suffering and without his restlessness, his eternal, breathless search for words, his brain would have held out much longer. Maybe he'd still be alive. He would have been eighty-four years old this year, on December 20."

Without asking a single word about who he was and without introducing herself to him, she had spoken of her brother, his suffering, his devotion, his passion and his death. All the things—her words and her changing expressions left no doubt—that had been most important in her life. And she had spoken of them so abruptly, as if she had a right to expect that Gregorius, in a lightning-fast, unearthly metamorphosis outside all time, turned into a denizen of her mind and an omniscient witness of her memories. He was someone who carried the book with the mysterious sign of the *Cedros vermelhos*, the red cedars, and that was enough to give him entry to the sacred region of her thoughts. How many years had she been waiting for someone like him to come by, someone she could talk to about the dead brother? Nineteen seventy-three had been the year of death on the tombstone. So, Adriana had lived alone in this house for thirty-one years, thirty-one years alone with the memories and the emptiness left behind by the brother.

So far she had held the kerchief together under her chin, as if to hide something. Now, she took her hand away; the crocheted kerchief divided and revealed a black velvet ribbon encircling her neck. Gregorius was never to forget this view of the dividing cloth, revealing the broad ribbon over the white lines of the neck; it congealed into a firm, precisely detailed image and later, when he knew what the ribbon hid, it became an icon of his memory, along with Adriana's gesture checking whether the ribbon was still there and sitting properly, a gesture that seemed to happen to her more than be performed by her, but at the same time was a gesture into which she sank completely and that seemed to say more about her than anything she did deliberately and consciously.

The kerchief had slipped far back and now Gregorius saw her graying hair, with still a few strands that still recalled the previous black. Adriana gripped the sliding kerchief, raised it and pulled it forward, embarrassed, paused a moment, and then ripped it off her head defiantly. Their looks met for a moment and hers seemed to say: *Yes, I've grown old.* She bent her head, a curl slid over her eyes, her torso collapsed and then, slowly and lost, she ran the hands with the dark purple veins over the kerchief in her lap.

Gregorius pointed to Prado's book, which he had put on the table. "Is that all Amadeu wrote?"

The few words worked a miracle. Everything exhausted and extinguished fell away from Adriana; she straightened up, threw her head back, ran both hands through her hair, and then looked at him. It was the first time a smile appeared on her features; mischievous and conspiratorial, it made her look twenty years younger.

"Venha, Senhor." Come. Everything overbearing had vanished from her voice, the words didn't sound like an order, not even like a demand, rather like the announcement that she would show him something, let him in on something hidden and mysterious and it suited the promised intimacy and complicity that she had apparently forgotten he didn't speak Portuguese.

She led him through the corridor to the second floor and up to the attic and took one stair after another, gasping. At one of the two doors, she stood still. It could have been merely a rest, but later, when Gregorius sorted out the images of his memory, he was sure it had also been a hesitation, a doubt, whether she really should show the stranger this holy of holies. At last she turned the knob, softly as if she were visiting a sickroom, and the care with which she opened the door only a crack at first and then pushed it open slowly, gave the impression that, as she climbed the stairs, she had gone back more than thirty years in time and was entering the room expecting to meet Amadeu in it, writing and meditating, maybe even sleeping.

Far back in consciousness, at its outermost edge and a little dim, Gregorius was grazed by the thought that he was dealing with a woman who was straying on a narrow ridge that separated her present, visible life from another whose invisibility and chronological distance was much more real for her, and that it would take only a feeble shove, almost only a gust of wind, to make her plunge and vanish irrevocably into the past of her life with the brother.

In fact, in the big room they now entered, time had stood still. It was furnished with ascetic sparseness. At one end, facing the wall, was a desk and a chair. At the other end, a bed with a small rug in front of it, like a prayer rug. In the middle was a reading chair with a standing lamp and next to it mountains of messy piles of books on the bare floorboards. Nothing else. The whole thing was a sanctuary, a chapel to the memory of Amadeu Inácio de Almeida Prado, doctor, resistance fighter and goldsmith of words. The cool, eloquent silence of a cathedral prevailed here, the impassive rustle of a room filled with frozen time.

Gregorius stood still in the door; that wasn't a room a stranger could simply walk around in. And even if Adriana now moved among the few objects, it was different from normal movement. Not that she walked on tiptoe or that her gait had anything artificial. But her slow steps had something ethereal, thought Gregorius, something dematerialized and almost timeless and spaceless. That also applied to the movements of arms and hands as she now went to the pieces of furniture and stroked them softly, barely touching them.

She did that first with the desk chair, a match for the chairs in the parlor with its round seat and curved back. It stood at an angle from the desk, as if someone had stood up hastily and pushed it back. Gregorius instinctively waited for Adriana to straighten it and only when she had affectionately gone over all corners without changing anything did he understand: the crooked position of the chair was where Amadeu had left it thirty years and two months before, and so a position that mustn't be changed at any cost, for it would have been as if someone were trying with Promethean arrogance to rescue the past from its inalterability or to overturn the laws of nature.

What was true of the chair was also true of the objects on the desk, which was slightly tilted to make it easier to read and write. On it, in a precarious position, was an enormous book open in the middle; in front of it, a pile of pages, the top one, as far as Gregorius could make out with an effort, with only a few words written on it. Adriana softly stroked the wood with the back of her hand and now touched the bluish porcelain cup on the red copper tray, along with a sugar bowl full of rock candy and an overflowing ashtray. Were these things also old? Thirty-year-old coffee grounds? Cigarette ashes more than a quarter century old? The ink in the open fountain pen must have crumbled to fine dust or have dried to a black lump. Would the lightbulb in the richly decorated table lamp with the emerald green shade still burn?

There was something that amazed Gregorius, but it took him a while to grasp it: There was no dust on the things. He shut his eyes and now Adriana was only a spirit with audible outlines sliding through the room. Had this spirit regularly wiped the dust, on eleven thousand days? And grown gray doing it?

When he opened his eyes again, Adriana was standing before a towering pile of books that looked as if it could topple over any minute. She was looking down at a thick, oversized book on top with a picture of the brain on the cover.

"O cérebro sempre o cérebro," she said softly and accusingly. The brain, always the brain. *"Porquê não disseste nada?"* Why did you say nothing?

Now there was anger in her voice, resigned anger, eroded by time and the silence with which the dead brother had answered for decades. He had told her nothing of the aneurysm, thought Gregorius, nothing of his fear and the awareness that life could come to an end any time. Only from the notes had she learned of it. And through all the grief, had been furious that he had denied her the intimacy of this knowledge.

Now she glanced up and looked at Gregorius, as if she had forgotten him. Only slowly did her mind come back to the present.

"Oh yes, come here," she said in French and, with firmer steps than before, she went back to the desk, where she pulled open two drawers. In them were thick piles of papers, pressed between cardboard covers and tied several times with red ribbons.

"He started that shortly after Fátima's death. 'It's a struggle against the internal paralysis,' he said, and a few weeks later: 'Why on earth didn't I start it before! You're not really awake when you don't write. And you have no idea who you are. Not to mention who you *aren't*.' Nobody was allowed to read it, not even me. He took out the key and always carried it with him. He was . . . he could be very distrusting."

She shut the drawers. "I'd like to be alone now," she said abruptly, almost hostilely, and as she went down the stairs, she didn't say another word. When she had opened the front door, she stood there mute, angular and stiff. She wasn't a woman to whom you gave your hand.

"Au revoir et merci," said Gregorius and turned hesitantly to leave.

"What's your name?"

The question came louder than necessary, it sounded a little like a hoarse bark that reminded him of Coutinho. She repeated the name: *Gregoriusch.*

"Where do you live?"

He told her the name of the hotel. Without a word of farewell, she shut the door and turned the key.

14

On the Tagus, the clouds were reflected. They chased the sun-glittering surfaces, slid over them, swallowed the light and let it pierce through the shadow in another place. Gregorius took off the glasses, and covered his face with his hands. The feverish change between dazzling brightness and threatening shadow pressing with unusual sharpness through the new glasses was a torment for the unprotected eyes. Just now, at the hotel, after he had woken up from a light and uneasy afternoon nap, he had tried the old glasses again. But now their dense heaviness felt disturbing, as if he had to push his face through the world with a tedious burden.

Uncertain and even a little strange to himself, he had sat on the edge of the bed a long time and tried to decipher and sort out the confusing experiences of the morning. In the dream, haunted by a mute Adriana with a marble pallor, the color black had prevailed, a black with the disconcerting quality of adhering to objects—all objects—no matter what their color or how much they shone in these other colors. The velvet ribbon around Adriana's neck that came up to the chin seemed to be choking her, for she was constantly tugging at it. Then she grasped her head with both hands again and she wasn't trying to protect the skull so much as the brain. Towers of books, one after another, collapsed and for a moment, when tense expectation blended with apprehension and the bad conscience of the voyeur, Gregorius had sat at Prado's desk where a sea of fossils lay and in the middle a half-written page, whose lines paled in a flash to illegibility when he aimed his eyes at them.

While he was busy remembering these dream images, it sometimes seemed to him that the visit to the blue office really hadn't taken place—as if the whole thing had been only an especially vivid dream, where—as an episode of tumbling delusion—a difference between waking and dreaming was faked. Then he grabbed his head too and when he recovered the sense of the reality of his visit and pictured the figure of Adriana clearly, stripped of all dreamlike elements, he mentally rehearsed the hour he had spent with her thought for thought, movement for movement, word for word. Sometimes he felt a chill when he thought of her stern, bitter look, with its irreconcilability toward distant events. An eerie feeling had crept over him when he saw her floating through Prado's room, completely turned to the past, and close to madness. Then he wanted to put the crocheted cloth gently back around her head to grant the tormented spirit a break.

The way to Amadeu de Prado led through this hard yet fragile woman, or rather: it led through her, through the dark corridor of her memory. Did he want to take that on? Was he up to it? He, called *The Papyrus* by his spiteful colleagues, because he had lived more in ancient texts than in the world?

It was crucial to find other people who had known Prado; not only seen, like Coutinho, and known as a doctor, like the limping man and the old woman of yesterday morning, but had really known, as a friend, perhaps as a comrade in the resistance. It would be hard, he thought, to learn anything from Adriana about it; she considered the dead brother her exclusive property, that had become clear at the latest when, looking down at the medical book, she had spoken to him. She would deny or use all means to keep away anybody who could question the only real picture of him—which was hers and only hers.

Gregorius had looked up Mariana Eça's number and called her after hesitating a long time. Would she have any objection if he visited João, her uncle, in the home? He now knew that Prado had also been in the resistance and perhaps João had known him. There was a silence and just as Gregorius wanted to apologize for the suggestion, she said pensively, "Of course I have nothing against it, on the contrary, a new face might be good for him. I'm only considering whether he'd accept it, he can be very brusque, and yesterday he was even more taciturn than usual. In any case, you mustn't take him straight on."

She was silent.

"I think I know something that might help. I wanted to bring him a record yesterday, a new recording of Schubert's sonatas. He wants to hear only Maria João Pires, I don't know whether it's the sound or the woman or a bizarre form of patriotism. But he will like this record. I forgot to take it. You can come by my house and bring it to him. As my messenger, as it were. Maybe you'll have luck then."

He had drunk tea at her house, a red-gold steamy Assam with rock candy, and told her about Adriana. He would have wanted her to say something about it, but she merely listened silently and, only once, when he spoke of the used coffee cup and the full ashtray that had apparently lasted three decades, she narrowed her eyes like somebody who suddenly thinks he's picked up a trace.

"Be careful," she said to him as they parted. "With Adriana, I mean. And tell me how it goes with João."

And now, with Schubert's sonatas in his bag, he sat on the boat and went over to Cacilhas to a man who had gone through the hell of torture without losing his direct look. Once again, Gregorius covered his face with his hands. A week ago, when he had sat in his Bern flat correcting Latin notebooks, if somebody had prophesied that seven days later, in a new suit and with new glasses, he would be sitting on a boat in Lisbon to learn something from a tortured victim of the Salazar regime about a Portuguese doctor and poet who had been dead for more than thirty years—he would have considered him crazy. Was he still Mundus, the myopic bookworm, who had gotten scared only because a few snowflakes had fallen in Bern?

The boat landed and Gregorius slowly climbed up to the home. How would they understand each other? Did João Eça speak anything but Portuguese? It was Sunday afternoon, people were paying their visits to the home, you could recognize them in the street by the bunches of flowers they carried. On the narrow balconies of the home, the old people sat in blankets in the sun that kept disappearing behind clouds. Gregorius got the room number at the gate. Before he knocked, he inhaled and exhaled slowly a few times, it was the second time this day that he had stood at a door with a pounding heart, not knowing what was in store for him.

His knock wasn't answered, not even the second time. He had already turned to go when he heard the door open with a slight squeak. He had expected a man in neglected clothing, who often didn't even really get dressed, but sat in his bathrobe at the chess board. The man who appeared in the cracked open door, noiseless as a ghost, was quite different. He wore a dark blue cardigan sweater over a sparkling white shirt with a red tie, trousers with an impeccable crease and shining black shoes. He kept his hands hidden in his sweater pockets, the bald head with the few cropped hairs over the protruding ears was turned slightly to the side like someone who doesn't want to deal with what's coming at him. From gray squinting eyes came a look that seemed to pierce whatever it met. João Eça was old and he may have been sick, as his niece had said; but a broken man he was not. It was better, thought Gregorius instinctively, not to have him as an enemy.

"Senhor Eça?" said Gregorius. *"Venho da parte de Mariana, a sua sobrinha. Trago este disco. Sonatas de Schubert."* Those were words he had looked up on the boat and had then said them to himself several times.

Eça stood still in the door and looked at him. Gregorius had never had to endure such scrutiny and after a while, he looked down. Now Eça pulled the door wide open and beckoned him in. Gregorius entered a meticulously cleared room furnished with what was most necessary and only what was most necessary. For a fleeting moment, he thought of the luxurious rooms where the ophthalmologist lived, and asked himself why she hadn't lodged her uncle in a better place. The thought vanished with Eça's first words:

"Who are you?" he asked in English. The words came light and hoarse and yet they had authority, the authority of a man who had seen everything and was nobody's fool.

Holding the record, Gregorius told in English about his origin and his profession and explained how he had met Mariana.

"Why are you here? Not because of the record, surely."

Gregorius put the record on the table and took a breath. Then he pulled Prado's book out of his pocket and showed him the portrait.

"Your niece thought you might have known him."

After a brief glance at the picture, Eça shut his eyes. He swayed a little, then, with eyes still shut, he went to the sofa and sat down.

"Amadeu," he said into the silence and then again: "Amadeu. *O sacerdote ateu.* The godless priest."

Gregorius waited. One wrong word, one wrong gesture, and Eça wouldn't say another word. He went to the chessboard and looked at the game in progress. He had to risk it.

"Hastings 1922. Alekhine beats Bogolyubov," he said.

Eça opened his eyes and looked at him in amazement.

"Tartakover was once asked whom he considered the greatest chess player. He said: 'If chess is a battle—Lasker; if it's a science—Capablanca; if it's an art—Alekhine.'"

"Yes," said Gregorius. "The sacrifice of both rooks reveals the imagination of an artist."

"Sounds like envy."

"It is. It simply wouldn't occur to me."

On Eça's weatherbeaten, peasant features, the trace of a smile appeared.

"If it makes you feel better, not to me either."

Their looks crossed, then each looked straight ahead. Either Eça was now undertaking something to continue the conversation, thought Gregorius, or the meeting was at an end.

"Up there in the alcove is some tea," said Eça. "I'd also like a cup."

At first, Gregorius was taken aback that he was told to do what the host usually did. But then he saw Eça's hands balled into fists in the sweater pockets, and now he understood: he didn't want Gregorius to see his disfigured shaking hands, the remaining marks of the horror. And so he poured tea for both of them. It steamed out of both cups. Gregorius waited. From the next room came the laughter of visitors. Then it was silent again.

The silent way Eça finally took his hand out of the pocket and took the cup was like his silent appearance in the door. He kept his eyes shut as if he thought the disfigured hand would thus be invisible for others too. The hand was covered with traces of burning cigarettes, two fingernails were missing, and it shook as with palsy. Now Eça glanced searchingly at Gregorius: Was he up to the sight? Gregorius's horror flowed over him like an attack of weakness; he held it in check, and brought his cup calmly to his mouth.

"You can only fill mine halfway."

Eça said it softly, strained, and Gregorius was never to forget these words. He felt a burning in his eyes that indicated tears and then he did something that was to shape the relationship between him and this flayed man forever: he took Eça's cup and poured half of the hot tea into himself.

Tongue and throat burned. It didn't matter. Calmly, he put the half-full cup back and turned the handle to Eça's thumb. Now the man looked at him at length, and this look too was etched deep in his memory. It was a look that blended incredulity and gratitude, a gratitude that was only tentative, for Eça had long ago given up expecting anything from others that called for gratitude. Shaking, he brought the cup to his lips, waited for a favorable moment and then drank in hasty sips. There was a rhythmic clinking when he put the cup on the saucer.

Now he took a pack of cigarettes out of his sweater pocket, put one between his lips and brought the trembling flame to the tobacco. He smoked in deep, calm drags and the shaking diminished. He held the hand with the cigarette so that the missing fingernails weren't seen. The other hand had once more disappeared in the sweater pocket. He looked out the window as he began to speak.

"I met him the first time in the fall of 1952, in England, on the train from London to Brighton. I was taking a language course for my firm; they sent me to learn foreign correspondence. It was the Sunday after the first week and I was going to Brighton because I missed the sea, I grew up on the sea, in the north, in Esposende. The compartment door opened and in came this man with the shining hair that sat on his head like a helmet, with these unbelievable eyes, bold, soft, and melancholy. He was making a long trip with Fátima, his bride. Money never mattered to him, not then and not later. I learned that he was a doctor, who was fascinated mainly by the brain. A diehard materialist, who had originally wanted to be a priest. A man who had a paradoxical attitude about a lot of things, not absurd, but paradoxical.

"I was twenty-seven, he was five years older. He was vastly superior to me in everything. In any case, that's how I felt on that trip. He the son of a noble Lisbon family, I the son of farmers from the north. We spent the day together, strolled on the beach, ate together. At some point, we came to talk about the dictatorship. *Devemos resistir,* we must resist, I said, I still remember the words, I remember because they seemed crass before a man who had the chiseled face of a poet and sometimes used words I had never heard of.

"He lowered his eyes, looked out the window, nodded. I had touched on a subject he was uncomfortable with. It was the wrong subject for a man traveling on his honeymoon with his bride. I spoke of other things, but he was no longer really involved, and left the conversation to Fátima and me. 'You're right,' he said when we parted, 'of course you're right.' And clearly he was talking of the resistance.

"When I thought of him on the way back to London, it seemed to me that he, or a part of him, wanted to go back to Portugal with me instead of continuing his trip. He had asked me for my address and it had been more than a courtesy toward a traveling acquaintance. In fact, they soon broke off the trip and returned to Lisbon. But that had nothing to do with me. Adriana, his older sister, had had an abortion and almost died from it. He wanted to check on it, he didn't trust the doctor. A doctor who distrusted doctors. That's how he was, that was Amadeu."

Gregorius pictured Adriana's bitter, unreconciled look. He was beginning to understand. And what about the younger sister? But that had to wait.

"Thirteen years passed until I saw him again," Eça went on. "It was in the winter of 1965, the year the secret police murdered Delgado. He had learned my new address from the company and one evening, he stood at my door, pale and unshaved. The hair that had once gleamed like black gold had become dull, and pain spoke from his look. He told how he had saved the life of Rui Luís Mendes, a high-ranking officer in the secret police, called the

Butcher of Lisbon, and how his previous patients were now avoiding him, he felt ostracized.

"'I want to work for the resistance,' he said.

"'To make up for it?'

"He looked down, embarrassed.

"'You haven't done anything wrong,' I said. 'You're a doctor.'

"'I want to do something,' he said. 'You understand: *do*. Tell me what I can do. You know your way around.'

"'How do you know that?'

"'I know it,' he said. 'I've known it since Brighton.'

"It was dangerous. For us much more than for him. Because for a resistance fighter, he didn't have—how should I put it—the right internal stature, the right character. You have to have patience, be able to wait, you have to have a head like mine, a peasant's skull, not the soul of a sensitive dreamer. Otherwise you risk too much, slip up, endanger everything. Cold-bloodedness, he did have that, almost too much of it, he tended to be daring. He lacked the persistence, the stubbornness, the ability to do nothing, even when the opportunity seems favorable. He sensed that I thought that, he sensed the thoughts of others even before they had begun to think them. It was hard for him; it was, I think, the first time in his life that anyone ever said to him: You can't do that, you lack the ability for that. But he knew I was right, he was anything but blind about himself, and he accepted that the tasks would be small and nondescript at first.

"I kept urging him that, above all, he had to resist the temptation to let his patients know he was working for us. He wanted it to atone for a supposed breach of loyalty toward Mendes's victims. And this plan really had meaning only if the people who blamed him for it learned of it. If he could manage to revise their contemptuous judgment. This wish was paramount in him, I knew that, and it was his and our greatest enemy. He flared up when I talked of it, acted as if I underestimated his intelligence, I, nothing but an accountant, and five years younger than he. But he knew that, on this point, I was right. 'I hate it when somebody knows as much about me as you do,' he said once. And grinned.

"He had overcome his yearning, his ludicrous yearning for forgiveness for something that hadn't been wrong, and made no mistakes, or none that had any consequences.

"Mendes secretly protected him, his lifesaver. In Amadeu's office, messages were passed, envelopes with money changed hands. There was never a search, as there usually was. Amadeu was furious about that, that's how he was, the godless priest, he wanted to be taken seriously, being spared wounded his pride, which had something of the pride of a martyr.

"For a while, that conjured up a new danger: the danger that he might want to provoke Mendes with daredevil acts so that he wouldn't be able to protect him anymore. I spoke to him about it. Our friendship hung on a silk thread. This time he didn't admit that I was right. But he became more controlled, more cautious.

"Shortly after, he brilliantly carried out two delicate operations that only someone like him could carry out, someone who knew the railroad network inside and out, and Amadeu did, he was crazy about trains, rails, and switches, knew all types of locomotives and above all he knew every railroad station in Portugal, even the smallest hole, he knew whether it had a signal box or not, for that was one of his obsessions: that you could determine the direction of the train by twisting a lever. This simple mechanical operation fascinated him enormously, and ultimately it was knowledge of these things, his crazy railroad patriotism that saved the lives of our people. The comrades who weren't happy that I accepted him, because they thought his exalted delicacy could be dangerous for us, changed their mind.

"Mendes must have been eternally grateful to him. In prison, I wasn't allowed any visits, not even Mariana, and certainly not comrades who were suspected of belonging to the resistance. With one exception: Amadeu. He could come twice a month and he could pick the day and even the hour. It violated all the rules.

"And he came. He always came and stayed longer than agreed, the guards were afraid of his furious look when they mentioned the time. He brought me medicines, some against pain and some for sleep. They let him through with that and took them away from me afterward, I never told him that, he would have tried to tear down the walls. Tears flowed over his cheeks when he saw what they had done to me. Tears that were naturally also tears of sympathy, but even more tears of impotent rage. It wouldn't have taken much for him to become violent toward the guards, his damp face was red with rage."

Gregorius looked at Eça and imagined his gray, piercing eyes watching the white-hot iron approaching that threatened to choke off all seeing in a hissing glow. He felt the unbelievable strength of this man who could be defeated only by snuffing him out physically, and even from his absence, his lack in the room, a resistance would still arise that wouldn't let his enemies sleep.

"Amadeu brought me the Bible, the New Testament. Portuguese and Greek. That and the Greek grammar he threw in were the only books they let through in the two years.

"'You don't believe a word of it,' I said to him when they came to take me back to the cell.

"He smiled. 'It's a beautiful text,' he said. 'An amazingly beautiful language. And pay attention to the metaphors.'

"I was amazed. I had never really read the Bible, knew only quotations, like everybody does. I was amazed at the strange blend of the relevant and the bizarre. Sometimes we talked about it. *A religion whose center is a scene of execution, I find disgusting,* he once said. *Just imagine if there had been a gallows, a guillotine or a garrote. Just imagine how our religious symbolism would look then.* I had never seen it like that. I was almost a little frightened, also because the sentence had a special weight in those walls.

"That's how he was, the godless priest: He thought things through to the end. He *always* thought them through to the end, no matter how black the consequences were. Sometimes it had something brutal, this way, something self-lacerating. Maybe that was why, except for me and Jorge, he had no friends, you had to be able to put up with some things. He was unhappy that Mélodie had parted ways with him, he loved his little sister. I saw her only once, she looked light and cheerful, a girl who didn't seem to touch the ground, I could imagine that she couldn't deal with her brother's melancholy side, he could be like a boiling volcano before the outburst."

João Eça shut his eyes. Exhaustion was written on his face. It had been a trip in time and he may not have talked so much in years. Gregorius would like to have asked more and more: about the little sister with the wonderful name, about Jorge and Fátima, and also whether he had started learning Greek then. He had listened breathlessly, forgetting his burning throat. Now it burned again and his tongue was thick. In the middle of his story, Eça had offered him a cigarette. He had the feeling he couldn't refuse it, it would have been as if he had ripped the invisible thread spun between them, he couldn't drink the tea from his cup and refuse his tobacco, that didn't work, who knows why, it simply didn't, and so he put the first cigarette of his life between his lips, watched the trembling flame in Eça's hand anxiously and then puffed timorously and sparingly not to cough. Only now did he feel how much the hot smoke had been poison to the burning in his mouth. He cursed his irrationality and at the same time he felt with amazement that he wouldn't want to miss the smoky burning.

A shrill signal startled Gregorius.

"Dinner," said Eça.

Gregorius looked at his watch: five-thirty. Eça saw his amazement and grinned scornfully.

"Much too early. Like in the slammer. It's not about the time of the inmates, it's about the time of the staff."

Might he visit him again, asked Gregorius. Eça looked over at the chess table. Then he nodded mutely. It was as if an armor of wordlessness had closed in around him. When he noticed that Gregorius wanted to give him his hand, he vigorously buried both hands in the sweater pocket and looked down.

Gregorius on the crossing back to Lisbon noticed little. He went through the Rua Augusta, through the chessboard of the Baixa, to Rossio. The longest day of his life seemed to be coming to an end. Later, in bed in the hotel room, he remembered how he had leaned his forehead against the fog-damp display window of the religious bookstore that morning and waited for the urgent hot wish to go to the airport to subside. Then he had met Adriana, drunk Mariana Eça's red-gold tea, and with her uncle had smoked his first cigarette with a burned mouth. Had all that really happened in one single day? He opened the picture of Amadeu de Prado. Everything new he had learned about him today changed his features. He began to live, the godless priest.

15

"*Voilà. Ça va aller?* It's not exactly comfortable, but . . . ," said Agostinha, the intern at DIÁRIO DE NOTÍCIAS, Portugal's traditional newspaper, somewhat embarrassed.

Yes, said Gregorius, that would do, and sat down in the gloomy alcove with the microfilm reader. Agostinha, who had been introduced to him by an impatient editor as a student of history and French, didn't want to go yet, he had just gotten the impression that, upstairs, where the phone was constantly ringing and the computer screens were flickering, she was tolerated more than needed.

"What are you looking for?" she asked now. "I mean, it's none of my business . . ."

"For the death of a judge," said Gregorius. "For the suicide of a famous judge in 1954, on June 9. He may have killed himself because he had Bechterev's disease and could no longer bear the back pains, but maybe also from the feeling that he made himself guilty because, during the dictatorship, he kept on administering the law and did not refuse to comply with the unjust regime. He was sixty-four when he did it. So, he didn't have long to go before retirement. Something must have happened that made it impossible for him to wait. Something with the back and the pains or something at court. That's what I'd like to find out."

"And . . . and why do you want to find this out? *Pardon . . .*"

Gregorius took out Prado's book and let her read:

PORQUÉ, PAI? WHY, FATHER? *"Don't take yourself so seriously," you used to say when somebody complained. You sat in your chair, where nobody could sit, the cane between your thin legs, the gouty deformed hands on the silver knob, the head—as always—stretched down and forward. (My God, if only I could see you once standing tall, head up, befitting your pride!* Only one single time! *But the thousandfold view of the twisted back, it extinguished every other memory, and not only that, it also paralyzed the imagination.) The many pains you had to endure in your life lent authority to your repeated admonition. No one dared contradict. Not only externally; internally, too, contradiction was forbidden. We children did parody your words, far away from you there was scorn and laughter, and even Mamã, when she scolded us about it, sometimes gave herself away with the trace of a smile we greedily pounced on. But the liberation was only make-believe, like the helpless blasphemy of the pious.*

Your words held. They held until that morning when I went off to school apprehensively, with wind-whipped rain in my face. Why wasn't my apprehension about the gloomy schoolrooms and the joyless cramming to be taken seriously? Why shouldn't I take it seriously that Maria João treated me like air, when I could think of hardly anything else? Why were your pains and the judiciousness they had bestowed on you the measure of all things? "Considered from the standpoint of eternity," you sometimes added, "that does lose significance." Full of rage and jealousy of Maria João's new friend, I left school, trudged home and sat down across from you after dinner. "I want to go to another school," I said in a voice that sounded more solid than it felt internally. "This one is unbearable." "You take yourself too seriously," you said and rubbed the silver knob of the cane.

"What, if not myself, should I take seriously?" I asked. "And the standpoint of eternity—there is none."

The room filled with a silence that threatened to explode. Such a thing had never happened. It was unheard of and coming from your favorite child made it even worse. Everyone expected an outburst with your voice cracking, as usual. Nothing happened. You put both hands on the knob of the cane. An expression appeared on Mamã's face that I had never seen. It made it clear—I later thought—why she had married you. You got up without a word, only a slight groan of pain was to be heard. You didn't appear at supper. Ever since this family had existed, that had never happened once. When I sat down to dinner the next day, you looked at me calmly and a little sadly. "What other school are you thinking of?" you asked. During recess, Maria João had asked me if I wanted an orange. "It's over," I said.

How can you tell whether to take a feeling seriously or treat it as a carefree mood? Why, Papá, didn't you talk to me before you did it? So that I would at least know why *you did it?*

"I understand," said Agostinha, and then she searched among the microfiches for a record of the death of Judge Prado.

"Nineteen fifty-four, that was the strictest censorship," said Agostinha, "I know about that, I wrote my senior essay on press censorship. What the DIÁRO prints doesn't have to be true. Especially if it was a political suicide."

The first thing they found was the obituary that appeared on June 11. Agostinha found it extremely terse for the Portuguese conditions of that time, so terse that it was tantamount to a mute cry. *Faleceue,* Gregorius knew the word from the cemetery. *Amor, recordação,* terse ritual formulas. Underneath, the names of the closest relatives: Maria Piedade Reis de Prado; Amadeu; Adriana; Rita. The address. The name of the church where the mass would be held. That was all. Rita, thought Gregorius—was that the Mélodie João Eça had spoken of?

Now they looked for an article. In the first week after June 9, there was nothing. "No, no, go on," said Agostinha when Gregorius wanted to give up. The article came on June 20, far back in the local section:

Yesterday, the minister of justice announced that Alexandre Horácio de Almeida Prado, who served as an outstanding judge on the Supreme Court for many years, died last week as the result of a long illness.

Next to it was a picture of the judge, a surprisingly big one, the size didn't suit the terse article. A severe face with a pince-nez and an eyeglass chain, a goatee and a mustache, a high forehead, as high as his son's, graying but still a full head of hair, white stand-up collar with folded corners, black tiepin, a very white hand supporting his chin, everything else was lost in the dark background. A cleverly taken photo, no trace of the torment of the crooked back, or of the gout in the hands, head and hand emerging silent and ghostly from the darkness, white and imperious, objection or contradiction was impossible, an image that cast a spell over a flat, a whole house, that could wallop with a spell and poison with its choking authority. A judge. A judge who couldn't have been anything but a judge. A man of iron rigidity and stony consistency, even toward himself. A man who would judge himself if he were lacking. A father whose smile usually failed. A man who had had something in common with António de Oliveira Salazar: not his cruelty, not his fanaticism, not his ambition and his desire for power, but the rigidity, even mercilessness toward himself. Was that why he had served him so long, the man in black with the strained face under the derby hat? And ultimately could he not forgive himself for promoting the cruelty, a cruelty that could be seen in the shaking hands of João Eça, hands that had once played Schubert?

Died as the result of a long illness. Gregorius felt himself growing hot with rage.

"That's nothing," said Agostinha, "that's nothing in comparison with the distortion I've usually seen. With silent lying."

On the way up, Gregorius asked her about the street noted in the obituary. He saw that she'd like to go along and was glad that she was apparently needed now in the editorial office.

"That you make the history of this family so much . . . so much your own . . . is . . . ," she said after they had shaken hands.

"Strange, you think? Yes it is strange. Very strange. For me, too."

16

It wasn't a palace, but a house for wealthy people who could spread out as much as they liked, one room more or less didn't matter, there would be two or three bathrooms. Here the hunched judge had lived, he had walked through this house on a cane with a silver knob, struggling grimly against the eternal pains, accompanied by the conviction that you shouldn't take yourself so seriously. Did he have his study in the square tower, whose arched windows were separated from one another with small pillars? There were so many balconies on the angular façade that you didn't think you could count them, each with its finely carved wrought-iron bars. Each of the five family members, Gregorius imagined, had one or two for himself, and he thought of the narrow, badly soundproofed rooms where they had lived, the museum guard and the cleaning woman with their nearsighted son, who sat in his room at a simple wooden table and defended himself with complicated Greek verb forms against the drone of the neighbors' radio. The tiny balcony, too narrow for a parasol, had been white hot in the summer and he had hardly ever entered it, for vapors of kitchen odors always wafted over it. The judge's house, on the other hand, was like a paradise of vastness, shadow and silence. Everywhere, high, spreading conifers with knotty trunks and interwoven branches that came together in small, shadowy roofs that sometimes looked like pagodas.

Cedars. Gregorius started. *Cedars. Cedros vermelhos.* Were they really cedars? *The* cedars soaked in red for Adriana? The trees whose imaginary color took on such meaning that they stood before her eyes when she sought a name for the invented publisher? Gregorius stopped passersby and asked if they were cedars. Shrugs and raised eyebrows, amazement at the question of a bizarre foreigner. Yes, said a young woman at last, they were cedars, especially big and beautiful ones. Now he imagined himself in the house, and looked out into the lush dark green. What could have happened? What could have changed the green into red? Blood?

Behind the tower window appeared a female figure in bright clothes, her hair up, light, almost hovering, she walked here and there, busy without haste, now she took a burning cigarette from somewhere, smoke rose to the high ceiling, she evaded a sunbeam that fell into the room through the cedars and apparently blinded her, then she suddenly vanished. *A girl who didn't seem to touch the ground,* João Eça had called Mélodie, whose real name must have been Rita. *His little sister.* Could there have been such a big difference in age that today she was a woman who could still move as nimbly and smoothly as the woman in the tower?

Gregorius went on and entered a coffee shop on the next street. Along with the coffee, he got a pack of cigarettes, the same brand he had smoked at Eça's yesterday. He puffed and pictured the students in Kirchenfeld standing in front of the bakery a few streets away, smoking and drinking coffee out of paper cups. When had Kägi introduced the ban on smoking in the teachers' lounge? Now he tried to inhale, a scorching cough took his breath away, he put the new glasses on the counter, coughed and rubbed the tears out of his eyes. The woman behind the counter, a chain-smoking matron, grinned. *"É melhor não começar,"* better not start, she said, and Gregorius was proud that he understood, even if the understanding came with hesitation. He didn't know what to do with the cigarette and finally put it out in the water glass next to the cup. The woman cleared away the glass with a lenient shake of her head, he was a bloody beginner, what could you do.

Slowly he went to the entrance of the cedar house, prepared to ring the bell of a door, once again uncertain. The door opened and the woman from just now came out with an impatient German shepherd on a leash. Now she wore blue jeans and running shoes, only the light blouse seemed the same. She walked the few steps to the door on tiptoe, pulled by the dog. *A girl who didn't seem to touch the ground.* Despite all the gray in the ash blond hair, she still looked like a girl even now.

"Bom dia," she said, raising her eyebrows inquiringly and looked at him with clear eyes.

"I . . . ," Gregorius began uncertainly in French and felt the unpleasant aftertaste of the cigarette, "a long time ago, a judge lived here, a famous judge, and I'd like . . ."

"That was my father," said the woman and blew a loose strand of hair off her face. She had a light voice that suited the watery gray of her eyes and the French words that came without an accent. *Rita* was good as a name, but *Mélodie* was simply perfect. "Why are you interested in him?" she asked.

"Because he was the father of this man," and now Gregorius showed her Prado's book.

The dog tugged at the leash.

"Pan, sit" said Mélodie. "Pan."

The dog sat down. She shoved the loop of the leash in the crook of her arm and opened the book. *"Cedros ver . . . ,"* she read, and from one syllable to the next, the voice grew softer, finally died out completely. She leafed through it and looked at the brother's portrait. Her light face, covered with tiny freckles, had become darker and swallowing seemed cumbersome for her. Intently, like a statue beyond space and time, she looked at the picture, and once she ran the tip of her tongue over the dry lips. Now she leafed some more, read two sentences, went back to the picture, then to the title page.

"Nineteen seventy-five," she said. "He was already two years dead. I didn't know anything about the book. Where did you get it?"

As Gregorius told, she ran her hand softly over the gray binding, the movement reminded him of the student in the Spanish bookshop in Bern. She didn't seem to be listening anymore and he broke off.

"Adriana," she said now. "Adriana. And not a single word. *É próprio dela,*" that's typical of her. At first, there was only amazement in the words, then came bitterness, and now the melodious name no longer suited her. She gazed into the distance, past the citadel, over the valley of the Baixa, to the hill of Bairro Alto. As if she wanted to strike the sister up there in the blue house with her angry look.

They stood mutely facing each other. Pan panted. Gregorius felt like an interloper, a voyeur.

"Come, we'll drink a coffee," she said, and it sounded as if she leaped light-footed over her resentment. "I want to look at the book. Pan, you're out of luck," and with these words, she dragged him into the house.

It was a house that breathed life, a house with toys on the steps, that smelled of coffee, cigarette smoke and perfume, with Portuguese newspapers and French magazines on the table, with open CD cases and a cat licking the butter on the breakfast table. Mélodie shooed the cat away and poured coffee. The blood that had just now shot into her face had subsided, only a few red spots still indicated the excitement. She reached for the glasses on the newspaper and began to read what the brother had written, here and there. Now and then, she bit her lips. Once, without taking her eyes off the book, she took off her jacket and blindly fished a cigarette out of the pack. Her breath was heavy.

"That part about Maria João and changing schools—that must have been before I was born, we were sixteen years apart. But Papá—he was like it says here, just like that. He was forty-six when I was born, I was an accident, conceived on the Amazon, on one of the few trips Mamã could tempt him to go on, I can't even imagine Papá on the Amazon. When I was fourteen, we celebrated his sixtieth birthday, it seems to me I knew him only as an old man, a stooped, strict old man."

Mélodie paused, lit another cigarette, and looked straight ahead. Gregorius hoped she would talk about the judge's death. But now her face lit up, her thoughts were moving in another direction.

"Maria João. So he knew her even as a kid. I didn't know. An orange. Apparently he loved her even then. Never stopped. The great, untouched love of his life. It wouldn't surprise me if he had never even kissed her. But nobody, no woman, measured up to her. She got married, had children. None of it mattered. When he had cares, real cares, he went to her. In a certain sense, she, only she, knew who he was. He knew how you create intimacy with shared secrets, he was a master at that art, a virtuoso. And we knew: if there was anybody who knew all his secrets, it was Maria João. Fátima suffered from it, and Adriana hated her."

Was she still alive, asked Gregorius. Recently she had lived outside in the Campo de Ourique, near the cemetery, said Mélodie, but it had been many years since she had met her there at his grave, a friendly yet cool encounter.

"She, a peasant girl, always kept her distance from us, the nobles. That Amadeu was also one of us—she acted as if she didn't know that. Or as if it was something accidental, external, that had nothing to do with him."

What was her last name? Mélodie didn't know. "She was simply Maria João to us."

She went out of the tower room to the flat part of the house, where there was a loom.

"I've done a thousand things," she laughed when she saw Gregorius's curious look. "I was always the flighty one, the unpredictable one, so Papá didn't know what to do with me."

For a moment, the light voice darkened as when a fleeting cloud pushes before the sun, then it was past, and she pointed to the photos on the wall showing her in the most varied surroundings.

"As a waitress in a bar; playing hooky, as a gas pump attendant; and here, you have to look at this: my orchestra."

It was a street orchestra with eight girls, all playing violins and all wearing Mao caps, the peak turned to the side.

"Do you recognize me? I've turned the peak to the left, all the others to the right, that means I was the leader. We made money, pretty good money. We played at weddings and parties; we were a hot item."

Abruptly she turned away, went to the window and looked out.

"Papá didn't like it, my drifting. Shortly before his death—I was on the road with the *moças de balão,* the balloon girls, as we were called—I suddenly see Papá's official car up on the curb with the chauffeur who picked him up every morning at ten to six and took him to the courthouse, he was always the first one in the courthouse. Papá sat in the back as always and now he looked at us. Tears shot into my eyes and I made one mistake after another in playing. The car door opened and Papá clambered out, laboriously, his face twisted with pain. With his cane he stopped traffic—even now he radiated the authority of a judge—came over to us, stood in back among the spectators for a while, then made his way to the open violin cases for the money and, without looking at me, he tossed in a handful of coins. The tears ran over my face and they had to finish the rest of the piece without me. Up there, the car drove on, and now Papá waved with his gouty hand, I waved back, sat down on the steps of a house and cried my eyes out, I don't know if it was more out of joy that he had come or out of sadness that he had come only now."

Gregorious let his gaze wander over the photos. She had been a girl who sat in everyone's lap and made everyone laugh and when she wept, it passed as quickly as a short downpour on a sunny day. She played hooky from school, but got through anyway because she charmed the teachers with her bewitching impudence. It was fitting that she now told how she had learned French overnight, as it were, and called herself after a French actress named Élodie, and the others turned it into Mélodie, a word invented for her, for her presence was as beautiful and fleeting as a melody, everybody fell in love with her, nobody could hold on to her.

"I loved Amadeu, or let's say: I would have liked to love him, for it was hard, the way you love a monument, and he was a monument, even when I was little, everybody looked up to him, even Papá, but most of all Adriana, who took him away from me with her jealousy. He was nice to me, the way you're nice to your kid sister. But I would have liked to be taken seriously by him, not just patted like a doll. I had to wait until I was twenty-five and was about to get married, only then did I get this letter from him, a letter from England."

She opened a desk and took out a full envelope. The yellowed stationery was written up to the margin with calligraphic letters in dark black ink. Mélodie read silently a while, then she began to translate what Amadeu had written to her from Oxford, a few months after his wife's death.

Dear Mélodie,

It was a mistake to make this trip. I thought it would help me if once again I saw things Fátima and I had seen together. But it hurts me and I'm coming back earlier than planned. I miss you and so I'm sending you what I wrote last night. Perhaps in this way, I can come closer to you with my thoughts.

OXFORD: JUST TALKING. *Why does the nocturnal silence among the cloistered buildings seem so lifeless to me, so queasy and desolate, so completely vapid and without charm? So completely different from the Rua Augusta, which flashes with life even at three or four in the morning when no human souls are out and about? How can it be, where the bright unearthly shining stone encloses buildings with sacred names, cells of scholarship, exquisite libraries, rooms of dusty velvet silence, where perfectly shaped sentences are spoken, weighed pensively, refuted, and defended? How can that be?*

"Come on," *said the red-haired Irish man to me as I stood before the poster announcing a lecture titled LYING TO LIARS,* "let's listen to this; might be fun." *I thought of Father Bartolomeu, who had defended Augustine: to repay lies with lies would be the same as repaying robbery with robbery, sacrilege with sacrilege, adultery with adultery. And that in view of what happened then in Spain and in Germany! We had quarreled as so often and he didn't lose his gentleness. He never lost it, this gentleness, not one single time, and when I sat down in the lecture hall next to the Irish man, all of a sudden I missed him terribly and felt homesick.*

It was unbelievable. The lecturer, a pointy nosed, pointy prissy spinster, sketched in a creaky voice a casuistic of lying that couldn't have been more nitpicking or farther from reality. A woman who must never have lived in the web of lies of a dictatorship where lying well can be a question of life or death. Can God create a stone He couldn't lift? If not, then He isn't almighty; if yes, then He isn't either, for now there is a stone He cannot lift. That was the kind of scholasticism that poured forth into the room from a woman made of parchment, with an artificial bird's nest of gray hair on her head.

But that wasn't what was really unbelievable. What was really incomprehensible was the discussion, as it was called. Cast into and enclosed in the gray lead frame of polite empty British phrases, the people spoke perfectly past one another. Constantly they said *they understood each other, answered each other. But it wasn't so. No one, not a single one of the discussants, showed the slightest indication of a change of mind in view of the reasons presented. And suddenly, with a fear I felt even in my body, I realized: that's how it* always *is.*

Saying something to another: how can we expect it to affect anything? The current of thoughts, images and feelings that flows through us on every side, has such force, this torrential current, that it would be a miracle if it didn't simply sweep away and consign to oblivion all words anyone else says to us, if they didn't by accident, sheer accident, suit our own words. Is it different with me? I thought. Did I really listen *to anybody else? Let him into me with his words so that my internal current would be diverted?*

"How did you like it?" asked the Irishman as we walked along Broad Street. I didn't say everything, I said only that I had found it eerie how everybody had been talking only to themselves. "Well," he said, "well." And after a while: "It's just talking, you know; just talking. People like to talk. Basically, that's it. Talking." "No meeting of minds?" I asked. "What?" he shouted and howled with laughter. "What!" And then he shot the soccer ball he had been carrying the whole time onto the sidewalk. I would like to have been the Irishman, an Irishman who dared to appear in All Souls College for the evening lecture with a bright red soccer ball. What wouldn't I have given to be the Irishman!

I think I know now why the nocturnal silence in this illustrious place is such a bad silence. The words, all of them destined to oblivion, have died out. That wouldn't matter, they die out in the Baixa too. But there, no one pretends that it's more than talk, people talk and enjoy talking, as they enjoy licking ice cream, so the tongue can take a break from words. While here, everyone always acts as if it were different. As if it were enormously important, *what they said. But they, too, have to sleep in their self-importance, and then a silence remains that smells rotten because cadavers of pomposity are lying around everywhere and stinking without words.*

"He hated them, the pompous asses, *os presunçosos,* whom he also called *os enchouriçados,* the windbags," said Mélodie and put the letter back in the envelope. "He hated them everywhere: in politics, medicine, journalism. And he was merciless in his condemnation. I liked his condemnation because it was incorruptible, relentless, even against himself. I didn't like it when it became murderous, destructive. Then I got out of his way, of my monumental brother."

Next to Mélodie's head, a photo hung on the wall that showed them dancing together, she and Amadeu. His movement wasn't really stiff, thought Gregorius; and yet you could see that he was strange to it. Later, when he thought about it, he came up with the right word: dancing was something *inappropriate* to Amadeu.

"The Irishman with the red ball in the sacred college," said Mélodie into the silence. "It moved me very much at that time, this passage in the letter. It seemed to me it expressed a longing he never spoke of otherwise: to be able to be a ball-playing boy just once. He learned to read at the age of four and from then on he read everything all over the place, in grammar school he was bored to death, and in the Liceu he skipped a grade twice. At twenty, he really knew everything and sometimes asked himself what was to come now. And yet he never knew how to play ball."

The dog barked and then children, who must have been her grandchildren, burst in. Mélodie gave Gregorius her hand. She knew he had wanted to learn much more, about *cedros vermelhos* for instance, and about the death of the judge. Her look proved that she knew it. It also proved that she wouldn't be willing to say anymore today, even if the children hadn't come.

Gregorius sat down on a bench at the Castelo and thought about the letter Amadeu had sent from Oxford to his little sister. He had to find Father Bartolomeu, the gentle teacher. Prado had had an ear for the various kinds of silence, an ear granted only to insomniacs. And he had said of the evening's lecturer that she was made of parchment. Only now was Gregorius aware that he winced at that comment and, for the first time, had recoiled internally from the godless priest with the murderous judgment. *Mundus, the Papyrus. Parchment and papyrus.*

Gregorius went down the hill toward the hotel. In a shop he bought a chess set. For the rest of the day, until late at night, he tried to win against Alekhine by not accepting the sacrifice of the two rooks, unlike Bogolyubov. He missed Doxiades and put on the old glasses.

17

They aren't texts, *Gregorius. What people say aren't* texts. *They simply talk.* It had been a long time since Doxiades had said that to him. It was often so unconnected and contradictory, what people said, he had complained to him, and they forgot so quickly what was said. The Greek found it touching. If, like him, you had been a taxi driver in Greece, and in Thessalonica to boot, then you knew—and knew it as certainly as only few things—that you couldn't tie people down to what they said. Often, they talked only to talk. And not only in the taxi. To want to take them at their word—that was something only a philologist could come up with, particularly a philologist of ancient languages, who dealt all day with immutable words, with texts that had thousands of commentaries.

If you couldn't take people at their word, what else should be done with their words? Gregorius had asked. The Greek had laughed aloud: "Take them as a chance to talk yourself! So that it keeps going on, talking." And now the Irishman in Prado's letter to his little sister had said something that sounded quite similar and he hadn't said it about fares in Greek taxis, but about professors in All Souls College in Oxford. He had said it to a man who was so disgusted by worn-out words that he wanted to be able to reset the Portuguese language.

Outside it was pouring, for two days now. It was as if a magical curtain shielded Gregorius from the outside world. He wasn't in Bern and he was in Bern; he was in Lisbon and he wasn't in Lisbon. He played chess all day long and forgot positions and moves, something that had never happened to him before. Sometimes he caught himself holding a piece in his hand and not knowing where it came from. Downstairs, at meals, the waiter had to keep asking him what he wanted, and once he ordered dessert before soup.

On the second day, he called his neighbor in Bern and asked her to empty the mailbox, the key was under the doormat. Should she send him the mail? Yes, he said, and then he called back and said no. Leafing through the notebook, he came on the phone number the Portuguese woman had written on his forehead. *Português.* He picked up the phone and dialed. When it rang, he hung up.

The Koiné, the Greek of the New Testament, bored him, it was too simple; but looking at the other, the Portuguese side in Coutinho's edition, had a certain appeal. He called various bookstores and asked for Aeschylus and Horace, or even Herodotus and Tacitus. They barely understood him and when he was finally successful, he didn't pick up the books because it was raining.

In the business directory, he looked for language schools where he could learn Portuguese. He called Mariana Eça and wanted to tell her about the visit with João, but she was in a hurry and not paying attention. Silveira was in Biarritz. Time stood still and the world stood still and that was because his will stood still as it had never before stood still.

Sometimes he stood gazing vacantly out the window, reviewing in his mind what the others—Countinho, Adriana, João Eça, Mélodie—had said about Prado. It was a bit as if the outlines of a landscape emerged out of the fog, still veiled, but recognizable, as in a Chinese pen-and-ink drawing. Only once in these days did he leaf through Prado's notes and got stuck on this passage:

AS SOMBRAS DA ALMA. THE SHADOWS OF THE SOUL. *The stories others tell about you and the stories you tell about yourself: which come closer to the truth? Is it so clear that they are your own? Is one an authority on oneself? But that really isn't the question that concerns me. The real question is: In such stories, is there really a difference between true and false? In stories about the outside, surely. But when we set out to understand someone on the inside? Is that a trip that ever comes to an end? Is the soul a place of facts? Or are the alleged facts only the deceptive shadows of our stories?*

On Thursday morning, under a clear blue sky, Gregorius went to the newspaper and asked Agostinha, the intern, to find out where there had been a Liceu in the thirties where you could learn ancient languages and where priests also taught. She searched eagerly and when she had it, she showed him the place on the city map. She found the appropriate office of the church, called and asked for Gregorius about a Father Bartolomeu, who had taught in that Liceu, it must have been about 1935. That could only have been Father Bartolomeu Lourenço de Gusmão, she was told. He was way over ninety and seldom received visits; what was it about? Amadeu Inácio de Almeida Prado? They would ask the priest and call back. The call came a few minutes later. The priest was willing to talk with someone who was interested in Prado after such a long time. He looked forward to the visit in the late afternoon.

Gregorius went to the former Liceu, where the student Prado had quarreled with Father Bartolomeu about Augustine's intransigent ban on lying without the priest ever losing his gentleness. It was in the east, beyond the city limits and was surrounded by high, old trees. The building with its pale yellow walls could almost have been taken for a former grand hotel of the nineteenth century, only the balconies were lacking and the narrow bell tower didn't fit. The building was thoroughly dilapidated. The plaster was peeling, the windowpanes were blind or smashed, shingles were lacking on the roof, the gutters were rusted and one corner was cracked off.

Gregorius sat down on the entrance steps, which had been mossy even in Prado's nostalgic visits. That must have been in the late sixties. Here he had sat and asked himself how it would have been if, thirty years before, at this fork in the road, he had taken a completely different turn. If he had resisted his father's touching but imperious wish and not gone to medical school.

Gregorius took out his notes and leafed through them . . . *the dreamlike, bombastic wish to stand once again at that point in my life and be able to take a completely different direction than the one that has made me who I am now . . . To sit once more on the warm moss and hold the cap—it's the absurd wish to go back behind myself in time and take myself—the one marked by events—along on this journey.*

Over there was the decomposing fence around the schoolyard where the boy at the bottom of the class had flung his cap in the pond with the water lilies after finals, more than sixty-seven years ago. The pond had long since dried up, only a hollow, carpeted with ivy, remained.

The building behind the trees must have been the girls' school, where Maria João had come over, the girl with brown knees and the fragrance of soap in the light dress, the girl who had become the great untouched love in Amadeu's life, the woman, who in Mélodie's estimation was the only one who knew who he had really been, a woman of such exclusive significance that Adriana had hated her, even though he may not have given her even one kiss.

Gregorius shut his eyes. He stood in Kirchenfeld, at the corner of the building where he could glance back unseen at the Gymnasium, after he had run away in the middle of class. Once more he had the feeling that had assailed him ten days before with unexpected force and had showed him how much he loved this building and all it stood for and how much he would miss it. It was the same feeling and it was different because it was no longer one and the same. It hurt him to feel that it was no longer one and the same and thus really no longer alike either. He stood up, let his eyes roam over the peeling, fading yellow of the façade, and now all of a sudden it didn't hurt anymore, the pain gave way to a hovering feeling of curiosity and he pushed open the door, which was now ajar and whose rusty hinges screeched as in a horror movie.

An odor of damp and mold struck him. After a few steps, he almost slipped, for the uneven, worn-out stone floor was covered with a film of damp dust and rotten moss. Slowly, his hand on the banister, he went up the worn stairs. The panels of the swinging door that opened to the upper floor were stuck together with so many spiderwebs that there was a dull sound of ripping when he pushed them open. He started, as frightened bats fluttered through the hall. Then there was a silence he had never before experienced: in it, you could hear the years.

The door to the Rector's office was easy to recognize, it was trimmed with fine wood carvings. This door was also stuck and gave way only after several shoves. He entered a room where there seemed to be only one thing: an enormous black desk on curved and carved legs. Everything else—the empty dusty bookshelves, the bare tea table on the naked rotting floorboards, the Spartan chair—had no reality beside that. Gregorius wiped off the seat of the chair and sat down behind the desk. The Rector at that time was named Senhor Cortês, the man with the measured pace and the strict expression.

Gregorius had stirred up dust; the fine particles danced in the cone of sunlight. The silencing time made him feel like an interloper and for a long moment he forgot to breathe. Then curiosity triumphed and he pulled open the drawers of the desk, one after another. A piece of rope, a moldy squiggle of wood from a sharpened pencil, a crinkled stamp from 1969, cellar smells. And then, in the bottom drawer, a Hebrew Bible, thick and heavy, bound in gray linen, faded, worn, with blisters of dampness on the cover, BIBLIA HEBRAICA in gold letters that had taken on black shadows.

Gregorius hesitated. The Liceu, as Agostinha had found out, had not been a religious school. The Marquês de Pombal had driven the Jesuits out of Portugal in the mid-eighteenth century, and something similar had happened again in the early twentieth century. In the late 1940s, orders like the Maristas had founded a few Colégios, but that had been after Prado finished school. Until then, there had only been public Liceus, which occasionally employed priests as teachers for ancient languages. So why this Bible? And why in the Rector's desk? A simple mistake, a meaningless accident? An invisible silent protest against those who had closed the schools? A subversive forgetting, directed against the dictatorship and unnoticed by its stooges?

Gregorius read. Carefully he turned the crinkly pages of thick paper that felt dank and moldy. The cone of sunlight shifted. He buttoned up the coat, pulled up the collar and shoved his hands in the sleeves. After a while, he stuck one of the cigarettes he had bought on Monday between his lips. Now and then he had to cough. Outside, before the half-open door, something swished by that must have been a rat.

He read in the Book of Job and he read with pounding heart. Eliphaz of Teman, Bildad of Shuah and Zofar of Na'ama. *Isfahan.* What would the name of the family have been where he would have taught? In the Francke bookshop in those days, there had been a picture book of Isfahan, of the mosques, the squares, the mountains all around veiled by sandstorms. He couldn't buy it and had therefore gone to Francke every day to leaf through it. After his dream of white-hot sand that would blind him had forced him to withdraw his application, he hadn't gone back to Francke for months. When he finally did go back, the picture book was no longer there.

The Hebrew letters had blurred before Gregorius's eyes. He rubbed his wet face, cleaned the glasses and read on. Something of Isfahan, the city of blinding, had remained in his life: he had read the Bible from the start as a poetic book, as poetry, linguistic music played faintly from the dark blue and gold of the mosques. *I have the feeling that you don't take the text seriously,* Ruth Gautschi had said and David Lehmann had nodded. Had that really been only last month?

Can there be anything more serious than poetic seriousness? he had asked the two of them. Ruth had looked down. She liked him. Not like Florence back then, in the first row; she would never have wanted to take off his glasses. But she liked him and now she was torn between this affection and the disappointment, perhaps even the horror, that he desecrated God's word by reading it as a long poem and hearing it as a series of oriental sonatas.

The sun had disappeared from Senhor Cortês's room and Gregorius was freezing. The desolation of the room had put everything in the past for hours, meanwhile he had sat in complete worldlessness, where only the Hebrew letters had projected as runes of a despondent dream. Now he stood up and walked stiffly out to the corridor and up the stairs to the classrooms.

The rooms were full of dust and silence. If they were distinct from each other, it was in the signs of dilapidation. In one there was an enormous water spot on the ceiling, in another, the washbasin hung crookedly because a rusted screw had broken, in a third a shattered glass lampshade lay on the floor, the bare bulb hung on a wire from the ceiling. Gregorius worked the light switch: nothing, neither here nor in the other rooms. Somewhere, a flat soccer ball lay in a corner, the pointy remains of the smashed windowpanes flashed in the afternoon sun. *And yet he never knew how to play ball,* Mélodie had said about her brother who had skipped two grades in this building because at the age of four he had already begun reading through the library.

Gregorius sat down in the place where he had sat as a student in the annex of the Bern Gymnasium. From here you could look over at the girls' school, but half the building was covered by the trunk of a gigantic pine tree. Amadeu de Prado would have chosen another seat where he could look over the whole bank of windows. So he could see Maria João at her desk no matter where she was sitting. Gregorius sat down in the seat with the best view and strained to see. Yes, he could have seen her in her bright dress that smelled of soap. They had exchanged looks and when she wrote an exam, he had wished he could guide her hand. Had he used an opera glass? In the aristocratic house of a Supreme Court judge, there must have been one. Alexandre Horácio wouldn't have used it if he ever sat in a box of the opera. But perhaps his wife, Maria Piedade Reis de Prado? In the six years she had lived after his death? Had his death been a liberation for her? Or had it made time stand still and made the feelings into formations of congealed emotional lava, as with Adriana?

The rooms were in long corridors like a barracks. Gregorius inspected them one after another. Once he tripped over a dead rat, then stood still, trembling, and wiped his hands, which had nothing to do with it, on his coat. Back on the ground floor, he opened a high, bare door. Here the students had eaten, there was a hatch and behind it the tiled room of the former kitchen, where only rusty pipes still remained, sticking out of the wall. The long dining table had been left. Was there an auditorium?

He found it on the other side of the building. Tightly screwed benches, a colored window missing two splinters, in front a raised lectern with a small lamp. A separate bench, probably for the school administration. The silence of a church, or no, simply the silence that mattered, a silence that wouldn't be ended with arbitrary words. A silence that made sculptures of words, monuments of praise, warning or scathing judgment.

Gregorius went back to the Rector's office. Undecided, he held the Hebrew Bible in his hand. He already had it under his arm and was on his way to the exit when he turned around. He lined the damp drawer where it had lain with his sweater and put the book inside. Then he made his way to Father Bartolomeu Lourenço de Gusmão who lived at the other end of the city, in Belém, in a church home.

18

"Augustine and the lies—that was only one of a thousand things we fought about," said Father Bartolomeu. "We fought a lot without ever getting into a fight. For, you see, he was a hothead, a rebel, and a boy with a quicksilver intelligence and a gifted speaker, who swept through the Liceu like a whirlwind for six years, and became a legend."

The priest was holding Prado's book and now ran the back of his hand over the portrait. It could have been a smoothing and it could have been a caress. Gregorius pictured Adriana, stroking Amadeus's desk with the back of her hand.

"He's older here," said the priest. "But it's him. That's how he was, exactly."

He put the book on the blanket around his legs.

"Back then, as his teacher, I was in my mid-twenties, it was an unbelievable challenge for me to have to stand up to him. He split the faculty into those who damned him to hell and those who loved him. Yes, that's the right word: some of us were in love with him—with his boldness, his overflowing generosity and tough determination, his brazen contempt for the world, his fearlessness, and his fanatical enthusiasm. He was full of audacity, an adventurer you could easily imagine on one of our historical ships, singing, preaching, and firmly resolved to protect the inhabitants of the distant continents against every degrading infringement of the occupation, with the sword if need be. He was willing to challenge everyone, even the devil, even God. No, it wasn't megalomania, as his opponents said, it was only flourishing life and a volcanic, raging outburst of awakening forces, a shower of sparks of flashing inspirations. No doubt he was full of arrogance, this boy. But it was so boisterous, so enormously great, this arrogance, that you forgot all resistance and viewed him in amazement like a natural wonder with its own laws. Those who loved him saw him as a diamond in the rough, an unpolished gem. Those who rejected him were offended by his lack of respect, which could wound, and by the mute but unmistakable self-righteousness of those who are quicker, clearer, and brighter than others and know it. They saw him as an aristocratic snotnose, favored by fate, showered not only with money, but also with talent, beauty and charm, as well as the irresistible melancholy that made the women love him. It was unjust that one was so much better off than the others, it was unfair and made him a magnet for envy and resentment. Yet even those who felt that were secretly full of admiration, for you couldn't shut your eyes to it: he was a boy who could touch heaven."

Memory had carried the priest far out of the room they were in, a room that was certainly spacious and full of books, no comparison with João Eça's miserable room up in Cacilhas, but nevertheless a room in a nursing home, as evidenced by the medical instruments and the bell over the bed. Gregorius had liked him from the start, the lanky, gaunt man with the snow-white hair and deep-set clever eyes. If he had taught Prado, he had to be well over ninety, but there was nothing senile about him, no sign that he had lost any of the alertness that countered Amadeu's impetuous challenges seventy years before. He had slim hands with long, finely shaped fingers, as if they were created to turn the pages of precious old books. With these fingers, he now leafed through Prado's book. But he didn't read; moving the paper was like a ritual to bring back the distant past.

"All the things he had read when he crossed the threshold of the Liceu at the age of ten in his small, tailor-made frock coat! Many of us caught ourselves secretly calculating whether we could keep up with him. And then, after class, he sat in the library with his phenomenal memory and his dark eyes soaking up all the thick books, line after line, page after page, with their incredibly concentrated, rapt look, whose steadfastness couldn't have been shaken by even the loudest bang. 'When Amadeu finishes reading a book,' said another teacher, 'it has no more letters. He devours not only the meaning, but also the printers' ink.'

"That's how it was: the texts seemed to disappear altogether in him and what stood on the shelf afterward were only empty husks. The landscape of his mind behind the impudent high forehead expanded with breathtaking speed; from one week to the next, new formations took shape in it, surprising formations of ideas, associations and fantastic linguistic inspirations that always amazed us. Sometimes he hid in the library and went on reading all night with a flashlight. The first time, his mother was in sheer panic when he didn't come home. But more and more she got used to the fact that her boy tended to violate all the rules and she took a certain pride in it.

"Many a teacher was afraid when Amadeu's concentrated look fell on him. Not that it was a rejecting, provoking or belligerent look. But it gave the explainer exactly one chance to get it right. If you made a mistake or showed uncertainty, his look wasn't lurking or contemptuous, you couldn't even read disappointment in it, no, he simply averted his eyes, didn't want to make you feel it, was polite and friendly as he left. But it was precisely this tangible desire not to wound that was destructive. I myself experienced it and others confirmed it: even when they were preparing, they pictured this testing look. For some it was the look of the examiner taking them back to the schoolroom; others managed to encounter it in the spirit of an athlete facing a strong opponent. I didn't know anybody who hadn't experienced it: that Amadeu Inácio de Almeida Prado, the precocious, alert son of the famous judge, was present in the study when you were preparing something difficult, something that could trip you up, even as a teacher.

"Nevertheless: he wasn't only demanding. He wasn't a monolithic whole. There were breaks in him, cracks and leaps, and sometimes you felt you didn't know your way around him at all. When he noticed what he had caused in his excessive, but also arrogant way, he was flabbergasted, dumbfounded, and tried everything to make up for it. And there was also the other Amadeu, the good, helpful comrade. He could sit with others all night to prepare them for an exam, revealing a modesty and an angelic patience that shamed everybody who had maligned him.

"The attacks of melancholy also belonged to another Amadeu. When they came upon him, it was almost as if a completely different soul had temporarily settled in him. He became extremely fearful, the slightest noise made him flinch, like a whip lash. In such moments, he looked like the embodied difficulty of being alive. And woe to anyone who tried a consoling or encouraging comment: Then he leaped on you with a furious hiss.

"He could do so much, this richly blessed boy. There was only one thing he couldn't do: celebrate, frolic, let go. His immense alertness and his passionate need for supervision and control got in his way. No alcohol. And no cigarettes, that came only later. But enormous amounts of tea, he loved the red-gold glow of a heavy Assam and brought a silver pot from home for it, which he ultimately gave to the cook."

There must have been this girl, Maria João, Gregorius interjected.

"Yes. And Amadeu loved her. He loved her in this inimitably chaste way that everybody smiled at, without being able to hide their envy, it was envy of a feeling that occurs really only in fairy tales. He loved her and adored her. Yes, that was it: he *adored* her—even if that's not usually said of children. But in Amadeu, so many things were different. And she wasn't an especially pretty girl, no princess, far from it. Nor was she a good student, as far as I know. Nobody really understood it, at least not the other girls in the school up there, who would have given anything to attract the eyes of the noble prince. Maybe it was simply that she wasn't dazzled by him, not overwhelmed like all the others. Maybe that was what he needed: somebody to face him with natural equality, with words, looks and movements that liberated him from himself with their naturalness and inconspicuousness.

"When Maria João came over and sat down next to him on the steps: he seemed to become completely calm all of a sudden, freed of the burden of his alertness and quickness, the weight of his incessant presence of mind, the torment of having constantly to outdo and surpass himself. Sitting next to her, he could listen to the ringing of the bells that called to class, and looking at him, you had the impression he'd like never to stand up again. Then Maria put her hand on his shoulder and pulled him back from the paradise of a precious effortlessness. It was always she who touched him; never did I see his hand rest on her. When she was about to go back to her school, she'd tie her shiny black hair into a ponytail with a rubber band. Every time, he looked at her as she did it as if he were under a spell, even the hundredth time, he must have loved it very much, this movement. One day, it was no longer a rubber band, but a silver barrette, and you could see on his face that it was a gift from him."

Like Mélodie, the priest couldn't remember the girl's last name either.

"Now that you ask me, it seems to me that we didn't *want* to know the name; as if it would have been *disturbing* to know it," he said. "A little bit the way you don't ask about the family names of saints. Or Diana or Electra."

A nurse in a nun's habit came in.

"Not now," said the priest when she reached for the blood pressure cuff.

He said it with gentle authority, and suddenly Gregorius understood why this man had been a stroke of luck for young Prado: he possessed precisely the kind of authority he had needed to assure himself of his limits, and maybe also to liberate himself from the strict, austere authority of the judging father.

"But we would like a cup of tea," said the priest and wiped away the nurse's nascent anger with his smile. "An Assam, and make it strong so the red gold glows properly."

The priest shut his eyes and was silent. He didn't want to let go of the distant time when Amadeu de Prado gave Maria João a silver barrette. Actually, thought Gregorius, he wanted to stay with his favorite student, with whom he had debated Augustine and a thousand other things. With the boy who could have touched the sky. The boy whose shoulder he would like to have put his hand on, like Maria João.

"Maria and Jorge," the priest went on with his eyes shut, "they were like his patron saints. Jorge O'Kelly. In him, the future pharmacist, Amadeu found a friend, and it wouldn't surprise me if he had been the only real friend, aside from Maria. In many respects, he was his complete opposite and sometimes I thought: he needs him to be *whole*. With his peasant skull, the tousled, eternally uncombed hair and his heavy, awkward manner, he could seem limited, and on parents' days, I saw noble parents of other students turn around amazed when he passed them in his poor clothing. He was so inelegant in his crumpled shirt, shapeless jacket and the same black tie he always wore askew in protest against the regulation.

"Once, in the school corridor, Amadeu and Jorge came toward us, me and my colleague, who said afterward: 'If I had to explain in a dictionary the definition of elegance and its polar opposite, I would simply depict these two boys. Any further commentary would be superfluous.'

"Jorge was one with whom Amadeu could rest and take a break from his fast pace. When he was with him, after a while, he also became slow; Jorge's ponderousness overcame him. As in chess. At first it made him crazy when Jorge brooded eternally over a move, and in his worldview, his quicksilver metaphysics, it wasn't right that somebody who needed so long for his thoughts could ultimately win. But then he began to inhale his calm, the calm of someone who always seemed to know who he was and where he belonged. It sounds crazy but I think it got to the point that Amadeu *needed* the regular defeats against Jorge. He was unhappy the few times he won, it must have been for him as if the rock face he could usually hold on to had given way.

"Jorge knew exactly when his Irish ancestors had come to Portugal, he was proud of the Irish blood and knew English well, even if his mouth wasn't really made for the English words. And in fact, you wouldn't have been surprised to meet him in an Irish farmyard or a country pub, and if you imagined that, he suddenly looked like the young Samuel Beckett.

"Even then, he was a die-hard atheist, I don't know how we knew that, but we did. Responding to that, he quoted unmoved the family device: *Turris fortis mihi Deus*. He read the Russian, Andalusian, and Catalan anarchists and played with the idea of crossing the border and fighting against Franco. That he later went into the resistance: anything else would have surprised me. All his life he was a romantic without illusions, if there is such a thing, and there must be. And this romantic had two dreams: to become a pharmacist and play a Steinway. The first dream he realized; even today he stands in a white labcoat behind the counter of the shop on the

Rua dos Sapateiros. Everybody laughed at the second dream, he most of all. For his coarse hands with the broad fingertips and the grooved nails, they were better suited to the school contrabass, which he tried for a while, until, in an attack of despair at his lack of talent, he sawed so violently on the strings that the bow broke."

The priest drank his tea and Gregorius noticed, disappointed, that the drinking became a slurping. Suddenly, he was an old man whose lips no longer obeyed him completely. His mood had also changed; grief and wistfulness were in the voice as he now spoke of the emptiness Prado had left behind when he finished school.

"Naturally, we all knew that, in the fall, when the heat subsided and a golden shadow lay on the light, we'd no longer meet him in the halls. But nobody talked about it. In parting, he shook hands with all of us, forgot no one, thanked with warm, refined words, I still know, that for a moment I thought: like a president."

The priest hesitated and then he said: "They shouldn't have been so well-formed, these words. They should have had something more halting, clumsy, groping. Something more like unhewn stone. A little less like polished marble."

And he should have said a good-bye to him, Father Bartolomeu, that was different from the others, thought Gregorius. With different, more personal words, perhaps with an embrace. He had hurt the priest by treating him like one of the others. It still rankled now, seventy years later.

"In the first days after the new school year began, I walked numbly through the halls. Numbed by his absence. I had to keep saying to myself: You can no longer expect to see the helmet of his hair show up, you must no longer hope that his proud figure will come round the corner and you can watch him explaining something to somebody and moving his hands in his inimitably eloquent way. And I'm sure it was the same with others, even though we didn't talk about it. Only one single time I heard somebody say: 'Everything's so different ever since.' There was no question he was talking about the absence of Amadeu. That his soft baritone voice was no longer heard in the halls. It wasn't only that you didn't see him anymore, meet him anymore. *You saw his absence* and encountered it as something tangible. His not being there was like the sharply outlined emptiness of a photo with a figure cut out precisely with scissors and now the missing figure is more important, more dominant than all the others. That's exactly how we missed Amadeu: through his precise absence.

"It was years before I met him again. He was studying up in Coimbra and now and then I heard something about him through a friend who assisted one of the professors of medicine in the lectures and dissecting courses. Even there, Amadeu had quickly become a legend. Not as brilliant, though. Experienced professors, with prizes for excellence, leading authorities in their field, felt tested by him. Not because he knew more than they did, not yet. But he was insatiable in his need for explanations, and there must have been dramatic scenes in the lecture halls when he proved with his merciless Cartesian perspicacity that something propounded as an explanation really wasn't.

"Once he must have mocked a particularly vain professor by comparing his explanation with the information of a doctor ridiculed by Molière who had explained the soporific force of a potion with its *virtus dormitiva.* He could be merciless when he encountered vanity. Merciless. The knife opened in his pocket. *It's an unrecognized form of stupidity,* he would say, *you have to forget the cosmic meaninglessness of all our acts to be able to be vain and that's a glaring form of stupidity.*

"When he was in this mood, you better not have had him as an enemy. They soon discovered that in Coimbra. And they discovered something else: that he had a sixth sense for the planned reprisals of the others. Jorge also possessed such a sense, and Amadeu managed to copy it in himself and then to cultivate it independently. When he imagined that someone wanted to show him up, he sought the most remote chess move you could make for this purpose and prepared himself meticulously for it. It must have been the same for the faculty in Coimbra. In the lecture hall, when he was summoned to the board with glee and asked about arcane matters, he refused the chalk offered by the avenging professor with a malicious smile, and took his own chalk out of his pocket. "Aha," he must have said contemptuously on such occasions, and then he filled the board with anatomical sketches, physiological equations or biochemical formulas. '*Must* I know that?' he asked when he had once miscalculated. The other's grin couldn't be seen, but it could be heard. You just couldn't get to him."

For the last half hour, they had sat in the dark. Now the priest turned on the light.

"I buried him. Adriana, his sister, wanted it. He had collapsed on Rua Augusta, which he loved especially, at six in the morning, when his incurable insomnia drove him through the city. A woman who came out of the house with her dog called an ambulance. But he was already dead. The blood from a burst aneurysm in the brain had extinguished the radiant light of his consciousness forever.

"I hesitated, I didn't know what he would have thought of Adriana's request. *Burial is a matter for others, the dead have nothing to do with it,* he had once said. It had been one of his chilly sentences that made many people fear him. Was it still true?

"Adriana, who certainly could be a dragon, a dragon who protected Amadeu, was helpless as a little girl in the face of the things death demands of us. And so I decided to comply with her request. I would have to find words that could stand before his silent spirit. After decades when he had no longer looked over my shoulder when I prepared words, now he was there again. His life glow was extinguished, but it seemed to me that the white, irrevocably silent countenance demanded even more from me than the previous face that had challenged me so often in its multicolored vividness.

"My words at the grave had to stand not only before the dead man. I knew that O'Kelly would be there. In his presence, I couldn't possibly speak words dealing with God and what Jorge would call *His empty promises.* The way out was for me to talk about my experiences with Amadeu and of the inextinguishable traces he had left behind in all those who knew him, even his enemies.

"The crowd at the cemetery was unbelievable. All the people he had treated, little people he never charged. I allowed myself one single religious word: *Amen.* I pronounced it because Amadeu had loved the word and because Jorge knew that. The sacred word died away in the silence of the graves. Nobody moved. It started raining. The people wept, fell into each other's arms. Nobody turned to go. The heavens opened and the people were soaked to the skin. But they stood still. Simply stood still. I thought: they want to stop time with their leaden feet, they want to keep it from flowing away so it couldn't drive their beloved doctor away from them, as every second does with everything that happened before it. At last, after they may have stood there without moving for half an hour, there was movement that started with the oldest ones who could no longer stand on their feet. Then it took another hour for the cemetery to empty out.

"When I finally wanted to go too, something remarkable happened, something I later dreamed of sometimes, something with the unreality of a scene in a Buñuel film. Two people, a man and a young woman of restrained beauty, came toward each other from each end of the path to the grave. The man was O'Kelly, the woman I didn't know. I couldn't know it, but I felt it: the two knew each other. It seemed like an intimate knowing and as if this intimacy was linked with a catastrophe, a tragedy that also involved Amadeu. Each had to cover an equally long way to the grave and they seemed to adapt the speed of their steps precisely to one another, so they arrived at the same time. Their eyes did not meet one single time on the way, but were aimed at the ground. That they avoided looking at each other created a greater closeness between them than any crossing of looks could have. Nor did they look at each other when they stood next to each other at the grave and seemed to breathe in harmony. The dead man seemed to belong to them alone and I felt I had to go. To this day, I don't know what kind of secret bound the two people or what it had to do with Amadeu."

A bell rang, it must have been the signal for supper. A trace of anger hovered over the priest's face. He flung the blanket off his legs, went to the door and locked it. Back in his chair, he reached for the light switch and turned off the lamp. A cart dragging crockery rolled through the corridor and went off. Father Bartolomeu waited until it was silent again before he went on.

"Or perhaps I do know something, or imagine it. That is, a good year before his death, Amadeu suddenly stood at my door in the middle of the night. All his self-assurance was gone. His features were agitated and so were his breath and his movements. I made tea and he smiled fleetingly when I brought out the rock candy he had been crazy about as a student. Then the tormented expression reappeared on his face.

"Clearly I couldn't press him, couldn't even ask anything. I was silent and waited. He was struggling with himself as only he could: as if victory and defeat in this struggle would decide life and death. And perhaps it was really so. I had heard rumors that he was working for the resistance. As he gazed straight ahead, breathing with an effort, I considered what growing old had made of him: the first age spots on the slim hands, the weary skin under the sleepless eyes, the gray strands in the hair. And suddenly, I became aware with terror: he looked neglected. Not like an unwashed bum. The neglect was more inconspicuous, softer: the untended beard, little hairs growing out of his ears and nose, carelessly cut nails, a yellowish glow on the white tie, unpolished shoes. As if he hadn't been home for days. And there was an irregular twitch of the eyelids that looked like the summary of a lifelong strain.

"'One life for many lives. You can't calculate like that. Can you?' Amadeu spoke in a strained voice, and behind the words were both outrage and the fear of doing something wrong, something unforgivable.

"'You know what I think about that,' I said. 'I haven't changed my mind since then.'

"'And if it were *really* many?'

"'Do *you* have to do it?'

"'On the contrary, I have to *prevent* it.'

"'He knows too much?'

"'She. She's become a danger. She wouldn't hold out. She would talk. The others think so.'

"'Jorge too?' It was a shot in the dark and it hit.

"'I don't want to talk about that.'

"Silent minutes passed. The tea grew cold. It was tearing him up. Did he love her? Or was it simply because she was a human being?

"'What's her name? *Names are the invisible shadows with which others clothe us and we them.* Do you still know?'

"Those were his own words in one of the many remarks he had amazed us all with.

"For a brief moment, the memory freed him and he smiled.

"'Estefânia Espinhosa. A name like a poem, isn't it?'

"'How will you do it?'

"'Over the border. In the mountains. Don't ask me where.'

"He disappeared through a garden gate and that was the last time I saw him alive.

"After what happened in the cemetery, I kept thinking about this nocturnal conversation. Was the woman Estefânia Espinhosa? Did she come from Spain, where she had gotten the news of Amadeu's death? And when she walked toward O'Kelly, was she walking to the man who had wanted to sacrifice her? Did they stand not moving and not looking at the grave of the man who had sacrificed a lifelong friendship to save the woman with the poetic name?"

Father Bartolomeu turned on the light. Gregorius stood up.

"Wait," said the priest. "Now that I have told you all these things, you should also read this." And from a bookcase, he took an ancient folder, held together by faded ribbons. "You're a classical philologist, you can read this. It's a copy of Amadeu's speech at the graduation ceremony, he made it especially for me. Latin. Magnificent. Unbelievable. You saw the lectern in the auditorium, you say. There he delivered it, right there.

"We were prepared for something, but not such a thing. From the first sentence, a breathless silence prevailed. And it became more silent and more breathless, this silence. The sentences from the pen of a seventeen-year-old iconoclast, who spoke as if he had already lived a whole life, were like whiplashes. I began to ask myself what would happen when the last word died out. I was afraid. Afraid for him who knew what he was doing and yet didn't know. Afraid for this thin-skinned adventurer, whose vulnerability was every bit equal to his verbal force. But also afraid for us who might not be up to it. The teachers sat there very stiff, very erect. Some had shut their eyes and seemed to be busy raising a protective wall internally against this barrage of blasphemous accusations, a bulwark against a blasphemy that wouldn't have been considered possible in this room. Would they still talk with him? Would they resist the temptation to defend themselves with a condescension that made him back into a child?

"The last sentence, you'll see, contains a threat, touching and frightening, for you imagined a volcano behind it spitting fire, and if it didn't, it might be destroyed by its own fervor. Amadeu didn't utter it loudly or with a clenched fist, this sentence, but softly, almost gently, and to this day I don't know if it was a calculation to increase the force or if, after all the firmness with which he had spoken the bold, ruthless sentences into the silence, he suddenly lost his nerve and, with the gentleness in his voice, he wanted to ask for forgiveness in advance, certainly not deliberate, but perhaps this wish impelled him from inside, for outside he was wide awake, not yet inside.

"The last word had died out. Nobody moved. Amadeu straightened the sheets of paper, slowly, his eyes aimed at the lectern. Now there was nothing more to straighten. There was nothing there for him to do, absolutely nothing. But you can't go away from such a lectern after such a speech without the audience taking sides in some sense. It would be a defeat of the worst sort: as if you hadn't said anything at all.

"I felt like standing up and applauding. If only because of the brilliance of this daredevil speech. But then I felt: you can't applaud blasphemy, polished as it may be. No one can, least of all a priest, a man of God. And so I remained sitting. The seconds passed. It couldn't have lasted much longer, otherwise it was a catastrophe, for him as for us. Amadeu raised his head and stretched his back. His glance went to the colored window and stayed there. It wasn't intentional, no dramatic trick, I'm sure of that. It was completely instinctive and illustrated, as you will see, his speech. It showed that he *was* his speech.

"Maybe that was enough to break the ice. But then something happened that seemed to everyone in the hall like a joking proof of God's existence: a dog started barking outside. At first, it was a short, dry bark that scolded us for our petty, humorless silence; then it turned into a long drawn-out howl and wail referring to the misery of the whole subject.

"Jorge O'Kelly burst out laughing, and after a second of fear, others followed him. I think that Amadeu was taken aback a moment; humor was the last thing he had counted on. But it was Jorge who had started, so it had to be all right. The smile that appeared on his face was a little forced, but it lasted, and as other dogs now chimed into the howling and wailing, he left the lectern.

"Only now did Senhor Cortês, the Rector, wake up from his paralysis. He stood up, went to Amadeu and shook his hand. Can you see in a handshake that someone is glad to know that it will be the last? Senhor Cortês said a few words to Amadeu, which were drowned out by the dogs' wailing. Amadeu answered, and as he spoke, he recovered his self-confidence, you could see that in his movements as he shoved the scandalous manuscript into the pocket of his frock coat; that is, they weren't movements of humble hiding, but the movements of stowing something precious in a safe place. Finally, he bent his head, looked the Rector straight in the eye, and turned to the door where Jorge was waiting for him. O'Kelly put his arm around his shoulders and pushed him out.

"Later, I saw the two of them in the park. Jorge was talking and gesticulating, Amadeu was listening. The two of them reminded me of a trainer going over a fight with his protégé. Then Maria João came up. Jorge touched his friend with both hands on his shoulders and pushed him, laughing, toward the girl.

"The teachers hardly spoke of the speech. I wouldn't say that it was hushed up. Rather it was that we didn't find the words or the tone to exchange views about it. And maybe many were also glad about the unbearable heat that day. So we didn't have to say: 'Impossible!' or 'There may be some truth in it.' Instead we could say: 'What a scorcher!'"

19

How could it be, thought Gregorius, that he was riding in the hundred-year-old trolley through the Lisbon evening with the feeling that he was departing now, thirty-eight years too late, to Isfahan? Coming from Father Bartolomeu, he had got out on the way and finally picked up the dramas of Aeschylus and the poems of Horace at the bookstore. Then as he walked to the hotel, something had bothered him and his steps became slower and more hesitant. For some minutes, he had stood in the steam of a chicken coop and had braved the repulsive odor of rancid fat. It had seemed enormously important to stand still *now* and find out what was pressing up to the surface. Had he ever before tried so intensely to track down himself?

Outside he was wide awake, but not yet inside. It sounded like something quite obvious when Father Bartolomeu had said that about Prado. As if every grown-up simply knew about inside and outside alertness. *Português.* Gregorius had pictured the Portuguese woman on the Kirchenfeldbrücke leaning on the ledge with outstretched arms, her heels sliding out of her shoes. *Estefânia Espinhosa. A name like a poem,* Prado had said. *Over the border. Into the mountains. Don't ask me where.* And then, suddenly, without understanding how it happened, Gregorius knew what he had felt in himself without recognizing it: He didn't want to read Prado's speech in the hotel room, but outside in the abandoned Liceu, where he had delivered it. There, where the Hebrew Bible lay in the drawer on his sweater. There, with rats and bats.

Why had this perhaps bizarre but harmless wish appeared to him as if something important was decided in him? As if it would have far-reaching consequences if, instead of going on to the hotel, he now went back to the streetcar? Shortly before it closed, he had slipped into a hardware shop and bought the strongest flashlight they had. And now he sat again in one of these old trolleys and rattled to the underground that would take him out to the Liceu.

The school building was completely sunk into the dark of the garden and looked abandoned, as no building ever before. When he set off just now, Gregorius had had before his eyes the cone of sunlight that had strayed into Senhor Cortês's office at noon. What he now had before him was a building that lay silent like a sunken ship on the bottom of the sea, lost for people and untouchable for time.

He sat down on a rock and thought of the student who had broken into the Bern Gymnasium at night a long time ago, and from the Rector's office had made phone calls all over the world for thousands of Francs, out of revenge. Hans Gmür was his name and he had worn his name like a garrote. Gregorius had paid the bill and persuaded Kägi not to press charges. He had met with Gmür in town and tried to find out what he wanted to avenge. It didn't work. "Just revenge," the boy simply kept saying. He looked exhausted behind his apple cake and seemed devoured by a resentment as old as himself. When they parted, Gregorius had watched him for a long time. Somehow, he admired him a little, he later told Florence, or envied him.

"Just imagine: he sits in the dark at Kägi's desk and calls Sydney, Belém, Santiago, even Peking. Always the embassies where they speak German. He has nothing to say, absolutely nothing. He simply wants to hear the open line buzz and feel the sinfully expensive seconds pass. Somethig splendid, isn't it?"

"And you of all people say that? A man who would like to pay his bills even before they're written? And not owe anybody anything?"

"Exactly," he had said. "Exactly."

Florence had adjusted her ultrastylish glasses, as always when he said such things.

Now Gregorius switched on the flashlight and followed the beam of light to the entrance. In the dark, the creaking of the door sounded much louder than in the daytime, and it sounded much more like something forbidden. The sound of startled bats flooded through the building. Gregorius waited until it had subsided before he went through the swinging door to the ground floor. He swept the light like a broom over the stone floor of the halls to keep from stepping on a dead rat. It was chilly in the cooled-off walls and he went first to the Rector's office to get his sweater.

He looked at the Hebrew Bible. It had belonged to Father Bartolomeu. In 1970, when the Liceu was closed as a hotbed of red cadres, the priest and Senhor Cortês's successor had stood in the Rector's empty office, furious and impotent. "We needed to do something, something symbolic," the priest had said. And so he had put his Bible in the desk drawer. The Rector had looked at him and grinned. "Perfect. The Lord will get them," he had said.

Gregorius sat down in the auditorium on the bench for the school administration, where Senhor Cortês had followed Prado's speech with a stony expression. He took Father Bartolomeu's folder out of the bookstore bag, removed the bands and took the staples out of the sheets Amadeu had straightened on the lectern after the speech, enveloped in embarrassed, horrified silence. They were the same calligraphic letters in dark black ink he had seen on the letter

Prado had sent to Mélodie from Oxford. Gregorius aimed the beam of the flashlight at the shimmering yellowish paper and began to read.

REVERENCE AND LOATHING FOR THE WORD OF GOD

I would not like to live in a world without cathedrals. I need their beauty and grandeur. I need them against the vulgarity of the world. I want to look up at the illuminated church windows and let myself be blinded by the unearthly colors. I need their luster. I need it against the dirty colors of the uniforms. I want to let myself be wrapped in the austere coolness of the churches. I need their imperious silence. I need it against the witless bellowing of the barracks yard and the witty chatter of the yes-men. I want to hear the rustling of the organ, this deluge of ethereal tones. I need it against the shrill farce of marches. I love praying people. I need the sight of them. I need it against the malicious poison of the superficial and the thoughtless. I want to read the powerful words of the Bible. I need the unreal force of their poetry. I need it against the dilapidation of the language and the dictatorship of slogans. A world without these things would be a world I would not like to live in.

But there is also another world I don't want to live in: the world where the body and independent thought are disparaged, and the best things we can experience are denounced as sins. The world that demands love of tyrants, slave masters, and cutthroats, whether their brutal boot steps reverberate through the streets with a deafening echo or they slink with feline silence like cowardly shadows through the streets and pierce their victims in the heart from behind with flashing steel. What is most absurd is that people are exhorted from the pulpit to forgive such creatures and even to love them. Even if someone really could do it: it would mean an unparalleled dishonesty and merciless self-denial whose cost would be total deformity. This commandment, this crazy, perverse commandment to love your enemy is apt to break people, to rob them of all courage and self-confidence and to make them supple in the hands of the tyrants so they won't find the strength to stand up to them, with weapons, if necessary.

I revere the word of God for I love its poetic force. I loathe the word of God for I hate its cruelty. The love is a difficult love for it must incessantly separate the luminosity of the words and the violent verbal subjugation by a complacent God. The hatred is a difficult hatred for how can you allow yourself to hate words that are part of the melody of life in this part of the world? Words that taught us early on what reverence is? Words that were like a beacon to us when we began to feel that the visible life can't be all of life? Words without which we wouldn't be what we are?

But let us not forget: These are the same words that call on Abraham to slaughter his own son like an animal. What do we do with our rage when we read that? What should we think of such a God? A God who blames Job for arguing with Him, he who knows and understands nothing? Who, after all, was it who created him like that? And why is it less unjust if God hurls someone into misery for no reason than if a common mortal does? In fact, isn't Job's complaint perfectly justified?

The poetry of the divine word is so overwhelming that it silences everything and every protest becomes wretched yapping. That's why you can't just put *away the Bible, but must* throw *it away when you have enough of its unreasonable demands and of the slavery it inflicts on us. It is a joyless God far from life speaking out of it, a God who wants to constrict the enormous compass of a human life—the big circle that can be drawn when it is left free—to the single, shrunken point of obedience. Grief ridden and sin laden, parched with subjugation and the indignity of confession, with the cross of ashes on our forehead, we are to go to the grave in the thousandfold refuted hope of a better life at His Side. But how could it be better on the side of One who just robbed us of all joy and freedom?*

And yet they are bewitchingly beautiful, the words that come from Him and go to Him. How I loved them as an altar boy! How drunk they made me in the glow of the altar candles! How clear, how evident it seemed that these words were the measure of all things! How incomprehensible it seemed to me that other words were also important to people, where every one of them could mean only damnable dissipation and the loss of the essential! Even today I stand still when I hear a Gregorian chant and for an idle moment I am sad that the old drunkenness has been wiped out irrevocably by rebellion. A rebellion that shot up in me like a flame the first time I heard these two words: sacrificium intellectus.

How are we to be happy without curiosity, without questions, doubt and arguments? Without joy in thinking? The two words like a sword stroke cutting off our head, they mean nothing less than a demand to live our feelings and acts against our thinking, they are the summons to a complete split, the order to sacrifice what is the core of our happiness: the internal unity and coherence of our life. The slave in the galley is chained, but he can think what he wants. But what He, our God, demands of us is that we force our slavery into our depths with our own hands and do it willingly and joyfully. Can there be a greater mockery?

In His omnipresence, the Lord observes us day and night, every hour, every minute, every second, He keeps a ledger of our acts and thoughts, He never lets us alone, never spares us a moment completely to ourselves. What is man without secrets? Without thoughts and wishes that only he, he alone, knows? The torturers, of the Inquisition and of today, they know: cut off his retreat, never turn off the light, never leave him alone, deprive him of sleep and silence: he will talk. That torture steals our soul means it demolishes the solitude with ourselves that we need like air to breathe. Did the Lord our God not consider that He was stealing our soul with His unbridled curiosity and revolting voyeurism, a soul that should be immortal?

Who could in all seriousness want to be immortal? Who would like to live for all eternity? How boring and stale it must be to know that what happens today, this month, this year, doesn't matter: endless more days, months, years will come. Endless, literally. If that was how it was, would anything count? *We would no longer need to calculate time, nothing could be missed, we wouldn't have to rush. It would be the same if we did something today or tomorrow, all the same. A million omissions would become nothing before eternity, and it would make no sense to regret something for there would always be time to make up for it. Nor could we live for the day, for this happiness lives on the awareness of passing time, the idler is an adventurer in the face of death, a crusader against the dictate of haste. When there is always and everywhere time for all and everything: How should there still be room for the joy of wasting time?*

A feeling is no longer the same when it comes the second time. It dies through the awareness of its return. We become tired and weary of our feelings when they come too often and last too long. In the immortal soul, a gigantic weariness and a flagrant despair must grow in view of the certainty that it will never end, never. Feelings want to develop and we through them. They are what they are because they retreat from what they used to be and because they flow toward a future where they will diverge. If this stream flowed into infinity: thousands of feelings must emerge in us that we, used to a foreseeable time, cannot even imagine. So that we really don't know what is promised us when we hear of the eternal life. How would it be to be us in eternity, devoid of the consolation of being someday released from the need to be us? We don't know, and it is a blessing that we never will. For one thing we do know: it would be hell, this paradise of immortality.

It is death that gives the moment its beauty and its horror. Only through death is time a living time. Why does the Lord, *the omniscient God, not know that? Why does He threaten us with an endlessness that must mean unbearable desolation?*

I would not like to live in a world without cathedrals. I need the luster of their windows, their cool stillness, their imperious silence. I need the deluge of the organ and the sacred devotion of praying people. I need the holiness of words, the grandeur of great poetry. All that I need. But just as much I need the freedom and hostility against everything cruel. For the one is nothing without the other. And no one may force me to choose.

Gregorius read the text three times with increasing amazement. A Latin rhetorical ability and stylistic elegance equal to Cicero. A force of thought and an honesty of feelings reminiscent of Augustine. A seventeen-year-old. Comparable virtuosity on an instrument, he thought, would have had people talking of a child prodigy.

As for the closing sentence, Father Bartolomeu was right: it was moving, the threat. Who did it refer to? He would always choose hostility to the cruel, this boy. If necessary, he would sacrifice cathedrals to it. The godless priest would build his own cathedrals, if only those of golden words, to defy the vulgarity of the world. His hostility against cruelty would become even more bitter.

Perhaps the threat was not so empty? When he stood there, had Amadeu unknowingly anticipated what he would do thirty-five years later: refuse to comply with the plans of the resistance movement, and Jorge's plans, and save Estafânia Espinhosa?

Gregorius wished he could hear his voice and feel the molten lava on which his words flowed. He took out Prado's notes and aimed the flashlight beam on the picture. An altar boy he had been, a child whose first passion had been for the altar candles and the biblical words that had seemed sacrosanct in their bright glow. But then words from other books had come between, words that had run riot in him until he had become someone who placed all strange words on the gold scales and crafted his own.

Gregorius buttoned his coat, shoved his cold hands in the opposite sleeves and lay down on the bench. He was exhausted. Exhausted from the effort of listening and the fever of understanding. But also exhausted from the alertness inside that went along with this fever and sometimes seemed to him nothing but the fever itself. For the first time he missed the bed in his Bern flat where, reading, he would wait for the moment when he could finally fall asleep. He thought of Kirchenfeldbrücke before the Portuguese woman had entered and transformed it. He thought of the Latin books on the desk in the classroom. Ten days ago now. Who had introduced the *ablativus absolutus* in his place? Explained the structure of the Iliad? In the Hebrew class, they had recently discussed Luther's choice of words when he decided to let God be a *jealous* God. He had explained to the students the enormous distance between the German and the Hebrew text, a breathtaking distance. Who would now continue this discussion?

Gregorius was freezing. The last underground train had left long ago. There was no telephone or taxi and it would take hours to walk to the hotel. Before the door of the auditorium, the soft sweeping rustle of the bats was heard. Now and then, a rat squeaked. In between, the silence of the tomb.

He was thirsty and was glad to find a piece of candy in his coat pocket. When he shoved it in his mouth, he pictured Natalie Rubin's hand holding the bright red candy to him. For a split second, it had looked as if she wanted to put the candy in his mouth herself. Or had he only imagined that?

She stretched and laughed when he asked her how he was to find Maria João, when nobody seemed to know her last name. They had been standing for days in a chicken coop at the cemetery of Prazeres, he and Natalie, for it had been there that Mélodie had last seen Maria. It became winter and it started snowing. The train to Geneva started moving in the Bern railroad station. Why had he boarded, asked the stern conductor, and in first class to boot. Freezing, Gregorius searched all his pockets for the tickets. When he woke up and sat up with stiff limbs, it was growing light outside.

20

In the first underground train, he was the only passenger for a while and the train seemed to be just another episode in the silent, imaginary world of the Liceu where he had begun settling in. Then Portuguese people came in, working people, who had nothing to do with Amadeu de Prado. Gregorius was grateful for their sober, surly faces akin to the faces of people who got on the bus on the Länggasse early in the morning. Could he live here? Live and work, whatever that might be?

The hotel porter observed him anxiously. Was he all right? Did something happen to him? Then he handed him an envelope of thick paper with a red wax seal. It had been brought yesterday afternoon by an old woman who had waited for him until late at night.

Adriana, thought Gregorius. Of the people he had met here, only she would seal a letter. But the porter's description didn't suit her. And she wouldn't have come herself, not a woman like her. It must have been the housekeeper, the woman whose task would be to remove all the dust from Amadeu's room in the attic so that nothing indicated the passage of time. Everything was fine, Gregorius assured him once again and went upstairs.

Queria vê-lo! I would like to see you. *Adriana Soledade de Almeida Prado.* That was all that was on the expensive stationery. Written with the same black ink he knew from Amadeu, with letters that looked both awkward and snooty. As if the writer had had a hard time remembering every letter in order to put it down with rusty grandeur. Had she forgotten that he knew no Portuguese and that they had spoken French with each other?

For a moment, Gregorius was scared by the laconic words that sounded like an order summoning him to the blue house. But then he saw the pale face and black eyes with the bitter look, he saw the woman walking on the rim of the abyss through the room of the brother, whose death could not be, and now the words no longer sounded imperious, but rather like a cry for help from the hoarse throat with the mysterious black velvet ribbon.

He considered the black lion, apparently the heraldic animal of the Prados, embossed on top of the stationery, right in the middle. The lion suited the father's sternness and the dreariness of his death, it suited Adriana's black shape, and it also suited the merciless audacity in Amadeu's nature. But it had nothing to do with Mélodie, on the other hand, the light-footed, flighty girl, who had come about because of unusual carelessness on the bank of the Amazon. Or with the mother, Maria Piedade Reis? Why didn't anybody talk about her?

Gregorius showered and slept until noon. He was pleased that he had managed to think about himself first and let Adriana wait. Could he have done that in Bern?

Later, on the way to the blue house, he passed by Júlio Simões's secondhand bookshop and asked him where he could get a Persian grammar. And what was the best language school if he should decide to learn Portuguese.

Simões laughed. "All at the same time, Portuguese and Persian?"

Gregorius's anger lasted only a moment. The man couldn't know that, at this point in his life, there was no difference between Portuguese and Persian; that in a certain sense, they were one and the same language. Simões also asked how far he had gotten in his search for Prado and whether Coutinho had been able to help him. An hour later, going on four o'clock, Gregorius rang the bell of the blue house.

The woman who opened the door might have been in her mid-fifties.

"Sou Clotilde, a criada," she said, I'm the maid.

She ran one hand, marked by a life of housework, through gray hair and checked whether the bun was right.

"A Senhora está no salão," she said and led the way.

Like the first time, Gregorius was overwhelmed by the size and elegance of the parlor. His eye fell on the grandfather clock. It still showed six twenty-three. Adriana was sitting at the table in the corner. The acrid smell of medicine or perfume hung in the air again.

"You're late," she said.

The letter had prepared Gregorius for such stern words. As he sat down at the table, he felt astonished at how well he coped with this old woman's acrid style. How easy it was for him to see her whole manner as an expression of pain and loneliness.

"I'm here now," he said.

"Yes," she said. And then, after a while, once more: "Yes."

Without a sound and unnoticed by Gregorius, the maid had come to the table.

"Clotilde," said Adriana, *"liga o aparelho,"* turn on the machine.

Only now did Gregorius notice the box. It was an ancient tape recorder, a monster with tape spools as big as plates. Clotilde pulled the tape through the slit in the tape head and fastened it in the empty spool. Then she pushed a button and the spools began to turn. She went out.

For a while, only crackling and swooshing were heard. Then a woman's voice said:

"Porque não dizem nada?" Why do you say nothing?

Gregorius didn't understand any more, for what now came out of the machine was to his ears a chaotic jumble of voices, covered by swooshing and loud sounds that must have come from clumsy handling of the microphone.

"Amadeu," said Adriana as a single male voice was heard. Her usual hoarseness had intensified as she uttered the name. She ran her hand over her throat and tightened the black velvet ribbon as if she wanted to press it tighter to her skin.

Gregorius put his ear to the loudspeaker. The voice was different from what he had imagined. Father Bartolomeu had talked of a soft baritone voice. The pitch was right, but the timbre was acrid, you felt that this man could speak with cutting sharpness. Did it also have something to do with the fact that the only words Gregorius understood were *"não quero,"* I don't want to?

"Fátima," said Adriana, when a new voice emerged from the jumble. The contemptuous way she uttered the name said everything. Fátima had been in the way. Not only in the conversation. In every conversation. She hadn't been worthy of Amadeu. She had illegitimately appropriated the dear brother. It would have been better if she had never entered his life.

Fátima had a soft, dark voice and you observed that it wasn't easy for her to prevail. In the softness, was there also the demand to be listened to with special attention and leniency? Or was it merely the swooshing that produced this impression? Nobody interrupted her, and ultimately the others let what she said die out.

"Everyone is always so considerate of her, so damn considerate," said Adriana, as Fátima was still speaking. "As if her lisp were a dreadful fate that excused everything, all religious sentimentalism, simply everything."

Gregorius hadn't heard the lisp, it had drowned in the accompanying static.

The next voice belonged to Mélodie. She talked at a fast clip, seemed to blow deliberately into the microphone and then burst out laughing. Adriana turned away in disgust and looked out the window. When she heard her own voice, she quickly reached for the switch and turned it off.

For a few minutes, Adriana looked at the machine that made the past into the present. It was the same look as on Sunday, when she had looked down at Amadeu's books and had spoken to the dead brother. She had heard the recording hundreds, perhaps thousands of times. She knew every word, every rustle, every crack and swoosh. Everything was as if now, too, she still sat with the others, over in the family home where Mélodie now lived. So why should she speak except in the present tense or in a past tense that was as if it were only yesterday?

"We didn't believe our eyes when Mamã brought the thing home. She's impossible with machines, just impossible. Afraid of them. Always thinks she'll break them. And then she brings home a tape recorder of all things, one of the first ones you could buy.

"'No, no,' said Amadeu when we talked about it later. 'It's not because she wants to immortalize our voices. It's something quite different. It's to make us pay attention to her again.'

"He's right. Now that Papá is dead and we have the office here, her life must seem empty to her. Rita hangs around and seldom visits her. Fátima does go to her every week. But that doesn't help Mamã much.

"'She'd prefer to see you,' she says to Amadeu when she comes back.

"Amadeu doesn't want to anymore. He doesn't say it, but I know. He's a coward when it comes to Mamã. The only cowardice in him. He, who usually doesn't evade unpleasant things, none of them."

Adriana gripped her throat. For a moment, it seemed as if she'd start talking about the secret hidden behind the velvet ribbon, and Gregorius held his breath. But the moment passed and now Adriana's look came back to the present.

Could he hear again what Amadeu says on the tape, asked Gregorius.

"Não me admira nada," that doesn't surprise me, Adriana began to quote and then repeated every one of Amadeu's words from memory. It was more than a quotation. Even more than a copy, as a good actor manages in a moment of glory. The closeness was much greater. It was perfect. Adriana *was* Amadeu.

Gregorius understood *não quero* again and could make out something new: *ouvir a minha voz de fora,* hearing my voice from outside.

As she came to the end, Adriana began to translate. That the whole thing was possible, no, that didn't surprise him, said Prado. He knew the technical principle from medicine. *But I don't like what it does with words.* He didn't want to hear his voice from outside, he didn't want to inflict that on himself, he disliked himself enough. And the coagulation of the spoken word: you usually spoke in the liberating awareness that most of it would be forgotten. He found it frightening to have to think that everything will be preserved, every thoughtless word, every tasteless remark. It reminds him of the indiscretion of God.

"He only mutters that," said Adriana. "Mamã doesn't like such things and it confuses Fátima."

The machine, it destroyed the freedom of forgetting, Prado said. *But I'm not scolding you, Mamã, it's also a lot of fun. You mustn't take everything your wiseguy son says so seriously.*

"Why the hell do you always mean to console her and have to take back everything?" Adriana flew off the handle. "When she tortured you so much in her gentle way! Why can't you simply stand up for what you think? When you always do! *Always!*"

Could he hear the tape once more, for the voice, asked Gregorius. The request touched her. As she rewound the tape, she had the face of a little girl, surprised and happy that the grown-up also found important what she does.

Gregorius kept listening to Prado's words. He put the book with the portrait on the table and heard the voice into the face until it really belonged to the face. Then he looked at Adriana and was scared. She must have been looking at him constantly and as she did her face had opened, all the severity and bitterness was gone and what remained was an expression welcoming him into the world of her love and admiration for Amadeu. *"Be careful. With Adriana, I mean,"* he heard Mariana Eça say.

"Come," said Adriana. "I'd like to show you where we work."

Her step was firmer and faster than before when she led the way to the ground floor. She was going to her brother in the office, she was needed, no time to lose, *someone who has pain or fear can't wait*, Amadeu used to say. Unerringly, she put the key in the lock, opened all the doors and turned on all the lights.

Thirty-one years ago, Prado had treated his last patients here. A fresh paper cloth was spread on the examining table. On the instrument cabinet were the sort of syringes no longer used today. In the middle of the desk the open patient card file, one of the cards inserted at an angle. Next to it the stethoscope. In the wastebasket a wad of bloody cotton left over from then. On the door, two white coats. Not a particle of dust.

Adriana took one of the white coats off the hook and put it on. "His always hangs his on the left, he's left-handed," she said as she did up the buttons.

Gregorius began to fear the moment when she got stuck in the past where she moved like a sleepwalker. But it wasn't yet time for that. With a relaxed face, that began to glow with a zeal for work, she opened the medicine cabinet and checked the stocks.

"We're almost out of morphine," she murmured. "I have to call Jorge."

She closed the cabinet, stroked the paper cover on the examining table, straightened the scales with her toes, checked whether the washbasin was clean, and then stood still at the desk with the card file. Without touching the crooked card or even looking at it, she began talking about the patient.

"Why did she go to this bungler, this backstreet abortionist. Well, she doesn't know how awful it was for me. But everybody knows that Amadeu takes good care of you in such cases. That he doesn't give a damn about the law when a woman's in trouble. Etelvina and another child, that's quite impossible. Next week, says Amadeu, we have to decide whether she has to get follow-up treatment in the hospital."

His older sister had an abortion and had almost died from it, Gregorius heard João Eça say. It was eerie to him. Here, downstairs, Adriana sank even deeper into the past than upstairs in Amadeu's room. Upstairs was a past she could attend only from outside. With the book, she had erected a belated memorial to it. But when he had sat there smoking and drinking coffee at the desk, the old-fashioned fountain pen in his hand, she couldn't get to him, and Gregorius was sure she had burned with jealousy of the solitude of his thoughts. Here, in the office, it had been different. She had heard everything he said, had spoken with him about the patients and had assisted him. There he was all hers. For many years, this had been the center of her life, the place of her most living present. Her face, which, despite the traces of age—behind them, as it were—was young and beautiful at this moment, expressed her wish to be able to remain forever in that present, not to have to leave the eternity of those happy years.

The moment of awakening wasn't far off. Adriana's fingers groped uncertainly to make sure the white coat was buttoned up. The gleam of the eyes began to die out, the slack skin of the old face drooped, the bliss of time past departed the room.

Gregorius didn't want her to wake up and go back to the cold solitude of her life, where Clotilde had to put on the tape for her. Not now; it would be too cruel. And so he risked it.

"Rui Luís Mendes. Did Amadeu treat him here?"

It was as if he had taken a syringe from the tray and shot her with a drug that raced through the dark veins. A wave of trembling went through her, the bony body shook feverishly a few moments, the breath came heavy. Gregorius was scared and cursed his venture. But then the convulsions subsided, Adriana's body grew firm, the flickering look became solid, and now she went over to the treatment table. Gregorius waited for the question of how he knew about Mendes. But Adriana was a long way back in the past.

She put her flat hand on the paper of the treatment table. "It was here. Right here. I see him lying as if it were only minutes ago."

And then she began to tell. The museum-like rooms came alive with the force and passion of her words, the heat and the disaster of that distant day came back into the office, where Amadeu Inácio de Almeida Prado, lover of cathedrals and merciless enemy of all cruelty, had done something that would never leave him, something he couldn't cope with and couldn't bring to a conclusion even with the merciless clarity of his intellect. Something that lay like a sticky shadow over the last years of his smoldering life.

It had happened on a hot, damp August day in 1965, shortly after Prado's forty-fifth birthday. In February, Humberto Delgado, the former candidate of the left-middle opposition in the presidential election of 1958, was murdered when he tried to return from Algerian exile and get into the country over the Spanish border. The Spanish and Portuguese police were blamed for the murder, but everybody was convinced that it had been the work of the secret police, the Polícia Internacional de Defesa do Estado, P.I.D.E., that had controlled everything ever since António de Salazar's senility had become obvious. In Lisbon, illegally printed fliers circulated placing responsibility for the bloody act on Rui Luís Mendes, a feared officer of the secret police.

"We also had a note in the mailbox," said Adriana. "Amadeu stared at the photo of Mendes as if he wanted to annihilate him with his look. Then he tore the note into little shreds and flushed it down the toilet."

It was early afternoon, and a silent, ominous heat lay over the city. Prado had lay down for his afternoon nap, which he took every day, and that lasted half an hour almost to the minute. It was the only point in the whole cycle of day and night when he managed to fall asleep easily. In these minutes, he always had a deep and dreamless sleep, was deaf to all noise, and if anything ripped him out of the sleep, he was disturbed and disoriented for a while. Adriana guarded this sleep like a shrine.

Amadeu had just fallen asleep when Adriana heard shrill shouts in the street shredding the midday silence. She dashed to the window. A man lay on the sidewalk in front of the house next door. The people who stood around him and blocked Adriana's view were yelling at one another and gesticulating wildly. It seemed to Adriana that one of the women kicked the body with the tips of her shoes. Two big men finally managed to push the people back, they picked up the man and carried him to the door of Prado's office. Only now did Adriana recognize him and her heart stopped: it was Mendes, the man on the flyer, whose photo was labeled: *o carniceiro de Lisboa,* the butcher of Lisbon.

"At that moment, I knew exactly what would happen. I knew it down to the last details, it was as if the future had already happened—as if it were already contained in my fear as an existing fact, and now it would simply be a matter of expanding chronologically. It was even horribly clear to me that the next hours would mean a deep incision in Amadeu's life and represent the hardest test he had ever had to endure."

The men who carried Mendes leaned on the doorbell and it seemed to Adriana that, with the shrill sound that kept starting over and swelling to something unbearable, the violence and brutality of the dictatorship which so far—not without a bad conscience—they had been able to stave off, now made its way into the elegant, guarded silence of her house. For two or three seconds, she considered simply doing nothing and playing dead. But she knew: Amadeu would never forgive her for that. So she opened the door and went to wake him.

"He didn't say a word, he knew: I wouldn't have woke him up if it weren't a matter of life and death. 'In the office,' I simply said. Barefoot he staggered down the stairs and rushed to the washbasin where he scooped cold water onto his face. Then he went to this examining table, where Mendes lay.

"He was petrified and for two or three seconds he stared unbelieving at the leaden, limp face with the fine pearls of sweat on the forehead. He turned around and looked at me for confirmation. I nodded. For a moment, he raised his hands to his face. Then a jolt went through my brother. With both hands, he ripped off Mendes's shirt popping the buttons. He put his ear on the hairy chest, then listened to it with the stethoscope I handed him.

"'Digitalis!'

"He said only this one word and in his tight voice was all the hatred he fought against, a hatred like flashing steel. As I filled the syringe, he massaged Mendes's heart, I heard the dull crack when the ribs broke.

"When I handed him the syringe, our eyes met for a split second. How I loved him at that moment, my brother! With the enormous force of his inflexible iron will, he struggled against the wish to simply let the man on the examining table die, the man who almost certainly had torture and death on his conscience and bore the whole merciless oppression of the state in his fat, sweaty body. How easy it would have been, how unbelievably easy! A few seconds of inaction would have been enough. Just to do nothing! *Nothing!*

"And really: after Amadeu had disinfected the spot on Mendes's breast, he hesitated and shut his eyes. Never, neither before nor after, have I observed a person mastering himself like that. Then

Amadeu opened his eyes and thrust the needle directly into Mendes's heart. It looked like the death blow and I froze. He did it with the breathtaking certainty with which he gave every injection, you had the feeling that, in such moments, human bodies were made of glass for him. Without the slightest tremor, with enormous steadiness, he now pressed the drug into Mendes's heart muscle to start it up again. When he pulled out the syringe, all violence had been wiped out of him. He stuck a bandage on the site of the puncture and listened to Mendes with the stethoscope. Then he looked at me and nodded. 'The ambulance,' he said.

"They came and carried Mendes out on a stretcher. Shortly before he got to the door, he came to, opened his eyes, and encountered Amadeu's look. I was amazed to see how calmly, even objectively, my brother looked at him. Maybe it was also exhaustion, in any case, he leaned against the door like someone who has weathered a tough crisis and can now count on having peace.

"But the opposite happened. Amadeu knew nothing of the people who had just gathered around the collapsed Mendes, and I had forgotten them. So, it took us by surprise when we suddenly heard hysterical voices shouting: *'Traidor! Traidor!'* They must have seen that Mendes was still alive on the orderlies' stretcher, and now they were shouting their rage at the one who had snatched him from the death he deserved and whom they saw as betraying the just punishment.

"As before, when he had recognized Mendes, Amadeu raised his hands to his face. But now, it happened slowly and, having so far carried his head high as always, he now lowered it, and nothing could have expressed better his weariness and grief at what he saw was in store for him.

"But neither weariness nor grief could dull his mind. With a confident grip, he took the white coat he hadn't had time to put on before, off the hook, and slipped it on. Only later did I grasp the somnambulistic certainty in this act: he knew, without thinking, that he had to appear to the people as a doctor and that they would recognize him best as that, if he wore the eloquent garment.

"When he appeared in the front door, the shouting fell silent. For a while, he just stood there, his head down, his hands in the pockets of the coat. Everybody waited for him to say something in his defense. Amadeu raised his head and looked around. It seemed to me as if his bare feet didn't simply touch the pavement, as if he pressed them into it.

"*'Sou médico,'* he said and once again, imploring, *'Sou médico.'*

"I recognized three or four of our patients from the neighborhood, who looked down embarrassed.

"*'É um assassino!'* someone now yelled.

"*'Carniceiro!"* yelled another.

"I saw Amadeu's shoulders lift and drop in heavy breaths.

"*'É um ser humano, uma pessoa,'* he is a human being, a person, he said loud and clear, and probably only I, who knew every nuance of his voice, heard the soft tremor when he repeated *'Pessoa.'*

"Right after that, a tomato burst on the white coat. As far as I know, it was the first and only time anyone had ever attacked Amadeu physically. I can't say how much this attack had to do with what happened to him next—how much it contributed to the deep shock triggered in him by this scene at the door. But I suppose it wasn't much in comparison with what now occurred: a woman emerged out of the crowd, stood before him, and spat in his face.

"If it had only been a single spitting, it might have been seen as an impulsive act, like a furious, uncontrollable twitch. But the woman spat several times and kept on spitting, as if she were spitting her soul out of her body and drowning Amadeu in the slime of her disgust trickling slowly down his face.

"He withstood this new attack with his eyes shut. But, just like me, he must have recognized the woman: it was the wife of a patient who had died of a cancer he had treated for years in countless house calls, for which he hadn't taken a Centavo. What ingratitude! I thought at first. But then I saw in her eyes the pain and despair that came out behind the rage, and I understood: she was spitting at him *because* she was grateful for what he had done. He had been a hero, a guardian angel, a divine emissary, who had guided her through the darkness of the disease where, if she had been left alone, she would have gotten lost. And it was he, he of all people, who had stood in the way of justice that wouldn't have let Mendes survive. This thought had caused such turmoil in the soul of this misshapen, rather limited woman that she could relieve herself only with an outburst, and, the longer it lasted, the more it took on something mythical, a significance that went far beyond Amadeu.

"As if the crowd felt that a line had been crossed, it dissolved, the people went away, eyes down. Amadeu turned around and came to me. I washed the worst off his face with a handkerchief. Over there, at the washbasin, he held his face under the stream of water and opened the faucet so far that the water sprayed out of the basin in all directions. The face he rubbed dry was pale. I believe that, at that moment, he would have given anything to be able to weep. He stood there and waited for the tears, but they wouldn't come. Since Fátima's death four years before, he hadn't wept anymore. He took a few stiff steps to me, it was as if he had to learn how to walk again. Then he stood before me, in his eyes the tears that wouldn't flow, he grabbed my shoulders with both hands and leaned his forehead against mine. We may have stood like that for three or four minutes, and they are some of the most precious minutes of my life."

Adriana fell silent. Once again, she lived these minutes. Her face twitched, but her tears wouldn't come either. She went over to the washbasin, let water run into her cupped palms and dipped her face in it. Slowly, she passed the towel over her eyes, cheeks, and mouth. As if the story demanded a fixed position of the narrator, she went back to the same place before she continued. She also put her hand again on the examining table.

Amadeu, she said, showered and showered. Then he sat down at the desk, took a fresh sheet of paper and screwed off the top of the fountain pen.

Nothing happened. Not a single word appeared.

"That was the worst of all," said Adriana, "to have to watch how the event had made him mute so that he threatened to choke on it."

When asked if he wanted something to eat, he nodded absently. Then he went into the bathroom and washed the tomato spots off the coat. He came to dinner—that had never happened before—in the coat, incessantly wiping the wet spots. Adriana felt that it came out of great depths, this wiping, and seemed just to happen to Amadeu, not that he performed it deliberately. She was afraid he would lose his mind right before her eyes and sit there like that forever, a lost-looking man, always trying in thought to wipe away the filth pelted at him by people he had given all his skill and all his vitality to, day and night.

Suddenly, in the middle of chewing, he ran into the bathroom and vomited in a seemingly endless series of retching convulsions. He wanted to rest, he said flatly afterward.

"I would like to have taken him in my arms," said Adriana. "But it was impossible, it was as if he were burning and everyone who came near him would be seared."

The next two days, it was almost as if nothing had happened. Prado was only a little more tense than usual and his kindness to the patients had something ethereal and unreal. Now and then he stopped in the middle of a movement and gazed straight ahead with an empty, vague look, like an epileptic during a seizure. And when he went to the door of the waiting room, there was a hesitation in his movements as if he were afraid to find someone from the crowd who had accused him of treason.

On the third day, he fell ill. Adriana found him trembling at the kitchen table at dawn. He seemed to have aged and didn't want to see anyone. He gratefully turned everything over to her to arrange and sank into a deep, ghostly apathy. He didn't shave or get dressed. The only visitor he allowed was Jorge, the pharmacist. But he hardly said a word to him either, and Jorge knew him too well to urge him. Adriana had told him how it had come about, and he had nodded silently.

"A week later, a letter came from Mendes. Amadeu put it on the night table, unopened. It lay there two days. Early on the morning of the third day, he stuck it, still unopened, in an envelope and addressed it to the sender. He insisted on taking it to the post office himself. They didn't open until nine, I objected. Nevertheless, he walked on the empty streets, the big envelope in his hand. I watched him and then waited at the window until he came back hours later. He walked more erect than when he left. In the kitchen he checked whether he could bear coffee again. He could. Then he shaved, got dressed and sat down at the desk."

Adriana fell silent and her face was extinguished. She looked forlorn at the examining table where Amadeu had stood when he pushed the lifesaving needle into Mendes's heart with a movement like a death blow. As the story came to an end, time also came to an end for her.

In the first moment, it seemed to Gregorius, too, as if time had been cut off right before his nose, and he had the impression of being able to catch a brief glance at the hardship Adriana had lived with for more than thirty years: the hardship of having to live in a time that had long ago come to an end.

Now she took her hand off the examining table and as she ended the touch, she also seemed to lose the link to the past, which was her only present. At first, she didn't know what to do with her hand, then she thrust it in the pocket of the white coat. The movement made the coat stand out as something special, now it looked to Gregorius like a magical wrap where Adriana had fled to disappear from her silent, uneventful present and to be revived in the distant flaming past. Now that it was extinguished, this past, the coat looked as forlorn on her as a costume in the prop room of an abandoned theater.

Gregorius could no longer bear the sight of her lifelessness. He would have liked to run off, into the city, to a pub with a lot of voices, with laughter and music. To the kind of place he usually avoided.

"Amadeu sits down at the desk," he said. "What does he write?"

The glow of her former life returned to Adriana's face. But her joy of being able to speak of him again was mixed with something else, something Gregorius recognized only slowly. It was anger. Not a short-winded anger kindled by a trifle that flames up and soon goes out, but a profound, creeping anger, like a smoldering fire.

"I wished he hadn't written it. Not even thought it. It was a creeping poison that pulsed in his veins from that day on. It changed him. Destroyed. He didn't want to show it to me. But he was so different afterward. I took it out of his drawer and read it while he slept. It was the first time I did such a thing, and the last time. For now a poison was also in me. The poison of offended respect, of destroyed trust. And it was never the same between us afterward.

"If only he hadn't been so mercilessly honest with himself! So possessed by the struggle against self-deception! *Bearing the truth about himself can be demanded of man,* he used to say. It was like a religious confession. A vow that bound him with Jorge. A credo that ultimately undermined even that sacred friendship, that damned sacred friendship. I don't know the details of how it came about, but it had something to do with the fanatic ideal of self-knowing that, even as students, the two priests of truth carried like the crusaders' banner."

Adriana went to the wall next to the door and leaned her forehead on it, her hands clasped on her back, as if someone had shackled them. Mutely, she quarreled with Amadeu, with Jorge, and with herself. She braced herself against the irrevocable fact that the drama of Mendes's rescue, which gave her those precious minutes of intimacy with the brother, soon set in motion something that changed everything. She leaned all the weight of her body against the wall, the pressure on her forehead must have hurt. And then, quite suddenly, she took her hands off her back, raised them high and punched the wall with the raised fists, over and over, an old woman who wanted to turn back the wheel of time; it was a desperate drumfire of muted blows, an eruption of helpless fury, a desperate assault against the loss of a happy time.

The blows grew weaker and slower, the excitement subsided. Exhausted, Adriana leaned a while on the wall. Then she walked backward into the room and sat down on a chair. The forehead was covered with white plaster from the wall; now and then a grain came loose and rolled over her face. Her look went back to the wall, Gregorius followed the look and now he saw it: Where she had stood just now, there was a big square lighter than the rest of the wall. The trace of a picture that must have hung there before.

"For a long time I didn't understand why he took away the map," said Adriana. "A map of the brain. It had hung there eleven years, ever since we had set up the practice. Covered with Latin names. I didn't dare ask why, he loses his temper when you ask him the wrong thing. I didn't know anything about the aneurysm, he kept it from me. With a time bomb in your brain, you don't bear the sight of such a map."

Gregorius was surprised by what he did now. He went to the washbasin, took the towel and approached Adriana to wipe her forehead. At first she sat there stiffly, defensively, but then she let her exhausted head drop gratefully to the towel.

"Would you take what he wrote then?" she asked when she sat up. "I don't want to have it here in the house anymore."

As she went to get the pages she blamed for so much, Gregorius stood at the window and looked out at the street where Mendes had collapsed. He imagined standing in the door, an incensed mob before him. A mob from which a woman broke loose, who spat at him, not once, but over and over again. A woman who had accused him of treason, he who had always demanded so much of himself.

Adriana had put the pages in an envelope.

"I often thought of burning it," she said and gave him the file.

Silently she led him to the door, still in the white coat. And then, quite suddenly, he was already halfway out, he heard the fearful voice of the little girl she also was: "Will you bring me back the pages? Please, they are his after all."

As Gregorius went down the street, he imagined her taking off the white coat sometime and hanging it next to Amadeu's. Then she would turn off the light and lock up. Clotilde would be waiting for her upstairs.

21

Breathlessly, Gregorius read what Prado had written. At first, he only skimmed it to know as soon as possible why Adriana had felt his thoughts as a curse on subsequent years. Then he looked up every word. Finally he wrote down the text to understand better what it had been for Prado to think it.

Did I do it for him*? When I wanted him to survive—was it for his sake? Can I honestly say that that was my wish? That's how it is with my patients, even with those I don't like. At least, I hope it is and I wouldn't like the idea that, behind my back, my action is guided by quite different motives than those I think I know. But with* him*?*

My hand, it seems to have its own memory, and it seems to me that this memory is more trustworthy than every other source of self-examination. And this memory of the hand, which stuck the needle in Mendes's heart, it says: it was the hand of a tyrant's murderer who brought the already dead tyrant back to life in a paradoxical act.

Here what experience always kept teaching me is confirmed, quite against the original temperament of my thought: that the body is less corrupt than the mind. The mind is a charming arena of self-deception, woven of beautiful, soothing words that give us the illusion that we have an unerring familiarity with ourselves, a closeness of discerning that shields us from being surprised by ourselves. How boring it would be to live in such effortless self-knowledge!

So, in reality, did I do it for myself? *To stand before myself as a good doctor and a brave person who has the strength to master his hatred? To celebrate a triumph of self-control and to revel in the frenzy of self-mastering? So, from moral vanity and even worse: from quite normal vanity? The experience in those seconds—it wasn't the experience of appreciative vanity, I'm sure of that; on the contrary, it was the experience of acting against myself and not indulging in the obvious feelings of satisfaction and spite. But maybe that's no proof. Maybe there is a vanity that isn't felt and that hides behind opposing feelings?*

I am a doctor—that is what I argued to the furious mob. I could also have said: I have taken the Hippocratic Oath, it is a sacred oath, and I will never break it, never, no matter how things are. I feel: I like to say it, I love it, they are words that excite me, exhilarate me. Is that because they are like the words of a priestly vow? So was it really a religious act when I gave back to the butcher the life he had already lost? The act of someone who secretly regrets that he can no longer trust in dogma and liturgy? Who still mourns the unearthly glow of the altar candles? So not an enlightened act? Is there, in my soul, unnoticed by me, a brief, but violent, bitter struggle between the former pupil of the priest and the tyrant-murderer, who has never taken action? Thrusting the needle with the lifesaving poison into his heart, was it an act in which priest and murderer were two of a kind? A movement, in which both got what they longed for?

If I had been in the place of Inês Salomão, who spat at me: What could I have said to me?

"It wasn't a murder that we demanded of you," I could have said. "Not a crime, either legally or morally. If you had left him his death: no judge could have prosecuted you and nobody could have judged you by the Sixth Commandment: Thou shalt not murder. No, what we could expect was something plain and simple, obvious: that you wouldn't keep a man alive with all your might, a man who has

brought us misery, torture, and death, and whom compassionate nature finally wanted to get off our back, and that you wouldn't make sure he could go on practicing his bloody regime."

How could I have defended myself?

"Everyone deserves help to remain alive, no matter what he's done. He deserves it as a person, as a human being. We don't have to judge over life and death."

"And if that means the death of others? Don't we shoot somebody we see shooting somebody? Wouldn't you prevent the obviously murdering Mendes from murdering, with a murder if necessary? And doesn't that go much further than what you could have done: nothing?"

How would it be for me now if I had let him die? If, instead of spitting at me, the others had acclaimed me for my fatal omission? If from the street, an exuberant sigh of relief had come at me instead of an enraged poisonous disappointment? I am sure: it would have haunted my dreams. But why? Because I can't be without something unconditional, absolute? Or simply because it would have meant an alienation from myself to let him die in cold blood? But what I am, I am by accident.

I imagine: I go over to Inês, I ring the bell and say:

"I couldn't have done differently, this is how I am. It might have turned out differently, but in fact, it didn't, and now I am how I am and so I couldn't help doing what I did."

"It doesn't matter how you are with yourself," she could say, "that's completely irrelevant. Just imagine: Mendes is healthy, he puts on his uniform and gives his murderous orders. Imagine. Imagine it precisely. And now judge yourself."

What could I answer her? What? WHAT?

I want to do something, Prado had said to João Eça, *you understand*: do. *Tell me what I can do.* What exactly was it that he wanted to make up for? *You haven't committed a crime,* Eça had said to him, *you're a doctor.* He himself had so argued to the accusing mob and had also said it to himself, certainly hundreds of times. It hadn't done anything to soothe him. It had seemed too simple to him, too glib. Prado was a man of deep distrust of everything glib and superficial, a man contemptuous and hostile to stock sentences like: *I am a doctor.* He had walked on the beach and wished for icy winds to sweep away everything that sounded like mere linguistic habit, a malicious kind of habit that prevented thinking by producing the illusion that it had already taken place and found its conclusion in the hollow words.

When Mendes lay before him, he had seen him as this particular, individual person whose life was at stake. Only as this individual person. He couldn't have seen this life as something that had to be calculated in terms of others, as a factor in a bigger calculation. And it was precisely this that the woman accused him of in her monologue: that he hadn't thought of the consequences also affecting individual lives, many individual lives. That he hadn't been ready to sacrifice one individual for many individuals.

When he had joined the resistance, thought Gregorius, it had also been to learn such thinking. He had failed. *One life for many lives. You can't calculate like that. Or could you?* he had said to Father Bartolomeu years later. He had gone to his former mentor to have his feelings confirmed. But he couldn't have done anything different anyway. And then he had taken Estefânia Espinhosa over the border, out of reach of those who thought they had to sacrifice her to prevent something worse.

The internal gravity that made him who he was had not allowed any other action. But a doubt had remained because suspicion of the moral indulgence was not to be dispelled, a suspicion that weighed heavily on a man who hated vanity like the plague.

It was this doubt that Adriana cursed. She had wanted the brother all to herself and had felt that you can never have for yourself someone who isn't on good terms with himself.

22

"I don't believe it!" said Natalie Rubin on the phone. "I simply don't believe it! Where are you?"

He was in Lisbon, said Gregorius and he needed books, German books.

"Books," she laughed. "What else!"

He listed: the biggest German-Portuguese dictionary there was; a detailed Portuguese grammar, dry as a Latin book, without any junk to make it easy to learn; a history of Portugal.

"And then something that may not exist: a history of the Portuguese resistance movement under Salazar."

"Sounds like an adventure," said Natalie.

"It is," said Gregorius. "Somehow."

"Faço o que posso," said she. I do what I can.

At first Gregorius didn't understand, then he was jolted. That one of his students knew Portuguese—that mustn't be. It obliterated the distance between Bern and Lisbon. It destroyed the magic, the whole crazy magic of his trip. He cursed the phone call.

"Are you still there? My mother is Portuguese, in case you're wondering."

He also needed a grammar of modern Persian, said Gregorius, and he named the book that had once cost thirteen Francs thirty, forty years before. In case the book was still available, or else another. He said it like a defiant boy who doesn't want his dream taken away.

Then he took her address and gave her the name of his hotel. He'd put the money in the mail, he said. If anything was left over—well, maybe he'd need something else later.

"You're opening an account with me, so to speak? I like that."

Gregorius liked the way she said that. If only she didn't know any Portuguese.

"You caused one hell of a turmoil here," she said, when he remained silent on the line.

Gregorius didn't want to hear anything about that. He needed a wall of ignorance between Bern and Lisbon.

So what happened, he asked.

"He's not coming back," Lucien von Graffenried had said into the amazed silence when Gregorius had closed the classroom door behind himself.

"You're crazy," others had said. "Mundus doesn't just run away, not Mundus, never in his life."

"You just can't read faces," von Graffenried had replied.

Gregorius wouldn't have thought von Graffenried was capable of that.

"We went to your house and rang the bell," said Natalie. "I would have sworn you were there."

His letter to Kägi had arrived only on Wednesday. All day Tuesday, Kägi had asked the police about accident reports. The Latin and Greek classes were canceled, the students sat perplexed outside on the steps. Everything was off kilter.

Natalie hesitated. "The woman . . . I mean . . . we found that thrilling, somehow. Excuse me," she added when he was silent.

And on Wednesday?

"At recess, we found a notice on the blackboard. Until further notice, you would no longer be teaching, it said, Kägi himself would take over the classes. A delegation went to Kägi and asked about it. He was sitting behind his desk with the letter in front of him. He was quite different from his usual self, much more modest, gentler, not like a Rector. 'I don't know if I should do that,' he said, but then he read the passage from Marcus Aurelius you had quoted. Did he think you were sick, we asked. He was silent a long time and looked out the window. 'I can't know that,' he said at last, 'but I really don't think so. I think he suddenly felt something, something new. Something soft and yet revolutionary. It must have been like a silent explosion that changed everything.' We told about . . . about the woman. 'Yes,' said Kägi. 'Yeees.' I had the feeling it was somehow envious. 'Kägi is cool,' said Lucien afterward, 'I wouldn't have expected that of him.' Right. But the class is so boring. We . . . we wish you were back."

Gregorius felt a burning in his eyes and took off the glasses. He swallowed. "I . . . I can't say anything about that now," he said.

"But you're . . . you're not sick? I mean . . ."

No, he said, he wasn't sick. "A little crazy, but not sick."

She laughed as he had never heard her laugh, altogether without the sound of the courtly maiden. It was a contagious laugh and he laughed too, surprised by his outrageous, unknown carefree laugh. For a while, they laughed in harmony, he reinforced her and she him, they kept laughing, for a long time, the reason was no longer important, but only the laughing, it was like train rides, like the feeling that the banging sound on the rails, a sound of safety and future, might never stop.

"Today is Saturday," said Natalie quickly, when it was over. "So the bookstores are only open until four. I'm off."

"Natalie? I'd like to keep this conversation between us. As if it had never taken place."

She laughed. "What conversation? *Até logo.*"

Gregorius looked at the candy wrapper he had put back in his coat pocket at night in the Liceu and had touched this morning when he groped in the pocket. He picked up the receiver and turned it around. Information had given him three numbers for the name Rubin. The second had been the right one. He had felt as if he were jumping off a cliff into emptiness when he dialed. You couldn't say that he had done it rashly or out of blind impulse. Several times he had had the receiver in his hand, had hung up again, and had gone to the window. Monday was March first, and the light was different this morning, the first time it was the light he had imagined when the train left the Bern railroad station in the snowstorm.

Nothing was in favor of calling the girl. A candy wrapper in the coat pocket was no reason to call a student out of the blue with whom you had never exchanged a personal word. Especially not if you had run away and a call meant a little drama. Was that what had decided the matter: that nothing was in favor of it and everything was against it?

And now they had laughed together, for some minutes. It had been like a touch. A light, hovering touch without resistance, something that made every physical touch look like a clumsy, ridiculous maneuver. He had once read an article in the paper about a policeman who had let a convicted thief get away. *We laughed together,* the policeman had said as an excuse; *so I could no longer lock him up. It simply didn't work.*

Gregorius called Mariana Eça and Mélodie. No answer. He set out for the Baixa, for Rua dos Sapateiros, where Jorge O'Kelly, as Father Bartolomeu had said, still stood behind the counter of his pharmacy. It was the first time since he arrived that you could wear your coat open. He felt the mild air on his face and noticed how glad he was that he hadn't reached the two women on the phone. He had no idea what he had wanted to say to them.

In the hotel, they had asked him how long he was planning to stay. *"Não faço ideia,"* no idea, he had said, and then he had paid his bill so far. The woman at reception had watched him to the door, he had seen it in the mirror on the pillar. Now he walked slowly to Praça do Rossio. He pictured Natalie Rubin going to the Stauffacher bookstore. Did she know you had to try Haupt on Falkenplatz for the Persian grammar?

At a kiosk a map of Lisbon was spread out, with all the churches marked. Gregorius bought the map. Prado—Father Bartolomeu had said—had known all churches and everything about them. He had been in some of them with the priest. *You would have to rip them out!* he had said, when they had gone past the confessional. *Such a humiliation!*

The door and window frames of O'Kelly's pharmacy were dark green and gold. Over the door was a staff of Aesculapius, in the window an old-fashioned scale. When Gregorius entered, several bells rang, and together they produced a soft, clanking melody. He was glad he could hide behind the many customers. And now he saw what he wouldn't have thought possible: a pharmacist behind the counter *smoking.* The whole shop smelled of smoke and medicine and O'Kelly soon lit a new cigarette with the butt of the old one. Then he drank a sip of coffee from a cup on the counter. Nobody seemed surprised. In his rasping voice, he explained something to the customers or made a joke. Gregorius had the impression that he called them all by their first names.

So that was Jorge, the confirmed atheist and disillusioned romantic, whom Amadeu de Prado needed to be whole. The man whose superiority in chess had been so important for him, the superior one. The man who was the first to burst out laughing when a barking dog had ended the embarrassed silence after Prado's heretical speech. The man who could saw a contrabass until the bow broke because he felt he was hopelessly untalented. And finally, the man whom Prado had resisted when he realized he had condemned Estefânia Espinhosa to death, the woman who—if Father Bartolomeu's assumption was correct—he had approached years later in the cemetery, and didn't meet her eye.

Gregorius left the pharmacy and sat down in the café across the street. He knew there was a note in Prado's book that began with a call from Jorge. Now, in the middle of the street noise and surrounded by people who were conversing or letting the spring sun shine on them with their eyes shut, when he leafed through the dictionary and began to translate, he sensed that something great and really unprecedented was happening with him: he was occupied with the written word amid voices, street music, and coffee steam. *But you, too, sometimes read the newspaper in the café,* Florence had objected when he explained to her that texts demanded protecting walls that kept the noise of the world away, at best the thick, solid walls of an underground archive. *Come on, newspapers,* he had replied, *I'm talking about texts.* And now, all at once, he no longer missed the walls, the Portuguese words before him merged with the Portuguese words next to him and behind him, he could imagine Prado and O'Kelly sitting at the next table and interrupted by the waiter, and that didn't matter to the words.

AS SOMBRAS DESCONCERTANTES DA MORTE. THE DISCONCERTING SHADOWS OF DEATH. *"I woke up with a start and was afraid of death," said Jorge on the phone. "And even now I'm still in a sheer panic." It was shortly before three in the morning. His voice sounded different from when he spoke with customers in the pharmacy, offered me something to drink, or said: "It's your move." You couldn't say the voice quavered, but it was husky like a voice covering powerful feelings, controlled only with difficulty, that threaten to burst out.*

He had dreamed he was sitting on the stage at his new Steinway grand piano and didn't know how to play. Just recently, he, the passionate rationalist, had done something bewitchingly mad: with the money left him by his brother killed in an accident, he had bought a Steinway even though he hadn't yet played a single bar on the piano. The salesman had been amazed that he simply pointed to the shiny grand piano, without even opening the keyboard cover. Since then, the piano stood in a museum shine in his solitary flat and looked like a monumental tombstone. "I woke up and suddenly knew: being able to play the grand piano as it deserves—that's no longer within the span of my life." He sat across from me in his dressing gown and seemed to sink deeper into the chair than usual. Embarrassed, he rubbed his eternally cold hands. "You must be thinking: that was clear from the start. And somehow, I naturally knew it. But you see: when I woke up, I knew it really *for the first time. And now I'm so scared."*

"Scared of what?" I asked and waited until he, a master of the fearless, direct look, would look at me. "Of what exactly*?"*

A smile strayed over Jorge's face: Usually he's the one who urges me to be precise and it is his analytically trained mind that counters my tendency to leave final things in hovering uncertainty.

For a pharmacist, it couldn't possibly be fear of pain and the agony of dying, I said, and as for the humiliating experience of physical and mental decay—well, we had often enough talked about ways and means in case the border of the bearable was crossed. So what was the object of his fear?

"The grand piano—since last night, it has reminded me that there are things I can no longer do on time." He shut his eyes as always when he wanted to forestall a mute objection from me. "It's not about unimportant little joys and fleeting pleasures as when you toss down a glass of water in dusty heat. It's about things you want to do and experience because only they would make your own, this very special life whole *and because without them, life remains incomplete, a torso and a mere fragment."*

But from the moment of death on, he would no longer be there to suffer and mourn this lack of completion, I said.

Yes, of course, said Jorge—he sounded irritated as always when he had heard something that seemed irrelevant to him—but it was about the current, living awareness that life would remain incomplete, fragmentary, and without the coherence we hope for. This knowledge, that's what was bad—the fear of death itself.

But the distress was not that his life now, *as they spoke, didn't yet possess this internal completion. Or was it?*

Jorge shook his head. He wasn't speaking of regret at not yet having experienced everything that had to be part of his life, so that it would be whole. If the awareness of the current lack of completion of his own life were taken as a misfortune, everyone necessarily always had to be unhappy in his life. The awareness of openness, on the other hand, was a condition that it was living and not yet dead life. So, it had to be something different that constituted unhappiness: the knowledge that even in the future *it would no longer be possible to have those rounding off, perfecting experiences.*

But if it wasn't true for one moment, I said, that the incompleteness in it could turn it into an unhappy moment—why shouldn't that also be true of all those moments filled with the awareness that wholeness was no longer to be achieved? It looked as if the desired wholeness was desirable only in the future, *as something you went toward and not something you arrived at. "I want to put it in yet other words," I added: "From which point of view is the unreachable wholeness to be lamented and a possible object of fear? If it is not the point of view of the fleeting moments for which the missing wholeness is not an evil, but rather an incentive and a sign of life?"*

Granted, said Jorge, to be able to feel the kind of fear he had woken up with, you had to take another point of view than that of the usual, forward-looking moments: to be able to recognize your missing wholeness as an evil, you had to view your life as a whole, consider it from its end, so to speak—just as you did when you thought of death.

"But why should this view be a reason for panic?" I asked. "As experienced, the current imperfection of your life is not an evil, that much we agreed on. It almost seems as if it is an evil only as an imperfection you will no longer experience, as one that can be perceived only from beyond the grave. For as an experiencer, you can't, after all, rush ahead into the future in order, from an end that hasn't yet occurred, to feel dispair about a defeciency of your life, which must still creep up to that

anticipated end. So your mortal fear seems to have a peculiar object: an imperfection of your life you will never be able to experience."

"I would have liked to be someone who could make the piano ring," said Jorge. "One who—let's say—can play Bach's Goldberg Variations on it. Estefânia—she can, she played them all alone for me, and ever since, I have carried in me the wish to do it too. Until an hour ago, I had, it seems, lived with the vague, never examined feeling that I would still have time to learn it. Only the dream of the stage made me wake up with the certainty: my life will end without playing the Variations."

All right, I said, but why fear? *Why not simply pain, disappointment, sadness? Or even rage? "One is afraid of something that's still coming, that's still in store; but your knowledge about the forever mute grand piano is already there, we're talking about it in the present. This evil can last, but it can't grow bigger so that there could be a logical fear of its growth. So, your new certainty may depress and stifle, but it is no reason for panic."*

That was a misunderstanding, Jorge countered: the fear applied not to the new certainty, but to its object: to what was indeed only a future, but nonetheless already fixed imperfection of his life, which, because of its greatness, turned certainty to fear from within.

The wholeness of life, whose anticipated absence drives one to the sweat on the forehead—what can it be? What can it consist of when you recall how rhapsodic, variable, and capricious our life is, outside and inside? We're not monolithic, not at all. Are we simply talking of the need to be sated with experience? Was what tormented Jorge the unattainable feeling of sitting at a shining Steinway and making Bach's music his own, which is only possible if it rises from his hands? Or was it the need to have experienced enough things to narrate *life as a whole?*

Is it ultimately a question of self-image, the determining idea one has made for oneself a long time ago of what one had to have accomplished and experienced so that it would be a life one could approve? Fear of death as fear of the unfulfilled then lay—it seems—completely in my hand, for it is I who draw the image of my own life as it was to be fulfilled. What is more obvious than the thought: Then I'll change the image so my life might now fit it—and the fear of death ought to disappear immediately. If it sticks to me nonetheless, then it's because of this: the image, even though made by me and nobody else, rises not from temperamental capriciousness and isn't available for random change, but is anchored in me and grows out of the play of forces of my feeling and thought that I am. So, the fear of death might be described as the fear of not being able to become whom one had planned to be.

The bright awareness of finitude that assaulted Jorge in the middle of the night and that I have to inflame in many of my patients with the words announcing the fatal diagnosis to them, disturbs us like nothing else because, often without knowing it, we live toward such wholeness and because every moment we live to the fullest draws its liveliness from the fact that it represents a piece in the puzzle of that unknown wholeness. If the certainty befalls us that it will never more be achieved, this wholeness, we suddenly don't know how to live the time that can no longer be part of a whole life. That is the reason for a strange, distressing experience of some of my doomed patients: they no longer know what to do with their time, however short it has become.

When I went into the street after the conversation with Jorge, the sun was just rising and the few people coming toward me looked like silhouettes against the light, faceless mortals. I sat down on a window ledge at ground level and waited for the faces of the passersby to open to me. The first one to approach was a woman with a swaying gait. Her face, I now saw, was still veiled in sleep, but it was easy to imagine it opening in the sunlight and looking hopefully and expectantly at the events of the day, the eyes full of future. An old man with a dog was the second one who passed by me. Now he stood still, lit a cigarette and let the dog off the leash so it could run over to the park. He loved the dog and his life with the dog, his features left no doubt of that. The old woman with the crocheted kerchief, who came a while later, was also attached to her life, even though it was hard for her to walk with her swollen legs. She held tight to the hand of the boy with the schoolbag, a grandson perhaps, whom—it was the first day of school—she brought to school early so he wouldn't miss this important beginning of his new future.

All of them would die and all were afraid of it, when they thought of it. Die sometime—but not now. I tried to remember the labyrinth of questions and arguments I strayed through with Jorge half the night, and the clarity that had been close to being grasped in order to escape at the last moment. I watched the young woman stretching, the old man frolicking with the dog leash, and the hobbling grandmother stroking the child's hair. Wasn't it obvious, simple and clear what their horror would consist of if, at this moment, they received tidings of their impending death? I held the haggard face in the morning sun and thought: they simply want more of the stuff of their life, no matter how light or heavy, sparse or lush this life may be. They don't want it to end, even if they can no longer miss the absent life after the end—and know that.

I went home. How does complicated, analytical thought relate to intuitive certainty? Which of the two should we trust more?

In the consulting room, I opened the window and looked at the pale blue sky above the roofs, the chimneys and the laundry on the line: How would it be between Jorge and me after last night? Would we sit across from each other at chess as always, or different? What does the intimacy of death do with us?

It was late afternoon when Jorge came out of the pharmacy and locked it. For an hour, Gregorius had been freezing and drinking one cup of coffee after another. Now he put a bill under the cup and followed O'Kelly. When he passed by the pharmacy, he realized that a light was still burning inside. He looked through the window: no one was there anymore, the antiquated cash register was covered with a dingy wrapper.

The pharmacist turned the corner, Gregorius had to hurry. They walked on the Rua da Conceição across the Baixa and further into the Alfama quarter, past three churches that rang the hour, one after another. In the Rua da Saudade, Jorge stamped out the third cigarette, before he disappeared in the door of a house.

Gregorius crossed the street. In none of the flats did a light go on. Hesitantly, he went back across the street and entered the dark vestibule. It must have been there, behind the heavy wooden door, that Jorge had disappeared. It didn't look like the door of a flat, rather like the door of a bar, but there were no signs of a tavern. Gambling? Was that conceivable for Jorge, after everything he knew about him? Gregorius stood still at the door, his hands in his coat pockets. Now he knocked. Nothing. When he turned the handle, it was like this morning when he had dialed Natalie Rubin's number: like a leap into emptiness.

It was a chess club. In a low, smoky room, dimly lit, there were a dozen games going on, all were men. In a corner was a small counter with drinks. There was no heating, the men had on coats and warm jackets, some wore berets. O'Kelly had been expected, and when Gregorius saw him behind a veil of smoke, his partner was holding the pieces in his fist to choose. At the next table sat a lone man who now looked at the clock and then drummed his fingers on the table.

Gregorius flinched. The man looked like the man back then in Jura he had played with for ten hours, only to lose in the end. It had been at a tournament in Moutier, on a cold weekend in December, where it never became light and the mountains seemed to arch over the town, as in a mountain fortress. The man, a local who spoke French like a moron, had the same square face as the Portuguese man over there at the table, the same stubbly haircut as from a lawn mower, the same receding forehead, the same jug ears. Only the Portuguese man's nose was different. And the gaze. Black, jet black under bushy brows, a gaze like a cemetery wall.

With this look, he now looked at Gregorius. *Not against this man,* thought Gregorius, *by no means against this man.* The man beckoned to him. Gregorius approached. Thus he could see O'Kelly playing at the next table. He could observe him inconspicuously. That was the price. *This damn holy friendship,* he heard Adriana say. He sat down.

"Novato?" asked the man.

Gregorius didn't know: Did that simply mean *new here* or did it mean *beginner*? He decided on the first and nodded.

"Pedro," said the Portuguese man.

"Raimundo," said Gregorius.

The man played even slower than the man in Jura back then. And the slowness began at the first move, a leaden, paralyzing slowness. Gregorius looked around. Nobody was playing with a clock. Clocks were out of place in this room. Everything except chessboards was out of place here. Even talk.

Pedro laid his forearms flat on the table, leaned his chin on his hands and looked at the board from below. Gregorius didn't know what bothered him more: this strained, epileptic look with the iris sliding up on a yellowish background or the manic lip chewing that had made him crazy with the man from Jura back then. It would be a struggle against impatience. Against the man from Jura, he had lost this struggle. He cursed all the coffee he had drunk.

Now he exchanged the first look with Jorge next to him, the man who had woke up from fear of death and had survived Prado for thirty-one years so far.

"Atenção!" said O'Kelly and pointed with his chin to Pedro. *"Adversário desagradável."* Unpleasant opponent.

Pedro grinned without raising his head, and now he looked like a moron. *"Justo, muito justo,"* quite right, he murmured, and fine bubbles formed in the corners of his mouth.

As long as it was a simple calculation of moves, Pedro wouldn't make any mistakes, Gregorius knew that after an hour. You mustn't be deceived by the receding forehead and the epileptic look: he calculated everything thoroughly, ten times if need be, and he calculated it out to at least ten moves. The question was what happened if you made a surprising move. A move that not only seemed not to make sense but in fact didn't. Gregorius had often put strong opponents off with that. Only with Doxiades the strategy didn't work. "Nonsense," the Greek simply said and didn't let go of the advantage.

Another hour had passed when Gregorius decided to cause confusion by sacrificing a pawn without attaining the slightest advantage of position.

Pedro pushed his lips in and out several times, then raised his head and looked at Gregorius. Gregorius wished he were wearing the old glasses, which were like a bulwark against such looks. Pedro blinked, rubbed his temples, ran his short, pudgy fingers over his hair stubble. Then he let the pawn alone. *"Novato,"* he murmured, *"diz Novato."* Now Gregorius knew: it meant beginner.

That Pedro hadn't taken the pawn because he considered the sacrifice a trap had maneuvered Gregorius into a position he could attack from. Move after move, he advanced his army and cut off all possibility of defense for Pedro. The Portuguese man started snuffling noisily every few minutes, Gregorius didn't know if it was deliberation or slovenliness. Jorge grinned when he saw how the disgusting noise annoyed Gregorius, the others seemed to know Pedro's habit. Whenever Gregorius thwarted one of Pedro's plans, even before it became visible, his look became a nuance harder, his eyes were now like glowing slate. Gregorius leaned back and glanced calmly at the game: even if it lasted for hours, nothing more could happen.

His look aimed ostensibly at the window where a streetlamp swung softly on a loose cable, he began to observe O'Kelly's face. In Father Bartolomeu's tale, the man had only been a figure of light at first, a figure of light without brilliance, anything but a show-off, but an incorruptible, fearless boy, who called things by name.

But, then at the end there had been the tale of Prado's night visit to the priest. *She. She has become the danger. She wouldn't resist. She would talk. The others think so. Jorge too? I don't want to talk about that.*

O'Kelly took a drag of the cigarette before he went across the board with the bishop and captured his opponent's rook. The fingers were yellow with nicotine and black under the nails. His big, fleshy nose with the open pores disgusted Gregorius, it looked to him like an outgrowth of ruthlessness. It fit the spiteful grin. But everything that could disgust was abolished by the weary and kind look from the brown eyes.

Estefânia. Gregorius was jolted and felt hot. The name had stood in Prado's text this afternoon, but he hadn't made the connection *. . . the Goldberg Variations . . . Estefânia—she can, she played all alone for me, and ever since, I've carried in me the wish to be able to do it too.* Could that have been *this* Estefânia? The woman Prado had to save from O'Kelly? The woman on whom the friendship between the two, the damn holy friendship, had smashed?

Gregorius began calculating feverishly. Yes, it could be. Then, however, it was the cruelest thing you could imagine: that someone was willing to sacrifice to the resistance movement the woman who had reinforced with Bach's notes the wonderful, bewitching Steinway illusions he had harbored even in the Liceu.

What had happened back then in the cemetery between the two, after the priest had gone? Had Estefânia Espinhosa gone back to Spain? She would have been younger than O'Kelly, so much younger that Prado could have fallen in love with her back then, ten years after Fátima's death. If that were so, then the drama between Prado and O'Kelly had been not only a drama of different morality, but also a drama of love.

What did Adriana know about this drama? Could she have even allowed it in her thoughts? Or did she have to seal her mind against it, as against so many other things? Did the untouched, crazy Steinway still stand in O'Kelly's flat?

Gregorius had made the last moves with the routine, perfunctory concentration he had played with in Kirchenfeld at the simultaneous tournaments against the students. Now he saw Pedro grinning insidiously and after a careful look at the board, he was jolted. The advantage was gone and the Portuguese man had set in motion a dangerous attack.

Gregorius shut his eyes. Leaden weariness washed over him. Why didn't he just get up and go? How did it happen that he was sitting in Lisbon in an unbearably low room in stifling smoke and playing against a disgusting man who didn't matter to him in the least and with whom he couldn't exchange a word?

He sacrificed the last bishop and thus opened the end game. He couldn't win anymore, but it could come to a draw. Pedro went to the toilet. Gregorius looked around. The room had emptied. The few people who had remained approached his table. Pedro came back, sat down and snuffled. Jorge's opponent had gone, he himself had sat down so that he could follow the end game at the next table. Georgorius heard his rattling breath. If he didn't want to lose, he had to forget the man.

Alekhine had once won an end game, even though he was three pieces down. Incredulous, Gregorius, as a student back then, had played over the end game. And afterward, for months he had played every end game he came across. Ever since, he saw at a glance what had to be done. He saw it now too.

Pedro considered half an hour and then, nevertheless, walked into the trap. He saw it as soon as he had moved. He could no longer win. He pushed his lips back and forth, back and forth. He stared at Gregorius with his stony look. *"Novato,"* he said, *"Novato."* Then he stood up quickly and went out.

"Donde és?" asked one of those standing around. Where do you come from?

"De Berna, na Suiça," said Gregorius and added: *"gente lenta,"* slow people.

They laughed and offered him a beer. He should come back.

On the street, O'Kelly stepped up to him.

"Why are you following me?" he asked in English.

When he saw the amazement in Gregorius's face, he laughed harshly.

"There were times when my life depended on noticing when somebody was following me."

Gregorius hesitated. What would happen if the man suddenly saw Prado's portrait in front of him? Thirty years after he had parted from him at the grave? Slowly, he took the book out of his coat pocket, opened it and showed O'Kelly the picture. Jorge blinked, took the book out of Gregorius's hand, went under the streetlamp and held the picture close to his eyes. Gregorius was never to forget the scene: O'Kelly, who observed the picture of his lost friend in the light of the swaying streetlamp, unbelieving, frightened, a face that threatened to fall apart.

"Come with me," said Jorge in a hoarse voice that sounded imperious only to hide the shaking; "I live nearby."

His step as he walked ahead now was stiffer than before and more uncertain, he was now an old man.

His flat was a cave, a smoky cave with walls plastered with photographs of pianists. Rubenstein, Richter, Horowitz, Dinu Lipati, Murray Perahia. A gigantic portrait of Maria João Pires, João Eça's favorite pianist.

O'Kelly went through the living room and turned on an endless series of lamps, one spotlight after another, bringing up photos from the dark. A single corner of the room remained unlit. There was the grand piano, whose silent black shaded off in the gleam of the many lamps and reflected dimly. *I wish I could make the piano ring. . . . My life will end without playing the Variations.* For decades this grand piano had stood there, a dark fata morgana of polished elegance, a black monument to the unfulfilled dream of a rounded life. Gregorius thought of the untouchable things in Prado's room, for there didn't seem to be a particle of dust on O'Kelly's grand piano either.

Life is not what we live; it is what we imagine we are living, said a note in Prado's book.

O'Kelly sat in the chair he seemed always to sit in. He looked at Amadeu's picture. His look, interrupted only seldom by a blink, stopped the planets. The black silence of the grand piano filled the room. The howls of the motorcycles outside bounced off the silence. *Human beings can't bear silence,* said one of Prado's brief notes, *it would mean that they would bear themselves.*

Where did he get the book, Jorge asked now, and Gregorius told him. *Cedros vermelhos,* Jorge read aloud.

"Sounds like Adriana, like her kind of melodrama. He didn't like it, this style, but he did everything to keep Adriana from noticing. 'She's my sister, and she helps me live my life,' he said."

Did Gregorius know what the red cedars were supposed to mean? Mélodie, said Gregorius; he had had the impression she knew. How did he know Mélodie and why did all that interest him, asked O'Kelly. The tone of the question wasn't really sharp, but Gregorius thought he heard the echo of a sharpness that had once been in the voice, at a time when you had to be on guard and wide awake when something strange appeared.

"I'd like to know what it was like to be him," he said.

Jorge looked at him in amazement, dropped his eyes to the portrait and then shut them.

"Can you do that? Know what it is like to be another person? Without *being* the other person?"

At least you could find out what it was like when you imagined being the other person, said Gregorius.

Jorge laughed. It must have sounded like that when he had laughed about the dog at the graduation ceremony in the Liceu.

"And that's why you ran away? Absolutely crazy. I like it. *A imaginação, o nosso último santuário,* imagination is our last sanctuary, Amadeu used to say."

Pronouncing Prado's name, a change came over O'Kelly. *He hasn't pronounced it in decades,* thought Gregorius. Jorge's fingers trembled when he lit a cigarette. He coughed, then opened Prado's book where Gregorius had stuck the receipt from the café between the pages that afternoon. His gaunt rib cage rose and fell, the breath rattled softly. Gregorius would have preferred to leave him alone.

"And I'm still alive," he said and put the book aside. "And the fear, the badly understood fear of back then, is still there. And the grand piano is still standing there, too. Today it's no longer a memorial, it's simply it, the grand piano, all itself, without a message, a mute companion. The conversation Amadeu writes about was in late 1970. Even then, yes, I would have sworn that we could never lose each other, he and I. We were like brothers. More than brothers.

"I remember the first time I saw him. It was the beginning of school, he came to class a day late, I forget why. And he came late to the lesson, too. Even then he wore a frock coat that made him into a boy from a rich house, for you can't buy such things off the rack. He was the only one without a schoolbag, as if he wanted to say: *I have everything in my head.* It fit his inimitable self-confidence as he sat down in the empty place. No trace of arrogance or haughtiness. He simply had the certainty there was nothing he couldn't learn easily. And I don't think he *knew* anything of this certainty, that would have diminished it, no, he *was* this certainty. As he stood up, said his name, and sat down again: fit for the stage, no, not fit for the stage, the boy wanted no stage and needed none, it was charm, pure grace, that flowed from his movements. Father Bartolomeu stopped short when he saw it and for a while, he couldn't go on."

He had read his graduation address, said Gregorius, when O'Kelly sank into silence. Jorge stood up, went into the kitchen and came back with a bottle of red wine. He poured and drank two glasses, not fast, but like someone who needs it.

"We worked on it night after night. Meantime he lost his nerve. Then rage helped. 'God punishes the Egyptians with plagues because Pharaoh is obstinate,' he then shouted, 'but it was God Himself who made him like that! And He made him like that so He could demonstrate His own power! What a vain, complacent God! What a show-off!' I loved him when he was full of this rage and offered God the forehead, his high, beautiful forehead.

"He wanted to title it: Reverence and Loathing of the *Dying* Word of God. That was bombastic, I said, bombastic metaphysics, and in the end he left it. He tended to bombast, he didn't want to admit it, but he knew it, and therefore he fought against kitsch, wherever there was an opportunity, and he could be unjust in that, horribly unjust.

"The only one he spared his anathema was Fátima. She could do everything. He waited on her hand and foot the whole eight years they were married. He needed someone he could wait on hand and foot, he was like that. It didn't make her happy. She and I, we didn't talk about it, she didn't like me especially, maybe she was also jealous of the intimacy between him and me. But once, I bumped into her in the city, in a café, she was reading the help-wanted ads in the newspaper and had circled a few. She packed the paper away when she saw me, but I had come from behind and had already seen it. 'I wish he thought more of me,' she said in that conversation. But the only woman he really thought more of was Maria João. Maria, my God, yes, Maria."

O'Kelly took a new bottle. His words began to blur around the edges. He drank and was silent.

What was Maria João's last name, asked Gregorius.

"Ávila. Like Saint Teresa. That's why, in school, they called her *a santa*, the saint. She threw things when she heard it. Later, when she married, she took a thoroughly normal, inconspicuous name, but I forgot it."

O'Kelly drank and was silent.

"I really thought we could never lose each other," he suddenly said into the silence. "I thought it was impossible. Once I read somewhere the sentence *Friendships have their time and end.* Not with us, I thought then, *not with us.*"

O'Kelly kept drinking faster now and his mouth no longer obeyed him. He stood up laboriously and went out of the room on uncertain legs. A while later, he came back with a sheet of paper.

"Here. We once wrote this together. In Coimbra when the whole world seemed to belong to us."

It was a list titled: LEALDADE POR. Prado and O'Kelly had noted all the reasons for loyalty:

Guilt toward the other; common steps of development; shared suffering; shared joy; solidarity of mortals; common intentions; common struggle against the outside; common strengths, weaknesses; common need for closeness, common taste; common hatred; shared secrets; shared fantasies, dreams; shared enthusiasm, shared humor; shared heroes; common decisions made; common successes, failures, victories, defeats; shared disappointments; common errors.

He missed love on the list, said Gregorius. O'Kelly's body grew taut and for a while, behind the smoke, he was wide awake again.

"He didn't believe in it. Avoided even the word. Considered it kitsch. There were these three things, and only them, he used to say: *desire, pleasure, and security.* And all of them were transitory. Most ephemeral was desire, then came pleasure, and unfortunately, security, the feeling of being safe with someone, also shattered eventually. The impositions of life, all the things we had to cope with, were simply too numerous and too powerful for our feelings to be able to weather them intact. That's why loyalty was important. It was not a feeling, he thought, but a will, a decision, a partisanship of the soul. Something that turned the accident of encounters and the contingency of feelings into a necessity. *A breath of eternity*, he said, *only a breath, but all the same.*

"He was wrong. We were both wrong.

"Later, when we were back in Lisbon, he was often preoccupied with the question of whether there was something like loyalty toward oneself. The duty not to run away from yourself. Neither in idea nor in fact. The willingness to stand for yourself even if you don't like yourself. He would have liked to recompose himself and then make sure that truth came out of the recomposition. *I can bear myself only when I'm working,* he said."

O'Kelly was silent, the tension in his body slackened, the look grew dull, his breath slowed like that of a sleeper. It was impossible simply to go now.

Gregorius stood up and looked at the bookshelves. A whole row of books about anarchism, Russian, Andalusian, Catalonian. A lot of books with *justiça* in the title. Dostoevsky and more Dostoevsky. Eça de Queirós, O CRIME DO PADRE AMARO, the book he had bought on his first visit to Júlio Simões's secondhand bookshop. Sigmund Freud. Biographies of pianists. Chess books. And finally, in an alcove, a narrow shelf with the schoolbooks from the Liceu, some almost seventy years old. Gregorius took out the Latin and Greek grammars and leafed through the crumbly pages with the many inkstains. The dictionaries, the workbooks. Cicero, Livy, Xenophon, Sophocles. The Bible, battered and full of notes.

O'Kelly woke up, but when he started talking, it was as if the dream he had just experienced was continuing.

"He bought me the pharmacy. A whole pharmacy in the best location. Just like that. We meet in the café and talk about everything under the sun. Not a word about the pharmacy. He was a virtuoso of mystery, a goddamned, lovable virtuoso of mystery, I haven't known anybody who mastered the art of mystery like him. It was his form of vanity—even if he didn't want to hear that. On the way back, he suddenly stands still. 'You see this pharmacy?' he asks. 'Naturally I see it,' I said, 'so what?' 'It belongs to you,' he says and holds a bunch of keys before my nose. 'You always wanted your own pharmacy, now you've got it.' And then he also paid for all the equipment. And you know what? It didn't even embarrass me. I was overwhelmed, and at first, I rubbed my eyes every morning. Sometimes I called him and said: 'Just imagine, I'm standing in my own pharmacy.' Then he laughed, a relaxed, happy laugh that became rarer from one year to the next.

"He had a troubled, complicated relationship to all the money in his family. He could throw money out the window expansively, unlike the judge, his father, who didn't allow himself anything. But then he saw a beggar and was upset, it was the same thing every time. 'Why do I give him only a few coins?' he said. 'Why not a bundle of bills? Why not *everything*? And why him and not all the others too? It's a pure, blind accident that we pass by him and not another beggar. And anyway: How can you buy an ice cream and a few steps away is someone who has to bear this humiliation? That simply doesn't work! *You simply can't have it!*' Once he was so furious about this muddle—*this damn, sticky muddle,* as he called it—that he stamped off, ran back and threw a big bill in the beggar's hat."

O'Kelly's face, which been relaxed in memory as with someone whose long pain has gone off, darkened again and grew old.

"When we had lost each other, at first I wanted to sell the pharmacy and give him back the money. But then I realized: it would have been like canceling everything that had been, the long happy time of our friendship. Like retrospectively poisoning our past closeness and the earlier trust. I kept the pharmacy. And a few days after this decision, something amazing happened: it was suddenly much more my pharmacy than before. I didn't understand it. I still don't understand it to this day."

He had left the light burning in the pharmacy, said Gregorius in parting.

O'Kelly laughed. "That's on purpose. The light is always burning. *Always*. The pure extravagance. My vengeance for the poverty I grew up in. Light only in a single room, you went to bed at dark. The few Centavos of pocket money I got, I put into batteries for a flashlight to read by at night. Books I stole. Books mustn't cost anything, that's what I thought then and still do. They kept turning the electricity off in our house because of unpaid bills. *Cortar a luz,* I will never forget the threat. Those are simple things you never get over. How something smelled; how it burned after a smack; how it was when the sudden dark flooded the house; how harsh Father's curse sounded. At first, the police sometimes came to the pharmacy because of the light. Now everybody knows it and they leave me alone."

23

Natalie Rubin had called three times. Gregorius called back. The dictionary and the Portuguese grammar had been no problem at all, she said. "You'll *love* this grammar book! Like a law book and heaps of lists with exceptions, the man is nuts about exceptions. Like you, sorry."

The history of Portugal had been harder, there were several and she had decided on the most condensed. All that was on the way. The Persian grammar he had mentioned was still in print, Haupt could get it by the middle of the week. The history of the Portuguese resistance, on the other hand—that was a real challenge. The libraries would be closed when she came. She could go back only on Monday. At Haupt, they advised her to inquire in the department of Romance literature and she knew who to ask on Monday.

Gregorius was frightened by her enthusiasm, even though he had seen it coming. She would prefer to come to Lisbon and help him with his research, he heard her say.

Gregorius woke up in the middle of the night and wasn't sure she had said it only in a dream or also in reality. *Cool,* Kägi and Lucien von Graffenried had said all the time he was playing against Pedro, the man from Jura, who pushed his pieces over the board with his forehead and banged his head furiously on the table when

Gregorius outfoxed him. To play against Natalie had been strange and weird, for she played without pieces and without light. "I know Portuguese and could assist you!" she said. He tried to answer her in Portuguese and felt as if he were taking an exam when the words didn't come. *Minha Senhora,* he kept starting over, *Minha Senhora,* and then he didn't know how to go on.

He called Doxiades. No, he hadn't woke him up, said the Greek, it's so hard with sleep once again. And not only with sleep.

Gregorius had never heard such a sentence from him, and he was scared. What was it? he asked.

"Oh, nothing," said the Greek. "I'm just tired, I'm making mistakes in my practice, I'd like to stop."

Stop? He and *stop*? Then what?

"Go to Lisbon, for example," he laughed.

Gregorius told of Pedro, his receding forehead and the epileptic look. Dixoiades remembered the man from Jura.

"After that, you played miserably for a while," he said. "For you."

It was already light when Gregorius fell asleep again. When he woke up two hours later, a cloudless sky arched over Lisbon and people were walking around without coats. He took the ship and went over to Cacilhas to João Eça.

"I thought you'd come today," he said and from his narrow mouth, the sparse words sounded like enthusiastic fireworks.

They drank tea and played chess. Eça's hand trembled when he moved, and there was a clack when he put the piece down. At every one of his moves, Gregorius was scared again about the burn scars on the backs of his hands.

"It's not the pain and the wounds that are the worst," said Eça. "The worst is the humiliation. The humiliation when you feel you're going in your pants. When I got out, I burned with a need for revenge. White hot. Waited in hiding until the torturers came off duty. In a plain coat and with a briefcase, like people going to an office. I followed them home. To get even. What saved me was the disgust at touching them. And it would have had to be that, shooting was much too good. Mariana thought I had undergone a process of moral maturation. Not a bit. I always rejected becoming mature, as she called it. Didn't like maturity. Considered this so-called maturity opportunism or pure fatigue."

Gregorius lost. After a few moves, he felt that he didn't *want* to win against this man. The art was not letting him sense that, and he decided on daredevil maneuvers a player like Eça would see through, but only a player like him.

"Next time, don't let me win," said Eça when the signal for food came. "Otherwise I'll get mad."

They ate the insipid boiled lunch of the home. Yes, that's how it always was, said Eça, and when he saw Gregorius's face, he laughed a real laugh for the first time. Gregorius learned something about João's brother, Mariana's father, who had married wealth, and about the doctor's failed marriage.

This time he didn't ask at all about Amadeu, said Eça.

"I'm here for your sake, not his," said Gregorius.

"Even if you haven't come for his sake," said Eça as evening fell, "I have something I'd like to show you. He gave it to me after I had asked him one day what he was writing. I've read it so often I know it almost by heart." And he translated the two sheets for Gregorius.

O BÁLSAMO DO DESILUSÃO. THE BALM OF DISAPPOINTMENT. *Disappointment is considered bad. A thoughtless prejudice. How, if not through disappointment, should we discover what we have expected and hoped for? And where, if not in this discovery, should self-knowledge lie? So, how could one gain clarity about oneself without disappointment?*

We shouldn't suffer disappointment sighing at something our lives would be better without. We should seek it, track it down, collect it. Why am I disappointed that the adored actors of my youth all now show signs of age and decay? What does disappointment teach me about how little success is worth? Many need a whole life to admit the disappointment about their parents to themselves. What did we really expect from them? People who have to live their life under the merciless rule of pain are often disappointed at how others behave, even those who endure with them and feed them the medicine. It's too little, what they do and say, and also too little, what they feel. "What do you expect?" I ask. They can't say it and are dismayed that, for years, they have carried around an expectation that could be disappointed and they don't know details of it.

One who would really like to know himself would have to be a restless, fanatical collector of disappointments, and seeking disappointing experiences must be like an addiction, the all-determining addiction of his life, for it would stand so clearly before his eyes that disappointment is not a hot, destroying poison, but rather a cool, calming balm that opens our eyes to the real contours of ourselves.

And it should not only be disappointments concerning others or circumstances. When you have discovered disappointment as the guide to yourself, you will be eager to learn how much you are disappointed about yourself: about lack of courage and inadequate honesty, or about the horribly narrow borders drawn by your own feelings, acts, and sayings. What was it we expected and hoped from ourselves? That we were boundless, or quite different than we are?

One could have the hope that he would become more real by reducing expectations, shrink to a hard, reliable core and thus be immune to the pain of disappointment. But how would it be to lead a life that banished every long, bold expectation, a life where there were only banal expectations like "the bus is coming"?

"I never knew anybody who could get so thoroughly lost in his daydreams as he," said Eça. "And who hated so much to be disappointed. What he writes here—he writes it *against himself.* As he also often *lived* against himself. Jorge would deny that. Have you met Jorge? Jorge O'Kelly, the pharmacist, in whose shop the light burns day and night? He knew Amadeu much longer than I, much longer. And yet.

"Jorge and I . . . well. Once we played a game. A single time. A draw. But when it came to plans of operations, and especially shrewd deceptions, we were an unbeatable team, like twins who understand each other blindly.

"Amadeu was jealous of this blind understanding, he felt he couldn't keep up with our deviousness and unscrupulousness. *Your phalanx,* he called our alliance, which was sometimes an alliance of silence, even against him. And then you felt: he would like to have broken through it, this phalanx. Then he made assumptions. Sometimes he hit the nail on the head. And sometimes he was completely off. Especially when it was about something that . . . yes, that concerned himself."

Gregorius held his breath. Would he now learn something about Estefânia Espinhosa? He could *ask* neither Eça nor O'Kelly about her, that was out of the question. Had Prado been wrong in the end? Had he taken the woman to safety from a danger that didn't exist? Or did Eça's hesitation concern a completely different memory?

"I've always hated Sundays here," said Eça in parting. "Cake without taste, whipped cream without taste, gifts without taste, phrases without taste. The hell of convention. But now . . . the afternoons with you . . . I could get used to that."

He took his hand out of his jacket pocket and held it out to Gregorius. It was the hand with the missing fingernails. Gregorius felt its solid pressure all the way on the ship.

PART III
THE ATTEMPT

24

On Monday morning, Gregorius flew to Zurich. He had woken up at dawn and had thought: *I am losing myself.* It wasn't that he first woke up and then had thought this thought out of a neutral awareness, an awareness that wouldn't have existed without it. It had been vice versa: first the thought had been there and then the waking. So this special, transparent awareness, which was new to him and different from the awareness that had filled him on the trip to Paris as something new, had, in a certain sense, been nothing but that thought. He wasn't sure he knew what he thought with it and in it, but, with all its vagueness, the thought had possessed an imperious distinctness. Panic seized him and he had begun to pack with trembling hands, jumbling books and clothes wildly. When the suitcase was done, he forced himself to calm down and stood at the window for a while.

It would be a radiant day. In Adriana's parlor, the sun would illuminate the parquet floor. In the morning light, Prado's writing desk would look even more deserted than usual. On the wall above the desk hung notes with faded, barely legible words, known from the distance only by a few points where the pen had come down harder on them. He would like to have known what the doctor's words were supposed to have reminded him of.

Tomorrow or the day after, perhaps even today, Clotilde would come to the hotel with a new invitation from Adriana. João Eça was counting on him to come for chess on Sunday. O'Kelly and Mélodie would be amazed that they never heard anything from him again, from the man who had emerged out of nothing and had asked about Amadeu as if his salvation depended on understanding who he had been. Father Bartolomeu would find it strange that he sent back the copy of Prado's valedictory address in the mail. Nor would Mariana Eça understand why he had disappeared off the face of the earth. And Silveira. And Coutinho.

She hoped there was nothing bad that made him leave so suddenly, said the woman at the reception desk when he settled the bill. He didn't understand a single word of the taxi driver's Portuguese. When he paid at the airport, he found in his coat pocket the note on which Júlio Simões, the secondhand bookdealer, had written down the address of a language school. He looked at it a while and then threw it into the wastepaper basket at the door of the departure lounge. The flight at ten was half empty, they told him at the counter, and gave him a window seat.

In the waiting room at the gate, he heard only Portuguese. Once he also heard the word *português*. Now it was a word that scared him but he couldn't have said why. He wanted to sleep in his bed on Länggasse, he wanted to walk on Bundesterrasse and over the Kirchenfeldbrücke, he wanted to talk about the *ablativus absolutus* and the Iliad, he wanted to stand on Bubenbergplatz, where he knew his way around. He wanted to go home.

At the approach to Kloten, he woke up at a stewardess's Portuguese question. It was a long question, he understood it without an effort and answered in Portuguese. He looked down on the Lake of Zurich. Large parts of the landscape lay under dirty snow. Rain pelted on the wings.

After all, it wasn't Zurich where he wanted to be, it was Bern, he thought. He was glad he had Prado's book with him. When the plane landed and everyone else put away their books and newspapers, he took it out and began to read.

JUVENTUDE IMORTAL. IMMORTAL YOUTH. *In youth we live as if we were immortal. Knowledge of mortality capers around us like a brittle paper ribbon that barely touches our skin. When in life does that change? When does the ribbon start twining around us tighter, until it ends by strangling us? How do we recognize its soft, but unrelenting pressure that makes us know it will never again subside? How do we recognize it in others? And how in ourselves?*

Gregorius wished the flight were a bus where you could simply sit still at the final stop, go on reading and then return. He was the last one out.

At the ticket counter, he hesitated so long that the woman turned her bracelet impatiently.

"Second class," he said at last.

As the train left the main railroad station in Zurich and reached its full speed, it occurred to him that Natalie Rubin was searching in the libraries today for a book on the Portuguese resistance and that the other books were on their way to Lisbon. In the middle of the week, long after he was living on Länggasse again, she would go to the Haupt book store only a few houses away and then take the Persian grammar to the post office. What could he say to her if he should run into her? What could he say to the others? Kägi and the other colleagues? The students? Doxiades would be the easiest, and yet: what would be the right words, the words that got it? When Bern cathedral came into view, he had the feeling he'd be entering a forbidden city in a few minutes.

In the flat, it was icy cold. Gregorius pulled up the Venetian blind in the kitchen that he had pulled down two weeks ago in order to hide. The record of the language course was still on the phonograph, the cover on the table. The telephone receiver was turned around on the cradle and reminded him of the night conversation with Doxiades. *Why do traces of the past make me sad even when they're traces of something cheerful?* Prado had asked himself in one of his laconic notes.

Gregorius unpacked the suitcase and put the books on the table. O GRANDE TERRAMOTO. A MORTE NEGRA. He turned on the heat in all the rooms, put on the washing machine, and then started reading about the Portuguese plague in the fourteenth and fifteenth centuries. It wasn't difficult Portuguese and he progressed well with it. After a while, he lit the last cigarette from the pack he had bought in the café near Mélodie's house. In the fifteen years he had lived here, this was the first time cigarette smoke hung in the air. Now and then, when a passage in the book came to an end, he thought of his first visit to João Eça and it was as if he felt in his throat the burning tea he had poured into himself to make it easier for Eça's trembling hands.

When he went to the closet to get a heavier sweater, he recalled the sweater he had wrapped the Hebrew Bible in at the abandoned Liceu. It had been good to sit in Senhor Cortês's room and read the Book of Job, while the cone of sunlight wandered through the room. Gregorius thought of Eliphaz of Teman, Bildad of Shuah, and Zophar of Na'ama. He pictured the railroad station sign of Salamanca and felt how, in preparation for Isfahan, he wrote the first Persian words on the board in his room a few hundred meters from here. He took a sheet of paper and set off on a search for the memory of his hand. A few lines and loops came, a dot for the vocalization. Then he ripped it up.

He was startled when the doorbell rang. It was Frau Loosli, his neighbor. She had seen from the change in the doormat that he was back, she said, and gave him the mail and the mailbox key. Did he have a good trip? And was there always a school vacation this early in the year?

The only thing in the mail that interested Gregorius was a letter from Kägi. Contrary to habit, he didn't use the letter opener, but ripped the letter open quickly.

Dear Gregorius,

I didn't want to let the letter you wrote me die out mutely. It touched me too much. And I assume that, wherever your travels take you, you will have the mail forwarded sometime.

The most important thing I'd like to tell you is this: our Gymnasium is remarkably empty without you. How empty may be revealed by the fact that Virginie Ledoyen said quite suddenly in the teachers' lounge today: "I sometimes hated him for his blunt, uncouth way; and it really wouldn't have hurt if he had sometimes dressed a little better. Always this worn-out, baggy stuff. But I must say, I must say: Somehow I miss him. Étonnant.*" And what the esteemed French colleague says is nothing in comparison to what we hear from the students. And as I may add, from a few female students. When I stand before your classes now, I feel your absence as a big, dark shadow. And what will happen now with the chess tournament?*

Marcus Aurelius, indeed. We, my wife and I, if I may confide this to you, have recently and increasingly had the feeling of losing our two children. It's not a loss through sickness or accident, it's worse: they reject our whole way of life and aren't at all squeamish about expressing it. There are moments when my wife looks as if she's falling apart. So your reminder of the wise emperor was right on target. And let me add something you hopefully won't sense as importunate: whenever I see the envelope with your letter that won't disappear from my desk, I feel a twinge of envy. Simply to get up and go: what courage! "He just got up and went," the students keep saying. "Just got up and went."

Your position is still open, you should know that. I've taken over some of the instruction, for the rest, we've found students as substitutes, even for Hebrew. As for the financial aspect, you'll be sent the necessary papers by the school administration.

What should I say in conclusion, dear Gregorius? Perhaps simply this: we all wish that your trip really takes you where you want to go, outside and inside.

Yours,
Werner Kägi

P.S. Your books are in my cabinet. Nothing can happen to them. In practical matters, I have one more request: at some time—no hurry—would you let me have your keys?

Kägi had added by hand: *Or would you like to keep them? In case?*

Gregorius sat still a long time. Outside it grew dark. He wouldn't have thought that Kägi would write him such a letter. A long time ago, he had seen him in the city with the two children, they had laughed, everything seemed to be fine. He liked what Virginie Ledoyen had said about his clothes and he was almost a little unhappy when he looked down at the pants of the new suit he had worn on the trip. *Blunt,* yes. But *uncouth*? And aside from Natalie Rubin and maybe Ruth Gautschi, which girl students missed him?

He had returned because he wanted to be back in the place where he knew his way around. Where he didn't have to speak Portuguese or French or English. Why did Kägi's letter make this plan, the simplest of all plans, suddenly seem hard? Why was it now more important to him than a while ago in the train that it was night when he went down to Bubenbergplatz?

An hour later, when he stood in the square, he had the feeling he couldn't touch it anymore. Yes, even though it sounded strange, that was the right word: he couldn't *touch* Bubenbergplatz anymore. He had already walked around the square three times, had waited at the traffic signals and looked in all directions: to the cinema, the post office, the memorial, the Spanish bookstore where he had come on Prado's book, straight ahead at the trolley stop, at Heiliggeistkirche and the Loeb department store. He had stood aside, shut his eyes and concentrated on the pressure his heavy body exerted on the pavement. The soles of his feet had become warm, the street seemed to come toward him, but it was still the same: he no longer succeeded in touching the square. Not only the streets, the whole square with its decades of familiarity had grown toward him, but the streets and buildings, the lights and sounds no longer managed to really reach him, to overcome the last, filmy gap, to reach him completely, and present themselves to his memory as something he not only *knew,* knew by heart, but as something he *was,* as he had always been in a way that dawned on him only now that he failed to be.

The stubborn, inexplicable gap didn't protect him, it wasn't like a buffer that could have meant distance and composure. Instead, it made Gregorius panic, it was the fear that in losing the familiar things he had evoked to recapture himself he was also losing himself and experiencing the same thing here as at dawn in Lisbon, only more pernicious and much much more dangerous, for while there had been Bern behind Lisbon, behind the lost Bern there was no other Bern. With his eyes aimed at the solid yet receding ground, when he ran into a passerby, he was dizzy afterward, for a moment everything was spinning, he grasped his head with both hands as if to hold on to it, and when he was certain and calm again, he saw a woman glance back at him, in her look a question of whether he might not need help.

The clock on Heiliggeistkirche showed shortly before eight, traffic subsided. The cloud cover had parted, you could see the stars. It was cold. Gregorius went through the Kleine Schanze and on to the Bundesterrasse. Excited, he saw the moment approaching when he could turn onto the Kirchenfeldbrücke, as he had done every morning for decades at quarter to eight.

The bridge was blocked. Overnight, until early morning, trolley tracks were being repaired. "A bad accident," said somebody when he saw Gregorius staring bewildered at the sign.

With the feeling that something strange had become habit, he entered Hotel Bellevue and went into the restaurant. The subdued music, the waiter's light beige jacket, the silver. He ordered something to eat. *The Balm of Disappointment.* "He had often joked," João Eça had said of Prado, "that we humans consider the world a stage concerned with us and our wishes. He considered this illusion the origin of all religion. 'No trace of it is true,' he used to say, 'the universe is simply there, and it's completely indifferent, really completely indifferent to what happens to us.'"

Gregorius took out Prado's book and looked for a title with *cena.* When the food came, he had found what he was looking for:

CENA CARICATA. COMICAL STAGE. *The world as a stage, waiting for us to produce the important and sad, funny and meaningless drama of our imaginations. How touching and charming it is, this idea! And how inevitable!*

Gregorius walked slowly to Monbijou and from there over the bridge to the Gymnasium. It had been many years since he had seen the building from this direction and it seemed peculiarly strange to him. He had always entered it through the back door, now the main entrance was before him. Everything was dark. The church bell rang nine-thirty.

The man who now parked the bicycle, went to the entrance, unlocked it and disappeared inside, was Burri, the major. He sometimes came in the evening to prepare a physics or chemistry experiment for the next day. In back, the light went on in the lab.

Without a sound, Gregorius slipped into the building. He had no idea what he wanted here. On tiptoe he sneaked up to the first floor. The classroom doors were locked and the high door to the auditorium couldn't be opened either. He felt locked out, even if, obviously, that made no sense at all. His rubber soles squeaked softly on the linoleum. The moon shone through a window. In its pale light he looked at everything as he had never looked at it before, not as a teacher and not as a student either. The door handles, the banister, the student lockers. They cast back at him the thousandfold looks from earlier times, and stood out from behind them as objects he had never yet seen. He put his hand on the doorhandles, felt their cool resistance and slid on through the corridor as a big, sluggish shadow. On the ground floor, at the other end of the building, Burri dropped something, the sound of smashing glass reverberated through the hall.

One of the doors yielded. Gregorius stood in the room where, as a student, he had seen the first Greek words on the blackboard. That was forty-three years ago. He had always sat in the back on the left and he sat in that seat now, too. Back then, Eva, Unbelievable, sat two rows in front of him, her red hair in a ponytail, and he could watch the tail swishing from shoulder to shoulder over blouse and sweater for hours. Beat Zurbriggen, who had sat next to him all the years, had often fallen asleep in class, and was teased about it. Later, they learned that it was connected with a metabolic disorder that killed him in his youth.

When Gregorius left the room, he knew why it was so strange to be here: in the corridor and in himself, he was running around as the former student and forgot that for decades he had walked through the halls as a teacher. Could you, as the latter, forget the former, even though the latter was the stage where you performed the dramas of the former? And if it wasn't forgetting, what was it?

Downstairs, Burri ran through the hall cursing. The door he slammed had to be the door to the teachers' lounge. Now Gregorius heard the entrance door fall shut. The key was turned. He was locked in.

It was as if he woke up. But it was no awakening into the teacher, no return to Mundus, who had spent his life in this building. The alertness was that of the secret visitor who hadn't managed to touch Bubenbergerplatz earlier that evening. Gregorius went down to the teachers' lounge, which Burri in his anger had forgotten to lock.

He looked at the chair where Virginie Ledoyen always sat. *I must say, I* must *say: somehow I miss him.*

For a while, he stood at the window and looked out at the night. He pictured O'Kelly's pharmacy. On the glass of the green-gold door stood the words IRISH GATE. He went to the phone, called information and had himself connected to the pharmacy. He felt like letting it ring all night in the empty, brightly lit pharmacy, until Jorge had slept off his drunkenness, entered the pharmacy, and lit the first cigarette behind the counter. But after a while the busy signal came and Gregorius hung up. When he called information again, he asked for the Swiss embassy in Isfahan. A foreign, hoarse male voice answered. Gregorius hung up. *Hans Gmür,* he thought, *Hans Gmür.*

Next to the back door, he climbed out a window and dropped down to the ground. When he blacked out, he held on to the bicycle stand. Then he went to the annex and from outside approached the window he had once climbed out during Greek class. He saw Unbelievable turn to her neighbor to point out to her the unbelievable event of his climbing out. Her breath moved the neighbor's hair. The freckles seemed to increase her amazement and the eyes with the squint seemed to expand. Gregorius turned away and walked toward Kirchenfeldbrücke.

He had forgotten that the bridge was closed. Annoyed, he went through Monbijou. As he came to the Bärenplatz, midnight was ringing. Tomorrow morning was market day, market day with market women and cashboxes with money. *Books I stole. Books mustn't cost anything, that's what I thought then and still do,* he heard O'Kelly say. He went on toward Gerechtigkeitsgasse.

In Florence's flat, there was no light. She never went to bed before one o'clock. Had never gone to bed. Gregorius crossed to the other side of the street and waited behind a pillar. The last time he had done that was more than ten years ago. She had come home alone and her step had been tired, listless. When he saw her coming now, she was with a man. *You really might buy something new for a change. After all, you don't live alone. And Greek isn't enough for that.* Gregorius looked down at his new suit: he was better dressed than the other man. When Florence stepped into the street and the streetlamp light fell on her hair, he was shocked: she had grown gray in the ten years. And in her mid-forties, she was dressed as if she were at least fifty. Gregorius felt anger rise in him: hadn't she ever been back to Paris? Had the sloppy guy next to her, who looked like a neglected tax clerk, killed off her sense of elegance? Afterward, when Florence opened the window upstairs and leaned out, he was tempted to emerge from behind the pillar and wave to her.

Later, he went over to the doorbell. Florence de l'Arronge was her maiden name. If he interpreted the order of the bells correctly, her name was now Meier. He wasn't even worth a *y*. How elegant the doctoral student had looked back then, sitting in LA COUPOLE! And how dowdy and fizzled out the woman had looked now! On the way up to the railroad station and on to Länggasse, he kept getting caught up in a rage he understood less with each step. It subsided only when he stood before the shabby house where he had grown up.

The door was locked, but a piece of cloudy glass was missing from the entry door. Gregorius put his nose to the opening: even today it smelled of cabbage. He looked for the window of the room where he had written Persian words on the board. It had been enlarged and had acquired another frame. It could make his blood boil when the mother imperiously called him to eat, while he was excitedly reading the Persian grammar. He saw the sentimental novel by Ludwig Ganghofer on her night table. *Kitsch is the most pernicious of all prisons,* Prado had noted. *The bars are covered with the gold of simplistic, unreal feelings so that you take them for the pillars of a palace.*

That night, Gregorius didn't sleep much and the first moment he woke up, he didn't know where he was. He rattled many doors of the Gymnasium and climbed through many windows. When the city woke up in the morning and he stood at the window, he was no longer sure if he really had been in Kirchenfeld.

In the editorial offices of the big Bern newspaper, they weren't very nice to him and Gregorius missed Agostinha of the DIÁRIO DE NOTÍCIAS in Lisbon. An advertisement from April 1966? Reluctantly, they left him alone in the archive and at noon he had the name of the industrialist who had once sought a tutor for his children. In the phone book, there were three Hannes Schnyders, but only one licensed engineer. An address in the Elfenau.

Gregorius went there and rang the bell with the feeling of doing something completely absurd. The Schnyders in the impeccable villa apparently considered it a welcome change to drink tea with the man who had almost become their children's tutor back then. The two of them were going on eighty and spoke of the wonderful times under the Shah when they had become rich. Why had he withdrawn his application back then? A boy studying ancient languages—that would have been exactly what they were looking for. Gregorius spoke of his mother's illness and changed the subject for a while.

How was the climate in Isfahan, he asked finally. Hot? Sand storms? Nothing you needed to be afraid of, they laughed, at least not when you had a house as they had. And then they brought out photos. Gregorius stayed until evening and the Schnyders were amazed and pleased at his interest in their memories. They gave him a picture book of Isfahan.

Before he went to bed, Gregorius looked at the mosques of Isfahan and listened to the record of the Portuguese language course. He fell asleep feeling that both Lisbon and Bern had failed him. And that he no longer knew how it was when a place *didn't* fail you.

When he woke up at about four, he felt like calling Doxiades. But what could he have said to him? That he was here but not here?

That he had misused the teachers' lounge of the Gymnasium as a switchboard for his crazy wishes? And that he wasn't even sure it had all really taken place?

To whom, if not the Greek, could he have told that? Gregorius thought of the strange evening when they had tried out a first name basis.

"My name's Constantine," the Greek had said all at once during the chess game.

"Raimund," he had replied.

There had been no ritual confirmation, no glass, no handshake, they hadn't even looked at each other.

"But that's nasty of you, Raimund" said the Greek when Gregorius snapped a trap shut.

It didn't sound right, and Gregorius had the impression that they both felt it.

"You shouldn't underestimate my nastiness, Constantine," he said.

For the rest of the evening, they avoided that form of address.

"Good night, Gregorius," said the Greek in parting, "sleep well."

"You too, Doctor," said Gregorius.

There it had stayed.

Was that a reason not to tell the Greek about his floating confusion as he stumbled through Bern? Or was the distancing closeness between them precisely what was needed for such a tale? Gregorius dialed and hung up on the second ring. Sometimes the Greek had this rough way typical of taxi drivers in Thessalonica.

He took out Prado's book. As he sat at the kitchen table with the Venetian blind pulled down and read as he had two weeks before, he had the feeling that the sentences the Portuguese aristocrat had written in the attic room of the blue house helped him to be in the right place: neither in Bern nor in Lisbon.

AMPLIDÃO INTERIOR. INTERNAL EXPANSE. *We live here and now, everything before and in other places is past, mostly forgotten and accessible as a small remnant in disordered slivers of memory that light up in rhapsodic contingency and die out again. This is how we are used to thinking about ourselves. And this is the natural way of thinking, when it is others we look at: they really do stand before us here and now, no other place and no other time, and how should their relationship to the past be thought of if not in the form of internal episodes of memory, whose exclusive reality is in the present of their happening?*

But from the perspective of our own inside, it's quite different. We're not limited to our own present, but, expanded far into the past. That comes through our feelings, especially the deep ones, those that determine who we are and how it is to be us. For these feelings know no time, they don't know it and they don't acknowledge it. It would naturally be false if I said: I am still the boy on the steps in front of the school, the boy with the cap in his hand, whose eyes strayed to the girls' school hoping to see Maria João. Naturally it is false, more than thirty years have passed since then. And yet it is also true. The heart pounding at difficult tasks is the heart pounding when Senhor Lançöes, the math teacher, entered the classroom; in the anxiety about all authorities, my bent father's words of authority resonate; and if the twinkling look of a woman strikes me, it takes my breath away as every time, from school window to school window, my look seemed to meet Maria João's. I am still there, at that distant place in time, I never left it, but live expanded in the past, or out of it. It is present, this past, and not simply in the form of brief episodes of flashing memory. The thousand changes that have driven time—measured by this timeless present of feeling, they are fleeting and unreal as a dream, and deceptive as dream images: they delude me into believing that I, a doctor that people come to with their pains and cares, possess fabulous self-confidence and fearlessness. And this anxious trust in the look of those who seek help forces me to believe in it as long as they stand before me. But as soon as they're gone, I'd like to shout: I'm still that scared boy on the school steps, it's absolutely irrelevant, really a lie, that I sit in the white coat behind the mighty desk and give advice, don't be deceived by what, in ridiculous superficiality, we call the present.

And not only in time are we expanded. In space, too, we stretch out far over what is visible. We leave something of ourselves behind when we leave a place, we stay there, even though we go away. And there are things in us that we can find again only by going back there. We go to ourselves, travel to ourselves, when the monotonous beat of the wheels brings us to a place where we have covered a stretch of our life, no matter how brief it may have been. When we set foot for the second time on the platform of the foreign railroad station, hear the voices over the loudspeaker, smell the unique odors, we have come not only to the distant place, but also to the distance of our own inside, to a perhaps thoroughly remote corner of our self which, when we are somewhere else, is completely in the dark and invisible. Otherwise, why should we be so excited, so outside ourselves when the conductor calls the names of the places, when we hear the screech of the brakes and are swallowed up in the suddenly appearing shadow of the railroad station? Otherwise, why should it be a magical moment, a moment of silent drama when the train comes to a complete halt with a final jolt? It is because, from the first steps we take on the strange and not strange platform, we resume a life we had interrupted and left, when we felt the first jolts of the moving train. What could be more exciting than resuming an interrupted life with all its promises?

It is an error, a nonsensical act of violence, when we concentrate on the here and now with the conviction of thus grasping the essential. What matters is to move surely and calmly, with the appropriate humor and the appropriate melancholy in the temporally and spatially expanded internal landscape that we are. Why do we feel sorry for people who can't travel? Because, unable to expand externally, they are not able to expand internally either, they can't multiply and so they are deprived of the possibility of undertaking expansive excursions in themselves and discovering who and what else they could have become.

When it grew light, Gregorius went down to the railroad station and took the first train to Moutier in the Jura. There were actually people traveling to Moutier. Real people. Moutier wasn't only the city where he had lost against the man with the square face, receding forehead, and crew cut, because he couldn't bear how slowly he moved. Moutier was a real city with a city hall, with supermarkets and tearooms. For two hours, Gregorius searched in vain for the place of the tournament. You couldn't search for something you didn't know anything about anymore. The waiter in the tearoom was surprised at his confused, incoherent questions and whispered afterward with his colleague.

In the early afternoon, he was back in Bern and took the lift up to the university. It was semester break. He sat down in an empty lecture hall and thought of the young Prado in the lecture halls of Coimbra. According to Father Bartolomeu, he could be merciless in the face of vanity. *Merciless. The knife opened in his pocket.* And he carried a few pieces of chalk with him if someone summoned him to the board to make a fool of him. It was many years ago that Gregorius had sat one day amid the surprised looks of the students in this lecture hall at a lecture on Euripides. He had been stunned at the high-flown gibberish tossed out. "Why don't you read the text again?" Gregorius had wanted to shout to the young lecturer. "Read! Just *read*!" As the man kept inserting into his talk more and more French notions that seemed fabricated to suit his pink shirt, he had left. Too bad, he thought now, that he hadn't really shouted at that fop back then.

Outside, he stood still after a few steps and held his breath. Up at Haupt bookstore, Natalie Rubin was coming out of the door. In the bag, he thought, was the Persian grammar and Natalie was now going toward the post office to send it to him in Lisbon.

Perhaps that in itself would not have been enough, Gregorius thought later. Perhaps he would have stayed there nevertheless and stood in Bubenbergplatz until he could have touched it again. But then, in the early dusk of the dull day, the light went on in all pharmacies. *Cortar a luz,* he heard O'Kelly say and, as the words wouldn't go away, Gregorius went to his bank and transferred a big sum to his checking account. "Well, at last you use some more of your money!" said the woman who managed his savings.

He told Frau Loosli, his neighbor, that he had to travel some more. Could she take in his mail again and forward it to him if he called and told her where? The woman would like to have known more, but didn't trust herself to ask. "Everything's fine," said Gregorius, and held out his hand.

He called the hotel in Lisbon and asked to reserve the same room as before for an indefinite time. Good that he called, they said, since a package had come for him and the old woman had brought another note for him. There had also been phone calls asking for him, they had written down the numbers. And they had found a chess set in the closet. Was it his?

In the evening, Gregorius went to dinner at the Bellevue, the safest place not to run into anybody. The waiter was gracious as with an old acquaintance. Afterward, Gregorius entered the Kirchenfeldbrücke, which was open again. He went to the place where the Portuguese woman had read the letter. When he looked down, he became dizzy. At home, he read the book about the Portuguese plague until late at night. He turned the pages feeling like someone who knew Portuguese.

The next morning, he took the train to Zurich. The plane to Lisbon left shortly before eleven. When it landed in the early afternoon, the sun appeared out of a cloudless sky. The taxi drove with the windows open. The hotel bellboy, who carried his suitcase and the package with Natalie Rubin's books to his room, recognized him and talked a blue streak. Gregorius didn't understand a word.

25

"Quer tomar alguma coisa?" Will you have a drink with me? said the note Clotilde had brought on Tuesday. And this time the signature was simpler and more familiar: *Adriana.*

Gregorius looked at the three phone messages. Natalie Rubin had called on Monday evening and had been confused when they told her he had left. Then, maybe she hadn't mailed off the Persian grammar he had seen her with yesterday?

He called her. A misunderstanding, he said, he had only made a small trip and was now back in the hotel. She told of her unsuccessful search for literature on the *Resistência.*

"If I were in Lisbon—I bet I'd find something," she said.

Gregorius said nothing.

He had sent her much too much money, she said into the silence. And: she was mailing his copy of the Persian grammar book today.

Gregorius was silent.

"You don't object if I study it, too?" she asked and suddenly there was a trepidation in her voice that really didn't suit the courtly maiden, much less than the laughter she had drawn him into again.

No, no, he said and strove for a cheerful tone; why should I.

"Até logo," she said.

"Até logo," he said too.

Tuesday night Doxiades and now the girl: Why was he suddenly like an illiterate about closeness and distance? Or had he always been, without noticing it? And why had he never had a friend as Jorge O'Kelly had been for Prado? A friend with whom he could have talked about things like loyalty and love, and about death?

Mariana Eça had called without leaving a message. José António de Silveira, on the other hand, left him a message inviting him for dinner if he should ever come back to Lisbon.

Gregorius opened the package of books. The Portuguese grammar was so similar to a Latin book that he had to laugh, and he read it until it grew dark. Then he opened the history of Portugal and discovered that Prado's life span had coincided almost exactly with the length of the Estado Novo. He read about Portuguese fascism and the secret police, P.I.D.E., which Rui Luís Mendes, the butcher of Lisbon, had belonged to. TARRAFAL, he learned, had been the worst camp for political prisoners. It had been on the Cape Verde Island of Santiago and its name had been a symbol for ruthless political persecution. But what interested Gregorius the most was what he read about the Mocidade Portuguesa, a paramilitary organization on the Italian and German pattern, which adopted the Roman greeting from the fascistic model. All the youth, from grammar school to university, had to join it. That started in 1936, at the time of the Spanish Civil War, when Amadeu de Prado was sixteen. Had he also worn the compulsory green shirt? Raised his arm, as they did in Germany? Gregorius looked at the portrait: inconceivable. But how had he gotten out of it? Had his father used his influence? The judge, who, despite Tarrafal, had his chauffeur pick him up at ten to six in the morning in order to be the first one in the courthouse?

Late at night, Gregorius stood in the Praça do Rossio. Would he ever be able to touch the square as he had once touched Bubenbergerplatz?

Before he went back to the hotel, he went to the Rua dos Sapateiros. In O'Kelly's pharmacy, a light was burning, and on the counter he saw the antiquated phone he had rung on Monday night from Kägi's office.

26

On Friday morning, Gregorius called Júlio Simões, the secondhand bookdealer, and got the address again of the language school, which he had thrown away before the flight to Zurich. The school administration was amazed at his impatience when he said he couldn't wait until Monday and wanted to start right way, if possible.

The woman, who soon entered the room for individual instruction, was dressed all in green, and even her eye shadow matched. She sat down behind a desk in the well-heated room and shivered as she pulled the scarf around her shoulders. Her name was Cecília, she said in a light, melodious voice that didn't fit the sullen, sleepy face. Please would he tell her who he was and why he wanted to learn the language. In Portuguese, naturally, she added with an expression that seemed to express profound boredom.

It wasn't until three hours later, when Gregorius went into the street, dizzy with exhaustion, that he realized what had happened in him at that moment: he had taken the sullen woman's impudent challenge as a surprise opening on the chess board. *Why do you never fight in life when you do it so well in chess!* Florence had said more than once. *Because I find fighting in life absurd,* he had answered; *you've got enough to fight with yourself.* And now he had himself actually gotten into the fight with the green lady.

Had she felt with unbelievable clairvoyance that she had to take him like that at this moment of his life? Sometimes it had seemed to him to be so, especially when, behind the sullen façade, a triumphant smile had appeared, with which she enjoyed his progress. *"Não, não,"* she had protested when he took out the grammar book, *"tem que aprender falando,"* you have to learn by speaking.

In the hotel, Gregorius lay down on the bed. Cecília had forbidden him the grammar book. Him, Mundus. She had even taken it away from him. Her lips moved incessantly and so did his lips and he had no idea where the words came from, *mais doce, mais suave,* she said constantly, and when she pulled the filmy green scarf over her lips, so that it blew when she spoke, he waited for the moment when he could see her lips again.

When he woke up, it was beginning to get dark, and when he rang Adriana's doorbell, it was night. Clotilde led him into the parlor.

"Where were you?" asked Adriana as soon as he entered the room.

"I bring back your brother's note," said Gregorius and handed her the envelope with the sheets.

Her features hardened, her hands remained in her lap.

"What did you expect?" asked Gregorius and it seemed like a bold move on the board whose consequences he couldn't estimate. "That a man like him wouldn't think about what was right? After an emotional shock like that? After an accusation that put everything he stood for in question? That he would simply go on with business as usual? You can't be serious!"

He was alarmed by the ferocity of his last words. He was prepared for her to throw him out.

Adriana's features smoothed out and an almost happy amazement slid over her face. She held out her hands to him and Gregorius gave her the envelope. For a while, she stroked it with the back of her hand, as she had done with the furniture on the first visit to Amadeu's room.

"Ever since then, he's been going to the man he met a long time ago in England, on the trip with Fátima. He told me about him when he . . . came back early, because of me. João is his name, João something. He often goes to him. Doesn't come home at night so I have to send the patients away. Lies upstairs on the floor and studies train routes. He's always been crazy about trains, but not like that. It's not good for him, you can see that, his cheeks are hollow, he lost weight, he's unshaven, it will be the death of him, I feel it."

In the end, her voice had become fretful again, an audible refusal to acknowledge the past as something that was irrevocably past. But before, when he had snapped at her, there was something in her face that could be interpreted as the willingness and even the yearning wish to shake off the tyranny of memory and be freed from the dungeon of the past. And so he risked it.

"He hasn't studied train routes for a long time, Adriana. He hasn't gone to João for a long time. He hasn't been practicing for a long time. Amadeu is dead, Adriana. And you know that. He died of an aneurysm. Thirty-one years ago, half a human lifetime. In the morning. On Rua Augusta. They called you." Gregorius pointed to the grandfather clock. "At six twenty-three. That's how it was, wasn't it?"

Dizziness gripped Gregorius, and he held tight to the back of the chair. He wouldn't have the strength to resist another outburst from the old woman, as he had experienced in the examining room a week before. As soon as the dizziness was past, he would go and never come back. Why, for God's sake, had he thought it was his duty to free this woman, with whom he really had nothing to do, from the frozen past and bring her back to a present, fluent life? Why had he seen himself as destined to break open the seals of her mind? How had he come up with this ludicrous idea?

They fell silent. The dizziness subsided and Gregorius opened his eyes. Adriana sat slumped on the sofa, had raised her hands to her face and was weeping, the gaunt body twitched, the hands with the dark veins shook. Gregorius sat down next to her and put his arm around her shoulders. Once more, the tears burst out of her, and now she clung to him. Then slowly, the sobs grew weaker and the calm of exhaustion set in.

When she sat up and reached for the handkerchief, Gregorius stood up and went to the clock. Slowly, as in slow motion, he opened the glass in front of the face and set the hands on the present time. He didn't dare turn around, one wrong move, one wrong look could make everything collapse. With a soft snap, the glass closed in front of the face. Gregorius opened the pendulum case and set the pendulum in motion. The ticking was louder than he had expected. In the first seconds, there seemed to be nothing in the parlor but this ticking. A new time had begun.

Adriana's look was directed at the clock and it was the look of an unbelieving child. The hand with the handkerchief had stopped in mid-motion and looked as if it were cut out of time. And then something happened that seemed to Gregorius like a motionless earthquake: Adriana's look flickered, smoldered, died out, came back and all of a sudden took on the certainty and brightness of a look thoroughly turned to the present. Their looks met and Gregorius put into his all the confidence he possessed so that he could hold hers when it began to flicker again.

Clotilde appeared and stood still in the door with the tea, her eyes directed at the ticking clock. *Graças a Deus!* she said softly. She looked at Adriana and when she put the tea on the table, her eyes glittered.

What kind of music did Amadeu hear, Gregorius asked after a while. At first Adriana didn't seem to understand the question. Her attention apparently had to travel a long way before she could get to the present. The clock ticked and, with every beat, seemed to announce the message that everything had become different. Then, all of a sudden, Adriana stood up without a word and put on a record of Hector Berlioz. *Les Nuits d'Été, La Belle Voyageuse, La Captive, La Mort d'Ophélie.*

"He could listen to it for hours," she said. "What am I saying—for days." She sat down on the sofa again.

Gregorius was sure she wanted to add something else. She pressed the cover of the record so hard her knuckles grew white. She swallowed. Fine drops formed in the corner of her mouth. She ran her tongue over her lips. Now she put her head back against the sofa, like someone yielding to fatigue. The black velvet ribbon slipped up and showed a small part of a scar.

"It was Fátima's favorite music," she said.

When the music had died away and the ticking of the clock stood out again in the silence, Adriana sat erect and straightened the velvet ribbon. Her voice possessed the amazed calm and relieved confidence of someone who has just surmounted an internal hurdle he had thought insurmountable.

"Cardiac arrest. At thirty-five. He couldn't believe it. My brother, who could adapt to everything new with tremendous, almost inhuman speed and whose presence of mind grew by leaps and bounds with a sudden challenge so that he seemed to be really alive only when he saw the avalanche of an unexpected event that seemed overpowering coming toward him—this man who could never get enough of reality, he couldn't believe, simply didn't want to admit that the white silence in her face was not only the calm of temporary sleep. He forbade the postmortem, the idea of the knife was unbearable to him, he kept postponing the funeral, shouted at people who reminded him of realities. He lost track of things, ordered a requiem mass, canceled it, forgot the cancellation and blasted the priest when nothing happened. *I could have known it, Adriana,* he said, *she had heart arhythmia, I didn't take it seriously, I'm a doctor and didn't take it seriously, in every patient I would have taken it seriously, in her I attributed it to nerves, there was an argument with the other women in the home, she wasn't a trained kindergarten teacher, they said, but only a spoiled daughter from a good family and the wife of a rich doctor, who didn't know how else to kill time, it hurt her, it hurt her terribly, for she could do it so well, she was a natural talent, the children ate out of her hand, the others were jealous, she managed to divert the grief over not having her own children, she managed so well, she really managed so well, and that's why it hurt her, she couldn't fight back, she ate herself up, and then the heart began tripping, sometimes it also looked like tachycardia, I should have taken it seriously, Adriana, why didn't I send her to a specialist, I knew one I studied with in Coimbra, he was a leading authority, all I had to do was call him, why didn't I, my god, why didn't I, I didn't ausculate her even once, just imagine, not even once.*

"So, one year after Mamã's death, we were again at a requiem mass, *she would have wanted it,* he said, *and besides you have to give death a form, at any rate, religions say that, I don't know,* suddenly his thoughts were unsettled, *não sei, não sei,* he said constantly. At the mass for Mamã, he had sat in a dark corner so they wouldn't notice that he wasn't taking part in the liturgy, Rita didn't understand it, *they're only gestures, a framework,* she said, *you were an altar boy, and it was all right in Papá's case.* Now, with Fátima, he was so off balance that one moment he participated and the next he sat still, frozen, instead of praying, and the worst thing was: he made mistakes in the Latin text. *Him! mistakes!*

"He never wept in public, and not at the grave either. It was February third, an unusually mild day, but he kept rubbing his hands, his hands were easily cold, and then, when the coffin began sinking into the grave, he buried his hands in his pockets and watched it, with a look I had never seen in him either before or after, the look of someone who has to bury everything he has, absolutely everything. Quite different from at the grave of Papá and Mamã, where he stood like someone who has prepared himself for this parting a long time and knows it also meant a step into his own life.

Everyone felt that he wanted to remain alone at the grave and so we left. When I looked back, he was standing next to Fátima's father, who had also remained, an old friend of Papá's, Amadeu had met Fátima in his house and had come home hypnotized. Amadeu embraced the big man who wiped his sleeve over his eyes and then went away with ostentatiously bold steps. My brother stood head down, eyes shut, and hands folded alone at the open grave, certainly for a quarter of an hour. I could swear he was praying, I really hope so."

I love praying people. I need the sight of them. I need it against the malicious poison of the superficial and the thoughtless. Gregorius pictured the student Prado as he had spoken in the auditorium of the Liceu about his love of cathedrals. *O sacerdote ateu,* he heard João Eça say.

Gregorius had expected her to give him her hand at parting, for the first time. But then, the old woman, whose gray strands now fell on her face, slowly came toward him until she stood right in front of him and he could smell the peculiar blend of perfume and medicine on her. He felt like withdrawing, but the way she shut her eyes now and ran her hands over his face had something imperious. Like a blind person, she ran along his features with cold, trembling fingers, that sought only the slightest touch. Touching the glasses, she faltered. Prado had worn glasses with round lenses in gold frames. He, Gregorius, was the foreigner, who had ended the standstill of time and had sealed the death of the brother. And he was also this very brother, who had come back to life in the telling. The brother—at that moment, Gregorius was sure of it—who also had something to do with the scar under the velvet ribbon and with the red cedars.

Adriana stood embarrassed before him, her arms at her sides, looking down. Gregorius grasped her shoulders with both hands. "I'll come back," he said.

27

He hadn't been in bed half an hour when the bellboy informed him he had a visitor. He didn't believe his eyes: it was Adriana, leaning on a cane, who stood in the middle of the hotel lobby, wrapped in a long black coat, the crocheted kerchief around her head. She offered the touching yet bombastic look of a woman who had left her house for the first time in years and was now standing in a world she no longer knew so that she didn't even trust herself to sit down in it.

Now she unbuttoned the coat and took out two envelopes.

"I . . . I'd like you to read that," she said stiffly and uncertainly, as if speaking outside in the world was more difficult, or something different, from inside. "One letter I found when we cleared out the house after Mamã's death. Amadeu came within a hairsbreadth of seeing it, but I had an idea when I took it from the secret compartment of Papá's desk and hid it. The other I found after Amadeu's death in his desk, buried under a pile of other papers." She looked at Gregorius shyly, dropped her eyes, looked at him again. "I . . . I wouldn't like to remain the only one who knows the letters. Rita, yes, Rita wouldn't understand them. And I don't have anybody else."

Gregorius shifted the envelopes from one hand to the other. He looked for words and didn't find them. "How did you get here?" he asked at last.

Outside in the taxi, Clotilde was waiting. When Adriana sank into the cushions of the backseat, it was as if this excursion into the real world had consumed all her strength. *"Adeus,"* she had said to him before she got in. She had given him her hand, he had felt the bones and the veins on the back of the hand, which yielded under the pressure. He was amazed to feel how strong and decisive her handshake was, almost like the handshake of someone who lived outside in the world from morning to night and shook dozens of hands every day.

This surprisingly strong, almost routine handshake reverberated in Gregorius as he watched the taxi. In his mind, he turned Adriana back into the forty-year-old woman described by old Coutinho when he mentioned the arrogant way she treated the patients. If there hadn't been the shock of the abortion and she had lived her own life afterward, instead of her brother's life: what a different person she would be today!

In the room, he first opened the thicker envelope. It was a letter from Amadeu to his father, the judge. A letter never sent, which had been constantly revised over many years; that could be inferred from the many corrections showing a development of the handwriting and the inks of different vintages.

Dear Father, was the original address, which later became *Honored feared Father,* even later Amadeu had added *beloved Papá,* and the last supplement had produced *secretly beloved Papá.*

When your chauffeur took me to the railroad station today and I sat in the cushions, where you sit every other morning, I knew I would have to capture in words all the contradictory feelings that threaten to rip me to pieces so as not to be only their victim. I believe that expressing a thing means keeping its force and taking away its terror, *writes Pessoa. At the end of this letter I will know if he is right. However, I will have to wait a long time for this knowledge; for as soon as I have begun, I feel that it will be a long and rocky road to the clarity I seek in writing. And I'm afraid when I think of something that Pessoa failed to mention: the possibility that expressing it can* miss *the thing. What happens then with its strength and its horror?*

I wish you a successful semester, *you said as every time I go back to Coimbra. Never—neither at this parting nor any other—have you used words that would have expressed the wish that the new semester might give me* satisfaction *or* pleasure. *In the car, when I stroked the lush cushions, I thought: Does he even know the word* prazer? *Was he ever young? Sometime he did meet Mamã. Sometime.*

But even though it was as always, this time it was also different, Papá. In a year, hopefully you'll come back, *you said when I was already outside. The sentence choked me and I felt I was stumbling. It was a sentence that came from the tormented man with the crooked back and not a sentence from the mouth of the judge. Sitting in the car, I tried to hear it as an expression of a pure and simple affection. But the sound failed for I knew: most of all he wants his son, the doctor, to be near him and help him in the fight against pain. "Does he sometimes talk of me?" I asked Enrique at the wheel. His answer was long in coming and he seemed to be preoccupied with traffic. "I believe he's very proud of you," he said finally.*

Gregorius knew that Portuguese children, even in the fifties, seldom addressed their parents familiarly, but used the indirect form with *o pai, a mãe.* He had learned that from Cecília, who had first called him *vocé,* but interrupted him after a while and suggested that they should say *tu,* the other was so stiff, after all it was the abbreviated form of V*ossa Mercê,* or *Your Grace.* In the letter the young Prado had taken a step beyond the usual, regarding both the familiar *tu* and the formal *você,* and had decided to alternate between the two extremes. Or had it not been a decision, but rather the natural, unthinking expression of his wavering feelings?

One sheet of the letter ended with the question to the chauffeur. Prado hadn't numbered the pages. The continuation was abrupt and written with different ink. Was that Prado's own order, or had Adriana determined the sequence?

You are a judge, Father—a person who judges, condemns, and punishes. "I no longer know how it came about," Uncle Ernesto once said to me; "it seems to me that it was fixed at his birth." Yes, I thought then; exactly.

I acknowledge: at home you didn't behave like a judge; you didn't speak your judgments more often than other fathers, rather, more seldom. And yet, Father, I often felt your taciturnity, your mute presence as judging, as judicial and juridical.

You are—I imagine—a just judge, filled with and determined by benevolence, not a judge whose harsh, unsparing judgments come from resentment at the deprivations and failures of his own life, or from the denied guilt of his secret failures. You exhaust the scope of leniency and mildness the law allows you. Nevertheless, I have always suffered from the fact that you are one who sits in judgment over others. "Are judges people who send others to prison?" I asked you after the first day of school, where I had to answer the question of my father's profession in class. That's what the others were talking about at recess. What they said didn't sound scornful or accusing; rather it was curiosity and the desire for sensation, pretty much like the curiosity about another student's father who worked in the slaughterhouse. From then on, I would endure every possible detour never again to have to pass by the prison.

I was twelve when I slipped past the guard into the courtroom to see you sitting in your robes on the judge's bench. At that time, you were a regular judge and not yet on the Supreme Court. What I felt was pride and at the same time I was deeply terrified. You were sentencing a habitual thief to prison, without probation because of recidivism. The woman was middle-aged, careworn and ugly, not a face that could charm. Nevertheless, everything in me contracted, every single cell, it seemed to me, was attacked by cramps and paralysis when she was led away and disappeared into the catacombs of the court, which I imagined as dark, cold and damp.

I thought the defense attorney didn't make a good case, a public defender probably, who washed down his sentences listlessly, you learned nothing about the woman's reasons, she couldn't explain herself, I wouldn't be surprised if she was illiterate. Later, I lay awake in the dark and defended her and it was less a defense against the state's attorney than a defense against you. I talked myself hoarse until my voice gave out and the stream of words ran dry. In the end, I stood before you with an empty head, paralyzed by a lack of words that seemed to me like a lack of consciousness. When I woke up, I realized that ultimately I had defended myself against a charge you had never raised. You never accused me, your idolized son, of anything serious, not one single time, and sometimes I think that I did everything I did for this reason: to forestall a possible charge I seemed to recognize, without knowing anything about it. Isn't that ultimately the reason why I became a doctor? To do what is humanly possible against the devilish affliction of vertebral arthritis in your back? To be protected from the reproach of not sympathizing enough with your mute suffering? A reproach meant to drive away Adriana and Rita.

But back to the court. Never will I forget the incredulousness and horror that gripped me when I saw the prosecuting attorney and the defense attorney go to each other after the verdict and laugh *together. I would have thought such a thing was* impossible *and, to this day, I can't* grasp *it. I'll say this for you: when you left the hall, with the books under your arm, your face was serious, regret could be read in it. How much I wished it was really possible in you, this regret that a heavy cell door would now close behind the thief and that enormous, unbearably loud keys would turn in the lock!*

I could never forget her, that thief. Many years later, I observed another thief in a department store, a young woman of bewitching beauty, an artist at making glittering things disappear into her coat pockets. Confused about the joyous feelings that accompanied my observation, I followed her through all the floors on her bold looting trek. Only very gradually did I grasp that, in my imagination, the woman was avenging that other thief you had sent to prison. When I saw a man approaching her with a lurking step, I hurried to her and whispered: "Cuidado!" *Her presence of mind left me speechless.* "Vem, amor," *she said and hung on to me, her head cuddling on my shoulder. On the street, she looked at me and now anxiety could be read in her eyes, in amazing contrast to her nonchalant, cold-blooded act.*

"Why?" The wind blew her abundant hair into her face and hid her look for a moment. I stroked it off her forehead.

"It's a long story," I said. "But to make it short: I love thieves. Assuming I know their names."

She pursed her lips and considered a moment. "Diamantina Esmeralda Ermelinda."

She smiled, pressed a kiss on my lips and disappeared around the corner. Afterward I sat at the table across from you with a feeling of triumph and the leniency of the surreptitious winner. In this moment, all the thieves in the world mocked all the law books in the world.

Your law books: as long as I can think, the uniform black leather volumes have instilled me with awe, a reverence. Those weren't books like the others and what was in them had a very special status and a unique dignity. They were so extraordinary that it surprised me to find Portuguese words in them—even though they were heavy, baroque, and squiggly words, concocted, it seemed to me, by denizens of a different, cold star. Their foreignness and distance were increased even more by the sharp smell of dust that penetrated from the shelf and made me think vaguely that it had to be part of the nature of these books that no one ever took them out and they kept their sublime content completely to themselves.

Much later, when I began to grasp what the arbitrariness of a dictatorship consisted of, I sometimes pictured the unused law books of childhood, and then I accused you in a childish play of thought for not taking them out to fling them in the face of Salazar's thugs.

You never pronounced a ban against taking them off the shelf, no, it wasn't you who pronounced it, it was the heavy, majestic volumes themselves who forbade me with draconian rigor to move them even in the slightest. How often as a little boy did I slip into your study and, with heart pounding, struggle against the wish to pick up a volume and cast a glance at the sacred contents! I was ten when I finally did it, with trembling fingers and after peeping several times into the hall to keep from getting caught. I wanted to track the mystery of your profession and understand who you were beyond the family, outside in the world. It was a powerful disappointment to see that the brittle, formal language prevailing between the covers had absolutely nothing of a revelation, nothing that could make you feel the hoped-for and feared shudder.

Back then, before you stood up after the trial of the thief, our eyes met. In any case, that's how it seemed to me. I had hoped—and it lasted for weeks, this hope—that you would bring it up yourself. Finally, the hope faded and became disappointment, which metamorphosed some more until it fell near protest and rage: Did you think I was too young for it, too limited? But that didn't fit with the fact that otherwise you demanded everything from me and expected it as natural. Was it painful for you that your son had seen you in your robes? But I never had the feeling that you were embarrassed by your profession. In the end, were you scared of my doubts? I would have them, even if I was still half a child; you knew that, you knew me well enough for that, at least I hope so. So, was it cowardice—a kind of weakness I otherwise never connected with you?

And I? Why didn't I bring it up myself? The answer is simple and clear: to take you to task—that was something one simply could not do. *It would have brought down the whole edifice, the entire scaffold, of the family. And it wasn't only something one couldn't* do; *it was something one couldn't even* think. *Instead of thinking and doing it,*

I superimposed in imagination the two images: the familiar, private father, ruler of muteness, and the man in the robes, who spoke with measured words and a sonorous, impeccable voice, overflowing with formal eloquence, into the courtroom, a hall where the voices triggered an echo that made me shiver. And whenever I went through this exercise of imagination, I was scared, for no consoling contradiction resulted but rather a monolithic figure. It was hard, Father, that everything fit together in this iron way and when I could no longer bear that you were present in me like a stony monument, I called for help on a thought I otherwise forbade myself because it defiled the sacredness of intimacy: that now and then you must have embraced Mamã.

Why did you become a judge, Papá, and not a defense attorney? Why did you come down on the side of the punishers? There must be judges, *you would probably say, and naturally I know that there is little to be done against this sentence. But why did my father, of all people, have to be one of them?*

So far, it was a letter to a father who was still alive, a letter the student Prado had written in Coimbra, you could imagine he had begun it right after the return he mentioned. On the next sheet, the ink and the handwriting changed. The pen stroke was now more self-confident, more relaxed, and as if it were refined by the professional routine of medical notes. And the verb forms indicated the time after the judge's death.

Gregorius calculated: there were ten years from the time Prado finished school to the time of his father's death. Had the mute conversation with the father come to a halt in the son for so long? In the depths of feelings, ten years were like a second, nobody knew that better than Prado.

Did the son have to wait until the father's death to continue writing the letter? When he finished school, Prado had returned to Lisbon where he worked in the neurological clinic, Gregorius knew that from Mélodie.

"I was nine then and glad he was back; today I would say it was a mistake," she had said. "But he was homesick for Lisbon, he was always homesick, as soon as he was away, he wanted to be back, there was in him both the crazy love of trains and this homesickness, he was full of contradictions, my big, beaming brother, there was the traveler in him, the man with wanderlust, he was fascinated by the Trans-Siberian Railroad, *Vladivostok* was a holy name in his mouth, and there was also the other in him, the one with this homesickness, *it's like thirst,* he'd say, *when it attacks me, homesickness, it's like an unbearable thirst, maybe I have to know all the train routes so I can come home any time, I couldn't bear it in Siberia, just imagine: the pounding of the wheels over many days and nights, it would take me farther away from Lisbon, ever farther.*"

It was already light out when Gregorius lay the dictionary aside and rubbed his burning eyes. He closed the curtain and lay down under the covers in his clothes. *I am losing myself,* that had been the thought that had made him go to Bubenbergplatz, which he could then no longer touch. When had that been?

And if I want *to lose myself?*

Gregorius slipped into a light sleep, swept by a whirlwind of thought slivers. The green Cecília constantly addressed the judge as *Your Grace,* she stole expensive glittering things, diamonds and other gems, but most of all she stole names, names and kisses carried by pounding wheels through Siberia to Vladivostok, much too far from Lisbon, the place of courthouses and pains.

A warm wind grazed him when Gregorius pulled the curtain back and opened the window at noon. He stood still a few minutes and felt his face dry and become hot under the onslaught of the desert air. For the second time in his life, he had food brought to his room and when he saw the tray before him, he thought of the other time, in Paris, on that crazy trip Florence had suggested after the first breakfast in his kitchen. *Desire, pleasure, and security.* Desire was the most fleeting, Prado had said, then came pleasure, and finally security also shattered. Therefore, it was loyalty that counted, a partisanship of the soul beyond feeling. *A breath of eternity. You never really meant me,* he had said to Florence at the end, and she hadn't said no.

Gregorius called Silveira, who invited him for supper. Then he wrapped up the picture book about Isfahan the Schnyders in Elfenau had given him, and asked the room clerk where he could buy scissors, pins, and tape. As he was about to leave, Natalie Rubin called. She was disappointed that the Persian grammar hadn't yet arrived, despite the express mail.

"I should have just brought it to you!" she said, and then, scared and a little embarrassed at her own words, she asked what he was doing over the weekend.

Gregorius couldn't resist. "I'm sitting without electricity in a school with rats and reading about the difficult love of a son for his father, who took his own life because of pain or guilt, nobody knows."

"You're pulling . . . ," said Natalie.

"No, no," said Gregorius, "I'm not pulling your leg. It's exactly as I say. Only: it's impossible to explain, simply impossible, and then there is also this wind from the desert . . ."

"You're hardly . . . hardly recognizable anymore. If I . . ."

"You said it, Natalie, I can't believe it myself sometimes."

Yes, he would call her as soon as the grammar had come.

"Will you also learn Persian in the fabulous rat school?" She laughed at her own linguistic creation.

"Naturally. That's where Persia *is*."

"I give up."

They laughed.

28

Why, Papá, did you never talk to me about your doubt, your inner struggles? Why didn't you show me your letters to the minister of justice, your requests to resign? Why did you destroy everything so that now it's as if you had never written them? Why did I have to learn of your attempts at liberation from Mamã, who told it to me with shame, even though it would have been a reason for pride?

If it was the pain that finally drove you to death: Well, I couldn't have done anything against that. With pain, the force of words is soon exhausted. But if it wasn't the pain that cast the decisive vote, but rather the feeling of guilt and failure because in the end you didn't muster the strength to break away from Salazar and no longer shut your eyes to blood and torture: Why didn't you talk with me? With your son who once wanted to be a priest?

Gregorius looked up. The hot air streamed out of Africa through the open window of Senhor Cortês's office. The wandering cone of light on the rotting floorboards was a stronger yellow today than recently. On the walls hung the pictures of Isfahan he had cut out. Dark blue and gold, gold and dark blue, and more and more of it, domes, minarets, markets, bazaars, women's faces veiled in dark black, eyes with a zest for life. Eliphaz of Teman, Bildad of Shuah, and Zophar of Na'ama.

The first thing he looked for was the Bible on his sweater, which already smelled of mold and mildew. *God punishes the Egyptians with plagues because Pharaoh is obstinate*, Prado had said to O'Kelly. *But it was God Himself who made him like that! And He made him like that so He could demonstrate His own power! What a vain, complacent God! What a show-off!* Gregorius reread the story: It was right.

For half a day, O'Kelly had said, they had argued about whether Prado should really talk about God as a show-off, a *gabarola* or *fanfarrão,* in his speech. Whether that wasn't going too far to place the LORD—even if only for the tiny length of a single impudent word—on a level with a bigmouth punk. Jorge had won out over Amadeu and he had left it out. For a moment, Gregorius had been disappointed in O'Kelly.

Gregorius went through the building, avoided the rats, sat down on the seat where he had recently imagined Prado making eye contact with Maria João, and finally found in the basement the former library where, according to Father Bartolomeu's report, young Amadeu had been locked up to be able to read through the night. *When Amadeu finished reading a book, it had no more letters.* The shelves were empty, dusty and filthy. The only book still there lay propping up a shelf to keep it from tipping over. Gregorius broke off the corner of a rotten floorboard and wedged it in instead of the book. Then he brushed off the book and leafed through it. It was a biography of Juana la Loca. He took it with him to Senhor Cortês's office.

It was much easier to be taken in by António de Oliveira Salazar, the aristocratic professor, than by Hitler, Stalin or Franco. With such scum, you would never have associated, you would have been immune to them through your intelligence and your unerring sense of style, and you never raised your arm, I'd stake my life on that. But the man in black with the intelligent, strained face under the bowler hat: sometimes I thought you may have felt a kinship with him. Not his merciless ambition or his ideological blindness, but the rigor vis-à-vis yourself. But Father: he made a pact with the others! And watched those crimes for which there will never be an appropriate word, as long as humans live! And we had Tarrafal! Tarrafal, Father! TARRAFAL! *Where was your imagination? Only one single time would you have had to look upon such hands as I saw on João Eça: burned, scarred, maimed hands that had once played Schubert. Why didn't you ever look at such hands, Father?*

Was it the anxiety of a sick person afraid out of physical weakness to pick a fight with the power of the state? And who therefore looked away? Was it your bent back that forbade you to show a backbone? But no, I refuse to accept such an interpretation, it would be unjust, for here where it counts, it would deprive you of the dignity you always proved: the strength never to surrender to your suffering in your thoughts and acts.

Once, Father, one single time, I was glad you could pull strings in the circle of well-dressed, top-hatted criminals, I have to admit that: when you managed to release me from the Mocedade. *You saw my horror when I imagined having to put on the green shirt and raise my arm.* It won't happen, *you said simply, and I was happy at the affectionate implacability in your look, I wouldn't have wanted to be your enemy. Of course, you yourself didn't want to imagine your son as a kitschy campfire proletarian either. Nevertheless I felt your act—whatever it may have been I don't want to know—as an expression of deep affection, and on the night after the release, the most passionate feelings flowed to you.*

It was more complicated when you kept me from the charge of bodily harm to Adriana. The judge's son: I don't know what strings you pulled, what conversations you held. I tell you today: I would rather have faced the judge and fought for the moral right to be able to put life above the law. Nevertheless, what you did moved me deeply, whatever it was. I couldn't explain it, but I was sure that neither of the two things I couldn't accept decided you: fear of scandal or the joy of being able to use your influence. You did it simply to protect me. I am proud of you, *you said when I explained the medical facts to you and showed you the passage in the textbook. Then you hugged me, the only time after childhood. I smelled the tobacco in your clothes and the soap on your face. I still smell them and I can still feel the pressure of your arms holding on longer than I had expected. I dreamed of these arms and they were imploring outstretched arms, stretched out with the fervent plea to the son to free him from the pains like a kindly magician.*

One element in this dream was the enormous expectation and hope that always appeared on your face when I explained the mechanism of your illness, the irreversible curvature of the spine named after Vladimir Bechterev, and when we spoke about the mystery of pain. Those were moments of great and deep intimacy when you hung your look on my lips and sucked in every word of the prospective doctor as a revelation. Then I was the knowing father and you the needy son. How had your father been to you, I asked Mamã after one of these conversations. "A proud, solitary, unbearable tyrant who ate out of my hand," she said. A fanatic advocate of colonialism he had been. "He would spin in his grave if he knew what you think of that."

Gregorius went to the hotel and changed for dinner with Silveira. The man lived in a villa in Belém. A maid opened the door and then Silveira came to him in the vast hall with the chandelier that looked like the entrance to an embassy. He noticed Gregorius looking around admiringly.

"After the divorce when the children moved out, everything was suddenly much too big. But I didn't want to move out either," said Silveira, on whose face Gregorius discovered the same weariness as in their first meeting on the night train.

Later, Gregorius no longer knew how it had come about. They were sitting over dessert and he was telling of Florence, of Isfahan, and of the crazy staying outside in the Liceu. It was a little bit as back then in the sleeping car when he had told this man how he had stood up in the classroom and left. "Your coat was damp when you took it from the hook, I remember precisely, it was raining," Silveira had said at the soup course, "and I also still know what light is in Hebrew:" Then Gregorius had told of the nameless Portuguese woman he had omitted back then in the sleeping car.

"Come with me," said Silveira after coffee and led him to the cellar. "Here, this was the camping equipment for the children. Everything of the finest, nothing lacking. One day they simply left the stuff, no more interest, no thanks, nothing. A heater, a standing lamp, a coffee machine, everything battery-operated. Why don't you just take it? For the Liceu? I'll tell the driver, he'll check the batteries and take it over there."

It wasn't only the generosity. It was the Liceu. Just a while ago, he had made him describe the abandoned school and had kept wanting to know more; but that could have been mere curiosity, a curiosity like that about the bewitched fairy-tale castle. The offer of the camping stuff, however, showed an understanding of his bizarre act—or, if not understanding, then respect—he hadn't expected that from anybody, least of all from a businessman whose life was calculated on money.

Silveira saw his surprise. "I simply like the business of the Liceu and the rats," he said smiling. "Something so completely different, something that doesn't pay. It seems to me it has something to do with Marcus Aurelius."

When he was alone in the living room for a while, Gregorius looked at the books. Lots of literature about porcelain. Commercial law. Travel books. Dictionaries of English and French business language. A lexicon of child psychology. A shelf with an odd assortment of novels.

On a little table in the corner was a photo of the two children, a boy and a girl. Gregorius thought of Kägi's letter. In the conversation that morning, Natalie Rubin had mentioned that the Rector canceled classes, his wife was in the hospital, in the Waldau.

There are moments when my wife looks as if she's falling apart, the letter had said.

"I called a business friend of mine who is often in Iran," said Silveira when he came back. "You need a visa, but otherwise it's no problem to travel to Isfahan."

He paused when he saw the expression that appeared on Gregorius's face.

"I see," he then said slowly. "I see. *Naturally.* It's not *this* Isfahan. And not Iran, but *Persia.*"

Gregorius nodded. Mariana Eça had been interested in his eyes and had seen the sleeplessness in him. But otherwise, Silveira was the only person here who had been interested in him. In *him.* The only one for whom he wasn't only an understanding mirror, as for the denizens of Prado's world.

As they stood again in the hall saying good-bye and the maid brought Gregorius's coat, Silveira's eyes wandered to the gallery and onto other rooms. He looked at the floor, then back up.

"The children's wing. Former wing. Do you want to see it?"

Two generous, light rooms with their own bath. Long rows of Georges Simenon on the bookshelves.

They stood on the gallery. Silveira suddenly seemed not to know what to do with his hands.

"If you like, you could live here. For free, of course. As long as you like." He laughed. "If you're not in Persia. Better than a hotel. You won't be disturbed, I'm away a lot. Like tomorrow morning again. Julieta, the maid, will take care of you. And someday I'll win a game against you."

"Chamo-me José," he said as they sealed the agreement with a handshake. *"E tu?"*

29

Gregorius packed. He was excited as if he were setting out on a trip around the world. He imagined clearing a few Simenons off the shelf in the boy's room and putting up his books: the two about the plague and the earthquake, the New Testament Coutinho had given him an eternity ago, Pessoa, Eça de Queirós, the picture biography of Salazar, Natalie Rubin's books. In Bern, he had packed Marcus Aurelius and his old Horace, the Greek tragedies and Sappho. At the last moment, also Augustine's *Confessions. Books for the next stretch of the way.*

The bag was heavy, and when he picked it up from the bed and carried it to the door, he became dizzy. He lay down. After a few minutes, it passed and he could carry on with Prado's letter.

I start trembling at the very thought of the unplanned and unknown, but inevitable and unstoppable force with which parents leave traces in their children that, like traces of branding, can never be erased. The outlines of parental will and fear are written with a white-hot stylus in the souls of the children who are helpless and ignorant of what is happening to them. We need a whole life to find and decipher the branded text and we can never be sure we have understood it.

And you see, Papá, that's also what happened to me with you. Not long ago it finally dawned on me that there is a powerful text in me that has dominated everything I have felt and done so far, a hidden white-hot text, whose insidious power lies in the fact that, despite all my education, it never occurred to me that it might not possess the validity I had unwittingly granted it. The text is brief and of Old Testament finality: OTHERS ARE YOUR COURT OF JUSTICE.

I can't prove it in court, but I know that, from an early age, I read this text in your eyes, Father, in the look that penetrated full of deprivation, pain and severity from behind your eyeglasses and seemed to follow me wherever I went. The only place it couldn't follow me was the big chair in the library of the Liceu, where I hid at night to be able to go on reading. The solid concreteness of the chair along with the darkness resulted in an impenetrable wall that protected me from all intrusions. There, your look didn't penetrate, and so neither was there a court of justice I had to account to when I read of the women with white limbs and all the things you may do only in secret.

Can you imagine my rage when I read in the Prophet Jeremiah: Can any hide himself in secret places that I shall not see him? saith the Lord. Do not I fill heaven and earth? saith the Lord.

"What do you want," said Father Bartolomeu. "He is God."

"Yes, and that's precisely what speaks against God: that he is God," I replied.

The priest laughed. He didn't hold it against me. He loved me.

How much, Papá, would I have liked to have a father to talk to about these things! About God and His complacent cruelty, about cross, guillotine and garrote. About the madness of turning the other cheek. About justice and revenge.

Your back, it couldn't bear the church pews, so that I saw you kneeling only one single time, at the requiem mass for Uncle Ernesto. The silhouette of your tortured body remains unforgettable to me, it had something to do with Dante and Purgatory, which I always imagined as a flaming sea of humiliation, for what is worse than humiliation, the fiercest pain is nothing compared to it. And we never got to talk about these things. I think I heard the word Deus *from you only in hackneyed idioms, never properly, never as if it were spoken from belief. And yet you didn't do anything against the mute impression that you bore not only the secular law books in you, but also the ecclesiastical ones from which the Inquisition emerged. Tarrafal, Father, TARRAFAL!*

30

Silveira's chauffeur came for Gregorius in the late morning. He had charged the batteries of the camping equipment and packed two blankets with coffee, sugar and cookies lying on top of them. In the hotel, they weren't happy he was moving out. *"Foi um grande prazer,"* they said.

It had rained during the night and fine sand from the desert wind lay on the car. Filipe, the driver, opened the door to the backseat of the big, shining car for Gregorius. *In the car, when I stroked the lush cushions*—that's where Prado's plan to write a letter to his father had been born.

Gregorius had ridden in a taxi with his parents a single time, on the way back from a vacation on Thunersee, where his father had sprained his foot, and they had to take a cab because of the luggage. He had seen from the back of his father's head how uneasy he was. For the mother, it had been like a fairy tale, her eyes lit up and she didn't want to get out.

Filipe went to the villa and then to the Liceu. The road where the delivery van used to bring supplies for the school kitchen was completely overgrown. Felipe the driver stopped. "Here?" he asked flabbergasted. The heavyset man with shoulders like a horse anxiously avoided the rats. In the Rector's office, he walked slowly along the walls, cap in hand, and looked at the pictures of Isfahan.

"And what are you doing in here?" he asked. "I mean, it's not my place . . ."

"Hard to say," said Gregorius. "Really hard. You know what daydreaming is. It's a little like that. But also quite different. More serious. And crazier. When a lifetime is short, no rules apply anymore. And then it looks as if you cracked up and are ripe for the loony bin. But basically it's the other way around: the ones who belong there are those who don't want to admit that time is short. Those who go on as if nothing was wrong. You understand?"

"Two years ago, I had a heart attack," said Felipe. "I found it strange to go back to work afterward. Now it comes back to me, I had completely forgotten it."

"Yes," said Gregorius.

When Felipe had gone, the sky clouded over, it became cool and dark. Gregorius put on the heater, turned on the light and made coffee. The cigarettes. He took them out of his pocket. What brand of cigarettes had he smoked the first time in his life, Silveira had asked him. Then he had stood up and come back with a pack of this brand. *Here. It was my wife's brand. Been lying for years in the drawer of the night table. On her side of the bed. Couldn't throw them away. The tobacco must be dry as dust.* Gregorius tore open the pack and lit one. By now he could inhale without coughing. The smoke was sharp and tasted like burned wood. A wave of dizziness washed over him and his heart seemed to skip a beat.

He read the passage in Jeremiah that Prado had written about and leafed back in Isaiah. *For my thoughts are not your thoughts, neither are your ways my ways, saith the Lord. For as the heavens are higher than the earth, so are my ways higher than your ways, and my thoughts than your thoughts.*

Prado had taken seriously the idea that God was a person who could think, will and feel. Then, as with any other person, he had heard what he said and had found: I won't have anything to do with such an arrogant character. Did God have a *character*? Gregorius thought of Ruth Gautschi and David Lehmann and of his own words about poetic seriousness, the greatest seriousness of all. Bern was far away.

Your remoteness, Father. Mamã as the interpreter, who had to translate your muteness to us. Why didn't you learn to talk about yourself and your feelings? I want to tell you: it was too comfortable for you, it was so wonderfully comfortable for you to hide behind the southern role of the aristocratic head of the family. And there was also the role of the taciturn sufferer in whom speechlessness is a virtue, that is, the greatness of not complaining about the pains. And so, your illness was absolution for your unwillingness to learn to express yourself. Your arrogance: others were to learn to guess you in your suffering.

Didn't you notice what you forfeited in autonomy, which we have only to the extent that we understand how to express ourselves?

Did you never think, Papá, that it could also be a burden for all of us that you didn't *talk about the pain and humiliation of the twisted back? That your mute, heroic endurance, which wasn't without vanity, could be more oppressive for us than if you had sometimes cursed and shed tears of self-pity we could wipe out of your eyes? For that meant that we children, and mainly I, the son, imprisoned in the jurisdiction of your bravery, we had no right to complain, every such right, even before it was claimed —even before one of us* thought *of claiming it—was absorbed, consumed, destroyed by your bravery and your bravely endured suffering.*

You didn't want any painkillers, you didn't want to lose your lucidity, you were dogmatic about that. Once, when you believed you were unobserved, I watched you through the crack in the door. You took one tablet and after a brief struggle, you also stuck the second one in your mouth. After a while, when I looked in again, you were leaning back in the chair, your head in the cushion, your glasses in your lap, your mouth slack. Naturally it was inconceivable: but how much would I have liked to go in and caress you!

Not once did I see you weep, with rigid countenance, you stood there when we buried Carlos, the beloved dog—even beloved by you. You weren't a soulless person, certainly not. But why did you act all your life as if the soul was something one had to be ashamed of, something unseemly, a place of the weakness that must be kept hidden, almost at any price?

Through you, we all learned from childhood on that we are first of all bodies and that there is nothing in our mind that wasn't first in the body. And then—what a paradox!—you withheld from us every education in affection so that we really couldn't believe that you came close enough to Mamã to beget us. It wasn't him, *Mélodie once said,* it was the Amazon. *Only once did I feel that you knew what a woman is: when Fátima came in. Nothing changed in you and everything changed. What a magnetic field is—I grasped that for the first time.*

Here the letter ended. Gregorius put the sheets back in the envelope. As he did, he noticed a penciled note on the back of the last page. *What did I know of your fantasies? Why do we know so little about the fantasies of our parents? What do we know of somebody if we know nothing of the images passed to him by his imagination?* Gregorius put the envelope away and went to João Eça.

31

Eça picked white, but didn't start. Gregorius had made tea and poured both of them half a cup. He smoked one of the cigarettes Silveira's wife had forgotten in the bedroom. João Eça also smoked. He smoked and drank and said nothing. Twilight descended over the city, they'd soon ring for supper.

"No," said Eça when Gregorius went to the light switch. "But lock the door."

It grew dark fast. The glow of Eça's cigarette expanded and contracted. When he started speaking, it was as if he had put a mute on his voice, as on an instrument, a mute that made the words not only softer and darker, but also rougher.

"The girl. Estefânia Espinhosa. I don't know what you know about her. But I'm sure you have heard of her. You've wanted to ask me about her for a long time. I feel that. You don't dare. I've been thinking about it since last Sunday. It's better if I tell you my story. It is, I think, only a part of the truth. If there is a truth here. But this part you should know. Whatever the others will say."

Gregorius refilled the teacup. Eça's hands shook as he drank.

"She worked in the post office. The post office is important for the resistance. Post office and railroad. She was young when O'Kelly met her. Twenty-three or twenty-four. That was 1970, in the spring. She had this unbelievable memory. Forgot nothing, neither what she had seen nor what she had heard. Addresses, phone numbers, faces. There was a joke about the phone book, which she knew by heart. She wasn't proud of it. 'How come you can't too?' she said. 'I don't understand how one can be so forgetful.' Her mother had run away or had died young, I don't know anymore, and the father was arrested and dragged off one morning, a railroad worker they suspected of sabotage.

"She became Jorge's lover. He was smitten with her, we were worried about it, such things are always dangerous. She liked him, but he wasn't her passion. That gnawed at him, made him edgy and sick with jealousy. 'Not to worry,' he said when I looked at him pensively. 'You're not the only one who's not a beginner.'

"The school for illiterates was her idea. Brilliant. Salazar had started a campaign against illiteracy, learning to read as a patriotic duty. We arranged for a room, stocked it with old benches and a desk. Enormous blackboard. The girl got hold of whatever educational materials there were, pictures illustrating letters, such things. Everybody could sit in a class of illiterates, every age. That was the trick: nobody needed to justify his presence to the outside, and moreover, with stool pigeons, you could insist on discretion, it's a stigma not to know how to read. Estefânia sent out the invitations, made sure they weren't opened, even though they said only: *Do we see each other on Friday? Kisses, Noëlia,* the imaginary name as a password.

"We met. Discussed plans. In case somebody from the P.I.D.E. should show up or any strange face, the girl would simply pick up a piece of chalk, she had prepared the board as if we were in the middle of a lesson. That was also part of the trick: we could meet openly, we didn't need to hide. We could do whatever we wanted with the pigs. Resistance isn't anything to laugh at. But sometimes we laughed.

"Estefânia's memory became increasingly important. We didn't have to write down anything, didn't have to leave a paper trail. The whole network was behind her forehead. Sometimes I thought: what if she got in an accident? But she was so young and so beautiful, flourishing life, you pushed the thoughts aside, we went on and landed one blow after another.

"One evening, it was in the fall of 1971, Amadeu entered the room. He saw her and was spellbound. When the meeting broke up, he went to her and spoke with her. Jorge waited in the door. She hardly looked at Amadeu, lowered her eyes immediately. I saw it coming.

"Nothing happened. Jorge and Estefânia stayed together. Amadeu didn't come to meetings anymore. Later, I found out that she went to his office. She was crazy about him. Amadeu rejected her. He was loyal to O'Kelly. Loyal to the point of self-denial. Through the winter, things stayed in this tense calm. Sometimes Jorge was seen with Amadeu. Something had changed, something intangible. When they walked beside each other, it was as if they were no longer walking in step as before. As if the solidarity had become an effort. And between O'Kelly and the girl, something had also changed. He controlled himself, but now and then irritability flashed, he corrected her, was refuted by her memory and left. Even so, things might have come to a head, but it would have been harmless, compared to what now happened.

"In late February, one of Mendes's minions burst into the meeting. He had opened the door silently and stood in the room, an intelligent, dangerous man, we knew him. Estefânia was unbelievable. As soon as she saw him, she broke off a sentence about a dangerous operation, picked up the chalk and the pointer and lectured about the *ç,* I don't know exactly that it was *ç*. Badajoz—that was the man's name, like the Spanish city—sat down, I can still hear the bench squeak in the breathless silence. Estefânia took off her jacket, although it was cool in the room. To be safe, she always dressed seductively at our meetings. With bare arms and the see-through blouse, she was . . . you could lose your mind on the spot. O'Kelly hated it. Badajoz crossed his legs.

"With a provocative spin of her body, Estefânia ended the would-be lesson. 'Until next time,' she said. The people stood up, you could feel the arduous self-control. Estefânia's music professor sitting next to me, stood up. Badajoz came to him.

"I knew it. I knew that was disaster.

" 'An illiterate professor,' said Badajoz and his face twisted into a nasty, repulsive grin. 'Something new, congratulations on the educational experience.'

"The professor turned pale and ran his tongue over his dry lips. But he held up well in the circumstances.

" 'I recently met someone who never learned to read. I knew of Senhora Espinhosa's course, she is my student, and I wanted to get an idea before I suggested to the person in question to try it,' he said.

" 'Aha,' said Badajoz. 'What's his name?'

"I was glad the others had disappeared. I didn't have my knife on me. I cursed myself.

" 'João Pinto,' said the professor.

" 'How original,' grinned Badajoz. 'And the address?'

"The address the professor gave didn't exist. They summoned him and kept him. Estefânia didn't go home anymore. I forbade her to stay at O'Kelly's place. 'Be reasonable,' I said to him. 'That's much too dangerous, if she's busted, you'll be busted with her.' I put her up with an old aunt.

"Amadeu asked me to come to the office. He had spoken with Jorge. He was out of his mind. Thoroughly beside himself. In this quiet, pale way that was peculiar to him.

" 'He wants to kill her,' he said flatly. 'He didn't say it in so many words, but it's clear: he wants to kill Estefânia. To wipe out her memory before they catch her. Just imagine: Jorge, my old friend

Jorge, my best friend, my only real friend. He's gone crazy, he wants to sacrifice his lover. *It's about many lives,* he kept saying. One life against many, that's his calculation. Help me, you must help me, it mustn't happen.'

"If I hadn't always known it—I realized in this conversation, at the latest: Amadeu loved her. Naturally, I couldn't know how it had been with Fátima, I had seen the two of them only that one time in Brighton, and yet I was sure: this was something completely different, something much wilder, white-hot lava shortly before the eruption. Amadeu was a walking paradox: self-confident and of fearless demeanor, but also one who constantly felt the look of others on him and suffered from it. That was why he had come to us, he wanted to defend himself against the accusation about Mendes. Estefânia, I think, was his chance to finally leave the courthouse, go out to the free, hot square of life, and live this one time completely according to his wishes, according to his passion, and the hell with the others.

"He knew of this chance, I'm sure of that, he knew himself relatively well, better than most, but there was this barrier, the iron barrier of loyalty to Jorge. Amadeu, he was the most loyal person in the universe, loyalty was his religion. Loyalty stood against freedom and a little happiness, nothing less. He had braced himself against the internal avalanche of desire and had averted his hungry eyes when he saw the girl. He wanted to keep being able to look Jorge in the eye, he didn't want a forty-year-old friendship to break up because of a daydream, however searing.

"And now, Jorge wanted to take away from him the girl who had never belonged to him. Wanted to destroy the unstable internal balance between loyalty and denied hope. That was too much.

"I talked with O'Kelly. He denied saying anything of the sort or even implying it. He had red spots on his unshaved face and it was hard to say if they were connected more with Estefânia or with Amadeu.

"He was lying. I knew it and he knew that I knew.

"He had started drinking, he felt that Estefânia was slipping away from him, with or without Amadeu, and he couldn't bear it.

" 'We could take her out of the country,' I said.

" 'They'll catch her,' he said. 'The professor is willing, but not strong enough, they'll crack him, then they'll know that everything is behind her forehead, and they'll hunt her down, they'll use everything they've got, it's simply *too* important, imagine, *the whole Lisbon network,* they won't rest until they have her, and they're an army.' "

The nurses had knocked on the door and called for dinner, Eça had ignored them and gone on talking. It was dark in the room and Eça's voice sounded to Gregorius as if it came from another world.

"What I say now will shock you: I understood O'Kelly. I understood both him and his arguments, for those were two different things. If they gave her an injection and cracked her memory, all of us were in it, some two hundred people, and it would be many times over, if they dragged every individual over the coals. It was inconceivable. You needed to imagine only a part of it and you thought: *She has to go.*

"In this sense, I understood O'Kelly. I still believe it would have been a justifiable murder. Whoever said no simply didn't get it. A lack of imagination, I'd say. The wish for clean hands as the highest principle. I find it repulsive.

"I think that, in this matter, Amadeu couldn't think clearly, he pictured her shining eyes, the unusual, almost Asian complexion, the contagious, thrilling laugh, the swaying walk, and he simply didn't want all that to die out, *he could not want it,* and I am glad he couldn't, for anything else would have made him a monster, a monster of self-denial.

"O'Kelly, on the other hand—I suspect that he also saw it as a redemption, redemption from the torment of not being able to keep her anymore and of knowing that passion drew her to Amadeu. And in that, too, I understood him, but in a completely different sense, that is, without approval. I understood him because I recognized myself in his feeling. It had been a long time, but I had also lost a woman to somebody else and she had also brought music into my life, not Bach as with O'Kelly, but Schubert. I knew what it meant to dream of such a redemption and I knew how much you can seek a pretext for such a plan.

"And precisely because of that, I threw a monkey wrench into O'Kelly's plan. I got the girl out of hiding and took her to the blue office. Adriana hated me for it, but she hated me even before, for her, I was the man who had hijacked her brother into the resistance.

"I spoke with people who knew their way around the mountains on the border, and instructed Amadeu. He stayed away a week. When he came back, he was sick. Estefânia I never saw again.

"They caught me shortly after, but that had nothing to do with her. They said she was at Amadeu's funeral. Much later, I heard that she was working in Salamanca, as a lecturer in history.

"With O'Kelly, I haven't spoken a word for ten years. Today it's all right again, but we don't seek each other out. He knows what I thought back then, that doesn't make it any easier."

Eça took a fierce drag on his cigarette, the burning ash ate along the paper that shimmered bright in the dark. He coughed.

"Every time Amadeu visited me in the slammer, I was tempted to ask him about O'Kelly, about their friendship. I didn't dare. Amadeu never threatened anybody, that was part of his credo. But, without knowing it, he could *be* a threat. The threat of shattering before the eyes of the others. Naturally, I couldn't ask Jorge either. Maybe today, after more than thirty years, I don't know. Can a friendship survive such a thing?

"When I came out, I looked for the professor. Since the day of the arrest, nobody had heard from him anymore. Those pigs.

Tarrafal. Have you ever heard of Tarrafal? I had counted on being sent there. Salazar was senile and the P.I.D.E. did what it wanted. I think it was an accident that it didn't come to that, accident is the brother of arbitrariness. In that case, I had planned to ram my head against the wall of the cell until the skull broke."

They fell silent. Gregorius didn't know what he could have said.

Finally, Eça stood up and turned on the light. He rubbed his eyes and made the opening move he always made. They played until the fourth move, then Eça pushed the board aside. The two men stood up. Eça took his hands out of the sweater pockets. They approached each other and embraced. Eça's body shook. A raw sound of animal strength and helplessness came out of his throat. Then he grew limp and held on tight to Gregorius. Gregorius stroked his head. When he softly unlocked the door, Eça was standing at the window and looking out into the night.

32

Gregorius stood in the parlor of Silveira's house and looked at a row of photographs, snapshots of a big party. Most of the men wore frock coats, the ladies long evening gowns whose trains brushed the shining parquet floor. José António da Silveira was also seen, many years younger, with a woman, a voluptuous blond who reminded Gregorius of Anita Ekberg in the Trevi Fountain. The children, maybe seven or eight, ran after one another under the endless buffet table. Over one of the tables the family coat of arms, a silver bear with a red sash. In another picture, they all sat in a parlor and listened to a young woman playing the grand piano, an alabaster beauty with a distant resemblance to the nameless Portuguese woman on the Kirchenfeldbrücke.

After arriving in the villa, Gregorius had sat on the bed for a long time and waited for the shock at parting from João Eça to subside. The raw sound from his throat, a dry sob, a cry for help, a memory of torture, everything together—he would never erase it from his memory. He wished he could pour so much hot tea into himself that would wash away the pain in Eça's breast.

Then, slowly, the details of the story about Estefânia Espinhosa came back into his mind. Salamanca, she had become a lecturer in Salamanca. The railroad station sign with the dark medieval name emerged before him. Then the sign disappeared and he thought of the scene Father Bartolomeu had described: how O'Kelly and the woman, without looking at each other, had walked toward each other and had then stood at Prado's grave. *That they avoided looking at each other created a greater closeness between them than any crossing of looks could have.*

Finally, Gregorius had unpacked the suitcase and put the books on a shelf. It was very quiet in the house. Julieta, the maid, had gone and put a note for him on the kitchen table where to find the food. Gregorius had never been in a house like this and everything seemed forbidden, even the sound of his steps. Switch after switch, he had turned on the lights. The dining room, where they had eaten together. The bathroom. Even into Silveira's study, he had cast a brief glance, only to close the door again right away.

And now he stood in the parlor where they had drunk coffee and said the word *nobreza* into the room, he liked it, it was terrific, and he kept repeating it. And *aristocracy*, he now became aware that he had always liked it, it was a word things flowed into, or vice versa. De l'Arronge—Florence's maiden name—had never made him think of aristocracy, and she didn't make anything of it either. Lucien von Graffenried: that was something else, old Bern aristocracy, he thought of a noble, impeccable sandstone structure, at the corner of Gerechtigkeitsgasse and that there had been a von Graffenried who had played some vague role in Beirut.

And naturally, Eva von Muralt, Unbelievable. It had only been a school party, not comparable with Silveira's photos in any way, and yet he had sweated with excitement in the high rooms. "Unbelievable!" Eva had said when a boy asked her if an aristocratic title could be bought. "Unbelievable!" she had also shouted when Gregorius wanted to wash the dishes at the end.

Silveira's record collection made a dusty impression. As if the period in his life when music had played a role was long gone. Gregorius found Berlioz, *Les Nuits d'Été, La Belle Voyageuse* and

La Mort d'Ophélie, the music Prado had loved because it reminded him of Fátima. *Estefânia was his chance to finally leave the courthouse, go out to the free, hot square of life.*

Maria João. He had to find Maria João. If anybody knew what happened on the flight back then and why Prado became sick after the return, it was she.

He spent an uneasy night, listening to every unfamiliar sound. The scattered dream images looked alike: they teemed with aristocratic women, limousines and chauffeurs. And they hunted Estefânia. They hunted her, and he didn't see even a single image of the hunt. He woke up with his heart racing, had to fight dizziness, and sat down at the kitchen table at about five with the other letter Adriana had brought him.

My esteemed, dear son,

Over the years, I have started so many letters to you and thrown them away, so that I don't know what number this one is. Why is it so hard?

Can you imagine how it is to have a son blessed with so much alertness and so many talents? A son powerful with words who gives his father the feeling that all he has left is silence so as not to sound like a bungler? As a law student, I enjoyed the reputation of being deft with words. And in the Reis family, your mother's family, I was introduced as an eloquent attorney. My speeches against Sidónio Pais, the gallant fraud in uniform, and for Teófilo Braga, the man with the umbrella in the streetcar, made an impression. So how come I fell silent?

You were four when you came to me with your first book to read me two sentences: Lisbon is our capital. It is a beautiful city. *It was Sunday afternoon, after a downpour, muggy, heavy air streamed in through the window, steeped with the smell of wet flowers. You had knocked on the door, stuck your head in and asked: "Do you have a minute?" Like the grown-up son of an aristocratic house who approaches the head of the family respectfully and requests an audience. I liked the precocious manners, but at the same time I was also scared. What had we done wrong that you didn't come crashing in like other children? Your mother hadn't told me anything about the book and I was flabbergasted when you read me the sentences without the slightest hesitation and with the clear voice of a lecturer. And it was not only clear, the voice, but also full of love for words, so that the two simple sentences sounded like poetry. (It is childish, but sometimes I thought that they were the origin of your homesickness, your legendary homesickness you savored, without it being any less true because of that; indeed you had never even been out of Lisbon, and couldn't possibly know the homesickness, you must have had it before you could have it, but who knows, you are capable of everything, even the inconceivable.)*

A radiant intelligence filled the room and I still know that I thought: How little the naïveté of the sentences suits his cleverness! Later, when I was alone again, pride gave way to another thought: from now on, his mind will be like a dazzling spotlight that mercilessly illuminates all my weaknesses. I believe that was the beginning of my fear of you. For yes, I was afraid of you.

How hard it is for a father to face up to his children! And how hard to endure the thought that one is registered in their souls with all his weaknesses, his blindness, his errors and his cowardice! Originally, I had these thoughts when I thought of the heredity of the Morbus Bechterev, which spared you, thank God. Later, I thought more of the soul, our inside, that is as receptive to impressions as a wax tablet and records everything with a seismographic precision. I stood before the mirror and thought: What will this stern face cause in them?

But what can you do to shape your face? Not nothing, for I don't mean the simple physiognomy. But not much. We aren't the sculptors of our facial features or the stage managers of our seriousness, our laughing and weeping.

From the first two sentences came hundreds, thousands, millions. Sometimes, it seemed as if the books you held belonged to you like the hands that held them. Once when you were reading outside on the steps, a ball from a children's game strayed to you. Your hands left the book and threw the ball back. How strange the movement of the hand was!

I loved you as a reader, I loved you very much. Even if you were strange to me in your consuming rage for reading.

Even stranger was your fervor as you carried the candles to the altar. Unlike your mother, I didn't believe for a moment that you could become a priest. You have the soul of a rebel and rebels don't become priests. So what goal would the ardor finally have, what object would it seek? That it possessed an explosive force, this ardor, that was palpable. I was afraid of the explosions it could produce.

I felt this fear when I saw you in court. I had to condemn the thief and send her to prison, the law demanded it. Why did you look at me at the table as if I were a torturer? Your look paralyzed me, I couldn't talk about it. Do you have a better idea of what we should do with thieves? Do you?

I saw you grow up, I was amazed at the drizzle of your mind, I heard your curses of God. I didn't like your friend Jorge, anarchists frighten me, but I was glad you had a friend, a boy like you, it could have been different, your mother dreamed of you pale and quiet behind the walls of an institution. She was deeply horrified at the text of your graduation address. "A blasphemous son, what did I do to deserve it?" she said.

And I read the text. And was proud! And jealous! Jealous of the independent thinking and of the upright walk that spoke from every one of your lines. They were like a shining horizon I would also like to reach, but never could, the leaden gravity of my upbringing was too great for that. How could I have explained my proud jealousy to you? Without making myself small, even smaller and more dejected than I already was?

It was crazy, thought Gregorius: both men, father and son, had lived on opposite hills of the city like opposing actors in an ancient drama, linked in an archaic fear of each other and in an affection they didn't find the words for and had written letters to each other that they didn't trust themselves to send. Clasped in a muteness neither understood, and blind to the fact that one muteness produced the other.

"Madam sometimes sat here, too," said Julieta, when she came in the late morning and found him at the kitchen table. "But she didn't read any books, only magazines."

She observed him. Hadn't he slept well? Or was there something wrong with the bed?

He was fine, said Gregorius, he hadn't felt so good in a long time.

She was glad there was someone else in the house now, she said, Senhor da Silveira had become so quiet and closed in. "I hate hotels," he had said recently when she had helped him pack. "Why do I go on? Can you tell me that, Julieta?"

33

He was the strangest student she ever had, said Cecília.

"You know more literary words than most people in the streetcar, but when you curse, shop, or book a trip, you have no idea. Not to mention flirting. Or do you know what you'd have to say to me?"

Shivering, she pulled the green shawl around her shoulders.

"And the man has the slowest quick-wittedness I've ever encountered. Slow and yet quick-witted—wouldn't have thought that possible. But with you . . ."

Under her withering look, Gregorius took out the grammar book and pointed to a mistake.

"Yes," she said and the green scarf in front of her lips billowed, "but sometimes the sloppy way is the right way. That was certainly so even with the Greeks."

On the way to Silveira's house, Gregorius drank a coffee across from O'Kelly's pharmacy. Now and then he saw the smoking pharmacist through the display window. *He was smitten with her,* he heard João Eça say. *She liked him, but he wasn't her passion. It made him edgy and sick with jealousy . . . Amadeu entered the room, she saw and was spellbound.* Gregorius took out Prado's notes and looked up something.

But when we set out to understand somebody's inside? Is that a trip that ever ends? Is the soul a place of facts? Or are the alleged facts only the deceptive shadows of our stories?

On the streetcar to Belém, all of a sudden he felt that his sense of the city had changed. So far, it had been exclusively the place of his investigations, and the time that had flowed through it had taken its shape from the plan to keep finding out more about Prado. Now, when he looked out through the window of the tram, the time when the car crept along creaking and groaning was all his, it was simply the time when Raimund Gregorius was living his new life. He saw himself standing again in the Bern tram depot and asking about the old cars. Three weeks ago, he had had the feeling of traveling here through the Bern of his childhood. Now he was traveling through Lisbon and only Lisbon. He felt as if something had been rearranged deep inside himself.

In Silveira's house, he called Frau Loosli and dictated his new address to her. Then he called the hotel and found out that the Persian grammar had come. The balcony was in the light of the warm spring sunshine. He listened to the people in the street and was amazed how much he understood. From somewhere came the smell of food. He thought of the tiny balcony of his childhood, where the vapors of repulsive cooking smells had hovered. Later, when he lay under the blanket in Silveira's son's room, he had fallen asleep after a few moments and found himself in a contest of quick-wittedness in which the slowest won. He stood with Eva von Muralt, Unbelievable, at the sink and washed the party dishes. Finally, he sat in Kägi's office and spent hours calling distant lands where nobody picked up the phone.

In Silveira's house, too, time began to be his own. For the first time since he was in Lisbon, he turned on the television and saw the evening news. He moved very close to the set so there was as little distance as possible between him and the words. He was surprised at everything that had happened in the meantime and what a different facet of the world was considered important here. On the other hand, it was also amazing that the familiar here was the same as at home. He thought: *I'm living here. Vivo aqui.* The film that came next, he couldn't follow. In the parlor, he put on the record of Berlioz's music that Prado had listened to for days after Fátima's death. It echoed through the whole house. After a while, he sat down at the kitchen table and finished reading the letter the judge had written to his feared son.

Sometimes, my son, increasingly more often, you seem to me a self-righteous judge who reproaches me for still wearing the robes. For seeming to shut my eyes to the cruelty of the regime. Then I feel your look on me as a searing light. And would like to pray to God to fill you with more understanding and take the executioner's glitter out of your eyes. Why didn't You grant him more imagination about me?—*I'd like to shout at Him and it would be a shout full of resentment.*

For you see: great, even excessive, as your imagination can be, you have no idea of what pain and a twisted back make of a person. Well, nobody *seems to have an idea of that except the victims.* Nobody. *You gave me a splendid explanation of what Vladimir Bechterev found. And I wouldn't want to miss a single one of these conversations, they are precious hours when I feel safe with you. But then it's past, and I return to the hell of being stooped and enduring. And the one thing you seem never to consider: that you can't expect the same thing from slaves of the humiliating curvature and the incessant pain as from those who can forget their body, in order to relish it when they come back to it.* That you can't expect the same thing from them! *And that they depend on* not having to say it themselves, *for that would be a new humiliation!*

The truth—yes the truth—is quite simple: I wouldn't know how I should have endured life if Enrique didn't pick me up every morning at ten to six. Sundays—you have no idea what a torture they are. Sometimes I don't sleep Saturday night because I anticipate how it will be. That even on Saturday at quarter after six, I enter the empty building: they joke about it. Sometimes I think that more cruelty is produced by thoughtlessness than by any other human weakness. I keep asking for a key for Sundays. They refused. Sometimes I wished they had my pains for one day, one single day, so they'd understand.

When I enter the office, the pain subsides a little, it's as if the room changes into a relieving prop inside the body. Until shortly before eight, it's quiet in the building. I usually study the files for the day, I have to be sure there are no surprises, a man like me is scared of that. Sometimes I also read poetry, my breath calms down, it's as if I were looking at the sea and sometimes that helps against the pain. Now do you understand?

But Tarrafal, you will say. Yes, Tarrafal, I know, I know. Should I give up the key because of that? I've tried it out, more than once. I took it off the key ring and put it on the desk. Then I left the building and walked through the streets as if I had really done it. I breathed into my back as the doctor recommended, the breathing grew louder and louder, I walked through the city gasping, hot with fear that someday the imaginary act could become real. With a sweaty shirt, I later sat at the judge's bench. Now do you understand?

It isn't only to you that I have written countless letters that disappeared. I've also kept writing to the minister. And one of the letters I put in the house mail. I caught the postman on the street before he delivered it to the minister. He was annoyed to have to rummage through his bag and he looked at me with the contemptuous curiosity many people show for an error. I threw the letter where the others went: into the river. So that the treacherous ink would be washed away. Now *do you understand?*

Maria João Flores, your loyal classmate, understood. One day, when I could no longer bear how you looked at me, I met her.

"He would like to worship you," she said and put her hand on mine; "worship and love as one loves a paragon. 'I don't want to see him as a sick man who is forgiven everything,' he said. 'It would then be as if

I no longer had a father.' He assigns a very definite role to others in his soul and is merciless when they don't fit it. A refined kind of egoism."

She looked at me and gave me a smile that came from the broad steppe of a keenly lived life.

"Why don't you try it with rage?"

Gregorius picked up the last sheet. The few sentences were written with another ink and the judge had dated it June 8, 1954, a day before his death.

The struggle is at an end. What, my son, can I say to you in farewell?

You became a doctor for my sake. What would have happened if there had not been the shadow of my life where you grew up? I am in your debt. You are not responsible that the pain remained and my resistance has now broken.

I left the key in the office. They'll blame it all on the pain. That a failure can also die—the idea is foreign to you.

Will my death satisfy you?

Gregorius was freezing and turned on the furnace. *Amadeu came within a hairsbreadth of seeing it, but I had an idea and hid it,* he heard Adriana say. The furnace didn't help. He turned on the television and sat still before a soap opera he didn't understand a word of, it could have been Chinese. In the bathroom, he found a sleeping pill. When it started to take effect, it was growing light outside.

34

There were two Maria João Floreses who lived in Campo de Ourique. The next day, after language school, Gregorius went there. At the first doorbell he rang, lived a young woman with two children hanging on her skirt. In the other house, he was told that Senhora Flores had gone away two days before.

He picked up the Persian grammar book in the hotel and went out to the Liceu. Migratory birds swooshed over the abandoned building. He had hoped the hot African wind would come back, but the mild March air remained, with a whiff of wintry sharpness.

In the grammar book was a note from Natalie Rubin: *I made it up to here!* The letters were tough, she had said when he called her to say that the book had arrived. For days, she had done nothing else, her parents were amazed at her diligence. When was he planning his trip to Iran? Wouldn't that be a little dangerous these days?

The year before, Gregorius had read in the newspaper an ironic commentary about a man who had started learning Chinese at the age of ninety. The author had made fun of the man. *You have no idea*—with this sentence, Gregorius had begun his draft of a letter to the editor. "Why do you waste the days with such things?" Doxiades had said when he saw his anger devouring him. He hadn't sent the letter. But Doxiades's casual manner had bothered him.

A few days ago, in Bern, when he had tested how many Persian letters he still remembered, only a few had come back to him. But now, with the book before his eyes, it went quickly. *I am still there, at that distant place in time, I never left it, but live expanded in the past, or out of it,* Prado had noted. *The thousand changes time has accelerated—they are, measured by this timeless present of feeling, fleeting and unreal as a dream.*

The cone of light in Senhor Cortês's office moved. Gregorius thought of the irrevocably silent face of his dead father. He would like to have gone to him back then with his fear of the Persian sandstorm. But he hadn't been such a father.

He made the long way to Belém on foot and arranged it so that he passed by the house where the judge had lived with his muteness, his pain, and the fear of his son's judgment. The cedars stood out in the black night sky. Gregorius thought of the scar under the velvet ribbon on Adriana's neck. Behind the lighted windows, Mélodie went from room to room. She knew whether these were the red cedars. And what they had to do with the fact that a court could have accused Amadeu of bodily injury.

It was now the third evening in Silveira's house. *Vivo aqui.* Gregorius went through the house, through the dark garden, to the street. He strolled through the neighborhood and looked at the people, cooking, eating, watching television. When he was back where he started, he looked at the pale yellow façade and the illuminated porch with columns. An elegant house in a wealthy neighborhood. *I live here now.* In the parlor, he sat down in a chair. What could that mean? He could no longer touch the Bubenbergplatz. Would he eventually be able to touch the ground of Lisbon? What kind of touch would it be? And how would his steps look on this ground?

To live for the moment: it sounds so right and so beautiful, Prado had remarked in one of his brief notes, *but the more I want to, the less I understand what it means.*

In all his life, Gregorius had never been bored. That somebody didn't know what to do with the time of his life: there were few things he found as incomprehensible as that. Even now he wasn't bored. What he felt in the silent, much-too-big house was something else: time stood still, or no, it didn't stand still, but it didn't pull him on with it, didn't approach any future, flowed by him indifferent, not touching.

He went into the boy's room and looked at the titles of the Simenon novels. *L'homme qui regardait passer les trains.* It was the novel whose stills had hung in the window of the Bubenberg Cinema, black-and-white pictures with Jeanne Moreau. It had been three weeks ago yesterday, Monday, when he had passed by there. The film must have been made in the sixties. Forty years ago. How long was that?

Gregorius hesitated to open Prado's book. Reading the letters had changed something. The father's letter even more than the son's. Finally, he started leafing through it. There weren't many pages left that he didn't know yet. How would it be after the last sentence? The last sentence he had always feared and from the middle of a book, he had always been tormented by the thought that there would inevitably be a last sentence. But this time, it was much harder with the last sentence than usual. It would be as if the invisible thread that had bound him with the Spanish bookstore on Hirschengraben would be broken. He would delay turning the last page and slow down his look, as best he could, it wasn't completely in your hands. The last look into the dictionary, more exhaustive than necessary. The last word. The last period. Then he would arrive in Lisbon. In Lisbon, Portugal.

TEMPO ENIGMÁTICO. ENIGMATIC TIME. *It took me a year to find out how long a month is. It was in October last year, on the last day of the month. What happens every year happened and what nevertheless throws me off every year, as if I had never before experienced it: The new faded morning light announced winter. No more burning light, no painful dazzle, no sweltering air you want to flee from to the shadows. A mild, conciliatory light that visibly contained the impending shortness of the days. Not that I would meet the new light as an enemy, as one who rejects and fights it in comical helplessness. It saves strength when the world loses the sharp corners of summer and shows us more blurred outlines that demand less resolve.*

No, it wasn't the pale, milky veil of the new light that made me flinch. It was the fact that the broken, weakened light once again indicated the irrevocable end of a period in nature and a temporal segment in my life. What had I done since the end of March, since the day when the cup on the table of the café had become hot in the sun again so that I winced when I picked it up? Had it been a lot of time that had flowed since then, or a little? Seven months—how long was that?

I usually avoid the kitchen, that's Ana's domain and there is something about her vigorous juggling of the pans that I don't like. But that day, I needed somebody to whom I could express my silent fear, even if I couldn't put a name to it.

"How long is a month?" I asked out of the blue.

Ana, who was about to light the gas, blew out the match.

"You mean?"

Her forehead was wrinkled like someone confronting an insoluble puzzle.

"What I say: how long is a month?"

Looking down, she rubbed her hands in embarrassment.

"Well, sometimes they're thirty days, sometimes . . ."

"I know that," I said gruffly. "But the question is: how long is that?"

Ana reached for the spoon to give her hands something to do.

"Once, I took care of my daughter for almost a month," she said hesitantly and with the caution of a psychiatrist afraid his words could cause a collapse in his patient that could never be restored. "Up and down the steps many times a day with the soup that mustn't be spilled—that was long."

"And how was it afterward, looking back?"

Now Ana risked a smile of relief that her answer apparently hadn't been wrong. "Still long. But somehow it kept getting shorter, I don't know."

"The time with all the soup—do you miss it now?"

Ana moved the spoon back and forth, then she took a handkerchief out of her apron and blew her nose. "Naturally I wanted to take care of the child, she really wasn't so sulky at the time. Nevertheless, I wouldn't like to have to do it again, I was constantly scared because we didn't know what it was or whether it was dangerous."

"I mean something else: whether you regret that that moment is past; that time has run out; that you can't do anything more with it."

"Well, yes, it's past," said Ana, and now she no longer looked like a pensive doctor, but like an intimidated schoolgirl.

"It's all right," I said and turned to the door. As I went out, I heard her strike a new match. Why was I always so short, so curt, so ungrateful for the words of others when it was something really important to me? Why the need to defend what's important rabidly against the others, when they really didn't want to take it away from me?

The next morning, the first day of November, I went at dawn to the arch at the end of Rua Augusta, the most beautiful street in the world. The sea in the wan morning light was like a smooth surface of flat silver. To experience with special alertness how long a month is—that was the idea that had driven me out of bed. In the café, I was the first one. When there were only a few sips left in the cup, I slowed down the usual pace of drinking. I was uncertain what I should do when the cup was empty. It would be very long, this first day, if I simply sat still. And what I wanted to know wasn't how long a month is for those who are completely inactive. But what was it I did *want to know?*

Sometimes I am so slow. Only today, when the light of early November breaks again do I notice that the question I asked Ana—about the irrevocability, the transience, the regret, the sadness—wasn't really the question that had preoccupied me. The question I had wanted to ask was completely different: What does it depend on when we have experienced a month as a fulfilled time, our time, instead of a time that has passed us by, which we only suffered, that ran through our fingers, so that it seems to us like a lost, past time, and we're not sad because it's past, but because we couldn't do anything with it? So, the question was not how long is a month, but rather: What can you do for yourself with the time of a month? When is it that I have the impression that this month was all mine?

So it is wrong when I say it took me a year to find out how long a month is. It was different: it took me a year to find out what I wanted to know when I posed the misleading question about the length of a month.

Early the next afternoon, when he came from language school, Gregorius ran into Mariana Eça. When he turned the corner and saw her coming toward him, he knew all at once why he had been afraid to call her: he would tell her about the attacks of dizziness, she would ponder aloud what it could be and he didn't want to hear that.

She suggested coffee and then told of João. "I waited all Sunday morning for him," he had said about Gregorius. "I don't know why, but I can talk to him about things that are weighing on me. Not that they would go away, but for a few hours, it gets easier." Gregorius told of Adriana and the clock, of Jorge and the chess club, and of Silveira's house. He was just about to mention the trip to Bern, but then he felt: that couldn't be told.

When he was done, she asked him about the new glasses and then she narrowed her eyes observantly. "You're sleeping too little," she said. He thought of the morning when she had examined him and he hadn't ever wanted to get up from the chair in front of her desk. Of the thorough examination. Of the boat trip together to Cacilhas and the red-gold Assam he had later drunk in her house.

"Recently I've been dizzy sometimes," he said. And after a pause: "I'm scared."

An hour later, he left her office. She had examined his visual acuity again and measured the blood pressure, he had to do knee bends and balancing exercises and she had him describe the dizziness very precisely. Then she had written down the address of a neurologist for him.

"It doesn't seem dangerous to me," she had said, "and it's not surprising when you think of how much has changed in your life in a short time. But the usual things have to be examined."

He pictured the empty square on the wall of Prado's office where the map of the brain had hung. She saw the panic in him.

"A tumor would bring completely different symptoms," she said and stroked his arm.

It wasn't far to Mélodie's house.

"I knew you'd come again," she said when she opened the door to him. "After your visit, Amadeu was quite present to me for a few days."

Gregorius gave her the letters to father and son to read.

"That's unjust," she said when she had read the last words of the father's letter. "Unjust. Unfair. As if Amadeu had driven him to death. His doctor was a shrewd man. He prescribed only small quantities of sleeping pills for him. But Papá could wait. Patience was his forte. A patience like a mute stone. Mamã saw it coming. She always saw everything coming. She didn't do anything to prevent it. 'Now it doesn't hurt him anymore,' she said when we stood at the open coffin. I loved her for these words. 'And he doesn't have to torment himself anymore,' I said. 'Yes,' she said, 'that, too.'"

Gregorius told of his visits to Adriana. She hadn't been in the blue house after Amadeu's death, said Mélodie, but she wasn't surprised that Adriana had made it into a museum and a shrine where time stood still.

"She admired him even as a little girl. He was the big brother who could do everything. Who dared to resist Papá! A year after he had gone to study in Coimbra, she transferred to the girls' school across from the Liceu. The same school Maria João had attended. There, Amadeu was the hero of the past and she enjoyed being the hero's sister. Nevertheless: things would have taken a different, more normal turn if not for the drama when he saved her life."

It had happened when Adriana was nineteen. Amadeu, who was soon to take the official exams, was at home and sat behind his books day and night. He came down only for meals. It was at one such family meal that Adriana choked.

"We all had food on our plate and didn't notice anything at first. Suddenly, a strange noise, a horrible gasp came from Adriana, she clasped her neck and stamped her feet. Amadeu was sitting next to me, steeped in preparation for the exam, we were used to him sitting there like a mute ghost and blindly shoveling in the food. I nudged him with my elbow and pointed to Adriana. He looked up confused. Adriana's face had turned purple, she wasn't getting any more air, and her helpless look went to Amadeu. We all knew the expression that appeared on his face, it was the expression of furious concentration he always had when there was something difficult he didn't understand immediately, he was used to understanding everything immediately.

"Now he jumped up, the chair toppled back, with a few steps he was next to Adriana, grabbed her under the arms and stood her up, turned her with her back to him, then he embraced her shoulders, took air in for a moment and jerked her torso back violently. A choked gasp came from Adriana. Nothing else. Amadeu jerked twice more in the same way, but the piece of meat lodged in her windpipe didn't move now either.

"What happened then was etched in all of us forever, second after second, movement after movement. Amadeu sat Adriana back on the chair and ordered me to come to him. He bent her head back.

"'Hold on,' he said in a strained voice. 'Tight.'

"Then he took the sharp meat knife from his place and wiped it on the napkin. We held our breath.

"'No!' shouted Mamã. 'No!'

"I don't think he even heard it. He straddled Adriana's lap and looked her in the eye.

"'I have to do this,' he said, and even now I'm amazed at how calm his voice was. 'Otherwise, you'll die. Take your hands away. Trust me.'

"Adriana took her hands off her neck. He groped with his index finger for the gap between thyroid cartilage and annular cartilage. Then he put the tip of the knife in the middle of the gap. A deep breath, a brief shutting of the eyes, then he stabbed.

"I was concentrating on holding Adriana's head tight as in a vise. I didn't see the blood spray, saw it only afterward on his shirt. Adriana's body convulsed. That Amadeu had found the way to the windpipe was heard in Adriana's whistling as she sucked in air through the new opening. I opened my eyes and saw with horror that Amadeu was turning the blade of the knife in the wound, it looked like an act of special brutality, I grasped only later that he had to keep the air passage open. Now, Amadeu took a ballpoint pen out of his shirt pocket, stuck it between his teeth, unscrewed the top with his free hand, ripped out the cartridge and put the bottom part in the wound as a cannula. Slowly, he pulled out the blade and held the pen tight. Adriana's breath was jerky and whistling, but she was alive and the color of the choking slowly subsided from her face.

"'Ambulance!' Amadeu ordered.

"Papá shook off his paralysis and went to the phone. We carried Adriana with the pen sticking out of her neck to the sofa. Amadeu stroked her hair.

"'It wouldn't work otherwise,' he said.

"The doctor, who appeared a few minutes later, put his hand on Amadeu's shoulder. 'That was close,' he said. 'This presence of mind. This courage. At your age.'

"When the ambulance had left with Adriana, Amadeu sat down at his place at the table in his bloodstained shirt. Nobody said a word. I think that was the worst thing for him: that nobody said anything. With his few words, the doctor had stated that Amadeu had done the right thing and had saved Adriana's life. And nevertheless, nobody said a word now, and the silence that filled the dining room was full of horrified amazement at his cold-bloodedness. 'The silence made me look like a butcher,' he said years later, the only time we talked of it.

"That we left him so completely alone at this moment he never got over, and it changed his relationship to the family forever. He came home less and then only as a polite guest.

"Suddenly, the silence shattered and Amadeu started shaking. He put his hands to his face and even now I still hear the dry sobs that racked his body. And again, we left him alone. I stroked his arm, but that was much too little, I was only the eight-year-old sister, he needed something quite different.

"That it didn't come was the last straw. All of a sudden, he leaped up, raced up to his room, ran back down with a medical textbook and banged the book down on the table with all his might, the cutlery hit the plates, the glasses clinked. 'Here,' he shouted, 'it says so here. The intervention is called a tracheotomy. Why are you gawking at me like that? You sat there like dummies! If not for me, we would have had to carry her out in a coffin!'

"They operated on Adriana and she stayed in the hospital for two weeks. Amadeu went there every day, always alone, he didn't want to go with us. Adriana was filled with an overwhelming gratitude, which was almost religious. With bandaged neck, she lay white on the pillows and kept going over the dramatic scene. When I was alone with her, she talked about it.

"'Shortly before he stabbed, the cedars in the window were red, bloodred,' she said. 'Then I blacked out.'"

She came out of the hospital, said Mélodie, with the conviction that she had to devote her life to the brother who had saved it for her. That gave Amadeu the creeps and he tried everything to talk her out of the idea. For a while, it seemed to work, she met a Frenchman who fell in love with her and the dramatic episode seemed to fade in her. But this love collapsed the moment Adriana got pregnant. And again Amadeu intervened. He gave up his trip with Fátima for it and came back from England. She had studied to be a physician's assistant, and three years later, when he opened the blue office, it was clear that she would work as his assistant. Fátima refused to let her live in the house. There were dramatic scenes when she had to go. After Fátima's death, it took less than a week for Adriana to move in. Amadeu was completely thrown by the loss and incapable of resistance. Adriana had won.

35

"Sometimes I thought Amadeu's mind was mainly language," Mélodie had said at the end of the conversation. "That his soul was made of words, in a way I had never experienced with anybody else."

Gregorius had shown her the note on aneurysms. She hadn't known anything about that either. But there had been something she remembered now.

"He flinched when anybody used words that had to do with going, flowing, passing, I remember mainly *correr* and *passar*. He was generally somebody who reacted to words as fiercely as if they were much more important than things. If you wanted to understand my brother, that was the most important thing you had to know. He talked of the dictatorship of the wrong and the freedom of the right words, of the invisible dungeon of language kitsch and the light of poetry. He was a person possessed by language, bewitched by language, a wrong word meant more to him than a knife stab. And then suddenly, the fierce reaction to words dealing with ephemerality and transience. After one of his visits when he revealed this new jumpiness, my husband and I racked our brains half the night. 'Not these words, please not these words,' he had said. We didn't dare ask about it. My brother, he could be like a volcano."

Gregorius sat down in a chair in Silveira's parlor and began reading the text by Prado that Mélodie had given him.

"He was in a panic that it could fall into the wrong hands," she had said. "'Maybe I should have destroyed it,' he said. But then he gave it to me for safekeeping. I couldn't open the envelope until after his death. The scales fell from my eyes."

Prado had written the text in the winter months after the mother's death and gave it to Mélodie shortly before Fátima's death in the spring. There were three texts begun on separate sheets and in different shades of ink. Even though they fit together into a farewell letter to his mother, there was no address. Instead, the text had a title like many of the notes in the book.

DESPEDIDA FALHADA À MAMÃ. FAILED FAREWELL FROM MAMA. *My farewell from you has to fail, Mamã. You aren't here anymore, and a real farewell would have to be an encounter. I have waited too long and naturally, that's no accident. What distinguishes an honest farewell from a cowardly one? An honest farewell from you—that would have been the attempt to come to some understanding with you about how it was with us, you and me. For that is the meaning of a farewell in the full, important sense of the word: that the two people, before they part, come to an understanding of how they have seen and experienced each other. What succeeded between them and what failed. That takes fearlessness: you have to be able to endure the pain of dissonance. It is also about acknowledging what was impossible. Parting is also something you do with yourself: to stand by yourself under the look of the other. The cowardice of a farewell resides in the transfiguration: in the attempt to bathe* what was *in a golden light and deny the dark. What you forfeit in that is nothing less than the acknowledgment of your self in those features produced by darkness.*

You played a trick on me, Mamã, and I now write down what I should have told you a long time ago: it was a perfidious trick that burdened my life like nothing else. That is, you let me know—in no *uncertain terms—that you expected from me, your son—*your *son—nothing less than that he be the best. Never mind what, just that whatever I did had to surpass the achievements of all others and not only surpass somehow, but tower high above them. The perfidy: you never* said *that to me. Your expectation was never explicit, which would have allowed me to take a position on it, to think about it and argue with my feelings about it. And yet I knew it, for that exists: a knowledge you drip into a defenseless child, drop by drop, day by day, without him noticing in the slightest this silently growing knowledge. The inconspicuous knowledge spreads in him like a pernicious poison, seeps into the tissue of body and soul and determines the colors and shades of his life. From this knowledge working unknown, whose power lay in its secrecy, an invisible, undiscoverable web emerged in me of inflexible, merciless expectations of myself, woven by the horrible spiders of an ambition born of fear. How often, how desperately and comically did I later lash out to free myself—only to be caught even more! It was impossible to defend myself against your presence in me: your trick was too perfect, too faultless, a masterpiece of overwhelming, breathtaking perfection.*

Part of its perfection was that you not only left your suffocating expectations unspoken, but hid them under words and gestures that expressed the opposite. *I'm not saying it was a conscious, cunning, insidious plan. No. You believed your* own *deceptive words and were a victim of the mask whose intelligence went far beyond yours. Since then, I've known how people can be entwined deeply with one another and present to one another without having the slightest idea of it.*

And there's something else about the intricate way you created me according to your will—like a wanton sculptress of an alien soul: the names you gave me. Amadeu Inácio. *Most people don't think anything of it, now and then somebody says something about the melody. But I know better, for I have the sound of your voice in my ear, a sound full of conceited devotion. I was to be a genius. I was to possess godlike grace. And at the same time—the same time!—I was to embody the murderous rigidity of the holy Ignacio and his abilities to perform as a priestly general.*

It's a nasty term, but it fits the case to a T: My life was determined by a maternal poisoning.

Was there in him, too, a secret, life-determining presence of parents, masked perhaps and turned into its opposite? Gregorius asked himself as he walked through the quiet streets of Belém. He pictured the narrow book where his mother wrote down what she earned by cleaning. The shabby eyeglasses with the cheap frames and the eternally dirty lenses over which she looked at him wearily. *If I could see the sea just once, but we simply can't afford that.* There had been something in her, something beautiful, even radiant, he hadn't thought about it for a long time: her dignity when she met on the street the people whose filth she had to deal with. Not a trace of obsequiousness, her look was on the same level as those who paid her for crawling around on her knees. *Could she do that?* he had asked as a little boy, only to be proud later on when he could observe it again. If only there hadn't been the sentimental novels of Ludwig Ganghofer she had picked up in the rare hours of reading. *Now you're also cursed with books.* She hadn't been a reader. It hurt, but she hadn't been a reader.

What bank will give me a loan, Gregorius heard the father saying, *and for such a thing.* He saw his big hand with the short fingernails, as he had counted out the thirteen francs thirty for the Persian grammar, coin after coin, into his hand. *Are you sure you want to go there?* he had said. *It's so far away, so far away from what we're used to. Even the letters, they're so different, not like letters at all. We won't know anything about you.* When Gregorius had given him back the money, the father had stroked his hair with the big hand, a hand much too seldom capable of affection.

The father of Eva, Unbelievable, old man von Muralt, had been a judge, had looked in briefly at the school party, a giant of a man. How would it have been, thought Gregorius, if he had grown up as the son of a strict, pain-plagued judge and an ambitious mother who lived her life through the life of the idolized son? Could he nevertheless have been Mundus, Papyrus? Could such a thing even be known?

When Gregorius came back to the heated house from the cold night air, he was dizzy. He sat down in the chair from before and waited until it was past. *Not surprising when you think of how much has changed in your life in a short time,* Mariana Eça had said. *A tumor would bring quite different symtoms.* He banished the doctor's voice from his head and went on reading.

My first big disappointment with you was that you didn't want to hear anything about the questions concerning Papá's profession. I asked myself: Did you—as a neglected wife in backward Portugal—declare yourself incapable of thinking about it? Because law and justice were things that concerned only men? Or was it worse: that you were simply without questions or doubts about Papá's work? That you simply weren't interested in the fate of the people of Tarrafal?

Why didn't you force Papá to talk to us, instead of being only a monument? Were you glad about the power you gained from that? You were a virtuoso of the mute, even denied complicity with your children. And you were also a virtuoso as a diplomatic intermediary between Papá and us. You liked the role and were not without vanity in it. Was that your revenge for the narrow range marriage left you? Compensation for the lack of social recognition and the burden of Father's pain?

Why did you buckle whenever I protested? Why didn't you hold out against me and teach me to endure conflicts? So that I could learn not playfully with a wink, but had to acquire it tediously as from the textbook, with grim thoroughness that often enough led me to lose proportion and overshoot the mark?

Why did you burden me with the encumbrance of my preferential treatment? Papá and you: Why did you expect so little from Adriana and Mélodie? Why didn't you sense the humiliation in the lack of confidence?

But it would be unjust, Mamã, if that were all I said to you in farewell. In the six years since Papá's death, I have encountered you with new feelings and I was glad to feel they were there. Your desolation at his grave moved me deeply and I was glad there were religious customs to shore up your spirit. I was really happy when the first signs of liberation became visible, much faster than expected. It was as if you had awoken to your own life for the first time. In the first year, you often came to the blue house and Fátima was afraid you would cling to me, to us. But no: now, when the old scaffolding of your life had collapsed, which had also determined the internal play of forces, now you seemed to discover what had been blocked for you by marrying much too early: your own life beyond the role in the family. You started asking about books, and leafed through them like a curious schoolgirl, awkwardly, inexperienced, but with glowing eyes. Once when you didn't notice me, I saw you standing at a shelf in the bookstore, an open book in hand. At this moment, I loved you, Mamã, and was tempted to go to you. But that would have been exactly the wrong thing: It would have pulled you back into the old life.

36

Gregorius paced back and forth in Senhor Cortês's room, called all things by their familiar German names. Then he walked through the dark cold corridors of the Liceu and did the same with everything he saw there. He spoke aloud and furiously, the guttural words resounding through the building, and an amazed observer would have judged that someone had gone astray in the abandoned building, who had become thoroughly demented about something.

It had begun in the morning in language school. Suddenly, he no longer knew the simplest things in Portuguese, things he knew from the first lesson on the first record of the language course, which he had heard before he left. Cecília, who appeared late because of a migraine, started an ironic comment, stopped, frowned and made a calming gesture.

"Sossega," she said, "calm down. That happens to everybody who studies a foreign language. Suddenly nothing works anymore. It passes. Tomorrow you'll be back up to snuff."

Then his memory went on strike with Persian, a language memory he had always been able to count on. In sheer panic, he had recited verses from Horace and Sappho to himself, had called up rare Homeric words and leafed frantically through Solomon's Song of Songs. Everything came as usual, nothing was lacking, there was no abyss of sudden memory loss. And yet he felt as if after an earthquake. Dizziness. Dizziness and memory loss. It would pass.

He had stood quietly at the window in the Rector's office. Today there was no cone of light wandering through the room. It was raining. All of a sudden, quite suddenly, he had become furious. It was a violent, hot fury, mixed with despair that the anger had no recognizable object. Only very slowly did he realize that he was experiencing a revolt, a resistance against all the linguistic foreignness he had inflicted on himself. At first it seemed to apply only to Portuguese, and maybe the French and English he had to speak here. Then gradually and reluctantly, he admitted to himself that the surge of rage also related to the ancient languages he had lived in for more than forty years.

He was alarmed at the depth of his rebellion. The ground swayed. He had to do something, hold on to something; he shut his eyes, stood on Bubenbergplatz and named the things he saw by their familiar German names. He talked to the things and to himself in slow, clear sentences of dialect. The earthquake subsided, he felt solid ground beneath his feet again. But the fear had an echo, he faced it with the fury of someone who has been exposed to a great danger, and so it happened that he strode through the corridors of the empty building like a lunatic, as if the essential thing was to defeat the spirits of the dark corridors with familiar German words.

Two hours later, when he sat in the living room of Silveira's house, the whole thing seemed to him like a nightmare, like something he may only have dreamed. Reading Latin and Greek was the same as always, and when he opened the Portuguese grammar, everything was there immediately and he made good progress with the rules of the conjunctive. Only the dream images still reminded him that something had broken open in him.

When he nodded off in the chair for a moment, he sat as the only student in an enormous classroom and defended himself with sentences in dialect against foreign language questions and demands aimed at him from the front by somebody he couldn't see. He woke up with his shirt damp, showered, and then made his way to Adriana.

Clotilde had reported that Adriana had changed since time and the present had returned to the blue house with the ticking clock in the living room. Gregorius had run into her on the streetcar coming from the Liceu.

"Sometimes," she had said and repeated the words patiently when he didn't understand, "she stands still at the clock as if she wanted to stop it again. But then she goes on and her walk has become faster and firmer. She gets up earlier. It is as if she would no longer . . . yes, as if she would no longer only endure the day."

She ate more and once she had asked Clotilde to take a walk with her.

When the door of the blue house opened, Gregorius experienced a surprise. Adriana wasn't wearing black. Only the black ribbon over the scar on her neck had remained. Skirt and jacket were a light gray with thin blue stripes and she had put on a shining white blouse. The trace of a smile showed that she enjoyed the amazement on Gregorius's face.

He gave her back the letters to father and son.

"Isn't it insane?" she said. "This speechlessness. *Éducation sentimentale,* Amadeu would say, would have to initiate us into the art of revealing feelings and into the experience that feelings become richer through words. How little that succeeded for him with Papá!" She looked at the floor. "And how little with me!"

He would like to read the notes on the scraps of paper on Amadeu's desk, said Gregorius. When they entered the attic room, Gregorius experienced the next surprise: the desk chair was no longer diagonal to the desk. After thirty years, Adriana had managed to get it out of the paralyzed past and straighten it so that it was no longer as if the brother was about to stand up from it. When he looked at her, she stood looking down, her hands in her jacket pockets, a devoted old woman who was at the same time like a schoolgirl who has solved a difficult task and waits for praise in bashful pride. Gregorius put his hand on her shoulder for a moment.

The blue china cup on the copper tray had been washed, the ashtray was empty. Only the rock candy was still in the sugar bowl. Adriana had screwed the top on the ancient fountain pen and now she turned on the desk lamp with the emerald green shade. She pushed the desk chair back and beckoned to Gregorius with a final hesitation to sit down.

The gigantic book open in the middle still lay on the reading desk and the stack of pages was still there, too. After a questioning glance at Adriana, he picked up the book to be able to see the author and title. JOÃO DE LOUSADA DE LEDESMA, O MAR TENEBROSO, the dark, dreadful sea. Big, calligraphic fonts, engravings of coasts, India ink drawings of seafarers. Gregorius looked at Adriana again.

"I don't know," she said, "I don't know why that suddenly interested him, but he was completely obsessed by books about the fear of people in the Middle Ages when they thought they were standing at the westernmost point of Europe and asked themselves what might be on the other side of the apparently endless sea."

Gregorius pulled the book to him and read a Spanish quotation: *Más allá no hay nada más que las aguas del mar, cuyo término nadie más que Dios conoce. Beyond that there is nothing except the water of the sea, whose borders no one knows but God.*

"Cabo Finisterre," said Adriana, "up in Galicia. The westernmost point of Spain. He was obsessed by that. The end of the world at the time. 'But here in Portugal there is a point that is even further west, so why Spain,' I said and pointed to it on the map. But he didn't want to hear anything about it and kept talking about

Finisterre, it was like an idée fixe. He had a haunted, feverish expression on his face when he spoke of it."

SOLIDÃO, LONELINESS, was at the top of last the page Prado had written on. Adriana had followed Gregorius's look.

"He often complained in his last year that he didn't understand what it really consisted of, the loneliness we all feared so much. *What is it that we call loneliness,* he said, *it can't simply be the absence of others, you can be alone and not lonely, and you can be among people and yet be lonely. So what is it?* It always concerned him that we could be lonely in the middle of the hustle and bustle. *All right,* he said, *it isn't only that others are there, that they fill up the space next to us. But even when they celebrate us or give advice in a friendly conversation, clever, sensitive advice: even then we can be lonely. So loneliness is not something simply connected with the presence of others or with what they do. Then what? What on earth?*

"He didn't talk to me about Fátima and his feelings for her, *Intimacy is our last sanctuary,* he used to say. Only one time did he get carried away with a remark. *I lie next to her, I hear her breath, I feel her warmth—and am horribly lonely,* he said. *What is it? WHAT?*"

Solidão par proscrição, loneliness through ostracism, Prado had written. *When others withdraw affection, respect and recognition from us: Why can't we simply say to them: 'I don't need all that, I satisfy myself?' Isn't it a horrible form of bondage that we can't do that? Doesn't it make us slaves of others? What feelings can be called up against it as a dam, a protecting wall? What sort must the internal firmness be?*

Gregorius bent over the desk and read the faded words on the notes on the wall.

Extortion through trust. "Patients confided the most intimate things to him, and also the most dangerous," said Adriana. "Politically dangerous, I mean. And then they expected him to divulge something too. So they wouldn't have to feel naked. He hated that.

He hated it from the bottom of his heart. *I don't want anybody to expect anything of me,* he said then and stamped his foot. *And why the devil is it so hard to keep my distance?* 'Mamã,' I was tempted to say, 'Mamã.' But I didn't. He knew it himself."

The dangerous virtue of patience. "*Paciência:* in the last years of his life he developed a real allergy to this word, his face darkened abruptly whenever anybody mentioned patience to him. *Nothing more than a blessed way of missing out on yourself,* he said annoyed. *Fear of the fountains that can shoot up in us.* I understood that properly only when I learned of the aneurysm."

The last note had more than the others: *If the surge of the soul is unavailable and more powerful than we are: why then praise and blame? Why not simply: "Was lucky," "had bad luck"? And it* is *more powerful than we are, this surge; it* always *is.*

"Before, the whole wall was filled with notes," said Adriana. "He was constantly writing down something and pinning it to the wall. Until that wretched trip to Spain a year and a half before his death. After that, he seldom picked up the pen; often he sat here at the desk and simply stared into space."

Gregorius waited. Now and then he glanced at her. She sat in the reading chair next to the mountain of books on the floor, which she hadn't changed, the big book with the reproduction of the brain was still on the stack there. She clasped her hands with the dark veins, released them, clasped them again. Things happened in her face. The resistance against remembering seemed to have gained the upper hand.

He would like to learn something about this time, too, said Gregorius. "To understand him even better."

"I don't know," she said and then relapsed into silence. When she started talking again, the words seemed to come from far away.

"I thought I knew him. Yes, I would have said: I know him, I know him inside and out, after all, I had seen him every day for years and heard him talk about his thoughts and feelings, even his dreams. But then he came home from this meeting, that was two years before his death, in December, he would have been fifty-one. It was one of those meetings where João also was, João something. The man who wasn't good for him. Jorge was also there, I think, Jorge O'Kelly, his holy friend. I wished he hadn't gone to these meetings. They weren't good for him."

"There, the people of the resistance met," said Gregorius. "Amadeu was working for the resistance, you must have known that. He wanted to do something, do something against people like Mendes."

"Resistência," said Adriana, and then again, *"Resistência."* She said the word as if she had never heard anything about it, and refused to believe such a thing could have been.

Gregorius cursed his need to force her to acknowledge reality, because for a moment it looked as if she would fall silent. But then the annoyance died out on her face and she was back with the brother who came home at night from a wretched meeting.

"He hadn't slept and was still wearing the clothes from the night before when I met him in the kitchen the next morning. I knew how he was when he hadn't slept. But this time it was different. He didn't look tormented as usual, despite the rings under his eyes. And he did something he never did: He had tipped the chair back and was teetering back and forth. Later, when I thought about it, I said to myself: It's as if he had set off on a trip. In the office, he was incredibly fast and light in everything, things succeeded for him as if by themselves, and he hit the wastebasket whenever he threw the used things in it.

"In love, you might think, weren't those clear signs that he was in love? Naturally, I also thought of that. But at one of those meetings, meetings of men? And it was so different from with Fátima. Wilder, more boisterous, lustier. Thoroughly unbridled, so to speak. He scared me. He was strange to me. Especially after I had seen her. As soon as she entered the waiting room, I felt that she wasn't simply a patient. Early to middle twenties. A remarkable blend of innocent maiden and vamp. Glittering eyes, Asian complexion, swaying walk. The men in the waiting room glanced at her furtively, the women narrowed their eyes.

"I led her into the consulting room. Amadeu was just washing his hands. He turned around and it was as if he was struck by lightning. The blood shot into his face. Then he got himself under control.

"'Adriana, this is Estefânia,' he said. 'Would you please leave us alone for a moment, we have something to discuss.'

"That had never happened. There had been nothing in this room I couldn't hear. *Nothing.*

"She came back, four or five times. He always sent me out, spoke with her and then escorted her to the door. Every time, his face was red and for the rest of the day, he was jumpy and his injections were off, he who was idolized for his sure hand. The last time, she didn't come to the office, but rang the bell up here, it was after midnight. He took his coat and went down. I saw the two of them turn the corner, he was talking intensely to her. An hour later, he came back with ruffled hair and he smelled.

"After that she stayed away. Amadeu had blackouts. As if a hidden force was sucking him into the depth. He was edgy and sometimes rough, even with patients. It was the first time I thought: He doesn't like the profession anymore, it's not good for him anymore, he'd like to run away from it.

"Once I came across Jorge and the girl. He had his arm around her waist, she didn't seem to like it. I was confused, Jorge acted as if he didn't know me and pulled the girl into a sidestreet. The temptation to tell Amadeu was great. I didn't. He was suffering. Once, on an especially bad evening, he asked me to play Bach's Goldberg Variations. He sat there with his eyes shut and I was absolutely sure he was thinking of her.

"The chess games with Jorge, which had become part of the

rhythm of Amadeu's life, were dropped. All winter long, Jorge didn't come to us a single time, not even on Christmas. Amadeu didn't speak of him.

"One evening in early March, O'Kelly stood at the door. I could hear Amadeu open it.

"'You,' he said.

"'Yes, me,' said Jorge.

"They went downstairs to the office so I wouldn't hear the conversation. I opened the door of the flat and eavesdropped. Nothing, not a single word. Later, I heard the front door slam. O'Kelly, his coat collar pulled up, a cigarette between his lips, vanished around the corner. Silence. Amadeu didn't come. Finally, I went downstairs. He was sitting in the dark and didn't move.

"'Leave me alone,' he said. 'I don't want to talk.'

"Late at night when he came up, he was pale, silent and thoroughly distraught. I didn't dare ask what was going on.

"The next day, the office was closed. João came. I didn't learn anything about the conversation. Ever since the girl had showed up, Amadeu lived past me, life had gone out of the hours of working together in the office. I hated this person, the long black hair, the swaying walk, the short skirt. I didn't play the piano anymore. I didn't count anymore. It was . . . it was humiliating.

"Two or three days later, in the middle of the night, João and the girl stood at the door.

"'I would like Estefânia to stay here,' said João.

"The way he said it, refusal was impossible. I hated him and his domineering way. Amadeu went into the office with her, he didn't say a word when he saw her, but he fumbled with the keys and dropped the key ring on the stairs. He made up a bed for her on the examining table, I saw it later.

"Toward morning, he came up, showered and made breakfast. The girl looked bleary-eyed and scared, she was wearing jeans or something, and everything provocative had disappeared. I controlled myself, made a second pot of coffee and another one for the road. Amadeu didn't explain anything to me.

"'I don't know when I'll be back,' he only said. 'Don't worry.'

"He stuffed a few things in a bag, put in a few medications, and then they went into the street. To my surprise, Amadeu took a car key out of his pocket and unlocked a car that hadn't been there the day before. But he can't drive, I thought, and then the girl got in behind the wheel. That was the last time I saw her."

Adriana sat still, her hands in her lap, her head on the back of the chair, her eyes closed. Her breathing was rapid, she was back in those events. The black velvet ribbon had slid up, Gregorius saw the scar on the neck, an ugly, jagged scar with a small bulge that gleamed grayish. Amadeu had sat astride her lap. *I have to do this,* he had said, *otherwise you'll die. Take your hands away. Trust me.* Then he had stabbed her. And half a lifetime later, Adriana had seen him sit down next to a young woman in a car and drive off for an undetermined time without any explanation.

Gregorius waited until Adriana's breathing calmed down. How had it been when Amadeu came back, he asked.

"He was getting out of the taxi as I happened to be standing at the window. Alone. He must have come back on the train. A week had passed. He didn't say a word about that time, not then and not later either. He was unshaven and hollow-cheeked, I think he had hardly eaten anything in those days. Famished, he devoured everything I put in front of him. Then he lay down upstairs in bed and slept a day and a night, he must have taken a pill, I found the package later.

"He washed his hair, shaved, and dressed carefully. I had cleaned the office in the meantime.

"'Everything's shining,' he said and attempted a smile. 'Thanks, Adriana. If I didn't have you.'

"We let the patients know that the office was open again and an hour later, the waiting room was full. Amadeu was slower than usual, maybe from the aftereffect of the sleeping pill, but maybe it was the onset of the illness. The patients felt he wasn't the same and looked at him uncertainly. In the middle of the morning, he asked for coffee, that had never happened before.

"Two days later, he got a fever and raging headaches. No medicine helped.

" 'No reason for panic,' he calmed me, his hands on his temples. 'After all, the body is also the mind.'

"But I observed him secretly, I saw the fear, he must have been thinking of the aneurysm. He asked me to put on Berlioz, Fátima's music.

" 'Turn it off!' he yelled after a few bars. 'Turn it off right now!'

"Maybe it was the headaches, maybe he also felt that he couldn't simply go back to Fátima after the girl.

"Then they caught João, we found out through a patient. Amadeu's headaches became so violent that he paced back and forth up here like a lunatic, both hands on his head. In one eye, a blood vessel burst, the blood dyed the eye dark red, he looked horrible, desperate and a bit brutalized. Shouldn't I get Jorge? I asked helplessly.

" 'Don't you dare!' he yelled.

"He and Jorge met again only a year later, a few months before Amadeu's death. In this year, Amadeu changed. After two or three weeks, the fever and the headaches disappeared. They left my brother as a man sunk in a deep melancholy. *Melancholia*—he had loved the word even as a little boy and later he read books about it. One of them said it was a typically modern phenomenon. 'Rubbish,' he cursed. He considered melancholy a timeless phenomenon and thought it was one of the most precious ones that humans knew.

" 'Because it shows all the fragility of man,' he said.

"It wasn't harmless. Naturally he knew that melancholy and clinical depression aren't the same. But when he had a depressed patient before him, he sometimes hesitated much too long before sending him to a psychiatrist. He talked with him as if it were melancholy and tended to transfigure the condition of such people and to offend them with his peculiar enthusiasm for their suffering. After the trip with the girl, this became stronger and sometimes bordered on gross negligence.

"His physical diagnoses remained sound to the end. But he was a marked man and when he had to deal with a difficult patient, sometimes he was no longer up to it. With women, on the other hand, he was self-conscious all of a sudden and sent them to specialists faster than before.

"Whatever happened on that trip, it distressed him like nothing else before, even more than Fátima's death. It was like a tectonic quake that shifted the deepest rock layers of his soul. Everything that rested on these layers had become shaky and swayed in the lightest breeze. The whole atmosphere in the house changed. I had to shelter and protect him as if we were living in a sanitorium. It was horrible."

Adriana wiped a tear from her eye.

"And wonderful. He belonged . . . he belonged to me again. Or he would have belonged to me if Jorge hadn't stood at the door one evening."

O'Kelly brought a chessboard and carved pieces from Bali.

"It's been a long time since we played," he said. "Too long. Much too long."

The first times they played, there was little talking. Adriana brought tea.

"It was a tense silence," she said. "Not hostile, but tense. They searched for each other. Searched in themselves for a possibility to be friends again."

Now and then they tried a joke or an idiom from their schooldays. It failed, the laughter died even before it had found its way to their faces. A month before Prado's death, they went down to the office after chess. It was a discussion that lasted late into the night. Adriana stood in the open door of the flat the whole time.

"The door of the office opened, they came out. Amadeu didn't turn on a light and the light from the office door barely illuminated the hall. They walked slowly, almost in slow motion. They seemed to stay unnaturally far apart. Then they were standing at the front door.

"'So,' said Amadeu.

"'Yes,' said Jorge.

"And then they fell . . . yes, they fell into each other, I don't know how I can express it better. They must have wanted to embrace each other, one last time, but then the movement once begun seemed impossible, but was not to be stopped altogether anymore, they stumbled to each other, groped for each other, clumsy as blind men, their heads butted into each other's shoulders, then they straightened up, recoiled, and didn't know what to do with their arms and hands. One, two seconds of horrible embarrassment, then Jorge ripped open the door and stormed out. The door fell shut. Amadeu turned to the wall, leaned his forehead against it and started sobbing. They were deep, raw, almost animal sounds, accompanied by violent twitches of his whole body. I know that I thought: How deep he has been in him, a whole lifetime! And will remain, even after this parting. It was the last time they met."

Prado's sleeplessness became even worse than usual. He complained of dizziness and had to take breaks between patients. He asked Adriana to play the Goldberg Variations. Twice he went to the Liceu and came back with traces of tears on his face. At the funeral, Adriana learned from Mélodie that she had seen him coming out of church.

There were a few days when he took up his pen. On those days he ate nothing. On the evening before his death, he complained of headaches. Adriana stayed with him until the sleeping pills worked. When she left, he looked as if he would fall asleep. But when she looked in on him at five in the morning, the bed was empty. He was on his way to the beloved Rua Augusta, where he collapsed an hour later. At six twenty-three, Adriana was notified. Later, when she came home, she put the clock back and stopped the pendulum.

37

Solidão por proscrição, loneliness through ostracism, that was what had preoccupied Prado at the end. That we depend on the respect and affection of others and that that makes us depend on them. How far he had come! Gregorius sat in Silveira's living room and reread the previous note about loneliness that Adriana had put into the book.

SOLIDÃO FURIOSA. FURIOUS LONELINESS. Is it so that everything we do is done out of fear of loneliness? Is that why we renounce all the things we will regret at the end of life? Is that why we so seldom say what we think? Why else do we hold on to all these broken marriages, false friendships, boring birthday parties? What would happen if we refused all that, put an end to the skulking blackmail and stood on our own? If we let our enslaved wishes and the fury at our enslavement rise high as a fountain? For the feared loneliness—what does it really consist of? Of the silence of absent reproaches? Of not needing to creep through the minefield of marital lies and friendly half-truths while holding our breath? Of the freedom not to have anybody across from us at meals? Of the fullness of time that yawns when the barrage of appointments falls silent? Aren't those wonderful things? A heavenly situation? So why the fear of it? Is it ultimately a fear that exists only because we haven't thought through its object? A fear we have been talked into by thoughtless parents, teachers and priests? And why are we so sure the others wouldn't envy us if they saw how great our freedom has become? And that they didn't seek our company as a result?

Then he hadn't yet known the icy wind of the ostracism he was later to feel twice: when he saved Mendes and when he took Estefânia Espinhosa out of the country. This earlier note showed him as the iconoclast who didn't forbid himself any thought, one who didn't shrink from delivering a blasphemous speech to a faculty of teachers, including priests. Back then he had written out of the security given him by his friendship with Jorge. This security, thought Gregorius, must have helped him get through the spit running over his face before the enraged mob. And then this security had broken away. The demands of life were simply too many and too massive for our feelings to survive them intact, he had said already at school in Coimbra. To Jorge, of all people.

Now his shrewd prediction had come true and he had remained in the chill of unbearable isolation, and even his sister's cares could do nothing against it. The loyalty he had considered an anchor against the tides of feelings—it too had turned out to be fragile. Never again did he go to meetings of the resistance, Adriana had said. He visited only João Eça in prison. Permission for that was the only mark of gratitude he took from Mendes. *His hands, Adriana,* he said when he came back, *his hands. They once played Schubert.*

He had forbidden her to air out the office to dispel the smoke from Jorge's last visit. The patients complained. The windows remained shut for days. He inhaled the stale air like a memory drug. When ventilation could no longer be avoided, he sat slumped on a chair and his life force seemed to leave the room along with the smoke.

"Come," Adriana had said to Gregorius. "I want to show you something."

They went down to the office. In a corner of the floor was a small rug. Adriana shoved it aside with her foot. The mortar had been broken open and one of the big tiles had been removed. Adriana went down on her knees and lifted out the tile. Underneath, a hollow had been chiseled into the floor where there was a folded chessboard and a box. Adriana opened the box and showed Gregorius the carved chess pieces.

Gregorius couldn't catch his breath, opened a window and inhaled the cool night air. He was overcome by dizziness and had to hold on to the windowsill.

"I surprised him at that," said Adriana. She had closed the opening back up and had come next to him.

"His face flushed flaming red. 'I only wanted . . . ,' he began. 'No reason to be embarrassed,' I said. That evening he was as vulnerable and fragile as a little child. Naturally, it *looked like* a grave for the chess set, for Jorge, for their friendship. But he hadn't *felt* it like that at all, I discovered. It was more complicated. And somehow, also more hopeful. He hadn't wanted to *bury* the set. He only wanted *to push it over the borders of his world,* without destroying it, and he wanted the certainty that he could take it out anytime. His world was now a world without Jorge. But Jorge was still there. He *was still there*. 'Now, where he no longer is, it is as if I were no longer either,' he had once said.

"After that, for days he was without self-confidence and almost servile to me. 'Such kitsch, the business with the chess set,' he finally burst out, as if I had made him speak."

Gregorius thought of O'Kelly's words: *He tended to bombast, he didn't want to admit it, but he knew it, and therefore he fought against kitsch at every opportunity, and he could be unjust in that, horribly unjust.*

Now, in Silveira's living room, he reread the note about kitsch in Prado's book:

Kitsch is the most pernicious of all prisons. The bars are covered with the gold of simplistic, unreal feelings so that you take them for the pillars of a palace.

Adriana had given him a pile of pages, one of the piles from Prado's desk, pressed between cardboard and tied with a red ribbon. "Those are things that aren't in the book. The world is not to know anything of them," she had said.

Gregorius untied the ribbon, pushed back the cover, and read:

Jorge's chess set. The way he handed it to me. Only he can do that. I don't know anyone who can be so compelling. *A compulsion I wouldn't miss for anything in the world. Like his compelling moves on the board. What did he want to make up for? Is it even right to say: he wanted to make up for something? He didn't say: 'You misunderstood me back then about Estefânia.' He said: 'I thought back then that we could talk about everything, everything that came into our head. That's how we had always done, didn't you remember?' After these words, I thought for a few seconds, only a few seconds, that we could find each other again. It was a hot, wonderful feeling. But it died out again. His gigantic nose, his tear ducts, his brown teeth. Earlier, that face had been in me, a part of me. Now it remained outside, stranger than the face of a stranger that had never been in me. There was such a rip in my breast, such a rip.*

Why should it be kitsch, what I did with the set? Really, a simple, genuine gesture. And I did it only for myself, not for an audience. If someone does something only for himself and unknown to him, a million people look at him and laugh in uproarious malice because they consider it kitsch: How would we judge?

An hour later, when Gregorius entered the chess club, O'Kelly was involved in a complicated end game. Pedro was also there, the man with the epileptic eyes and the snuffled snot, who reminded Gregorius of the lost tournament in Moutier. There was no free board.

"Sit down here," said O'Kelly and pulled an empty chair up to his table.

All the way to the club, Gregorius had asked himself what he expected of it. What he wanted from O'Kelly. Clearly he couldn't *ask* him what had happened back then with Estefânia Espinhosa and whether he would have been willing in all seriousness to sacrifice her. He hadn't found the answer, but he couldn't go back either.

Now, with the smoke of his cigarette in his face, he suddenly knew: He had wanted once more to make sure how it was to sit next to the man Prado had carried inside him for a lifetime, the man, as Father Bartolomeu had said, he had needed to be *whole*. The man he enjoyed losing to and to whom he had given a whole pharmacy without expecting gratitude. The man who was the first to laugh aloud when the barking dog had broken through the painful silence after his scandalous speech.

"Shall we?" asked O'Kelly after he had won the end game and parted from his partner.

Never had Gregorius played like that against anybody. It wasn't the game, but the presence of the other person. Only his presence. The question of how it must have been to be somebody whose life was filled with this man whose nicotine-stained fingers with the dirty nails moved the pieces with merciless precision.

"What I recently told you, about Amadeu and me, I mean: forget it."

O'Kelly looked at Gregorius with a look blending bashfulness and the furious willingness to throw everything away.

"The wine. Everything was quite different."

Gregorius nodded and hoped O'Kelly could see on his face his respect for that deep and complicated friendship. Prado had asked himself, he said, if the soul was a place of facts or whether the alleged facts were only the deceptive shadows of stories we tell ourselves, about others and about ourselves.

Yes, said O'Kelly, that had been what preoccupied Amadeu all his life. Inside a person, he said, it was much more complicated than our schematic, ridiculous explanations wanted to have us believe. *Everything is much more complicated. At every moment it is much more complicated. 'They got married because they fell in love and wanted to share their life'; 'she stole because she needed money'; 'he lied because he didn't want to hurt': What ridiculous stories! We are stratified creatures, creatures full of abysses, with a soul of inconstant quicksilver, with a mind whose color and shape change as in a kaleidoscope that is constantly shaken.*

That sounded as if there *were*, after all, psychological facts, even very complicated ones, Jorge had objected.

No, no, Amadeu protested, we could improve our explanations to infinity and they'd still be false. *And what is false is the assumption that there are truths to be discovered. The soul, Jorge, is a pure invention, our most brilliant invention, and its brilliance resides in the suggestion, the overwhelmingly plausible suggestion, that there is something in the soul to be discovered as in a real part of the world. The truth, Jorge, is quite different: we invented the soul to have a subject of conversation, something we can talk about when we meet one another. Just imagine if we couldn't talk about the soul: What should we talk about with one another? It would be hell!*

"He could work himself up into a state of intoxication about that, he then really glowed, and when he saw that I was enjoying his intoxication, he said: *You know, thinking is the second most beautiful thing. The most beautiful is poetry. If there were poetic thinking and thinking poetry—that would be paradise.* Later when he began with his notes: I think they were the attempt to pave the way to this paradise."

A damp shimmer lay in O'Kelly's eyes. He didn't see that his queen was in danger. Gregorius made an insignificant move. They were the last ones in the room.

"Once the thinking game became dead serious. It's none of your business, it's *nobody's* business."

He bit his lips.

"Neither is João's business up in Cacilhas."

He took a drag of the cigarette and coughed.

"'You're fooling yourself,' he said to me. 'You want it for another reason than the one you're staging for yourself.'

"Those were his words, his damned, insulting words: *the one you're staging for yourself.* Can you imagine how it is when somebody says that you're only *staging* your reasons? Can you imagine how it is when a *friend*, THE friend, says that?

"'How do you know that,' I yelled at him. 'I think there is no true or false, or don't you admit that anymore?'"

On O'Kelly's unshaved face red spots appeared.

"You know, I had simply believed we could talk about everything that came into our mind. *Everything.* Romantic. Damned romantic, I know. But that's how it was between us, more than forty years. Ever since the day he appeared in class in his expensive frock coat and without a schoolbag.

"*He* was the one who had no fear of any thought. *He* was the one who had wanted to talk of the dying word of God in the face of priests. And when I wanted to try out a bold and, I admit, horrible thought—I noticed that I had overestimated him and our friendship. He looked at me as if I was a monster. Otherwise he could always distinguish between a mere tried-out thought and one that actually set us in motion. *He* was the one who taught me this difference, this liberating difference. And suddenly he didn't know anything about it anymore. All the blood had drained out of his face. In this one single second, I realized that the most horrible thing had happened: our lifelong affection had turned into hate. That was the moment, the dreadful moment, when we lost each other."

Gregorius wanted O'Kelly to win the game. He wanted him to mate him with compelling moves. But Jorge didn't come back to the game and Gregorius arranged a draw.

"It's simply not possible, unlimited openness," said Jorge, when they shook hands in the street. "It's beyond us. Loneliness through the need to suppress, there's that too."

He exhaled smoke.

"It's been a long time, over thirty years. As if it were yesterday. I'm glad I have the pharmacy. I can live there in our friendship. And occasionally I succeed in thinking that we never lost each other. That he just died."

38

For a good hour, Gregorius had been sneaking around Maria João's house and asking himself why his heart was pounding. *The great untouched love of his life,* Mélodie had called her. *It wouldn't surprise me if he had never even kissed her. But nobody, no woman, measured up to her. If there was anybody who knew all his secrets, it was Maria João. In a certain sense, she, only she, knew who he was.* And Jorge had said that she had been the only woman Amadeu really had thought something of. *Maria, my God yes, Maria,* he had said.

When she opened the door, everything was clear to Gregorius all at once. She held a steaming cup of coffee in one hand and warmed the other one on it. The look in the clear brown eyes was scrutinizing but not threatening. She wasn't a radiant woman. She wasn't a woman you'd turn around to look at. Nor had she been such a woman in her youth. But Gregorius had never met a woman who radiated such inconspicuous and yet such perfect confidence and independence. She must have been over eighty, but it wouldn't have been surprising if she were still confidently practicing her profession.

"Depends on what you want," she said when Gregorius asked if he might come in. He didn't want to stand in a doorway again and produce the portrait of Prado as a calling card. The calm open look gave him the courage for a direct opening.

"I'm interested in the life and notes of Amadeu de Prado," he said in French. "I have learned that you knew him. Knew him better than anybody else."

Her look could make you think that nothing could throw her off. But it did happen now. Not on the surface. In her dark blue wool dress, she leaned on the door frame as sure and calm as before, and the free hand kept rubbing the warm mug, only a little slower. But the eyelashes beat faster, and on the forehead appeared lines of a concentration you need when you're suddenly confronted with something unexpected that could have consequences. She said nothing. For a few seconds, she shut her eyes. Then she had herself under control again.

"I don't know if I want to go back there," she said. "But it doesn't make sense for you to stand out here in the rain."

The French words came without hesitation, and her accent had the sleepy elegance of a Portuguese woman who speaks fluent French, without leaving her own language even a moment.

Who was he, she wanted to know after she had given him a cup of coffee, not with the affected movements of an attentive hostess, but with the sober, plain movements of someone carrying out the practical essentials.

Gregorius told of the Spanish bookstore in Bern and the sentences the bookdealer had translated for him. *Of the thousand experiences we have, we find language for one at most and even this one merely by chance and without the care it deserves. Buried under all the mute experiences are those unseen ones that give our life its form, its color, and its melody.*

Maria João shut her eyes. The chapped lips with traces of fever blisters began to shake imperceptibly. She sank a little deeper into the chair. Her hands clasped a knee and let go of it. Now she didn't know what to do with her hands. The lids with the dark veins twitched. Slowly her breath grew calmer. She opened her eyes.

"You heard that and ran away from school," she said.

"I ran away from school and heard that," said Gregorius.

She smiled. *She looked at me and gave me a smile that came from the broad steppe of a keenly lived life,* Judge Prado had written.

"Good. But it fit. It fit so well that you wanted to meet him. How did you get to me?"

When Gregorius had finished his story, she looked at him.

"I don't know anything about the book. I'd like to see it."

She opened it, saw the picture and it was as if a double force of gravity pressed her into the chair. Behind the veined, almost transparent eyelids, the pupils raced. She made another attempt, opened her eyes and riveted her look on the picture. Slowly, she ran the shriveled hand over it, once and then once more. Now she leaned her hands on her knees, stood up and went out of the room without a word.

Gregorius picked up the book and looked at the picture. He thought of the moment when he had sat in the café on Bubenbergplatz and had seen it for the first time. he thought of Prado's voice from Adriana's old tape recorder.

"So now I've gone back there," said Maria João sitting down in the chair again. "If it's about the soul, there is little we can do. He used to say."

Her face was more composed and she had combed the stray strands out of her face. She took the book and looked at the picture.

"Amadeu."

In her mouth, the name sounded completely different than in the mouths of the others. As if it were a completely different name that couldn't possibly belong to the same man.

"He was so white and quiet, so terribly white and quiet. Perhaps it was because he consisted so much of language. I couldn't, wouldn't believe it: that words would never more come from him. Never more. The blood from the burst vein had washed them away, the words. All words. A bloody break in the dam of destructive force. As a nurse, I've seen a lot of dead people. But never did death seem so horrible to me. As something that simply shouldn't have happened. As something absolutely unbearable. Unbearable."

Despite the noise of traffic outside the window, silence filled the room.

"I picture him coming to me, the hospital report in his hand, it was a yellowish envelope. He had gone there because of piercing headaches and dizziness. He was afraid it could be a tumor. Angiography, radiography. Nothing. Only an aneurysm. 'You could live to be a hundred with that,' the neurologist had said. But Amadeu was pale as a ghost. 'It can burst any minute, any minute, how should I live with this time bomb in my brain,' he said."

"He took the map of the brain off the wall," said Gregorius.

"I know, that was the first thing he did. What it meant, you can guess only if you know what unbounded admiration he had for the human brain and its enigmatic achievements. A proof of God's existence, he said, it's a proof of God's existence. Only there is no God. And now a life began for him in which he steered clear of every thought of the brain. Every clinical syndrome with the remotest connection to the brain he immediately referred to the specialists."

Gregorius pictured the big book that lay in Prado's room on top of the heap of books. *O cérebro sempre o cérebro,* he heard Adriana say. *Porquê não disseste nada?*

"Nobody but me knew about it. Not Adriana. Not Jorge."

The pride was barely audible, but it was there.

"Later we seldom talked about it, and never for long. There wasn't much to say. But the threat of a bloody deluge in his head lay like a shadow over the last seven years of his life. There were moments when he wished it would finally happen. To get rid of the fear."

She looked at Gregorius. "Come." She led the way into the kitchen. From the top shelf of a cabinet, she took a big flat box of lacquered wood, its cover embellished with marquetry. She sat down at the kitchen table.

"A few of his notes were written in my kitchen. It was another kitchen, but it was this table. The things I write here are the most dangerous, he said. He didn't want to talk about them. Writing is mute, he said. He'd sit here all night and then go to the office without any sleep. He ruined his health. Adriana hated it. She hated everything connected with me. 'Thanks,' he said when he left. 'With you it's in a quiet, protected port.' I always kept the sheets in the kitchen. They belonged here."

She opened the engraved clasp of the box and took out the top three sheets. After she had read a few lines to herself, she shoved the papers at Gregorius.

He read. Whenever he didn't understand, he looked at her and she translated.

MEMENTO MORI. Dark monastery walls, downcast look, snow-covered cemetery. Must it be that?

Reflecting on what you may really want. The awareness of limited, ephemeral time as a source of strength to withstand your own habits and expectations, but mostly the expectations and threats of others. So something that opens up and doesn't lock the future. Understood like this, the memento is a danger for the powerful, the oppressors who try to keep the oppressed from finding an ear for their wishes, not even in themselves.

"Why should I think about it, the end is the end, it comes when it comes, why do you tell me that, that doesn't change in the least."

What is the reply?

"Don't waste your time, do something worthwhile with it."

But what can that mean: worthwhile? Finally to start realizing long-cherished wishes. To attack the error that there will always be time for it later. The memento as an instrument in the struggle against indolence, self-deception and fear, linked with the necessary change. Take the long-dreamed-of trip, learn this language, read those books, buy yourself this jewelry, spend a night in that famous hotel. Don't miss out on yourself.

Bigger things are also part of that: to give up the loathed profession, break out of a hated milieu. Do what contributes to making you more genuine, moves you closer to yourself.

Lying on the beach or sitting in the café from morning to night: that can also be the answer to the memento, the answer of one who has only worked up to now.

"Think that you have to die someday, maybe this morning."

"I think of it all the time, and so I play hooky from the office and let myself bask in the sun."

The apparently gloomy warning doesn't lock us up in the snow-covered monastery garden. It opens the way out and wakes us to the present.

With death in mind straightening out the relationship with others. Ending a hostility, excusing yourself for an injustice done, expressing an acknowledgment that pettiness kept us from doing. Stop taking trivialities seriously, the jibes of others, their pompousness, their entire bad judgment of us. The memento as a demand to feel different.

The danger: relations are no longer genuine and alive because they lack the momentary seriousness assumed by a certain lack of distance. And: for much of what we experience, it is crucial not to be linked with thoughts of finitude, but rather with the feeling that the future will still be very long. It means nipping this experience in the bud if the awareness of impending death would seep in.

Gregorius told of the Irishman who dared appear at the evening lecture in All Souls College at Oxford with a bright red football.

"Amadeu noted: *What wouldn't I have given to be the Irishman!"*

"Yes, that fits," said Maria João, "that fits precisely. Above all, it fits the beginning, our first meeting, when, as I would say today, everything was already set. It was in my first year in the girls' school of the Liceu. We all were in awe of the boys over there. Latin and

Greek! One day, it was a warm morning in May, I simply went over there, I'd had enough of the stupid awe. They played, they laughed, they played. Only he didn't. He sat on the steps, had wrapped his arms around his knees and was looking at me. As if he had been waiting years for me. If he hadn't looked like that—I wouldn't have simply sat down next to him. But it seemed to be the most natural thing in the world.

"'You're not playing?' I said. He shook his head short and sweet, almost a little gruffly.

"'I read this book,' he said in the soft, irresistible tone of a dictator who doesn't yet know anything of his despotism and in a certain sense never would know it. 'A book about saints, Thérèse of Lisieux, Teresa of Ávila and so on. After that, everything I do seems so banal. Simply not *important* enough. You understand?'

"I laughed. 'My name's Ávila, Maria João Ávila,' I said.

"He laughed too, but it was a tormented laugh, he felt he wasn't taken seriously.

"'Not *everything* can be important, and not *always*,' I said. 'That would be awful.'

"He looked at me and now his smile wasn't tormented. The Liceu bell rang, we parted.

"'Will you come back tomorrow?' he asked. Not more than five minutes had passed, and there already existed an intimacy as after years.

"Naturally I went back over the next day and by then he knew everything about my last name and gave me a lecture about Vasco Ximeno and Count Raimundo de Borgonha, who had been dispatched to the town by King Alfonso VI of Castile, about Antão and João Gonçalves de Ávila, who brought the name to Portugal in the fifteenth century, and so on.

"'We could go to Ávila together,' he said.

"The next day, I looked out of the classroom to the Liceu and I saw two dazzling points of light in the window. It was the sunlight in the lenses of his opera glasses. Everything went so fast, everything always went so fast with him.

"At recess, he showed me the opera glasses. 'They belong to Mamã,' he said. 'She likes to go to the opera, but Papá . . .'

"He wanted to make me a good student. So I could become a doctor. I really didn't want that, I said, I wanted to be a nurse.

" 'But you . . . ,' he began.

" 'A nurse,' I said. 'A simple nurse.'

"It took him a year to accept it. That I stuck to my guns and couldn't be compelled by his—that shaped our friendship. For that's what it was: a lifelong friendship.

" 'You have such brown knees, and your dress smells so good of soap,' he said two or three weeks after our first encounter.

"I had given him an orange. The others in the class were really jealous: the aristocrat and the peasant girl. *Why Maria of all people?* one of them asked, not knowing I was nearby. They imagined things. Father Bartolomeu, the most important teacher for Amadeu, didn't like me. When he saw me, he turned around and went the other way.

"On my birthday, I got a new dress. I asked Mamã to shorten it a little. Amadeu didn't say anything about it.

"Sometimes he came over to us and we went for a walk at recess. He told of home, his father's back, his mother's silent expectations. I learned everything that moved him. I was his confidante. Yes, that's what I was: his lifelong confidante.

"He didn't invite me to the wedding. 'You'd only be bored,' he said. I stood behind a tree when they came out of the church. The expensive wedding of an aristocrat. Big, shiny cars, a gown with a long white train. Men in frock coats and derby hats.

"It was the first time I set eyes on Fátima. A well-proportioned, beautiful face, white as alabaster. Long black hair, a boyish figure. Not a doll, I'd say, but somehow . . . slow. I can't prove it, but I think he patronized her. Without noticing it. He was that sort of controlling man. Not a domineering nature, not at all, but controlling, glorious, superior. Basically, there was no place in his life for a woman. When she died, it was a deep shock."

Maria João fell silent and looked out the window. When she continued, it was hesitant, as with a bad conscience.

"As I said: a deep shock. No doubt. And yet . . . how should I put it: not a shock that would penetrate the ultimate, deepest depth. In the first days, he often sat with me. Not to be consoled. He knew that he . . . that he couldn't expect *that* from me. Yes, he knew that. He *must* have known. He simply wanted me to be there. That's how it was often: I had to be *there.*"

Maria João stood up, went to the window and stood still, her look outside, her hands clasped behind her back. When she went on talking, it was in the soft voice of secrecy.

"The third or fourth time, he finally found the courage, the internal need had become too great, he had to tell somebody. He couldn't produce any children. He had had an operation not to become a father under any circumstances. That was long before he met Fátima.

"'I don't want little, defenseless children, who have to bear the burden of my soul,' he said. 'I know how it was with me—and still is.'"

The outlines of parental will and fear are written with a white-hot stylus in the souls of the children who are helpless and ignorant of what is happening to them. We need a whole life to find and decipher the branded text and we can never be sure we have understood it. Gregorius told Maria João what was in the letter to the father.

"Yes," she said, "yes. What weighed on him wasn't the operation, he never regretted it. It was that he hadn't told Fátima about it. She suffered from the childlessness and he almost choked on his bad conscience. He was a brave man, a man of really extraordinary bravery. But here he was cowardly and he never got over this cowardice."

He's cowardly when it comes to Mamã, Adriana had said. *The only cowardice in him. He, who otherwise didn't avoid any unpleasant issue, none.*

"I understood it," said Maria João. "Yes, I believe I can say: I understood it. I found out how deep father and mother were in him. What they had done to him. And yet: I was upset. Also because of Fátima. But what upset me even more was the extremism, even brutality of his decision. Mid-twenties and he commits himself in this matter. Forever. It took me about a year to cope with it. Until I could say: He wouldn't be Amadeu if he couldn't do such a thing."

Maria João picked up Prado's book, put on a pair of glasses and started leafing through it. But her thoughts were still in the past and she took off the glasses.

"We never talked any longer about Fátima, about what she was for him. She and I once met in the café, she came in and felt obliged to sit down with me. Even before the waiter came, we both knew it was a mistake. Fortunately, it was only an espresso.

"I don't know if I understood the whole thing or if I didn't. I'm not even sure if *he* understood it. And here is *my* cowardice: I didn't read what he wrote about Fátima. 'You may read only after my death,' he said when he gave me the sealed envelope. 'But I don't want it to fall into Adriana's hands.' More than once, I've picked up the envelope. At some point, I decided forever: I don't want to know it. And so it is still here in the box."

Maria João put the text about the warning of death back in the box and pushed it aside.

"One thing I do know: When the thing happened with Estefânia, I wasn't surprised in the least. There is this: You don't know what someone is lacking until he gets it and then all of a sudden it's absolutely clear that that's what it was.

"He changed. For the first time in forty years he seemed embarrassed with me and to want to hide something about himself from me. I learned only that there was somebody, somebody from the resistance who was also connected with Jorge. And that Amadeu wouldn't allow it, couldn't allow it. But I knew him: he thought constantly of her. From his silence, it was clear: I was not to see her. As if I could learn something about him from looking at her that I wasn't to know. What no one was to know. Not even himself, so to speak. I went there and waited in front of the house where the resistance met. Only one single woman came out and I realized at once: That's her."

Maria Joâo's glance went through the room and fixed on a distant point.

"I won't describe her to you. I'll say only this: I could immediately imagine what had happened to him. That the world suddenly looked quite different for him. That the previous order had been turned upside down. That all of a sudden, quite different things counted. That's the kind of woman she was. And she was only in her mid-twenties. She wasn't only the ball, the red Irish ball in the college. She was much more than all red Irish balls together: He must have felt that she was the chance for him to be *whole*. As a man, I mean.

"That's the only way to explain that he staked everything on it: the respect of others, the friendship with Jorge, which had been sacred to him, even life. And that he came back from Spain, as if he . . . was destroyed. Destroyed, yes, that's the right word. He slowed down, had trouble concentrating. Nothing more of the earlier quicksilver in his veins, nothing more of his boldness. His life glow was extinguished. He spoke of having to learn life all over again.

"'I was out at the Liceu,' he said one day. 'Back then, everything was still ahead of me. So much was still possible. Everything was open.'"

Maria João had a lump in her throat, she cleared her throat, and when she went on, it sounded hoarse.

"He said something else. 'Why didn't we ever go to Ávila together,' he said.

"I thought he had forgotten it. He hadn't. We wept. It was the only time we wept together."

Maria João went out. When she came back, she had a scarf around her neck and a thick coat over her arm.

"I'd like to go to the Liceu with you," she said. "What's left of it."

Gregorius imagined her looking at the pictures of Isfahan and asking questions. He was amazed that he wasn't embarrassed. Not with Maria João.

39

She, the eighty-year-old woman, drove the car with the calm and precision of a cabdriver. Gregorius looked at her hands on the steering wheel and the gearshift. They weren't elegant hands, nor did she take the time to tend them. Hands that had cared for sick people, emptied bedpans, applied bandages. Hands that knew what they were doing. Why hadn't Prado made her his assistant?

They stopped and walked through the park. She wanted first to go to the girls' school.

"I haven't been here in thirty years. Not since his death. Back then I was here almost every day. I thought, the shared place, the place of the first meeting, could teach me to part from him. I didn't know how I was to do it: part from him. How do you part from somebody who shaped your own life like nobody else?

"He gave me something I didn't know before and never experienced after him either: his unbelievable ability to empathize. He was preoccupied a lot with himself, and he could be dreadfully self-referential. But at the same time, as far as others were concerned, he possessed an imagination so fast and precise it could make you dizzy. He seemed to tell me how I felt even before I had begun to look for the words. Wanting to understand others was a passion with him. But he wouldn't have been Amadeu if he hadn't also questioned the possibility of such an understanding, questioned so radically that it could make you dizzy in the opposite direction.

"It created an unbelievable, breathtaking closeness when he was like that with me. At my home, we weren't especially gruff, but we were very sober with each other, practical so to speak. And then came someone who could see inside me. It was like a revelation. And it let a hope emerge."

They stood in Maria João's classroom. There were no more benches here, only the board was still there. Blind windows, lacking a pane of glass here and there. Maria João opened a window, whose squeaking spoke of decades. She pointed to the Liceu.

"There. Over there, on the third floor, were the points of light of the opera glasses." She swallowed. "That someone, a boy from an aristocratic family, was looking for me with opera glasses: That . . . was really something. And as I said, it let a hope emerge. It still had a childish form, this hope, and naturally it wasn't clear what it was about. Nevertheless, it was, in a vague form, the hope for a shared life."

They went down the stairs, with a soapy film of damp dust and rotting moss, as in the Liceu. Maria João was silent until they had gone across the park.

"Somehow that's what it was then, too. A shared life, I mean. Shared in a close distance; in a distant closeness."

She looked up at the façade of the Liceu.

"There, at this window, he sat and because he already knew everything and was bored, he wrote me little notes on scraps he slipped to me at recess. They weren't . . . weren't billets-doux. There wasn't what I kept hoping for, in every note. They were his thoughts about something. About Teresa of Ávila and many other things. He made me into an inhabitant of his world of thought. 'Except for me only you live there,' he said.

"And nevertheless, what I grasped only very slowly and much later was true: He didn't want me to be involved in his life. In a sense that's very hard to explain, he wanted me to stay outside. I waited for him to ask me to work in the blue office. In my dreams, I worked there, many times, and it was wonderful, we understood each other without words. But he didn't ask, didn't even hint.

"He loved trains, they were a symbol of life for him. I would like to have traveled in his compartment. But he didn't want me there. He wanted me on the platform, he wanted always to be able to open the window and ask me for advice. And he wanted the platform to go along when the train started moving. Like an angel, I was to stand on the moving platform, on the angels' platform sliding there at exactly the same speed."

They entered the Liceu. Maria João looked around.

"Girls really weren't allowed in here. But he smuggled me in after classes and showed me everything. Father Bartolomeu caught us. He was fuming. But it was Amadeu, so he said nothing."

They were standing at Senhor Cortês's office. Now Gregorius was afraid. They entered. Maria João burst out laughing. The laughter of a merry schoolgirl.

"You?"

"Yes."

She went to the wall with the pictures of Isfahan and looked at him questioningly.

"Isfahan, Persia. As a student, I wanted to go there. To the *Morgenland.*"

"And now, where you have run away, you make up for it. Here."

He nodded. He hadn't known that there were people who grasp so fast. You could open the train window and ask the angel.

Maria João did something surprising. She came to him and put her arm around his shoulders.

"Amadeu would have understood that. And not only understood. He would have loved you for it. *A imaginação, o nosso ultimo santuário*, he used to say. Imagination and intimacy, aside from language, those were the only two sanctuaries he allowed. *And they have a lot to do with each other, a lot,* he said."

Gregorius hesitated. But then he opened the desk drawer and showed Maria João the Hebrew Bible.

"I bet that's your sweater!"

She sat down in a chair and put one of Silveira's blankets over her legs.

"Read to me from it, please. He also did. Naturally I didn't understand a thing, but it was wonderful."

Gregorius read the story of Creation. He, Mundus, read the story of Creation in a dilapidated Portuguese Gymnasium to an eighty-year-old woman he hadn't known yesterday and who didn't know a word of Hebrew. It was the craziest thing he had ever done. He enjoyed it as he had never before enjoyed anything. It was as if he had cast off all internal shackles to fight unhindered this one time like someone who knows his impending end.

"And now let's go into the auditorium," said Maria João. "It was locked back then."

They sat in the first row in front of the raised lectern.

"So that's where he gave his speech. His notorious speech. I loved it. It was so much from him. He *was* it. But there was something in it that scared me. Not in the version he presented, he took it out. You remember the conclusion, where he says that he needs both, the holiness of words and the hostility against everything cruel. Then comes: *And no one may force me to choose.* That was the last sentence he delivered. But originally, there was another sentence: *Seria uma corrida atrás do vento*, it would be reaching for the wind.

" 'What a wonderful image!' I shouted.

"Then he picked up the Bible and read to me from Ecclesiastes: *I have seen all the works that are done under the sun; and behold, all is vanity and reaching for the wind.* I was scared.

" 'You can't do that!' I said. 'The priests all know that immediately and will consider you a megalomaniac!'

"What I didn't say was that, at that moment, I was worried about his emotional health.

"'But why,' he said in amazement. 'It's just poetry.'

"'But you can't speak biblical poetry! *Biblical* poetry! In your name!'

"'Poetry trumps everything,' he said. 'It annuls all rules.'

"But he had become uncertain and deleted the sentence. He felt that I was worried, he always felt everything. We never talked about it again."

Gregorius told her of Prado's discussion with O'Kelly about the dying word of God.

"I didn't know that," she said and was silent a while. She folded her hands, released them, folded them again.

"Jorge. Jorge O'Kelly. I don't know. I don't know if he was good fortune or bad for Amadeu. A great misfortune disguised as great good fortune, there is that. Amadeu, he longed for Jorge's strength, a coarse strength. He really longed for his coarseness, which could be seen in his coarse, chapped hands, his unruly, tangled hair and the unfiltered cigarettes he then smoked nonstop. I don't want to do him an injustice, but I didn't like Amadeu's uncritical enthusiasm for him. I was a peasant girl, I know how peasant boys are. No reason for romanticism. When it came to the crunch, Jorge would think of himself first.

"What fascinated him about O'Kelly and even intoxicated him was that Jorge had no trouble keeping his distance from others. He just said no and grinned over his big nose. Amadeu, on the other hand, struggled for his borders as for his salvation."

Gregorius told of the letter to the father and the sentence: *Others are your court of justice.*

"Yes, exactly. It made him a profoundly uncertain person, the thinnest-skinned person you can imagine. He had this overwhelming need for trust and afterward to be accepted. He thought he had to hide this uncertainty and much that looked like courage and boldness was simply a headlong flight forward. He demanded infinitely too much from himself, much too much, and he became self-righteous and judgmental about it.

"Everyone who knew him closely talked of the feeling of never being able to satisfy him and his expectations, of always falling short. That he didn't think much of himself made everything even worse. You couldn't even defend yourself with the accusation of complacency.

"How intolerant he was of kitsch! Above all in words and gestures. And what fear he had of his own kitsch! 'You have to be able to accept yourself in your own kitsch to be free,' I said. Then he breathed more calmly, more freely for a while. He had a phenomenal memory. But such things he quickly forgot and then the strained breath took him back again into its icy, merciless grip.

"He had fought against the court. My God, he fought! And he lost. Yes, I think you have to say that he lost.

"In quiet times, when he simply practiced medicine and people were grateful to him, he sometimes looked as if he had done it. But then the story with Mendes. The spit on his face haunted him, to the last he kept dreaming of it. An execution.

"I was against him going into the resistance. He wasn't the man for it, didn't have the nerves, although he did have the mind. And I didn't see that he had to make up for anything. But there was nothing to do. *When it has to do with the soul, there's little we can do,* he said, I already told you these words.

"And Jorge was also in the resistance. Jorge, whom he finally lost this way. Listless, he brooded over it in my kitchen and didn't say a word."

They went upstairs and Gregorius showed her the school bench where he had seated Prado in his thoughts. It was the wrong floor, but otherwise almost right. Maria João stood at the window and looked over to her seat in the girls' school.

"Others are your court of justice. He had also experienced it when he cut open Adriana's neck. The others sat at the table and looked at him as a monster. And he did the only right thing. When I lived in Paris, I attended a course in emergency medicine and they showed us that. Tracheotomy. You have to split the *ligamentum conicum* and keep the windpipe open with a trachea canula. Otherwise the patient dies of bolus. I don't know if I could have done it or if I would have thought of a pen as a substitute for the canula. 'If you want to work here. . . ,' the doctors said to him who operated on Adriana afterward.

"For Adriana's life, it had devastating consequences. When you've saved somebody's life, especially then you must have a quick and easy parting. For others and through others for yourself, saving a life is a burden nobody can bear. Therefore, it should have been treated as a stroke of luck, something like a spontaneous cure. Something impersonal.

"Adriana's gratitude was hard for Amadeu. It had something religious, something fanatical. Sometimes he was disgusted by it, she could be as servile as a slave. But there was her unfortunate love affair, the abortion, the danger of isolation. Sometimes I tried to persuade myself that he didn't take me into his practice because of Adriana. But it's not the truth.

"With Mélodie, his sister Rita, it was completely different, light and easy. He had a photo of him wearing one of the Mao caps of her girls' orchestra. He envied her courage to be flighty. He didn't hold it against her that, as the unplanned latecomer, she felt much less of the emotional burden of the parents than the older siblings. But he could also be furious when he thought of how much easier his life as a son could have been.

"I was in his house only once. When we were still in school. The invitation was a mistake. They were nice to me, but we all felt that I didn't belong there, not in a rich, aristocratic house. Amadeu was unhappy about the afternoon.

"'I hope . . . ,' he said, 'I can't . . . '

"'It's not important,' I said.

"Much later, I once met with the judge, he had requested it. He felt that Amadeu was offended by his activity under a government that had Tarrafal on its conscience. *He loathes me, my own son loathes me,* he blurted out. And then he told of his pains and how his profession helped him go on living. He accused Amadeu of a lack of empathy. I told him what Amadeu had said to me: *I won't see him as a sick man who is forgiven everything. It would be as if I didn't have a father anymore.*

"What I didn't tell him was how unhappy Amadeu was in Coimbra. Because he had doubts about his future as a doctor. Because he wasn't sure if perhaps he wasn't only following his father's wish and missing out on his own will.

"He shoplifted in the oldest department store in the city, was almost caught, and then suffered a nervous breakdown. I visited him.

"'Do you know the reason?' I asked. He nodded.

"He never explained it to me. But I think it was connected with the father, the court and the sentence. A kind of helpless, encoded revolt. In the hospital corridor, I ran into O'Kelly.

"'If he had at least pinched something really valuable!' he only said. 'This junk!'

"I don't know if I liked him at this moment, or the opposite. To this day I don't know.

"The accusation of a lack of empathy was anything but justified. How often in my presence had Amadeu assumed the position of a Bechterev sufferer and held it until he got a backache! And then remained bent over, his head stretched forward like a bird, his teeth gnashing.

"'I don't know how he stands it,' he said. 'Not only the pain. The humiliation!'

"If his imagination failed somewhere, it was with the mother. The relationship to her remained a mystery to me. Pretty, well-groomed, but a nondescript woman. 'Yes,' he said. 'That's it. No one would believe it.' He blamed her for so much that it really couldn't be right. The unsuccessful demarcation; the passion for work; the excessive demands on himself; the inability to dance and play. Everything was supposed to be connected with her and her gentle dictatorship. But you couldn't talk to him about it. 'I don't want to talk, I want to be furious! Just furious! *Furioso! Raivoso!*'"

Twilight fell, Maria João was driving with her headlights on.

"Do you know Coimbra?" she asked.

Gregorius shook his head.

"He loved the Biblioteca Joanina at the university. Not a week went by that he wasn't there. And the Sala Grande dos Actos, where he received his certificate. He also kept going there later to see the rooms."

When Gregorius got out, he became dizzy and he had to hold on to the roof of the car. Maria João squinted.

"Do you have that often?"

He hesitated. Then he lied.

"You shouldn't take it lightly," she said. "Do you know a neurologist here?"

He nodded.

She drove off slowly as if she were considering coming back. Only at the intersection did she accelerate. The world was spinning and Gregorius had to hold on to the doorknob before he could unlock it. He drank a glass of milk from Silveira's refrigerator and then went upstairs slowly, step by step.

40

I hate hotels. Why do I keep doing it? Can you tell me that, Julieta? On Saturday noon, when Gregorius heard Silveira unlock the door, he thought of these words of his, which the maid had told him. Silveira's actions fit his words: he simply dropped his suitcase and coat, sat down in a chair in the hall and shut his eyes in exhaustion. When he saw Gregorius coming down the stairs, his face lit up.

"Raimundo. You're not in Isfahan?" he asked laughing.

He had a cold and was sniffling. The business deal in Biarritz hadn't gone as expected, he had lost twice to the sleeping car waiter and Felipe, the chauffeur, hadn't showed up on time at the railroad station. Moreover, Julieta was also off today. Exhaustion was written on his face, an exhaustion greater and deeper than back then on the train. *The problem is,* Silveira had said back then when the train stood in the railroad station of Valladolid, *that we have no panorama of our life. Neither forward nor backward. If something goes well, we simply had good luck.*

They ate what Julieta had prepared yesterday and then drank coffee in the living room. Silveira saw Gregorius's look go to the photos of the noble party.

"Dammit," he said. "I completely forgot that. The party, the damn family party."

He wasn't going, *he simply wasn't going,* he said and banged the fork on the table. Something in Gregorius's face made him stop.

"Then you're coming along," he said. "A stiff family party of the nobility. The last one! But if you like . . ."

It was close to eight when Felipe picked them up and was amazed to see them standing in the hall and shaking with laughter. He had nothing suitable to wear, Gregorius had said an hour earlier. Then he had tried on Silveira's things, which were all tight. And now he looked at himself in the big mirror: a pair of pants that were too long, lying in folds on the unsuitable, thick shoes, a smoking jacket that didn't close, a shirt whose collar choked him. He was jolted when he saw himself, but then was carried away by Silveira's fit of laughter and now he began to enjoy the clowning. He couldn't have explained it, but he had the feeling that he was taking revenge on Florence with this masquerade.

Yet the obscure revenge didn't really get going until they entered Silveira's aunt's villa. Silveira enjoyed introducing his snooty relatives to his friend from Switzerland, Raimundo Gregorio, a real scholar, who mastered countless languages. When Gregorius heard the word *erudito,* he flinched like an imposter just before he's exposed. But at the table, he suddenly felt an attack of mischief and, to prove his multilingualism, he spoke a wildly jumbled blend of Hebrew, Greek and Bern German and got drunk on the abstruse combinations of words that became crazier from one minute to the next. He hadn't known he had so much wordplay, he seemed to be carried away by imagination into a bold, broad loop in space, farther and higher, until he crashed somewhere. Dizziness gripped him, a pleasant dizziness of crazy words, red wine, smoke and background music, he *wanted* this dizziness and did everything to keep it going, he was the star of the evening, Silveira's relatives were glad not to have to be bored with themselves, Silveira chain-smoked and enjoyed the show, the women watched Gregorius with looks he wasn't used to, he wasn't sure whether they meant what they seemed to mean, but it didn't matter, what did count was that there were such ambiguous looks at him, Mundus, the man of the most brittle parchment, called Papyrus.

Sometime during the night he stood in the kitchen and washed dishes, it was the kitchen of Silveira's relatives, but it was also the kitchen of the von Muralts, and Eva, Unbelievable, watched what he was doing in horror. He had waited until the two maids had gone, then he had slipped into the kitchen and now he was standing there, dizzy and swaying, leaning on the sink and polishing the plates. He wanted not to fear the dizziness now, he wanted to enjoy the lunacy of the evening, the luxury of making up after forty years for what he couldn't have done back then at the school party. Can you buy a title of nobility in Portugal, he had asked at dessert, but the expected embarrassment had failed to appear, they considered the question the stammering of someone who didn't know the language. Only Silveira had grinned.

The glasses were steamy with hot dishwater, Gregorius groped in the emptiness and dropped a plate that fell to pieces on the stone floor.

"Espera, eu ajudo," said Silveira's niece Aurora, who suddenly stood in the kitchen. Together, they crouched down and gathered up the slivers of china. Gregorius still didn't see anything and bumped into Aurora, whose perfume, he thought later, suited his dizziness to a T.

"Não faz mal," never mind, she said when he apologized and he was amazed to feel her press a kiss on his forehead. What was he doing here, she asked, when she stood up again and pointed giggling at the apron he had tied around himself. Washing dishes? He? The guest? The polyglot scholar? *"Incrível!"* Unbelievable!

They danced. Aurora had taken off his apron, turned on the kitchen radio, taken hold of his hand and shoulder, and now she waltzed him around the kitchen. Gregorius had fled from dancing school back in his youth after one and a half lessons. Now he spun like a bear, stumbling over the pants that were too long, gripped by vertigo, *I'm going to fall,* he tried to hold on to Aurora, who didn't seem to notice anything and whistled to the music, his knees buckled, and it was only Silveira's strong grip that prevented the fall.

Gregorius didn't understand what Silveira said to Aurora, but from his tone he was clearly bawling her out. He helped Gregorius sit down and brought him a glass of water.

Half an hour later, they left. He had never seen anything like that, said Silveira in the back of the car. Gregorius had stood this whole stiff company on its head. Well, Aurora always had this reputation . . . But the others . . . He simply had to bring Gregorius along the next time, they had instructed him!

They let the chauffeur drive himself home, then Silveira sat down behind the wheel and they went to the Liceu. "It seems right now, somehow, doesn't it?" Silveira had suddenly said on the way.

In the light of the camping lamp, Silveira looked at the pictures of Isfahan. He nodded. He glanced at Gregorius and nodded again. On a chair lay the blanket as Maria João had folded it. Silveira sat down. He asked Gregorius questions no one here had asked, not even Maria João. How had he come to ancient languages? Why wasn't he at the university? He still remembered everything Gregorius had told him about Florence, but hadn't there been any other woman afterward?

And then Gregorius told him about Prado. It was the first time he talked about him with someone who hadn't known him. He was amazed at everything he knew about him and how much he had thought about him. Silveira warmed his hands on the camp stove and listened without once interrupting. Could he see the book of the red cedars? he asked at the end.

He kept looking at the portrait for a long time. He read the introduction about the thousand mute experiences. He reread it. Then he began leafing through. He laughed and read aloud: *Petty bookkeeping about generosity: there is that, too.* He leafed some more, stopped, leafed back and read aloud:

AREIAS MOVEDIÇAS. QUICKSAND. *When we have understood that in every effort it's a matter of pure luck whether we succeed or not; so when we have understood that in every act and experience we are quicksand before ourselves and for ourselves: What then happens with all the intimate and praised feelings like pride, remorse and shame?*

Now Silveira stood up and paced back and forth, Prado's text before his eyes. Feverishly. He read aloud: *To understand yourself: Is that a discovery or a creation?* He leafed on and read aloud again: *Is anyone really interested in* me, *and not only in his interest in me?* He had come on a longer piece of text, sat down on the edge of Senhor Cortês's desk and lit a cigarette.

PALAVRAS TRAIÇOEIRAS. TREACHEROUS WORDS. *When we talk about ourselves, about others, or simply about things, we want—it could be said—to* reveal *ourselves in our words: We want to show what we think and feel. We let others have a glimpse into our soul.* (We give them a piece of our mind, *as they say in English. An Englishman said that to me when we stood at a ship's railing. That's the only good thing I brought from that absurd country. Maybe also the memory of the Irishman with the red ball in All Souls.) In this understanding of the case, we're the sovereign director, the self-appointed dramaturge as far as opening our self is concerned. But maybe this is absolutely false? A self-deception? For not only do we* reveal *ourselves with our words, we also* betray *ourselves. We give away a lot more than what we wanted to reveal, and sometimes it's the exact opposite. And the others can interpret our words as symptoms for something we ourselves may not even know. As symptoms of the sickness of being us. It can be amusing when we regard others like this, it can make us more tolerant, but also put ammunition in our hands. And the moment we start speaking, if we think that others are doing the very same thing with us, the word can stick in our throat and fear can make us mute forever.*

On the way back, they stopped at a building with a lot of steel and glass.

"That's my office," said Silveira. "I'd like to make a photocopy of Prado's book."

He turned off the motor and opened the door. A look at Gregorius's face made him stop.

"I *see*. Yes. This text and a copy machine—they don't go together." He ran his hand along the steering wheel. "And besides, you want to keep the text all to yourself. Not only the *book*. The *text*."

Later, when Gregorius lay awake, he kept thinking of these sentences. Why hadn't there been anybody before in his life who understood him so fast and so easily? Before they went to bed, Silveira had embraced him for a moment. He was a man he could tell about his dizziness. The dizziness and the fear of the neurologist.

41

When João Eça stood in the door of his room in the home on Sunday, Gregorius saw in his face that something had happened. Eça hesitated before asking him in. It was a cold March day, yet the window was wide open. Eça straightened his trousers before he sat down. He struggled with himself as he set up the pieces with shaking hands. The struggle, Gregorius later thought, was about both his feelings and the question of whether he should talk about them.

Eça moved the pawns. "I went in bed last night," he said in a rough voice. "And I didn't notice it." He kept his eyes lowered to the board.

Gregorius moved. He couldn't be silent for too long. He had reeled dizzily last night through a strange kitchen and almost landed in the arms of a hysterical woman, unintentionally, he said.

That was something different, Eça was irritated.

Because it didn't concern the lower body? asked Gregorius. In both cases, it was about losing the usual control of the body.

Eça looked at him. Things were going on in him.

Gregorius made tea and poured him a half cup. Eça saw the look that fell on his shaking hands.

"A dignidade," he said.

"Dignity," said Gregorius. "I have no idea what that really is. But I don't think it's something that gets lost just because the body fails."

Eça botched the opening.

"When they led me to torture, I went in my pants and they laughed at it. It was a horrible *humiliation;* but I didn't feel I was losing my *dignity*. But what is it *then*?"

Did he believe he would lose his dignity if he had talked, asked Gregorius.

"I didn't say a word, not a single word. I locked away all the possible words in me. Yes, that's it: I *locked* them away and bolted the door irrevocably. So it was *impossible* for me to talk, it was no longer *negotiable*. That had a peculiar effect: I stopped experiencing the torture as a *behavior* of the others, as an *act*. I sat there like a mere body, a heap of flesh stabbed by pains like a hailstorm. I stopped acknowledging the torturers as actors. They didn't know it, but I *degraded* them, degraded to scenes of a blind happening. That helped me make the torture into an agony."

And if they had loosened his tongue with a drug?

He had often asked himself that, said Eça, and he had dreamed of it. He had come to the conclusion that they could have *destroyed* him with that, but they could never take away his *dignity* in this way. To lose your dignity, you had to *forfeit* yourself.

"And then you get worked up about a dirtied bed?" said Gregorius and shut the window. "It's cold and it doesn't smell, not at all."

Eça ran his hand over his eyes. "I don't want any tubes, any pumps. Only to make it last a few weeks longer."

That there are things a person wouldn't do or allow at *any* price: maybe that's what dignity consisted of, said Gregorius. It didn't need to be moral boundaries, he added. You could forfeit your dignity in other ways. A teacher who played the crowing cock in the variety show out of subjection. Asskissing for the sake of a career. Unbounded opportunism. Duplicity and avoiding conflict to save a marriage. Such things.

"The beggar?" asked Eça. "Can a person be a beggar with dignity?"

"Maybe, if there's an inevitability in his story, something unavoidable, he can't do anything about. And if he stands by it. Stands by himself," said Gregorius.

To stand by yourself—that was also part of dignity. That way, a person could get through a public flaying with dignity. Galileo. Luther. Even somebody who admitted his guilt and resisted the temptation to deny it. Something politicians couldn't do. Honesty, the courage for honesty. With others and yourself.

Gregorius stopped. You knew what you thought only when you expressed it.

"There's a disgust," said Eça, "a very special disgust you feel when you face someone who deceives himself incessantly. Maybe that's a disgust over the lack of dignity. I sat in school next to someone who kept wiping his sticky hands on his pants, and I still picture this special behavior: as if it wasn't *true* that he wiped them. He wanted to be my friend. It didn't work. And not because of the pants. That's how he was *in general*."

In partings and pardons, too, there was a question of dignity, he added. Amadeu had spoken of that sometimes. He had been particularly concerned with the difference between a forgiveness that leaves the other his dignity and one that takes it away from him. *It must not be forgiveness that demands subordination,* he said. *Thus, not as in the Bible, where you must understand yourself as a servant of God and Jesus. A servant! That's what it says!*

"He could get white hot with rage," said Eça. "And often afterward he also spoke of the lack of dignity in the New Testament attitude about death. *To die in dignity means to die acknowledging the fact that dying is the end. And to resist all immortality kitsch.* On Ascension Day, his office was open, and he worked even more than usual."

Gregorius went back to Lisbon on the Tagus. *When we have understood that in every act and experience we are quicksand . . .* What did that mean for dignity?

42

On Monday morning, Gregorius sat in the train to Coimbra, the city where Prado had lived with the tormenting question of whether studying medicine had perhaps been a great mistake because he was mainly following his father's wish and giving up his own will. One day, he had gone into the oldest department store in the city and stolen goods he didn't need. He who could allow himself to give his friend Jorge a complete pharmacy. Gregorius thought of his letter to his father and the beautiful thief, Diamantina Esmeralda Ermelinda, who Prado's imagination had assigned the role of avenging the thief sentenced by his father.

Before he went, he had called Maria João and asked her about the street where Prado had lived back then. He had given an evasive answer to her worried question about his dizziness. This morning, he hadn't been dizzy. But something was different. It was as if he had to overcome a paper-thin air cushion of the softest resistance in order to touch things. He could have experienced the layer of air to be pierced as a protective cover if not for the flickering fear that the world was incessantly slipping past him. On the railroad platform in Lisbon, he had walked back and forth firmly to assure himself of the stony resistance. It had helped and when he took a seat in the empty train compartment, he was calmer.

Prado had made this trip countless times. On the telephone, Maria João had spoken of his passion for railroads, which João Eça had also described when he told how his knowledge of these things, *his crazy patriotism for the railroad,* had saved the lives of people in the resistance. It had been the working of the switches that fascinated him especially, he had reported. Maria João had emphasized something else: train travel as a riverbed of imagination, a movement where fantasy liquefied and passed you images from closed chambers of the soul. The conversation with her this morning had lasted longer than planned, the particular, precious trust that had emerged when he had read to her from the Bible yesterday had remained. Gregorius again heard O'Kelly's sighing words: *Maria, my God, yes, Maria.* Exactly twenty-four hours had passed since she had opened the door to him, and it was already perfectly clear to him why Prado had written the thoughts he considered most dangerous in her kitchen and nowhere else. What was it? Her fearlessness? The impression that this was a woman who, in the course of her life, had found an internal demarcation and independence that Prado could only dream of?

They had talked on the phone as if they were still sitting in the Liceu, he at Senhor Cortês's desk, she in the chair with the blanket over her legs.

"Concerning travel, he was remarkably split," she had said. "He wanted to travel, ever farther, he wanted to lose himself in the space opened up to him by fantasy. But, as soon as he was away from Lisbon, he became homesick, a horrible homesickness, you couldn't bear to see it. 'Look, Lisbon is indeed beautiful, but . . . ,' people said to him.

"They didn't understand that it wasn't really about Lisbon, but about him, Amadeu. That is, his homesickness wasn't the yearning for the familiar and beloved. It was something much deeper, something that concerned his core: the wish to flee back behind the solid, reliable dams inside that protected him from the dangerous breakers and malicious undercurrents of his soul. He knew from experience that the internal dikes were solid mainly when he was in Lisbon, in his parents' house, in the Liceu, but above all in the blue office. *Blue is the color of my security,* he said.

"That it was about protection from himself explains why his homesickness always smacked of panic and catastrophe. When it came over him, he had to go very fast and then he broke off a trip from one moment to the next and fled home. How often Fátima was disappointed when it happened!"

Maria João had hesitated before she added:

"It's good that she didn't understand what his homesickness was about. Otherwise, she would have had to think: I apparently don't manage to rid him of his fear of himself."

Gregorius opened Prado's book and read for the nth time a note that seemed like none other to be the key to all the others.

ESTOU A VIVER EM MIM PRÓPRIO COMO NUM COMBOIO A ANDAR. I LIVE IN MYSELF AS IN A MOVING TRAIN. *I didn't board voluntarily, didn't have the choice and don't know the name of the destination. One day in the distant past I woke up in my compartment and felt rolling. It was exciting, I listened to the pounding of the wheels, held my head in the wind and savored the speed of the things passing by me. I wished the train would never interrupt its journey. By no means did I want it to stop somewhere forever.*

It was in Coimbra, on a hard bench in the lecture hall that I became aware: I can't get off. I can't change the tracks or the direction. I don't determine the pace. I don't see the locomotive and can't see who's driving it and whether the engineer makes a reliable impression. I don't know if he reads the signals correctly and notices if a switch is worked wrong. I can't change the compartment. In the corridor, I see people passing by and think: Maybe it looks completely different in their compartment than in mine. But I can't go there and see, a conductor I never saw and never will see has bolted and sealed the compartment door. I open the window, lean far out and see that everybody else is doing the same thing. The train makes a soft curve. The last cars are still in the tunnel and the first are going on. Maybe the train is traveling in a circle, over and over, without anybody noticing it, not even the engineer? I have no idea how long the train is. I see all the others craning their neck to see and understand something. I call a greeting, but the wind blows away my words.

The lighting in the compartment changes and I can't determine it. Sun and clouds, twilight and again twilight, rain, snow, storm. The light on the ceiling is dim, grows lighter, a glistening glow, it begins flickering, goes out, comes back, it's a miserable light, a chandelier, a dazzling colored neon light, all in one. The heating doesn't work right. It might heat when it's hot and break down when it's cold. If I move the switch, it clicks and clacks, but doesn't change anything. Strangely, my coat doesn't always warm me evenly either. Outside, things seem to take their usual, reasonable course. Maybe in the other compartments, too? In mine, in any case, it's different from what I expected, completely different. Was the designer drunk? A madman? A diabolical charlatan?

Train schedules are available in the compartment. I want to see where we'll stop. The pages are empty. At the railroad stations where we stop, place signs are missing. The people outside glance curiously at the train. The windowpanes are murky from frequent fierce storms. I think: they distort the image of what is inside. Suddenly I'm overcome by the need to put things right. The window's stuck. I shout myself hoarse. The others bang indignantly on the wall. Beyond the station comes a tunnel. It takes my breath away. Leaving the tunnel, I ask myself if we really did stop.

What can you do on the trip? Tidy up the compartment. Fasten things so they don't rattle. But then I dream that the wind billows up and smashes the windowpanes. Everything I have carefully straightened up flies away. I dream a lot on the endless journey, dreams of missed trains and wrong information in the schedules, of stations that vanish when you arrive, of level crossing attendants and stationmasters in red caps suddenly standing in the emptiness. Sometimes I fall asleep out of sheer weariness. Falling asleep is dangerous, only seldom do I awake refreshed and am glad about the changes. What usually happens is that I'm bothered by what I find on awakening, both inside and out.

Sometimes I'm startled and think: the train can go off the rails anytime. Indeed I usually frighten myself with the thought. But in rare, incandescent moments, it flashes through me like a blessed lightning bolt.

I wake up and the landscape of the others draws past. Sometimes at breakneck speed so that I hardly keep up with their moods and their exuberant nonsense; then again with tormenting slowness when they keep saying and doing the same thing. I'm glad about the windowpane between them and me. So I see their wishes and plans but they can't open fire on me unhindered. I'm glad when the train picks up speed and they disappear. The wishes of others: What do we do with them when they strike us?

I press my forehead to the compartment window and concentrate with all my might. I would like once, one single time, to grasp what is going on outside. Really grasp *it. So that it doesn't slip away from me again immediately. It fails. Everything goes much too fast, even when the train stops between stations. The next impression wipes away the last one. Memory is overheated, I'm breathlessly busy retrospectively assembling the fleeting images of the event into an illusion of something intelligible. I always come too late, how fast the light of attention to things scurries off. Everything is always already past. I'm always left behind empty-handed. Never am I* there. *Not even when the inside of the compartment is reflected at night in the windowpane.*

I love tunnels. They're the symbol of hope: sometime it will be bright again. If by chance it is not night.

Sometimes I get a visit in the compartment. I don't know how that's possible despite the bolted and sealed door, but it does happen. Usually the visit comes at the wrong time. They're people from the present, often also from the past. They come and go as they like, they're inconsiderate and bother me. I have to talk with them. It's all temporary, not binding, doomed to oblivion; conversations on a train. A few visitors disappear without a trace. Others leave sticky and stinking traces, ventilating doesn't help. Then I'd like to rip out all the furnishings of the compartment and replace them with new ones.

The trip is long. Some days I wish it were endless. Those are rare, precious days. Other days I'm glad to know that there will be a last tunnel, where the train will come to a halt forever.

When Gregorius got off the train, it was late afternoon. He took a room in a hotel on the other side of the Mondego, where he had a view of the old city on the Alcáçova Hill. The last sunbeams bathed the majestic buildings of the university towering over everything in a warm, golden light. Up there, in one of the steep narrow streets, Prado and O'Kelly had lived in a República, one of the student dorms dating from the Middle Ages.

"He didn't want to live differently from the others," Maria João had said. "Even though the noise from the room next door sometimes drove him to despair, he wasn't used to that. But the family wealth from the big estates of previous generations sometimes weighed heavily on him. There were two words that got him hot like no others: *colónia* and *latifundiário*. Then he looked like a person who's ready to shoot.

"When I visited him, his clothes were ostentatiously casual. Why didn't he wear the yellow ribbon of the school like the other medical students, I asked him.

" 'You know I don't like uniforms, even the cap in the Liceu was repulsive to me,' he said.

"When I had to go back and we were standing in the railroad station, a student came on the platform wearing the dark blue ribbon of literature.

"I looked at Amadeu. 'It's not the *ribbon*,' I said. 'It's the *yellow* ribbon. You'd gladly wear the *blue* ribbon.'

"'You do know,' he said, 'that I don't like people to see through me. Come again soon. Please.'

"He had a way of saying *por favor*—I would have gone to the ends of the earth to hear it."

The street where Prado had lived was easy to find. Gregorius glanced into the entryway of the dorm and went up a few stairs. *In Coimbra, when the whole world seemed to belong to us.* That's how Jorge had described that time. So in this house he and Prado had written down what it was that endowed *lealdade,* loyalty between people. A list that lacked love. *Desire, pleasure, security.* All feelings that disintegrate sooner or later. Loyalty was the only one that lasted. *A will, a decision, a resolution of the soul.* Something that changed to necessity by the chance of encounters and the contingency of feelings. *A breath of eternity, only a breath, but all the same,* Prado had said. Gregorius pictured O'Kelly's face. *He deluded himself. We both deluded ourselves,* he said with the slowness of a drunk.

In the university, Gregorius wanted to go immediately to the Biblioteca Joanina and the Sala Grande dos Actos, the rooms that had kept Prado coming back here. But that was possible only at certain times, and those had passed today.

The Capela de São Miguel was open. Gregorius was alone and looked at the overwhelmingly beautiful baroque organ. *I want to hear the rustling of the organ, this deluge of ethereal tones. I need it against the shrill absurdity of marches,* Prado had said in his speech. Gregorius recalled the times he had been in church. Confirmation lessons, the parents' funerals. *Our Father . . .* How dull, joyless and naïve it had sounded! And all that, he thought now, had nothing to do with the sweeping poetry of the Greek and Hebrew texts. Nothing, absolutely nothing!

Gregorius started. Without meaning to, he had banged his fist on the bench and now looked around ashamed, but he was still alone. He dropped to his knees and did what Prado had done with his father's twisted back: he tried to imagine how the posture felt from within. *You would have to rip them out,* Prado had said when he had passed the confessionals with Father Bartolomeu. *Such humiliation!*

When Gregorius straightened up, the chapel was spinning rapidly. He clung to the bench and waited until it had passed. Then, as students rushed past him, he walked slowly along the corridors and entered a lecture hall. Sitting in the last row, he thought first of the lecture on Euripides where he had once failed to tell the lecturer his opinion aloud. Then his thoughts slid back to the lectures he had attended as a student. And finally, he imagined the student Prado standing up in the lecture hall and posing critical questions. Staid, prizewinning professors, leading authorities in their field, felt tested by him, Father Bartolomeu had said. But Prado had sat here not as an arrogant, know-it-all student. He had lived in the purgatory of doubt, tormented by the fear that he could miss himself. *It was in Coimbra, on a hard bench in the lecture hall, that I became aware: I can't get off.*

It was a lecture in jurisprudence, Gregorius didn't understand a word and left. He stayed until night on the grounds of the university and kept trying to be aware of the confusing feelings that accompanied him. Why did he think that here, in the most famous university of Portugal, all of a sudden he might have liked to stand in a lecture hall and share his comprehensive philosophical knowledge with students? Had he perhaps missed a possible life, one he could easily have lived with his abilities and knowledge? Never before, not for a single hour, had he considered it a mistake that, as a student, he had stayed away from lectures after a few semesters and devoted all his time to the ceaseless reading of texts. Why now all of a sudden this particular nostalgia? And was it really nostalgia?

He had ordered a meal in a small pub. But when it arrived, it revolted him and he wanted to be out in the cool night air. The paper-thin cushion of air that had enclosed him this morning was back again, a little thicker and with a resistance that was a trace stronger. As at the train platform in Lisbon he walked with exaggerated firmness and that helped now, too.

JOÃO DE LOUSADA DE LEDESMA, O MAR TENEBROSO. The big volume leaped to his eyes as he walked along the walls of books in a secondhand bookshop. The book on Prado's desk. The last thing he read. Gregorius took it off the shelf. The big calligraphic font, the engravings of coasts, the India ink drawings of seafarers. *Cabo Finisterre,* he heard Adriana say, *up in Galicia. It was like an idée fixe. He had a haunted, feverish expression on his face when he spoke of it.*

Gregorius sat down in a corner and leafed through it until he came on the words of the twelfth-century Muslim geographer El Edrisi: *From Santiago we went to Finisterre, as the peasants call it, a word that means the end of the world. You see nothing more than sky and water, and they say that the sea is so stormy that no one could travel on it, and so you can't know what is on the other side. They told us that some, eager to fathom it, disappeared with their ships and none ever came back.*

It took a while for the thought to take shape in Gregorius. *Much later I heard that she was working in Salamanca as a lecturer in history,* João Eça had said about Estefânia Espinhosa. When she was working for the resistance, she was in the post office. After the flight with Prado, she had stayed in Spain. And had studied history. Adriana had seen no connection between Prado's trip to Spain and his sudden fanatical interest in Finisterre. Was there a link? If he and Estefânia Espinhosa had traveled to Finisterre because she had always been interested in the medieval fear of the endless stormy sea, an interest that had led to her studies? Did something happen on this trip to the end of the world that upset Prado and moved him to return?

But no, it was too absurd, too preposterous. And it was just as ridiculous to assume that the woman had also written a book about the fearsome sea. He really couldn't waste the secondhand bookdealer's time with that.

"Let's see," said the secondhand bookdealer. "The same title—that's almost out of the question. Violates good academic morals. We'll check it with the name."

Estefânia Espinhosa, said the computer, had written two books, both dealt with the beginnings of the Renaissance.

"Not so far away, eh?" said the secondhand bookdealer. "But we can get much more precise information. Watch," and he called up the history department of the University of Salamanca.

Estefânia Espinhosa had her own Web page, and right at the start they came on the list of publications: two entries about Finisterre, one in Portuguese, the other in Spanish. The secondhand bookseller grinned.

"Don't like the machine, but sometimes . . ."

He called a specialized bookshop and they had one of the two books.

The shops would soon close. Gregorius, the big book about the dark sea under his arm, took off. Was there a picture of the woman on the cover? He almost ripped the book out of the saleswoman's hand and turned it over.

Estefânia Espinhosa, born 1948 in Lisbon, currently a professor at the University of Salamanca of early modern Spanish and Italian history. And a portrait that explained everything.

Gregorius bought the book and on the way to the hotel he stood still every few feet to look at the picture. *She wasn't only the ball, the red Irish ball in the college. She was much more than all red Irish balls together: He must have felt that she was the chance for him to be whole. As a man, I mean,* he heard Maria João say. And the words of João Eça could not have been more apt: *Estefânia, I think, was his chance to get out of the courthouse at last, go out to the free, hot place of life and live for this one time completely according to his wish, to his passion, and to hell with others.*

So she had been twenty-four when she sat down behind the steering wheel in front of the blue house and drove across the border with Prado, twenty-eight years older, away from O'Kelly, away from danger, into a new life.

On the way back to the hotel, Gregorius passed by the psychiatric clinic. He thought of Prado's nervous breakdown after the shoplifting. Maria João had said that in the ward, he was interested mainly in those patients who, blindly entangled in themselves, paced back and forth and talked to themselves. He kept his eye on such people even later and was amazed how many of them there were on the street, in the bus, on the Tagus, who shouted out their rage at imaginary opponents.

"He wouldn't have been Amadeu if he hadn't spoken to them and listened to their stories. That had never happened to them and when he made the mistake of giving them the address, they ran to his door the next day and Adriana had to throw them out."

In the hotel, Gregorius read one of the few notes of Prado's book he didn't yet know.

O VENENO ARDENTE DO DESGOSTO. THE WHITE HOT POISON OF ANGER. *When others make us angry at them—at their shamelessness, injustice, inconsideration—then they exercise power over us, they proliferate and gnaw at our soul, then anger is like a white-hot poison that corrodes all mild, noble and balanced feelings and robs us of sleep. Sleepless, we turn on the light and are angry at the anger that has lodged like a succubus who sucks us dry and debilitates us. We are not only furious at the damage, but also that it develops in us all by itself, for while we sit on the edge of the bed with aching temples, the distant catalyst remains untouched by the corrosive force of the anger that eats at us. On the empty internal stage bathed in the harsh light of mute rage, we perform all by ourselves a drama with shadow figures and shadow words we hurl against enemies in helpless rage we feel as icy blazing fire in our bowels. And the greater our despair that it is only a shadow play and not a real discussion with the possibility of hurting the other and producing a balance of suffering, the wilder the poisonous shadows dance and haunt us even in the darkest catacombs of our dreams. (We will turn the tables, we think grimly, and all night long forge words that will produce in the other the effect of a fire bomb so that now he will be the one with the flames of indignation raging inside while we, soothed by* schadenfreude, *will drink our coffee in cheerful calm.)*

What could it mean to deal appropriately *with anger? We really don't want to be soulless creatures who remain thoroughly indifferent to what they come across, creatures whose appraisals consist only of cool, anemic judgments and nothing can shake them up because nothing really bothers them. Therefore, we can't seriously wish not to know the experience of anger and instead persist in an equanimity that wouldn't be distinguished from tedious insensibility. Anger also teaches us something about who we are. Therefore this is what I'd like to know: What can it mean to train ourselves in anger and imagine that we take advantage of its knowledge without being addicted to its poison?*

We can be sure that we will hold on to the deathbed as part of the last balance sheet—and this part will taste bitter as cyanide—that we have wasted too much, much too much strength and time on getting angry and getting even with others in a helpless shadow theater, which only we, who suffered impotently, knew anything about. What can we do to improve this balance sheet? Why did our parents, teachers and other instructors never talk to us about it? Why didn't they tell something of this enormous significance? Not give us in this case any compass that could have helped us avoid wasting our soul on useless, self-destructive anger?

Gregorius lay awake a long time. Now and then he stood up and went to the window. The upper part of the city with the university and the bell tower now, after midnight, looked barren, sacred, and a little menacing. He could imagine a surveyor waiting in vain to be allowed into the mysterious district.

His head leaning on a mountain of pillows, Gregorius reread the sentences where Prado had opened himself and revealed himself more than in all others: *Sometimes I'm startled and think: The train can go off the rails anytime. Yes, I usually scare myself with the thought. But in rare, incandescent moments, it flashes through me like a blessed lightning bolt.*

He didn't know where the image came from, but all at once, Gregorius saw this Portuguese doctor who had dreamed of poetic thinking as paradise sitting among the pillars of a cloister, that had become a silent shelter for the derailed. His derailment had been that the incandescent lava of his tormented soul had seared and washed away with stunning force everything of enslavement and strain in him. He had disappointed all expectations and broken all taboos, and that was his bliss. In the end, he was at peace with the bent judging father, the soft dictatorship of the ambitious mother, and the lifelong stifling gratitude of the sister.

And with himself, too, he had finally found peace. The homesickness was over, he no longer needed Lisbon and the blue color of safety. Now that he had let go of the internal storm tide and had become one with it, there was no longer any reason to erect the dike. Unhampered by himself, he could travel to the other end of the world. At last, he could travel the snowy steppes of Siberia to Vladivostok without having to think at every pounding of the wheels that he was going away from his blue Lisbon.

Now the sunlight fell into the cloister garden, the pillars grew lighter and lighter and finally turned completely pale so that only a shining depth remained where Gregorius lost his hold.

He woke with a start, reeled to the bathroom and washed his face. Then he called Doxiades. The Greek had him describe all details of the dizziness. Then he was silent a while. Gregrorius felt a creeping fear.

"It can mean anything," said the Greek finally in his calm doctor voice. "Mostly it's harmless, nothing that can't be brought under control quickly. But tests have to be made. The Portuguese can do that just as well as we can here. But my gut feeling is: you should come home. Talk to the doctors in your mother tongue. Fear and foreign languages don't go well together."

When Gregorius finally fell asleep, the first glimmer of dawn was visible behind the university.

43

There were three hundred thousand volumes, said the tourist guide, and her spike heels clacked on the marble floor of the Biblioteca Joanina. Gregorius hung back and looked around. Never had he seen anything like it. Rooms paneled in gold and tropical woods, linked by arches reminiscent of triumphal arches, topped by the coat of arms of King João V, who had founded the library in the early eighteenth century. Baroque shelves with galleries of delicate pillars. A portrait of João V. A red carpet that enhanced the impression of splendor. It was like a fairy tale.

Homer, the Iliad and the Odyssey, several editions in magnificent bindings that made them into sacred texts. Gregorius let his eyes glide on.

After a while, he felt his look slipping by the shelves carelessly. His thoughts had stayed with Homer. It must have been the thoughts that made his heart pound, but he couldn't figure out what they were about. He went into a corner, took off his glasses and shut his eyes. In the next room, he heard the guide's shrill voice. He pressed the palms of his hands on his ears and concentrated on the muffled silence. The seconds passed by, he felt his blood throbbing.

Yes. What he had been looking for, without noticing, was a word that appeared in Homer only one single time. It was as if something behind his back, hidden in the wings of memory, wanted to test whether his ability to remember was still as good as ever. His breath speeded up. The word didn't come. *It didn't come.*

The guide moved through the room with the group, the people were chattering. Gregorius pushed past them as far back as he could. He heard the door to the library shut and the key turn.

His heart pounding, he ran to the shelf and took out the Odyssey. The old, stiff leather cut his palms with its sharp edges. He leafed through it frantically and blew the dust into the room. The word wasn't where he had thought. *It wasn't there.*

He tried to breathe calmly. As if a bank of veil clouds went through him, he felt a dizziness that came and went. Methodically, he went through the whole epic in his mind. No other passage was possible. But the result of the exercise was that now the supposed certainty at the start of his search crumbled. The floor began to sway and this time it wasn't dizziness. Had he deceived himself in the worst way, and it was the Iliad? He took it off the shelf and leafed through it thoughtlessly. The movements of the leafing hand were empty and mechanical, the goal forgotten, more from one moment to the next, Gregorius felt the cushion of air surrounding him, he tried to stamp, flailed his arms, the book fell out of his hand, his knees gave way, and he slid to the floor in a soft, feeble motion.

When he came to, he struggled to find his glasses that lay an arm's length away. He looked at his watch. No more than a quarter of an hour could have passed. Sitting up, he leaned his back against the wall. Minutes went by when he only breathed, glad he hadn't hurt himself and that the glasses had remained intact.

And then, quite suddenly, panic flamed up in him. Was this forgetting the beginning of something? A first, tiny island of forgetting? Would it grow and would others join it? *We are gravel-covered slopes of forgetting,* Prado had written somewhere. And if an avalanche of gravel now came over him and ripped away all the precious words? He grabbed his head with his big hands and pressed as if he could thus keep more words from disappearing. Object after object, he examined the field of vision and gave every thing its name, first in dialect, then in High German, French and English and finally Portuguese. None was lacking and slowly he calmed down.

When the door was opened for the next group, he waited in the corner, mingled with the people for a moment and then disappeared through the door. A dark blue sky arched over Coimbra. At a café, he drank a chamomile tea in short, small sips. His stomach relaxed and he could eat something.

The students lay in the warm March sun. A man and a woman, entangled in each other, suddenly burst into loud laughter, threw away their cigarettes, got up with fluid, supple movements and started dancing, as light and loose as if there were no gravity. Gregorius felt the undertow of memory and let himself go. And suddenly it was there, the scene he hadn't thought about in decades.

No errors, but a bit clumsy, the Latin professor had said when Gregorius translated Ovid's *Metamorphoses* in the lecture hall. A December afternoon, snowflakes, electric light. Girls grinning. *A little more dancing!* the man in the bow tie and the red scarf over his blazer had added. Gregorius had felt the whole weight of his body on the bench. The bench had creaked when he moved. The remaining time when the others' turn came, he had sat there numb. The numbness had lasted until he went through the arbor decorated for Christmas.

After the holidays, he hadn't gone to this class anymore. He had avoided the man with the red scarf and evaded the other professors as well. From then on, he had studied only at home.

Now he paid and went through the Mondego, called *O Rio dos Poetas,* back to the hotel. *Do you find me boring? How? But Mundus, you can't ask me such questions!* Why did all these things hurt so much, even now? Why hadn't he managed in twenty, thirty years to *shake them off* ?

When Gregorius woke up in the hotel two hours later, the sun was just going down. Natalie Rubin had walked with clacking spike heels over the marble of the corridors in the University of Bern. Standing at the front of an empty lecture hall, he had delivered a lecture about words that appeared in Greek literature only one single time. He wanted to write down the words, but the board was so soapy the chalk slid off and when he wanted to say the words, he had forgotten them. Estefânia Espinhosa had also flitted through his fitful sleep, a figure with shining eyes and an olive complexion, flat at first, then as a lecturer lecturing under a gigantic, gold-covered dome about subjects that didn't exist. Doxiades had interrupted her. *Come home,* he had said, *we'll examine you on Bubenbergplatz.*

Gregorius sat on the edge of the bed. The Homeric word didn't come now either. And the uncertainty about the passage where it was began to torment him again. There was no point picking up the Iliad. It was in the Odyssey. It was *there*. He *knew* it. But where?

The next train to Lisbon, they had found out downstairs at the reception desk, wasn't until the next morning. He reached for the big book about the dark sea and read more of what El Edrisi, the Muslim geographer, had written: *Nobody knows—we are told—what is in this sea, nor can it be examined, for there are many obstacles that confront the ship voyage: the profound darkness, the high waves, the frequent storms, the countless monsters that inhabit it, and the violent winds*. He would have liked to make photocopies of Estefânia Esphinhosa's two articles about Finisterre, but had failed with the library staff because he lacked the words.

He sat still a while. *Tests have to be made,* Doxiades had said. And he also heard the voice of Maria João: *You shouldn't take it lightly.*

He showered, packed and asked the baffled woman at the reception desk to call a taxi. The rental car agency at the railroad station was still open. But they also had to count today, said the man. Gregorius nodded, signed for two more days and went to the parking lot.

He had gotten his driver's license as a student, with the money he earned from teaching. That had been thirty-four years ago. Since then, he hadn't driven, the yellowed license with the youthful photo and the bold stipulation about wearing corrective lenses and not driving at night, had lain unused in the folder of his travel documents. The man at the rental car agency had frowned, his look went back and forth between the photo and the real face, but he hadn't said anything.

Behind the wheel of the big car, Gregorius waited until his breath calmed down. Slowly, he tried all the knobs and switches. With cold hands he started the motor, put it in reverse, released the clutch and stalled the engine. Frightened by the violent jolt, he shut his eyes and waited again until his breath was calm. At the second attempt, the car lollopped along, but did go on and Gregorius backed out of the parking space. He took the curves to the exit ramp at a snail's pace. At a traffic signal at the exit from the city, the car died again. Then it kept getting better.

He did the highway to Viana do Castelo in two hours. He sat calmly behind the wheel and stayed in the right lane. He began to enjoy the trip. He managed to push the issue of the Homeric word so far into the background that it could almost be called forgetting. Becoming cocky, he pressed the accelerator and held the steering wheel with outstretched arms.

A car with blinding headlights came toward him in the opposite lane. Things began to spin, Gregorius let up on the gas, slid onto the shoulder at the right, pulled up onto the grass and came to a stop centimeters from the guard rail. Dashing cones of light flowed away above him. Later, at the next rest stop, he got out and carefully inhaled the cool night air. *You should come home. Talk to the doctors in your mother tongue.*

An hour later, beyond Valença do Minho, came the border. Two members of the Guardia Civil with machine guns waved him through. From Tui, he took the highway through Vigo, Pontevedra and further north to Santiago. Shortly before midnight, he stopped and studied the map as he ate. There was no other solution: if he didn't want to make an enormous detour through the Cape of Santa Eugenia, he had to go through Padrón on the mountain roads to Noia, the rest was clear, keep along the coast to Finisterre. He had never driven on mountain roads and pictures rose in him of the Swiss passes where the driver of the mail truck constantly had to swerve the steering wheel back and forth.

The people around him spoke Galician. He didn't understand a word. He was tired. He had forgotten the word. He, Mundus, had forgotten a word in Homer. Under the table, he pressed his feet on the floor to dissipate the cushion of air. He was afraid. *Fear and foreign language don't go well together.*

It was easier than he had thought. In sharp, blind curves, he slowed down to a walk, but at night, because of the headlights, you had better notice of oncoming cars than in the day. The traffic thinned out, it was after two o'clock. When he thought that, if the dizziness came, he couldn't simply stop on the narrow road, he panicked. But then, when a sign indicated that Noia was close, he grew bold and cut the curves. *A little hard. But Mundus, you can't ask me such things!* Why hadn't Florence simply lied! *You boring? Why,* absolutely *not!*

Did that really exist: that you simply shook off offenses? *We are expanded far into the past,* Prado had noted. *That comes through our feelings, that is the deep ones, those that determine who we are and how it is to be us. For these feelings know no time, they don't know it and they don't acknowledge it.*

From Noia to Finisterre, it was a hundred fifty kilometers of good roads. You didn't see the sea, but you imagined it. It was coming up on four o'clock. Now and then Gregorius stopped. It wasn't dizziness, he decided every time, it was simply that the brain seemed to be swimming in the skull with fatigue. After four dark gas stations, he finally found one that was open. How far was Finisterre, he asked the sleepy station attendant. *"Pues, el fin del mundo!"* he laughed.

When Gregorius entered Finisterre, dawn was beginning to break through a cloud-covered sky. The first customer, he drank a cup of coffee in a bar. Wide awake and very solid, he stood on the stone floor. The word would come back when he least expected it, that's how memory was, he knew that. He enjoyed making the crazy trip and being here now, and took the cigarette the innkeeper offered him. After the second drag, he felt slightly dizzy. *"Vértigo,"* he said to the innkeeper. "I'm an expert in dizziness, there are a whole lot of kinds and I know them all." The innkeeper didn't understand and wiped the counter vigorously.

Gregorius drove the few kilometers to the Cape with the window open. The salty sea air was wonderful and he drove very slowly like someone savoring anticipation. The road ended in a harbor with fishing boats. The fishermen had recently come back and were standing and smoking together. Later he no longer knew how it had happened, but all of a sudden, he was standing with the fishermen and smoking their cigarettes, it was like a group of regulars meeting out in the open.

Were they content with their life, he asked. Mundus, a Bern philologist of ancient languages, asked the Galician fishermen at the end of the world about their outlook on life. Gregorius enjoyed it, he enjoyed it enormously, joy at the absurdity blended with fatigue, euphoria and an unknown feeling of liberating boundlessness.

The fishermen didn't understand the questions, and Gregorius had to repeat them twice in his broken Spanish. *"Contento?"* one of them finally shouted. "We don't know anything else!" They laughed and kept laughing until it became a roaring laughter, Gregorius joining so passionately that his eyes began watering.

He put his hand on the shoulder of one of the men and turned him to the sea.

"Siempre derecho, más y más—nada!" he shouted into a gust of wind.

"America!" shouted the man. *"America!"*

From the inside pocket of his jacket, he took out the photo of a girl in blue jeans, boots, and a cowboy hat.

"Mi hija!" My daughter! He gestured toward the sea.

The others ripped the picture out of his hand.

"Qué guapa es!" How pretty she is, they shouted all together.

Gregorius laughed and gesticulated and laughed, the others tapped him on the shoulders, right and left and right, they were rough blows, Gregorius staggered, the fishermen were spinning around, the sea was spinning around, the roar of the wind became a roar of the ear, it swelled on and on, to disappear quite suddenly in a silence that swallowed up everything.

When he came to, he was lying on the bench in a boat with frightened faces above him. He sat up. His head hurt. He refused the bottle of liquor. It went away, he said, and added: *"El fin del mundo!"* They laughed with relief. He shook off calloused, gigantic hands, tottered his way slowly out of the boat, and sat down behind the steering wheel. He was glad the motor caught immediately. The fishermen, their hands in the pockets of their oil slicks, watched him go.

In the town, he took a room in a boardinghouse and slept until afternoon. It had cleared up in the meantime and become warmer. Nevertheless, he was freezing when he went to the cape at dusk. He sat down on a rock and watched the light in the west grow weaker until it finally died out completely. *O mar tenebroso.* The black waves crashed, the light foam washed over the beach with a menacing rustle. The word didn't come. *It didn't come.*

Was this word *there* at all? Was it ultimately not the memory, but the mind, that had gotten a fine lesion? How could a person almost lose his mind because a word, a single word, that occurred one single time, had escaped? He might torment himself in the lecture hall taking a test. But facing the raging sea? Shouldn't the black water merging seamlessly into the night sky simply wash away such cares as something completely meaningless, absurd, of concern only to someone who had lost all sense of proportion?

He was homesick. He shut his eyes. He came at quarter to eight from Bundesterrasse and entered Kirchenfeldbrücke. Through the arcades of Spitalgasse, Marktgasse and Kramgasse, he went down to the Bärengraben. In the cathedral, he heard the Christmas Oratorio. He got off the train in Bern and entered his flat. He took the record of the Portuguese language course off the phonograph and put it in the broom closet. He lay down on the bed and was glad to know: everything was as before.

It was quite unlikely that Prado and Estefânia Espinhosa had come here. More than unlikely. Nothing supported it, nothing in the least.

Freezing and his jacket damp, Gregorius went to the car. In the dark, the car looked enormous. Like a monster that nobody could drive back to Coimbra intact, least of all him.

Later, he tried to get something to eat across from the boardinghouse, but it didn't work. At the reception desk, he got a few sheets of paper. Then he sat down at the tiny table in the room and translated what the Muslim geographer had written, into Latin, Greek and Hebrew. He had hoped that writing Greek letters would bring back the lost word. But nothing happened, the space of memory remained mute and empty.

No, it wasn't that the rustling breadth of the sea made retaining and forgetting words meaningless. Nor retaining and forgetting phrases. It wasn't so, it wasn't so at all. A single word among words, a single phrase among phrases: they were untouchable, absolutely untouchable for the mass of blind, wordless water, and that would remain so even if the whole universe from today to tomorrow became a world of countless deluges, dripping out of all skies nonstop. If there was only one word in the universe, one single word, then it wouldn't be a *word,* but if it were one, it would be mightier and more illuminating than all floods beyond all horizons.

Slowly Gregorius calmed down. Before he went to sleep, he looked out the window down at the parked car. Tomorrow, during the day, it would work.

It worked. Exhausted and fearful after an uneasy sleep, he drove in short shifts. During the breaks, he was regularly haunted by dream images of the night. He had been in Isfahan and it had been on the sea. The city with its minarets and domes, with the shining dark blue and glittering gold, had risen against a bright horizon and therefore he was frightened when he looked at the sea and saw it raging black and roaring before the desert city. A hot, dry wind drove damp, heavy air into his face. For the first time, he had dreamed of Prado. The goldsmith of words did nothing, he was only present in the broad arena of the dream, wordless and elegant, and with his ear to Adriana's enormous tape recorder, Gregorius searched for the sound of his voice.

In Viana do Castelo, shortly before the highway to Porto and Coimbra, Gregorius felt that the lost word from the Odyssey was on the tip of his tongue. Behind the wheel, he shut his eyes instinctively and tried with all his might to keep it from sinking back into forgetting. Wild horns startled him. At the last second, he was able to turn the wheel sharply, get the car out of the oncoming lane where it had drifted, and prevent a head-on collision. At the next rest stop, he stopped and waited until the painful throbbing of the blood in his brain subsided. Then he drove behind a slow truck to Porto. The woman at the car rental agency was not exactly pleased that he wanted to return the car here and not in Coimbra. But after a long look at his face, she finally agreed.

When the train toward Coimbra and Lisbon started, Gregorius leaned his head back, exhausted. He thought of the farewells in store for him in Lisbon. *That's the meaning of a farewell in the full, important meaning of the word: that the two people, before they part from each other, come to an understanding of how they have looked and experienced each other,* Prado had written in his letter to the mother. *Parting is also something you do with yourself: to stand by yourself under the look of the other.* The train got under way. The fear of the accident he had missed by a hairsbreadth began to fade. Until Lisbon, he didn't want to think of anything anymore.

Just as he managed to let go of things, supported by the monotonous beat of the wheels, the lost word was suddenly there: λίστρον, an iron shovel for cleaning the floor of the hall. And now he also knew where it was: in the Odyssey, at the end of the twenty-second book.

The compartment door opened, a young man took a seat and unfolded a tabloid paper with enormous letters. Gregorius stood up, took his bag and went to the end of the train where there was an empty compartment. λίστρον, he said to himself, λίστρον.

When the train stopped in the railroad station of Coimbra, he thought of the hill of the university and of the surveyor who went over the bridge in his imagination with an old-fashioned doctor's bag, a thin, bent man in a gray smock, who thought about how he could make the people in the castle let him in.

When Silveira came home from the office that night, Gregorius met him in the hall. Silveira hesitated and narrowed his eyes.

"You're going home."

Gregorius nodded.

"Explain!"

44

"If you'd given me time—I'd have made a Portuguese out of you," said Cecília. "When you're back in your raw, guttural country, think of that: *doce, suave,* and we leap over the vowels."

She pulled the green scarf over her lips, it blew when she spoke. She laughed when she saw his look.

"The thing with the scarf, you like it. Don't you?" And she puffed.

She gave him her hand. "Your unbelievable memory. Because of that I won't forget you."

Gregorius held her hand too long. He hesitated. Finally he ventured.

"Is there any reason why . . ."

"You mean: why I always wear green? Yes, there is. You'll hear it when you come back."

Quando voltares. When you come back. *Quando,* she had said, not *se.* On the way to Vítor Coutinho, he imagined how it would be if he showed up at the language school on Monday morning. How her face would look. How her lips would move when she told him the reason for the eternal green.

"Que quer?" Coutinho's voice roared an hour later.

The door buzzed; the old man came down the steps with his pipe between his teeth. For a moment, he had to search in his memory.

"Ah, *c'est vous,*" he said then.

Today, too, it smelled of stale food, dust and pipe tobacco, and today, too, Coutinho wore a washed-out shirt of indefinable color.

Prado. *O consultório azul.* Had Gregorius found the man?

No idea why I give this to you, but that's how it is, the old man had said to him when he had given him the New Testament back then. Gregorius had it with him. It remained in his pocket. He didn't even mention it, the right words wouldn't come. *Intimacy, it is fleeting and deceptive as a mirage,* Prado had written.

He was in a hurry, said Gregorius, and gave the old man his hand.

"One more thing," the old man shouted at him through the courtyard. "Will you call the number now that you're here again? The number on your forehead?"

Gregorius made the sign of uncertainty and waved.

He went to the Baixa, the lower part of the city, and paced the chessboard of the streets. In the café across from O'Kelly's pharmacy, he ate something and kept waiting for the figure of the smoking pharmacist to appear behind the glass door. Did he want to talk with him once more? Did *he want to*?

All morning he felt that something wasn't right with his farewells. That something was lacking. Now he had it. He went to the photo shop and bought a camera with a telephoto lens. Back in the café, he aimed at the part of the door where O'Kelly appeared and shot a whole roll of film because his reaction was usually too long.

Later he went back to Coutinho's house in the Comitério dos Prazeres and photographed the dilapidated building overgrown with ivy. He aimed at the window, but the old man didn't appear.

Finally, he gave up and went to the cemetery where he took pictures of the Prado family plot. Near the cemetery, he bought more film and then took the old streetcar through the city to Mariana Eça.

Red-gold Assam with rock candy. Big dark eyes. Reddish hair. Yes, she said, it would be better if he could talk with the doctors in his mother tongue. Gregorius said nothing of fainting in the library of Coimbra. They talked about João Eça.

"His room is a little small," said Gregorius.

For a moment, anger flitted over her face, then she had herself under control again.

"I suggested other homes to him, more comfortable ones. But that's what he wanted. *It should be barren,* he said. *After everything that was, it has to be barren.*"

Gregorius left before the teapot was empty. He wished he hadn't said anything about Eça's room. It was ridiculous to do, as if, after four afternoons, he was closer to him than she, who had known him as a little girl. As if he understood him better. It was ridiculous. Even if it was right.

When he rested in Silveira's house that afternoon, he put on the old, heavy glasses. His eyes didn't want to.

It was too dark to take a picture when he came to Mélodie's house. The flash worked when he took a few pictures anyway. Today she wasn't seen behind the illuminated windows. *A girl who didn't seem to touch the floor.* The judge had gotten out of the car, had stopped traffic with his cane, made his way through the audience, and without looking at the daughter in the Mao cap, tossed a handful of coins in the open violin case. Gregorius looked up at the cedars that had looked bloodred to Adriana just before her brother stuck the knife in her throat.

Now Gregorius saw a man behind the window. That decided the issue of whether he should ring the bell. In the bar where he had once been, he drank a coffee and smoked a cigarette, as then.

Then he went over to the citadel and imprinted Lisbon at night in his memory.

O'Kelly was there to lock up the shop. A few minutes later, when he entered the street, Gregorius followed him at such a great distance that, this time, he couldn't discover him. He turned into the side street where the chess club was. Gregorius went back to take a picture of the lighted pharmacy.

45

On Saturday morning, Felipe drove with Gregorius to the Liceu. They packed up the camping gear and Gregorius took the pictures of Isfahan off the walls. Then he sent the chauffeur away.

It was a warm sunny day, April began next week. Gregorius sat down on the moss of the entrance steps. *I sat on the warm moss of the entrance steps and thought of my father's imperious wish that I might become a doctor—one who might release people like him from pain. I loved him for his trust and cursed him for the crushing burden he imposed on me with his touching wish.*

Suddenly Gregorius began to weep. He took off the glasses, buried his head between his knees and let the tears drip freely onto the moss. *Em vão, in vain,* had been one of Prado's favorite phrases, Maria João had said. Gregorius said the words and repeated them, slowly, then faster, until the words merged into one another and with the tears.

Later he went up to Prado's classroom and photographed the view of the girls' school. From the girls' school, he got the opposite view: the window where Maria João had seen the points of light in Prado's opera glasses.

He told Maria João of the pictures when he sat in her kitchen at noon. And then, all at once, it broke out of him, he talked of fainting in Coimbra, of forgetting the Homeric word, and of the panicky fear of a neurological examination.

Later they sat together at the kitchen table and read what Maria João's encyclopedia said about dizziness. It could have completely harmless causes, Maria João showed him the sentences, moving her index finger along, she translated, repeated the important words.

Tumor. Gregorius pointed mutely to the word. Yes, of course, said Maria João, but he had to read what it said there, mainly, that in this case dizziness doesn't appear without other, more serious phenomena of breakdown, which didn't appear in him.

She was glad, she said at parting, that he had recently taken her along on the trip to the past. In this way, she could feel the peculiar blend of closeness and distance that was in her where Amadeu was concerned. Then she went to the closet and took out the big box with the marquetry. She handed him the sealed envelope with Prado's notes about Fátima.

"I won't read it, as I said," she said. "And I think it's better off with you. Maybe, in the end, you're the one who knows him best of all of us. I'm grateful for the way you talk about him."

Later, when Gregorius sat on the ferry over the Tagus, he pictured Maria João waving good-bye until he had disappeared from view. She was the one he had met last, and she was the one he would miss most. Would he write and tell her how the examination had turned out? she had asked him.

46

When Gregorius stood before the door, João Eça squinted and his features hardened as with someone preparing for a great pain.

"It's Saturday," he said.

They sat down in the usual places. The chessboard wasn't there, the table looked naked.

Gregorius told of the dizziness, the fear, the fishermen at the end of the world.

"So you're not coming anymore," said Eça.

Instead of him and his worries, he spoke of himself, and in anyone else, that would have seemed strange to Gregorius. Not in this tortured, taciturn, lonely man. His words were some of the most precious he had heard.

If the dizziness turned out to be nothing and the doctors managed to get rid of it, he would come back, he said. To learn Portuguese properly and write the history of the Portuguese resistance. He said it in a firm voice, but the confidence he forced into it sounded hollow, and he was sure that it sounded hollow to Eça too.

With shaking hands, Eça took the chessboard off the shelf and lined up the pieces. For a while, he sat there with his eyes shut. Then he stood up and took a collection of chess games.

"Here. Alekhine against Capablanca. I'd like us to play it together."

"Art against science," said Gregorius.

Eça smiled. Gregorius wished he could have captured this smile on film.

Sometimes he tried to imagine how the last minutes were after you took the lethal tablets, Eça said in the middle of the game. First perhaps relief that it was now finally over and you had escaped from your undignified sickliness. A soupçon of pride at your own bravery. A regret that you hadn't been so brave more often. A final summing up, a final assurance that it was right and would be wrong to call the ambulance. Hope and composure to the last. Waiting for the cloudiness and numbness in fingertips and lips.

"And then suddenly a tremendous panic, a convulsion, the crazy wish that it might not be the end. An internal flooding, a hot ripping current of will to live that sweeps everything aside and makes all thoughts and decisions appear artificial, stilted, absurd. And then? What *then*?"

He didn't know, said Gregorius, and then he took out Prado's book and read aloud:

Wasn't it obvious, simple and clear what her horror consisted of when she received news of her impending death at this moment? I held the bleary-eyed face in the morning sun and thought: They simply wanted more of the stuff of their life, however light or heavy, barren or lush this life may be. They don't want it to end, even if they can no longer miss the lacking life after the end—and know that.

Eça took the book and read himself, first this passage, then the whole conversation with Jorge about death.

"O'Kelly," he said finally. "Smoking himself to death. 'So what?' he said when anyone mentioned it. I picture his face: *Kiss my ass.* And then fear got to him after all. *Merda.*"

It was beginning to grow dark when the game was over and Alekhine had won. Gregorius took Eça's cup and drank the last sip of tea. At the door, they stood facing each other. Gregorius felt himself shaking. Eça's hands grabbed his shoulders and now he felt his head on his cheek. Eça sobbed aloud, Gregorius felt the movement of his Adam's apple. With a violent shove that made Gregorius totter, Eça pushed away from him and opened the door, looking down. Before Gregorius turned the corner in the hall, he looked back. Eça stood in the middle of the hall and watched him. Never had he done that.

On the street, Gregorius went behind some bushes and waited. Eça came onto the balcony and lit a cigarette. Gregorius shot the whole roll of film.

He saw nothing of the Tagus. And saw and felt João Eça. From the Praça do Comércio, he walked slowly toward Bairro Alto and sat down in a café near the blue house.

47

He let one quarter hour after another pass. Adriana. That would be the hardest good-bye.

She opened the door and immediately interpreted his face correctly. "Something's happened," she said.

A routine medical examination with his doctor in Bern, said Gregorius. Yes, he might well come back. He was amazed at how calmly she took it, it almost offended him a little.

She didn't breathe frantically, but more conspicuously than before. Then she pulled herself together, stood up and took out a notebook. She'd like to have his phone number in Bern, she said.

Gregorius raised his eyebrows in surprise. Then she pointed to the little table in the corner where there was a telephone.

"Since yesterday," she said. And she wanted to show him something else. She led the way to the attic.

The mountains of books on the bare floorboards in Amadeu's room had disappeared. The books were now on a shelf in the corner. She watched him expectantly. He nodded, went to her and touched her arm.

Now she pulled out the drawer of Amadeu's desk, untied the ribbon holding the cardboard cover together and took out three sheets of paper.

"He wrote it afterward, after the girl," she said. Her gaunt breast rose and fell. "The letters are suddenly so small. When I saw it, I thought: he wanted to hide it from himself."

She slid her eyes over the text. "It destroys everything. *Everything.*"

She put the sheets in an envelope and handed it to Gregorius.

"He was no longer himself. I'd like . . . please take it. Far away. Very far away."

Later Gregorius cursed himself. He wanted to see once more the examining room where Prado had saved Mendes's life, where the map of the brain had hung and where he had buried Jorge's chess set.

"He really likes to work down here," said Adriana, when they stood in the office. "With me. With me together." She stroked the examination table. "They all love him. Love and admire him."

She smiled a ghostly light, distant smile.

"Many come, even when they don't need anything. They make up something. Just to see him."

Gregorius's thoughts raced. He went to the table with the antiquated syringes, and picked up one. Yes, this was the way syringes looked back then, he said. How different they were today!

The words didn't reach Adriana, she was tugging at the paper cloth on the examination table. A remnant of the smile from before still lay on her features.

Did she know what had become of the map of the brain, he asked. Today, it had to be a rarity.

"'Why do you need the maps,' I sometimes ask him. 'Bodies are like a glass for you.' 'It's just a map,' he says then. He loves maps. Land maps. Railroad maps. In Coimbra, when he was in school, he once criticized a sacred atlas of anatomy. The professors didn't like him. He is impudent. Simply superior."

Gregorius knew only one solution to her lapse into present tense. He looked at the clock.

"I'm late," he said. "Can I use your phone?"

He opened the door and went out, into the vestibule of the house.

Her face was distraught as she locked up. A vertical line divided her forehead and made her look like somebody ruled by darkness and confusion.

Gregorius went to the stairs.

"Adeus," said Adriana and unlocked the front door.

It was her acrid, hostile voice he had known on the first visit. She stood straight as a candle and faced the whole world brazenly.

Gregorius went to her slowly and stood still before her. He looked her in the eye. Her look was sealed and cold. He didn't hold out his hand. She wouldn't take it.

"Adieu," he said. "All the best." Then he was outside.

48

Gregorius gave Silveira the photocopy of Prado's book. He had wandered through the city for more than an hour until he found a store that was still open where you could make copies.

"That's . . . ," said Silveira in a hoarse voice. "I . . ."

Then they talked about the dizziness. His sister with the diseased eyes, said Silveira, had suffered from dizziness for decades, they couldn't find the cause, she simply got used to it.

"I was at the neurologist with her one time. And left the office with the feeling of being in the Stone Age. Our knowledge of the brain is still Stone Age. A few areas, a few models of activity, a few bits of material. We don't know more. I had the feeling they don't even know where they should *search*."

They spoke of the fear that comes of uncertainty. Suddenly Gregorius felt that something was bothering him. It lasted until he understood: the day before yesterday, on his return, the conversation with Silveira about the trip, today the conversation with João Eça, now Silveira again. Could two intimacies block, hinder, poison each other? He was glad he hadn't told Eça anything about the fainting in the library of Coimbra so that he had something he shared only with Silveira.

So what was the Homeric word he had forgotten, Silveira asked now. λίοτϛον, said Gregorius, an iron shovel to clean the floor of the hall.

Silveira laughed, Gregorius joined him, they laughed and laughed, they roared with laughter, two men, who, for a moment, were able to rise above all fear, all sadness, all disappointment and over all their weariness of life. Who were linked in laughter in a precious way, even if the fear, the sadness, and the disappointment were all their own and created their own loneliness for them.

When his laughter subsided and he felt the weight of the world again, Gregorius thought of how he had laughed with João Eça about the overcooked lunch of the home.

Silveira went into his study and came back with the napkin from the dining car on which Gregorius had written the Hebrew words: *And God said, Let there be light: and there was light.* He should read it to him once more, said Silveira. Then he asked him to write something from the Bible in Greek.

Gregorius couldn't resist and wrote: *In the beginning was the Word, and the Word was with God, and the Word was God. The same was in the beginning with God. All things were made by him; and without him was not any thing made that was made. In him was life; and the life was the light of men.*

Silveira picked up his Bible and read these opening sentences of the Gospel of Saint John:

"So the word is the light of men," he said. "And so things exist properly only when they are grasped in words."

"And the words have to have a rhythm," said Gregorius. "A rhythm as the words have in Saint John, for example. Only then, only when they are poetry, do they really shed light on things. In the changing light of the words the same things can look quite different."

Silveira looked at him.

"And therefore, when, faced with three hundred thousand books, one word is missing, it has to make you dizzy."

They laughed and laughed some more, they looked at each other and knew of each other that they were also laughing at the earlier laughter and because you laughed best about the most important things there were.

Would he leave him the photographs of Isfahan? Silveira asked later. They hung them in his study. Silveira sat down behind his desk, lit a cigarette and looked at the pictures.

"I wish my ex-wife and my children would see that," he said.

Before they went to bed, they stood silently in the hall a while.

"That's also past now," said Silveira. "Your stay here, I mean. Here in my house."

Gregorius couldn't fall asleep. He imagined how his train would start up the next morning, he felt the first, soft jolts. He cursed the dizziness and the fact that Doxiades was right.

He turned on a light and read what Prado had noted about intimacy:

INTIMEIDADE IMPERIOSA. IMPERIOUS INTIMACY. *In intimacy, we are clasped into one another, and the invisible bonds are liberating shackles. This clasping is imperious: it demands exclusivity. To share is to betray. But we want to love and touch not only one single person. What to do? Control the various intimacies? Strict bookkeeping of subjects, words, gestures? Mutual knowledge and secrets? It would be a silent trickling poison.*

It was already growing light when he slipped into a restless sleep and dreamed of the end of the world. It was a melodious dream without instruments or notes, a dream of sun, wind and words. The fishermen with their rough hands shouted rough things to one another, the salty wind blew away the words, and the word that had escaped him, too, now he was in the water and dove deep, he kept swimming deeper with all his might and felt the desire and warmth in his muscles when they braced against the cold, he had to leave the banana boat, it was rushing, he assured the fishermen it had nothing to do with them, but they defended themselves and looked at him strangely when he went to shore with the sailor's kitbag, accompanied by sun, wind, and words.

PART IV
THE RETURN

49

Silveira had long ago disappeared from sight, but Gregorius still kept waving. "Is there a company that produces porcelain in Bern?" he had asked on the platform. Gregorius had taken a picture from the compartment window: Silveira, sheltering the cigarette against the wind so he could light it.

The last houses of Lisbon. Yesterday in the Bairro Alto, he had gone once more to the religious bookstore where he had leaned his forehead on the foggy damp windowpane before ringing the doorbell of the blue house for the first time. Back then, he had had to struggle against the temptation to go to the airport and take the next plane to Zurich. Now he had to struggle against the temptation to get out at the next station.

If, with every meter the train left behind, a memory was extinguished, and if in addition, the world changed back piece by piece, so that, when he arrived at the railroad station of Bern, everything would be as before: Would the time of his stay also be destroyed?

Gregorius took out the envelope Adriana had given him. *It destroys everything. Everything.* What he would now read, Prado had written after the trip to Spain. *After the girl.* He thought of what she had said about his return from Spain: unshaved and hollow-cheeked, he had got out of the taxi, famished, had gulped down everything, taken a sleeping powder and slept for a day and a night.

As the train came to Vilar, where it would cross the border, Gregorius translated the text Prado had written in tiny letters.

CINZAS DA FUTILIDADE. ASHES OF FUTILITY. *It has been an eternity since Jorge called me in the middle of the night because he was assailed by the fear of death. No, not an eternity. It was in* a different time, *a* completely *different time. And it was hardly three years, three perfectly normal, boring calendar years. Estefânia. He spoke then of Estefânia. The Goldberg Variations. She had played them for him, and he wanted to play them himself on his Steinway.* Estefânia Espinhosa. *What an enchanting, bewitching name! I thought that night. I wanted never to see the woman, no woman could live up to this name, it had to be a disappointment. How could I know that it was the other way around: the name couldn't live up to* her.

The fear that life remained incomplete, a torso; the awareness of no longer being able to become the one we aimed to be. That's how we had finally interpreted the fear of death. But how, I asked, can the missing wholeness and coherence of life be feared when it's not experienced at all as soon as it has become an irrevocable fact? Jorge seemed to understand it. What did he say?

Why don't I leaf through, why don't I watch? Why don't I want to know what I thought and wrote back then? Whence this indifference? Is *it indifference? Or is the loss greater, deeper?*

To want to know how one thought before and how it became what one thinks now: that too, if it existed, was also part of the wholeness of a life. So had I lost what makes death fearsome? The belief in a coherence of life worth struggling for and which we try to wrest from death?

Loyalty, I tell Jorge, loyalty. That's how *we invent our coherence. Estefânia. Why couldn't the surf of accident wash her up someplace else? Why to us of all places? Why did she have to put us to a test we weren't up to? Which* neither *of us passed, each in his own way?*

"You're too hungry for me. It's wonderful with you. But you're too hungry for me. I can't want this trip. You see, it would be your *trip, yours alone. It couldn't be* ours.*" And she was right: you mustn't make others into the building blocks of your own life, into water bearers in the race for your own bliss.*

Finis terrae. *Never have I been so awake as there. And so sober. Since then, I know: my race is at an end. A race I didn't know I was running, always. A race without rivals, without purpose, without reward. Wholeness?* Espejismo, *say the Spaniards, I read the word in the newspapers on those days, it's the only one I still know. Mirage. Fata Morgana.*

Our life, those are fleeting formations of quicksand, formed by one gust of wind, destroyed by the next. Images of futility that blow away even before they have properly formed.

He was no longer himself, Adriana had said. And she wanted nothing to do with the strange, estranged brother. *Far away. Very far away.*

When was somebody himself? When he was as always? As he saw himself? Or as he was when the white hot lava of thoughts and feelings buried all lies, masks, and self-deceptions? Often it was others who complained that somebody was no longer himself. Perhaps this is what it really meant: He's no longer as we would like him to be? So was the whole thing ultimately not much more than a kind of rallying cry against a menacing shake-up of the usual, camouflaged as concern and worry about the alleged welfare of the other?

On the way to Salamanca, Gregorius fell asleep. And then something happened that he hadn't ever known: he woke up directly into dizziness. A flood of misguided nervous irritation sloshed through him. He threatened to fall into the depths and clutched the armrest of the chair. Shutting his eyes made it even worse. He buried his face in his hands. It was over.

λίοτϛoν. Everything's fine.

Why hadn't he flown? Tomorrow morning, in eighteen hours, he'd be in Geneva, three hours later at home. At noon with Doxiades, who would arrange for all the rest.

The train slowed down. SALAMANCA. And a second sign: SALAMANCA. Estefânia Esphinosa.

Gregorius stood up, heaved the suitcase down from the shelf and held on to it until the dizziness had passed. On the platform, he walked firmly to crush the cushion of air surrounding him.

50

Later, when he thought back on his first evening in Salamanca, he seemed to have struggled for hours against the dizziness, reeling through cathedrals, chapels and cloisters, blind to their beauty, but overwhelmed by their dark force. He looked at altars, domes, and choir stalls that immediately overlapped in his memory, wound up twice at mass and finally sat still in an organ concert. *I would not like to live in a world without cathedrals. I need their beauty and grandeur. I need them against the vulgarity of the world. I want to let myself be wrapped in the austere coolness of the church. I need their imperious silence. I need it against the witless bellowing of the barracks yard and the witty chatter of the yes-men. I want to hear the rustling of the organ, this deluge of ethereal notes. I need it against the shrill farce of marches.*

That had been written by the seventeen-year-old Prado. A boy who glowed. A boy who went soon after with Jorge to Coimbra, where the whole world seemed to belong to them and where he reprimanded the professors in the lecture hall. A boy who had not yet known anything of the tide of accident, of blowing quicksand and the ashes of futility.

Years later, he had written these lines to Father Bartolomeu: *There are things that are too big for us humans: pain, loneliness and death, but also beauty, sublimity and happiness. For them we created religion. What happens when we lose it? Those things are still too big for us. What is left for us is the poetry of the individual life. Is it strong enough to bear us?*

From his hotel room, Gregorius could see the old and the new cathedrals. When the hour rang, he went to the window and looked up at the illuminated facades. San Juan de la Cruz had lived here. Florence had traveled here several times when she was writing about him. She had gone with other students, and he had never felt like making the trip. He hadn't liked how she had gushed over the mystical poetry of the great poet, she and the others.

Over poetry, you didn't *gush*. You *read* it. You read it with the tongue. You lived it. You felt how it moved you, changed you. How it contributed to giving your own life a form, a color, a melody. You didn't talk about it and you certainly didn't make it into the cannon fodder of an academic career.

In Coimbra, he had asked himself if he hadn't missed a possible life in the university. The answer was no. He felt once again how he had sat in La Coupole in Paris and had put down Florence's chattering colleagues with his Bern tongue and his Bern knowledge. *No.*

Later he dreamed that Aurora whirled him around to organ music in Silveira's kitchen, the kitchen expanded, he swam rapidly down and was caught in a whirlpool until he lost consciousness and woke up.

He was the first one to breakfast. Afterward, he went to the university and asked for the history department. Estefânia Espinhosa's lecture was in an hour: Isabel la Católica.

In the inner courtyard of the university, students huddled under the arcades. Gregorius didn't understand a word of the rapid Spanish and went to the lecture hall early. It was a paneled room of bare, monastic elegance, with a raised lectern in the front. The room filled up. It was a big room, but even before time, every seat was taken and students sat on the floor at the sides.

I hated this person, the long black hair, the swaying walk, the short skirt. Adriana had seen her as a girl in her mid-twenties. The woman who came in now was in her late fifties. *He pictured her shining eyes, the unusual, almost Asian complexion, the contagious, thrilling laughter, the swaying walk, and he simply didn't want all that to die out, he could not want it,* João Eça had said of Prado.

Nobody could want that, thought Gregorius. Not even today. And especially not when he heard her speak. She had a dark, smoky alto voice and spoke the hard Spanish words with a remnant of Portuguese softness. Right at the beginning, she had turned off the microphone. It was a voice that would fill a cathedral. And a look that made you hope the lecture might never end.

Gregorius understood hardly anything of what she said. He listened to her as to a musical instrument, sometimes with his eyes shut, sometimes with his look concentrated on her gestures: the hand stroking the gray-streaked hair off her forehead, the other hand holding the silver pen and drawing a line in the air to emphasize things, the elbows leaning on the lectern, the two outstretched arms embracing the lectern when she raised something new. A girl who had originally worked in the post office, a girl with a phenomenal memory where all secrets of the resistance were kept, the woman who didn't like it when O'Kelly held her around the waist in the street, the woman who had got in behind the steering wheel in front of the blue house and had traveled for her life to the end of the world, the woman who hadn't let Prado take her on his trip, a disappointment and a setback that had provoked in him the greatest and most painful awareness of his life, the consciousness that the race for his bliss had finally been lost, the feeling that his life begun so glowingly had gone out and fallen into ashes.

The shoving of the students standing up startled Gregorius. Estefânia Espinhosa packed her papers in her briefcase and came down the steps from the podium. Students approached her. Gregorius went outside and waited.

He had placed himself to be able to see her from afar. To decide then if he would address her. Now she came, accompanied by a woman to whom she spoke as to an assistant. Gregorius's heart pounded in his throat when she passed by him. He followed the two upstairs and through a long corridor. The assistant went off and Estefânia Esphinhosa disappeared through a door. Gregorius went past the door and saw her name. *The name couldn't live up to* her.

Slowly he went back and held tight to the banister. He stood still downstairs for a moment. Then he ran back upstairs. He waited until his breath had calmed down, then he knocked on the door.

She had a coat on and was about to leave. She looked at him questioningly.

"I . . . can I speak French with you?" asked Gregorius.

She nodded.

He introduced himself falteringly and then, as so often in these days, he took out Prado's book.

Her light brown eyes narrowed, she stared at the book without reaching out her hand for it. The seconds passed.

"I . . . why . . . Come in."

She went to the phone and told someone in Portuguese that she couldn't come now. Then she took off the coat. She asked Gregorius to sit down and she lit a cigarette.

"Is there anything about me in there?" she asked and exhaled smoke.

Gregorius shook his head.

"How do you know about me?

Gregorius told. Of Adriana and João Eça. Of the book about the dark sea that Prado had read at the end. About the research of the secondhand bookseller. Of the blurb on her books. O'Kelly he didn't mention. Nor did he say anything about the handwritten note with the small letters.

Now she wanted to see the book. She read. She lit another cigarette. Then she looked at the portrait.

"That's how he looked earlier. I never saw a picture from this time."

He hadn't planned to get off here, said Gregorius. But then he couldn't resist. The picture of Prado, it was so . . . so incomplete without her. But naturally he knew that it was unreasonable to simply burst in here.

She went to the window. The phone rang. She let it ring.

"I don't know if I want to," she said. "To talk about those days, I mean. At any rate not here. Can I take the book with me? I'd like to read it. Think about it. Come to my house this evening. Then I'll tell you how I feel about it."

She gave him a card.

Gregorius bought a guide and visited monasteries, one after another. He wasn't a man who went sightseeing. If people gathered around something, he tended to stay outside in spite; that corresponded with his habit of reading bestsellers only years later. So, it wasn't tourist eagerness that drove him now. It took him until late afternoon to begin to understand: the preoccupation with Prado had changed his feelings about churches and monasteries. *Can there be anything more serious than poetic seriousness?* he had objected to Ruth Gautschi and David Lehmann. That linked him with Prado. Maybe it was even the strongest link. But the man, who had changed himself from a glowing altar boy to a godless priest, seemed to have gone a step further, a step that Gregorius tried to understand as he walked through cloisters. Had he managed to extend the poetic seriousness about the biblical words to the buildings that had been created from these words? Was *that* it?

A few days before his death, Mélodie had seen him coming out of church. *I want to read the mighty words of the Bible. I need the unreal force of their poetry. I love praying people. I need the sight of them. I need them against the malicious poison of the superficial and the thoughtless.* Those had been the feelings of his youth. With what feelings had the man entered the church, the man who was waiting for the time bomb in his brain to explode? The man for whom, after the trip to the end of the world, everything had become ashes.

The taxi that took Gregorius to Estefânia Esphinosa's address had to wait at a traffic signal. In the window of a travel agency, he saw a poster with domes and minarets. How would it have been if, in the blue Orient with its golden domes, he had heard the Muezzin every morning? If Persian poetry had been the background melody of his life?

Estefânia Espinhosa wore blue jeans and a dark blue sailor's sweater. Despite the strands of gray, she looked as if she were in her mid-forties. She had made sandwiches and poured Gregorius a cup of tea. She needed time.

When she saw Gregorius's eyes slide over the bookshelves, she said he could go closer. He picked up the thick history books. How little he knew of the Iberian Peninsula and its history, he said. Then he told of the books about the earthquake of Lisbon and the Black Plague.

She made him tell her about the philology of ancient languages and kept asking questions. She wanted to know, he thought, what kind of person it was whom she would tell about the trip with Prado. Or was it only that she needed even more time?

Latin, she said at last. In a certain sense, Latin had been the beginning. "There was this boy, this student, who helped out in the post office. A timid boy who was in love with me and thought I didn't notice it. He was studying Latin. *Finis terrae,* he said one day, when he picked up a letter to Finisterre. And then he recited a long Latin poem that also talked about the end of the world. I liked the way he recited Latin poetry while still sorting letters. He felt that I liked it and kept on doing it all morning.

"I started learning Latin secretly. He couldn't know anything about it, he would have misunderstood it. It was so improbable that somebody like me, a girl from the post office with a rotten education, would learn Latin. *So improbable!* I don't know what appealed to me more: the language or this improbability.

"It went fast, I have a good memory. I began getting interested in Roman history. Read everything I could get my hands on, and later books about Portuguese, Spanish, Italian history. My mother had died when I was a child, I lived with my father, a railroad man. He had never read books, first was upset that I did, then later proud, a touching pride. I was twenty-three, when the P.I.D.E. took him and sent him to Tarrafal for sabotage. But I can't talk about that, not even today.

"I met Jorge O'Kelly a few months later at a meeting of the resistance. Papá's arrest had been spoken about in the post office, and to my amazement, it turned out that a lot of my colleagues belonged to the resistance movement. As for political things, I had awakened to them all of a sudden because of Papá's arrest. Jorge was an important man in the group. He and João Eça. He fell head over heels in love with me. It flattered me. He tried to make me a star. I had this idea of the school for illiterates where everybody could meet unsuspected.

"And there it happened. One evening Amadeu entered the room. After that everything was different. A new light fell on all things. It was the same for him, I felt that the first evening.

"I wanted it. I didn't sleep anymore. I went to the office, kept going, despite his sister's hateful looks. He wanted to take me in his arms, inside him was an avalanche that could let go at any moment. But he rejected me. Jorge, he said, Jorge. I began to hate Jorge.

"Once I rang Amadeu's doorbell at midnight. We walked a few streets, then he pulled me under an archway. The avalanche broke. 'That mustn't happen again,' he said afterward and forbade me to come back.

"It was a long, tormenting winter. Amadeu didn't come to meetings anymore. Jorge was sick with jealousy.

"It would be an exaggeration to say I saw it coming. Yes, that would be an exaggeration. But I was, indeed, concerned that they were relying more and more on my memory. 'What if something happens to me,' I said."

Estefânia went out. When she came back, she looked changed. As before a contest, thought Gregorius. She had apparently washed her face and her hair was now tied in a ponytail. She stood at the window and smoked a whole cigarette with hasty drags, before she went on.

"The catastrophe occurred at the end of February. The door opened much too slowly. Silently. He was wearing boots. No uniform, but boots. His boots, that was the first thing I saw when the door opened. Then the intelligent, lurking face, we knew him, it was Badajoz, one of Mendes's people. I did what we had often discussed and started talking about the *ç*, explaining it to the illiterates. Later, for a long time, I couldn't see a *ç* without having to think of Badajoz. The bench creaked when he sat down. João Eça slipped me a warning look. *Now everything depends on you,* the look seemed to say.

"As always, I was wearing my see-through blouse, it was my working clothes, so to speak. Jorge hated it. Now I took off the jacket. Badajoz's looks on my body, they were supposed to save us. Badajoz crossed his legs, it was disgusting. I brought the lesson to an end.

"When Badajoz approached Adrião, my piano teacher, I knew it was over. I didn't hear what they said, but Adrião turned pale and Badajoz grinned deviously.

"Adrião didn't come back from the interrogation. I don't know what they did to him, I never saw him again.

"João insisted that I live with his aunt from then on. Safety, he said, it was about keeping me safe. By the first night, I realized that was so, but it wasn't only me, it was mainly my memory. What it could give up if they had caught me. In those days, I met with Jorge only once. We didn't touch, not even our hands. It was eerie, I didn't understand. I understood it only when Amadeu told me why I had to leave the country."

Estefânia came back from the window and sat down. She looked at Gregorius.

"What Amadeu said about Jorge—it was so monstrous, so inconceivably cruel that at first I simply laughed. Amadeu made up a bed for me in the office before we left the next day.

"'I simply don't believe it,' I said. 'Kill me.' I looked at him. 'We're talking about Jorge, your friend,' I said.

'Exactly,' he said flatly.

"What *precisely* did he say, I wanted to know, but he wasn't willing to repeat the words.

"Afterward, when I lay alone in the office, I went over everything I had experienced with Jorge. Was he *capable* of thinking such a thing? *Seriously* thinking it? I was tired and uncertain. I thought of his jealousy. I thought of moments when he had seemed brutal and inconsiderate, even if not to me. I didn't know it anymore. I didn't *know* it.

"At Amadeu's funeral, we stood next to each other at the grave, he and I. The others had left.

"'You didn't really *believe* it, did you?' he asked after a while. 'He *misunderstood* me. It was a misunderstanding, a simple misunderstanding.'

"'It's not important anymore now,' I said.

"We walked away from each other, without touching. I've not heard anything more of him. Is he still alive?"

After Gregorius's answer, there was silence for a while. Then she stood up and took off the shelf her copy of O MAR TENEBROSO, the big book that had lain on Prado's desk.

"And at the end he was reading that?" she asked.

She sat down and kept the book in her lap.

"It was simply too much, much too much for a twenty-five-year-old girl, as I was. Badajoz, spirited off to João's aunt, the night in Amadeu's office, the dreadful thoughts of Jorge, the trip next to the man who had robbed me of my sleep. I was a complete mess.

"The first hours, we drove without saying anything. I was glad I could operate a steering wheel and gears. We were to go north, to Galicia, over the border, João had said.

"'And then we drive to Finisterre,' I said and told him the story of the Latin student.

"He asked me to stop and embraced me. After that, he kept asking me, more frequently. The avalanche broke. He was searching for me. But it was just that: he wasn't searching for *me,* he was searching for *life*. He wanted more of it, and he always wanted it faster and greedier. Not that he was coarse or violent. On the contrary, before him, I hadn't known there was such tenderness. But he gulped me down in it, sucked me into himself, he had such a ravenous hunger for life, for its warmth, its lust. And he was just as hungry for my mind as for my body. He wanted, in a few hours, to know my whole life, my memories, thoughts, fantasies, dreams. *Everything*. And he grasped with a speed and a precision that, after an initial joyous amazement, began to scare me, for his quick mind tore down all protecting walls.

"In the years afterward, I fled whenever somebody began to understand me. That has subsided. But one thing has remained: I don't want anybody to understand me *completely*. I want to go through life unknown. The blindness of others is my safety and my freedom.

"Even though now it sounds as if Amadeu was really passionately interested in *me,* it wasn't so. For it wasn't an *encounter*. He sucked with everything he knew, mainly *material of life* he couldn't get enough of. To put it another way, I wasn't really *somebody* for him, but rather a *scene* of life he reached for as if he had previously been cheated of it. As if he wanted to live a whole life once more before death overtook him."

Gregorius told her of the aneurysm and the map of the brain.

"My God," she said softly.

They had sat on the beach in Finisterre. Outside, a ship had passed.

"'Let's take a ship,' he said, 'at best, one to Brazil. Belém, Manaús. The Amazon. Where it's hot and damp. I'd like to write about it, about colors, smells, sticky plants, the rain forest, animals. I've only written about the soul.'"

This man who could never get enough of reality, Adriana had said of him.

"It wasn't adolescent romanticism, or the kitsch of an aging man. It was *genuine,* it was *real.* But on the other hand, it had nothing to do with *me.* He wanted to take me along on a trip that would have been only *his* trip, his internal trip to the most neglected zones of his soul.

"'You're too hungry for me,' I said. 'I can't do it, I *can't.*'

"Back then, when he had pulled me into the doorway, I had been willing to follow him to the end of the world. But then I didn't yet know his horrible hunger. Then, somehow, it was also horrible, this hunger for life. Of devouring, destructive force. Terrifying. Dreadful.

"My words must have wounded him dreadfully. Quite dreadfully. He no longer wanted to take a double room, paid for two singles. Later, when we met, he had changed clothes. He looked composed and stood there stiff, very correct. I understood: my words gave him the feeling that he had lost his dignity, and the stiffness, the correctness were the helpless attempt to show that he had won it back. And I didn't see it like that at all, there had been nothing undignified in his passion, or in the lust, it isn't lust in and of itself that is undignified.

"I didn't shut my eyes, despite complete exhaustion.

"He would stay here a few days, he said abruptly the next morning, and nothing could have expressed his complete internal retreat better than this abruptness.

"In parting, we shook hands. His last look was sealed off inside. He went back to the hotel, without even turning around, and before I stepped on the gas, I waited in vain for a sign in the window.

"After an unbearable half hour behind the wheel, I drove back. I knocked. He stood calmly in the door, without hostility, almost without emotion, he had shut me out of his soul, forever. I have no idea when he went back to Lisbon."

"A week later," said Gregorius.

Estefânia gave him back the book.

"I read it all afternoon. First I was horrified. Not about him. About me. That I had no idea who he was. How aware he was of himself. And how sincere. Mercilessly sincere. Thus his verbal force. I was upset that I had simply said to such a man: 'You're too hungry for me.' But then I slowly realized: it was right to say that. It would have been right even if I had known his sentences."

It was going on midnight. Gregorius didn't want to go. Bern, the railroad, the dizziness—everything was far away. He asked how the girl working in the post office and learning Latin had become a professor. Her information was curt, almost cold. That could occur: that someone who opened herself completely about the distant past, would remain sealed about what came later and about the present. Intimacy had its time.

They stood in the doorway. Then he decided. He held out the envelope with Prado's last note.

"I think these sentences most likely belong to you," he said.

51

Gregorius stood at the display window of a real estate agent. In three hours, his train left for Irún and Paris. His bag was at the railroad station in a locker. He stood solidly on the pavement. He read the prices and thought of his savings. To learn Spanish, the language he had previously left to Florence. To live in the city of her holy hero. Attend Estafânia Espinhosa's lectures. Study the history of the many monasteries. Translate Prado's notes. Discuss the sentences with Estafânia, one by one.

In the agency, they set up three inspections within the next two hours. Gregorius stood in empty apartments that echoed. He examined the view, the traffic noise, he imagined the daily walk through the staircase. He promised to take two apartments. Then he rode back and forth through the city in the taxi. *"Continue!"* he said to the driver. *"Siempre derecho, más y más!"*

When he was finally back at the railroad station, he made a mistake about the locker at first, and finally had to run to catch the train.

In the compartment, he nodded off and woke up only when the train stopped in Valladolid. A young woman came in. Gregorius heaved her suitcase onto the shelf. *"Muito obrigada,"* she said, sat down next to the door and began reading a French book.

When she crossed her legs, there was the sound of a light, silky friction.

Gregorius looked at the sealed envelope Maria João hadn't wanted to open. *You may read that only after my death,* Prado had said. *And I don't want it to fall into Adriana's hands.* Gregorius broke the seal, took out the sheets, and began to read.

PORQUÉ TU, ENTRE TODAS? WHY YOU, OF ALL WOMEN? *A question that forms sometimes in everyone. Why does it seem dangerous to allow it, even if it happens only in silence? What is so frightening about the idea of contingency that is expressed in it and is not the same idea as those of randomness and interchangeability? Why can one not acknowledge this contingency and joke about it? Why do we think it would trivialize, really cancel affection, if we acknowledge it as something obvious?*

I saw you pass through the living room, past heads and champagne glasses. 'That is Fátima, my daughter,' said your father. 'I could imagine you passing through my rooms,' I said to you in the garden. 'Can you still imagine me in passing through your rooms?' you asked in England. And on the ship: 'Do you also think in passing we were destined for each other?'

No one is destined for another. Not only because there is no Providence and no one else who could arrange it. No: because there is simply no inevitability between people beyond accidental needs and the powerful force of habit. I had spent five years in a clinic, five years, when no one had passed through my rooms. I stood here absolutely by chance, you stood there absolutely by chance, between us the champagne glasses. That's how it was. No different.

It is good that you won't read that. Why did you think you had to ally with Mamã against my Godlessness? An advocate of contingency loves no less. Nor is he less loyal. Rather more.

The reading woman had taken off her glasses and cleaned them. Her face didn't look like the face of the nameless Portuguese woman on the Kirchenfeldbrücke. But they did have one thing in common: the unequal distance between the eyebrows and the bridge of the nose, with one eyebrow stopping before the other.

He would like to ask her something, said Gregorius. Whether the Portuguese word *glória,* aside from fame, could also mean *bliss* in the religious sense.

She thought, then she nodded.

And whether an unbeliever could use it when he wanted to speak of what remained when religious bliss was removed from religious bliss.

She laughed. *"Que c'est drôle! Mais . . . oui. Oui."*

The train left Burgos. Gregorius read on.

UM MOZART DO FUTURO ABERTO. A MOZART OF THE OPEN FUTURE. *You came down the steps. Like thousands of times before, I watched as more and more of you became visible, while the head remained hidden to the last behind the banister opposite. I had always completed what was still concealed in thoughts. And always the same.* It was certain, *who was coming down.*

On this morning, it was different all of a sudden. Children playing had thrown the ball against the colored window the day before and smashed the pane. The light on the stairs was different than usual—instead of the gold, veiled light, reminiscent of the illumination in a church, unbroken daylight flowed in. It was as if this new light made a breach in my usual expectations, as if something ripped open that demanded new thoughts from me. I was suddenly curious *about how your face would look. The sudden curiosity made me happy and yet also made me flinch. It was years since the time of wooing curiosity had come to an end and the door had shut on our shared life. Why, Fátima, did a window have to shatter for me to be able to meet you again with an open look.*

I also tried it with you, Adriana. But our familiarity had become leaden.

Just why is the open look so hard? We are sluggish creatures who need familiarity. Curiosity as a rare luxury on home ground. To be certain and be able to play with the openness, in every moment, it would be an art. You had to be a Mozart. A Mozart of the open future.

San Sebastian. Gregorius looked in the schedule. Soon he would have to change trains in Irún for Paris. The woman crossed her legs and went on reading. He picked up the last note from the sealed envelope.

MINHA QUERIDA ARTISTA NA AUTO-ILUSÃO. MY BELOVED VIRTUOSO OF SELF-DELUSION. *We are in the dark about so many of our wishes and thoughts, and others sometimes know more about them than we do. Who ever believed anything* different?

No one. No one who lives and breathes with another. We know each other down to the smallest twitches of body and words. We know and often don't want to know what we know. Especially when the gap between what we see and what the other believes becomes unbearably wide. It takes divine courage and divine strength to live with oneself in perfect truth. So much we know, even of ourselves. No reason for self-justification.

And if she is a true virtuoso of self-deception, always a step ahead of me? Would I have had to confront you and say: No, you're fooling yourself, you're not like that? *I owed you that. If I owed you.*

How does one know what he owes the other in this sense?

Irún. *Isto ainda não é Irún,* that's not yet Irún. Those had been the first Portuguese words he had said to anyone. Five weeks before, and also on the train. Gregorius heaved down the woman's suitcase.

Shortly after he had taken a seat in the train to Paris, the woman passed by his compartment. She had almost disappeared, then she paused, bent back, saw him, hesitated a moment and then came in. He put her suitcase on the shelf.

She had chosen this slow train, she said in reply to his question, because she wanted to read this book. LE SILENCE DU MONDE AVANT LES MOTS. Nowhere else did she read as well as on the train. Nowhere else was she so open to new things. So she had become an expert in slow trains. She was also traveling to Switzerland, to Lausanne. Yes, exactly, arrival tomorrow morning in Geneva. Obviously they had both chosen the same train.

Gregorius pulled his coat over his face. His reason for the slow train had been different. He didn't want to get to Bern. He didn't want Doxiades to pick up the phone and reserve a bed in the clinic. There were twenty-four stops to Geneva. Twenty-four opportunities to get out.

He dove ever deeper. The fishermen laughed as he danced with Estefânia Espinhosa through Silveira's kitchen. All these monasteries from which you entered all these empty, echoing apartments. Their echoing emptiness had extinguished the Homeric word.

He woke with a start. λίστςον. He went to the toilet and washed his face.

While he slept, the woman had turned off the ceiling light and turned on her reading lamp. She read and read. When Gregorius came back from the toilet, she looked up a moment and smiled remotely.

Gregorius pulled his coat over his face and imagined the reading woman. *I stand here completely by chance, you stand there completely by chance, between us the champagne glasses. That's how it was. No different.*

They could share a cab to the Gare de Lyon, said the woman, as they pulled into Paris shortly after midnight. LA COUPOLE. Gregorius breathed the perfume of the woman next to him. He didn't want to go to the clinic. He didn't want to smell clinic air. The air he had fought his way through when he had visited the dying parents in the sticky, overheated ward where the air always smelled of urine.

At close to four in the morning, when he woke up behind his coat, the woman had fallen asleep with the open book in her lap. He turned off the reading lamp over her head. She turned to the side and pulled the coat over her face.

It grew light. Gregorius didn't want it to grow light.

The dining car waiter passed by with the drinks cart. The woman woke up. Gregorius handed her a cup of coffee. Silently they watched the sun rise behind a fine veil of clouds. It was strange, said the woman suddenly, that *glória* could stand for two completely different things: external, noisy fame and internal, silent bliss. And after a pause: "Bliss—what are we really talking about?"

Gregorius carried her heavy suitcase through the Geneva railroad station. The people in the Swiss train were talking loud and laughing. The woman saw his anger, pointed to the title of her book and laughed. Now he laughed too. In the middle of his laughter, the loudspeaker voice announced Lausanne. The woman stood up, he took down her suitcase. She looked at him. *"C'était bien, ça,"* she said. Then she got off.

Fribourg. Gregorius gagged. He was climbing up the mountain and looking down on Lisbon at night. He was on the ferry over the Tagus. He was sitting with Maria João in the kitchen. He was going through the monasteries of Salamanca and sitting down in Estefânia Espinhosa's lecture.

Bern. Gregorius got out. He put down the suitcase and waited. When he picked it up and went on, it was as if he were wading through lead.

52

In the cold flat, he had put down the suitcase and had then gone to the photo shop. Now he sat in the living room. In two hours, he could pick up the developed pictures. What should he do until then?

The telephone receiver was still turned around on the cradle and reminded him of the conversation at night with Doxiades. Five weeks ago. Back then it had snowed, now people were walking around without coats. But the light was still pale, no comparison with the light on the Tagus.

The record of the language course was still on the phonograph. Gregorius turned it on. He compared the voices with the voices in the old streetcar of Lisbon. He went from Belém to the Alfama quarter and took the Metro on to the Liceu.

The doorbell rang. The doormat, she always knew from the doormat when he was there, said Frau Loosli. She gave him a letter from the school administration that had come the day before. The other mail was on the way to Silveira's address. He looked pale, she said. Was everything all right?

Gregorius read the numbers of the school administration and forgot them even as he read them. He came early to the photo shop and had to wait. He almost ran back.

A whole roll of film only for the lighted door of O'Kelly's pharmacy. He had almost always shot too late. Three times it had worked and the smoking pharmacist was seen. The tangled hair. The big, fleshy nose. The eternally slipped tie. *I began to hate Jorge.* Ever since he had known the story of Estafânia Espinhosa, thought Gregorius, O'Kelly's look seemed devious to him. Mean. As back then, when he saw at the next table how annoyed he was by the repulsive sound of Pedro snuffling snot in the chess club every few minutes.

Gregorius put his eyes right up to the photos. Where was the weary and kind look he had previously seen on the peasant face? The look with the grief for his lost friend? *We were like brothers. More than brothers. I really thought we could never lose each other.* Gregorius no longer found the earlier look. *It's simply not possible, unlimited openness. It's beyond us. Loneliness through having to suppress, there's that too.* Now they were back, the other looks.

Is the soul a place of facts? Or are the alleged facts only the deceptive shadows of our stories? Prado had asked himself. That's also true of looks, thought Gregorius. Looks weren't there and were read. Looks were always looks *read into.* Only as read into did they *exist.*

João Eça in the twilight on the balcony of the home. *I don't want any tubes, any pumps. Only to make it last a few weeks longer.* Gregorius felt the hot, burning tea he had drunk from Eça's cup.

The pictures of Mélodie's house had become nothing in the dark.

Silveira, on the platform, sheltering the cigarette against the wind to be able to light it. Today he went back to Biarritz and would ask himself, as so often, why he went on.

Gregorius went through the pictures once more. Then once again. The past began to freeze under his look. Memory would select, arrange, retouch, lie. The pernicious thing was that the omissions, distortions and lies were later no longer recognized. There was no point of view outside of memory.

A normal Wednesday afternoon in the city where he had spent his life. What should he do with it?

The words of the Muslim geographer El Edrisi about the end of the world. Gregorius took out the sheets on which he had translated his words into Latin, Greek and Hebrew in Finisterre.

Suddenly he knew what he wanted to do. He wanted to photograph Bern. To record where he had lived all the years. The buildings, streets, squares that had been much more than only the stage set of his life.

In the photo shop, he bought film and in the time until twilight he walked through the streets of the Länggasse, where he had spent his childhood. Now that he considered them from various angles and with the attention of the photographer, they were quite different, these streets. He photographed into sleep. Sometimes he woke up and didn't know where he was. Then when he sat on the edge of the bed, he was no longer sure if the distancing, calculating look of the photographer was the right look to take possession of the world of a life.

On Thursday, he went on. Down to the Old City he took the lift from the university terrace and the way through the railroad station. That way, he could avoid Bubenbergplatz. He shot one roll after another. He saw the cathedral as he had never seen it. An organist was practicing. The first time since his arrival, the dizziness came and Gregorius held tight to the pew.

He brought the film to be developed. When he then went to Bubenbergplatz, it was as if he were attempting something big, heavy. At the memorial he stood still. The sun had disappeared, a leaden gray sky arched over the city. He had expected to feel whether he could touch the square again. He didn't feel it. It wasn't as before, and it wasn't as on his short visit three weeks ago. How was it? He was tired and turned to go.

"How did you like the goldsmith's book?"

It was the bookdealer from the Spanish bookstore. He held out his hand to Gregorius.

"Did it keep its promise?"

Yes, said Gregorius, absolutely.

He said it stiffly. The bookdealer noted that he wasn't in the mood to talk and quickly took his leave.

In the Bubenberg Cinema, the program had changed, the Simenon with Jeanne Moreau was gone.

Gregorius waited impatiently for his film. Kägi, the Rector, turned the corner. Gregorius stood in the doorway of a shop. *There are moments when my wife looks as if she's falling apart,* he had written. Now she was in the psychiatric clinic. Kägi looked tired and seemed hardly to notice what was going on around him. For a moment, Gregorius felt the impulse to talk with him. Then the feeling passed.

The photos were ready, he sat down in the Hotel Bellevue restaurant and opened the envelopes. They were strange pictures, they had nothing to do with him. He put them back in the envelopes and as he ate, he tried in vain to find out what he had hoped.

On the stairs of his flat, a violent dizziness grabbed him and he had to hold on to the banister with both arms. After that, he sat next to the phone all evening and imagined what would inevitably happen when he called Doxiades.

Shortly before falling asleep, he was always afraid of sinking into dizziness and unconsciousness and waking up without memory. As it slowly became light over the city, he gathered all his courage. When Doxiades's receptionist appeared, he was already at the office.

The Greek came a few minutes later. Gregorius waited for an angry amazement at the new glasses. But the Greek only squinted a moment, led the way into the examination room and then heard everything about the new glasses and the dizziness.

First he saw no reason for panic, he said at last. But a series of tests was necessary, and the case had to be observed in the clinic for a while. He picked up the phone, let his hand rest on it, and looked at Gregorius.

Gregorius inhaled and exhaled a few times, then he nodded.

On Sunday evening, they'd take him, said the Greek after he had hung up. There was nobody better than this doctor for miles around, he said.

Gregorius walked slowly through the city, past the many buildings and squares that had been important to him. That was the right way to do it. He ate where he had usually eaten, and in the early afternoon he went to the cinema, where, as a student, he had seen his first film. The film bored him, but it still smelled as it had then and he stayed to the end.

On the way home, he ran into Natalie Rubin.

"New glasses!" she greeted him.

Neither of them had any idea how they should meet each other. The phone conversations were far back and were still present only as the echo of a dream.

Yes, he said, he might well go back to Lisbon. The examination? No, no, only a minor matter with his eyes.

Her Persian had ground to a halt, said Natalie. He nodded.

Had they gotten used to the new teacher, he asked finally.

She laughed. "A boring man by the grace of God!"

Both of them turned around after a few steps and waved.

On Saturday, Gregorius spent several hours picking up his Latin, Greek and Hebrew books. He looked at the many marginal notes and the changes his handwriting had undergone over the decades. In the end, a small pile of books lay on the table, which he packed in the handbag for the clinic. Then he called Florence and asked if he might visit her.

She had had a stillbirth and was operated on for cancer a few years before. The disease hadn't come back. She was working as a translator. She was not at all as tired and dowdy as he had recently thought when he had seen her come home.

He told of the monasteries in Salamanca.

"Back then, you didn't want to," she said.

He nodded. They laughed. He didn't tell her anything about the clinic. When he went to the Kirchenfeldbrücke afterward, he regretted that.

He went once all the way around the dark Gymnasium. As he did, he thought of the Hebrew Bible in Senhor Cortês's desk, wrapped in his sweater.

On Sunday morning, he called João Eça. What should he do this afternoon, said Eça, could he please explain that to him.

He was going to the clinic tonight, said Gregorius.

"Must be nothing," said Eça after a pause. "And if—nobody can keep you there."

In the afternoon, Doxiades called and asked if he wanted to come for chess, he would take him to the clinic afterward.

Did he still think of stopping, Gregorius asked the Greek after the first game. Yes, said the Greek, he thought of it often. But maybe it would pass. In the next month, he was going to Thessaloniki, it was more than ten years since he had been there.

The second game was over and it was time.

"What if they find something bad?" asked Gregorius. "Something that would make me lose myself?"

The Greek looked at him. It was a calm and solid look.

"I have a prescription pad," he said.

Silently, they drove in the twilight to the clinic. *Life is not what we live; it is what we imagine living,* Prado had written.

Doxiades gave him his hand. "It's probably nothing," he said. "And the man, as I said, is the best."

At the entrance to the clinic, Gregorius turned around and waved. Then he went in. As the door closed behind him, it started raining.

A GROVE PRESS READING GROUP GUIDE

NIGHT TRAIN TO LISBON

PASCAL MERCIER

ABOUT THIS GUIDE

We hope that these discussion questions will enhance your reading group's exploration of Pascal Mercier's *Night Train to Lisbon.* They are meant to stimulate discussion, offer new viewpoints and enrich your enjoyment of the book.

More reading group guides and additional information, including summaries, author tours and author sites for other fine Grove Press titles may be found on our Web site, www.groveatlantic.com.

QUESTIONS FOR DISCUSSION

1. In the first chapter we meet Raimund Gregorius, aka Mundus, aka Papyrus and learn about his essential habits. Now that you have finished the book, as the story progressed, and in light of what you learned about him, throughout, how are his nicknames appropriate? "That was the moment that decided everything," (p. 5). What do you think was decided?

2. After he leaves his classroom what makes Mundus head for the bookstore? Why does he have such an instinctive reaction to the book *Um Ourives das Palavras* by Amadeu Inácio de Almeida Prado? Cite some passages from *A Goldsmith of Words* to support your view.

3. Why did the woman on the bridge, strange as their interaction was, have such a lasting effect on Gregorius? What incident in Gregorius's past makes the consequences less surprising?

4. "That words could cause something in the world, make someone move or stop, laugh or cry: even as a child he had found it enigmatic and it had never stopped impressing him." (p. 42). Why is this small piece essential to our understanding of the puzzle that is Gregorius? How is his métier, teaching ancient languages, involved with everything he thinks? What is the importance of books in the life of Gregorius and Prado? How do books connect the two?

5. In Lisbon Mundus has an accidental collision with a rollerblader. Are there other fortuitous "collisions"? Because his glasses were broken by the rollerblader, he gets new lenses prescribed by Mariana Eça. "With the new glasses the world was bigger and for the first time, space really had three dimensions

where things could extend unhindered." (p. 88). Discuss Gregorius and his eyesight. Concern with his vision has led him to some very important links. Connect some of these links to make a chain encircling Amadeu Prado. What other physical changes besides new glasses does Gregorius make? Discuss chance vs. choice.

6. Mundus interacts with three different physicians, Doxiades, his Greek doctor and friend in Bern, Eça, his Portuguese ophthalmologist, and of course, Amadeu Prado the man he encounters only through his writing. Why is a man of the mind drawn to medical practitioners concerned with the body?

7. Only six days pass between the moment that Gregorius leaves his old life in Bern to the moment when he first encounters Prado's sister, Adriana, at the casa azul, "As if my whole future were behind this door," (p. 97). In this short time he has become immersed in another man's life, a life that was ended by an aneurysm thirty-one years before. How does time and memory have an effect on what he learns inside the house?

8. What is the nature of Adriana's relationship with her brother, before and after his death? What are the important events that formed their bond? Why does she always wear the black ribbon around her neck? Is she a reliable source?

9. Mundus wishes to meet Mariana's uncle João Eça because he knows that he had been in the resistance movement as had Prado. Mariana sets him up with an errand to deliver a recording of Schubert's sonatas. Prado and Eça had first met on a train during Amadeu and Fatima's honeymoon in England. Senhor Eça, as well as train journeys, in addition to the sonatas all take their place in the unraveling of some of

the mysteries of Prado's life. Is it all serendipity or is something else at work here? "Was he still Mundus, the myopic bookworm, who had gotten scared only because a few snowflakes had fallen in Bern?" (p. 114). Was he?

10. Once trust is established between João Eça and Gregorius he learns a great deal from the older man. What part does the game of chess play in their relationship? In what other personal associations does chess figure?

11. Prado appears to have had a very different relationship with his sister Rita/Melodie than with his sister Adriana. After his wife, Fatima's death, he writes a long letter to Melodie from Oxford in which he speaks of an Irishman with a red soccer ball. "No meeting of minds?" I asked. "What?" he shouted and howled with laughter. "What?" And then he shot the soccer ball he had been carrying the whole time onto the sidewalk. I would like to have been the Irishman, an Irishman, who dared to appear in All Souls College for the evening lecture with a bright red soccer ball." (p. 137). What is Amadeu trying to communicate to his sister? Why does he want to be like the Irishman? How would his life have been different if he had been?

12. In order to find out more about Prado's early days, Gregorius visits Father Bartolomeu, now in his nineties, who had been a teacher at the Liceu. Father Bartolomeu speaks of Prado's funeral. "Two people, a man and a young woman, of restrained beauty came toward each other from each end of the path to the grave. Each had to cover an equally long way to the grave and they seemed to adapt the speed of their steps precisely to one another, so they arrived at the same time. Their eyes did not meet one single time on the way but were aimed

toward the ground. To this day, I don't know what kind of secret bound the two people or what it had to do with Amadeu" (p. 160). Who were these people and what was their secret, and what did it have to do with Prado?

13. Father Bartolomeu gives Gregorius an envelope containing Amadeu Prado's "blasphemous" graduation speech. "I would not like to live in a world without cathedrals. I need the luster of their windows, their cool stillness, their imperious silence. I need the deluge of the organ and the sacred devotion of praying people" (p. 171). What does the speech reveal about Prado? Why was he sometimes called the "priest of truth"?

14. What does the note written by Prado about saving Mendes, "the doctor of death," reveal? "Here what experience always kept teaching me is confirmed, quite against the original temperament of my thought: that the body is less corrupt than the mind" (p. 193). Does Prado think of himself primarily as a doctor? The question of sacrificing one life for many arises once again in the case of Estafânia Espinhosa. Do you think that there is a consistency between the two instances? What is ironic about Estâfania? Did you find Prado's behavior inevitable?

15. Prado's close friendship with Jorge O'Kelly, would be pianist, Lisbon pharmacist, former resistance fighter, and accomplished chess player, began when they were boys and flourished even though they differed in significant ways. In order to understand Prado, Gregorius must understand O'Kelly. In what ways were they different? What drew them to each other? "All the blood had drained out of his face. In this one single second, I realized that the most horrible thing had happened: our lifelong affection had turned into hate. That was the

moment, the dreadful moment, when we lost each other" (p. 335). What split them apart?

16. Gregorius tracks down another close friend of Prado's from his school days, Maria João Ávila. "If there was anybody who knew all his secrets, it was Maria Joao. In a certain sense, she, only she, knew who he was." (p. 337). What does Gregorius perceive about her? How did this relationship develop? Was there any similarity to Prado's other liaisons with women?

17. Gregorius eventually leaves his hotel in Lisbon to live in the apartment of a man, Senhor Da Silveira, whom he had met and befriended on the night train. What are the parallels in the friendship between these two and Prado/O'Kelly? What else has changed about Gregorius besides his address? What are the parallels between Raimundo Gregorius and Amadeu Prado? Cite some specific events in the narrative to sustain your views.

18. Many letters are quoted in this book. Gregorius reads one of these from the father, Judge Prado, to his son Amadeu and from the son, Doctor Prado to his father. "It was crazy, thought Gregorius: both men, father and son, had lived on opposite hills of the city like opposing actors in an ancient drama, linked in an archaic fear of each other and in an affection they didn't find the words for, and had written letters to each other that they didn't trust themselves to send. Clasped in muteness neither understood, and blind to the fact that one muteness produced the other." (p. 291). What do the letters contain, and what is learned from them? What is the nature of the father-son relationship?

19. "And there's something else about the intricate way you created me according to your will-like a wanton sculptress of an alien soul: the names you gave me Amadeu Inacio. Most people don't think anything of it, now and then somebody says something about the melody. But I know better, for I have the sound of your voice in my ear, a sound full of conceited devotion. I was to be a genius. I was to possess godlike grace. And at the same time-the same time!-I was to embody the murderous rigidity of the holy Ignacio and his abilities to perform as a priestly general" (p. 312). What kind of a woman was Senhora Prado? What was the nature of the mother-son relationship?

20. "He had disappointed all expectations and broken all taboos, and that was his bliss. In the end, he was at peace with the bent judging father, the soft dictatorship of the ambitious mother, and the lifelong stifling gratitude of the sister." (p. 379). Gregorius sees this image of Prado late in the story when he himself may be facing death. When the bookseller from the Spanish bookstore asks him if the book kept its promise, Gregorius says that it did, absolutely. How have the memories of the doctor/poet's life helped him to bring together his own life and to find his own peace?

IF YOU LIKED THIS BOOK YOU MIGHT ALSO LIKE:

The Divine Husband by Francisco Goldman; *The Shadow of the Wind* by Carlos Ruiz Zafón; *The Dante Club* by Matthew Pearl; *Suite Française* by Irène Némirovsky; *The Sixth Lamentation* by William Brodrick; *The Grand Complication* by Alan Kurzweil; *Anil's Ghost* by Michael Ondaatje; *The Catastrophist* by Ronan Bennett; *The Reader* by Bernard Schlink; *The Club Dumas* by Arturo Pérez-Reverte

SOME FILMS YOU MIGHT ENJOY:

The Battle of Algiers; Grand Hotel; The Third Man; The Wind that Shakes the Barley; Syriana; The Constant Gardener